Footsteps into Crime

Sarah E. Hopkins

TSL Publications

In memory of my brother Laurence
who taught me that anything is possible

First published in Great Britain in 2025
By TSL Publications, Rickmansworth

Copyright © 2025 Sarah E. Hopkins

ISBN: 978-1-917426-23-7

Cover & photographs courtesy of :
Sarah E Hopkins

Prologue

1989

The atmosphere in the room was tense. Connie stood by the window watching her husband run around the small garden with two-year-old Jamie who was whooping in delight as Denny chased him. She envied the child for a minute. All that mattered to him was the delightful childhood innocence, playing in a sunny garden with his beloved uncle. As she watched them she momentarily forgot the cruel sadness that had brought them here today. In her mind she was sat in one of Brenda's stripy deckchairs with the warm sun on her body enjoying their antics. At one point Denny looked up and noticed her, a question in his eyes. She smiled and shook her head remembering with sad clarity why they were all here back on the estate where her life had begun and where Caroline's would end.

Darling Cath sat vigil by the bed softly crying. Of the three girls, she was the emotional one and Connie and Caroline loved her all the more for this endearing quality.

Connie knew that she would have to remain strong for what was to come. Not one for public displays of emotion, she discreetly wiped away a solitary tear with her perfectly manicured right hand. 'Cup of tea Cath?' It was a statement more than a question. The need to escape the raw tension of this room and the sickly aroma of imminent death was overwhelming.

Opening the creaky bedroom door she proceeded along the narrow hallway and down the stairs into the kitchen wrinkling her nose as an offensive smell hit her nostrils. The bin was overflowing so she swiftly dealt with that before making a necessary phone call.

'Mum, can you come and pick up Jamie please? It's almost time. Can you also call for the nurse?'

As she waited for the kettle to boil and for her mother to arrive she went into the front room and glanced at the photos that were dotted all around. Most of them were of Caroline and Denny with their parents Geoff and

Brenda whose death Connie knew had left a massive void in her friend's life. A big photo of Caroline with her beloved son hung over the fireplace and Connie was touched to see a few photos of the three friends which spanned the years. Their friendship had begun from birth and they had grown up like sisters. The smiling pictures of three happy girls made Connie feel nostalgic and sad but also grateful that she had been a part of a friendship that had been honest and pure.

As Connie studied the modest room, she once again felt confused that Caroline had always been adamant that she wanted to bring up her son in this house on this drab council estate. She had always insisted that it made her feel closer to her long dead parents even though Connie had offered her one of the rentals and Denny had said that he would buy her a lovely flat to live in. But Caroline had always flatly refused.

Connie knew in her heart that Caroline had never really approved of her brother's chosen career and didn't want to take 'dirty' money. She adored her big brother and had never actually come out with it but Connie had often seen the disapproval in her eyes as she had with her own mother over the years.

Deep in thought Connie didn't hear the scream at first but when it did register, she rushed back up the stairs as quickly as her four-inch heels would allow her shouting for Denny to come quickly.

Chapter 1

1967

Alan Stewart opened his weary eyes and smiled as he nestled into his wife Sonia's warm curves. It was December 1967 and the weather had so far been bitter thanks to the northerly winds moving across the country. He was so snug that the thought of moving from the warm cocoon of their bed into the cold ice box of their bedroom was not appealing at all. The curtains that covered the cracked windows were thin and he knew that there would be ice on the insides making the bedroom colder still.

'What time is it?' Sonia sleepily enquired.

'Go back to sleep, it's still early but I want to get to the pub early today as we have a delivery.'

The last thing that he wanted to do was stand in a cold cellar freezing his gonads off but needs must, the twins were due any day now and the final payment on the silver cross pram was looming. He gently eased himself out of bed and promptly stubbed his toe on Sonia's dressing table. Cursing quietly he carefully navigated his way around the darkened bedroom searching for his clothes and made his way downstairs. Going into the small front room he turned on a bar of the electric fire and feeling disgruntled studied his humble home. Granted they were better off than when they had lived in the tenements as children but Alan was ambitious and wanted more for his family.

Sonia kept the house clean and tidy but there was no escaping the fact that it was in desperate need of updating and that they would never have the money to do it. The couple were just managing to keep their heads above water now that Sonia had given up her cleaning job at the Town Hall and soon there would be two more mouths to feed. In all honesty, although Alan couldn't wait for the arrival of the twins, the financial responsibility worried him. Sonia never wanted to know about money and bills and always handed him the dreaded brown envelopes. She had no concept of money and although this sometimes frustrated him, he had always looked after her and always would. He just wasn't sure at this precise moment how. Growing up his younger brother David had often had his head in a book and Alan had always teased him, calling him a book worm, but now he felt as if David had had the last laugh as these days he was now a respectable doctor who owned his own home. Alan didn't know exactly how much his brother earned but was certain that it was more than he did and being a doctor was far more credible than a lowly barman in his eyes.

Alan loved his Sonia with a passion and while he sipped his tea he made a vow to himself that one day he would have a better job and they would live in a better area with more green spaces. His mind drifted off to when they had met and spoken properly for the first time during an air raid huddled together in Bethnal Green tube station.

Alan had grown up in a slum tenement block in East London during the hardships of World War Two.

One dark night in 1941 when he was eight years old Hitler's planes had determinedly rampaged over London, lighting up the sky with dozens of enemy aircraft. As the destruction of London grew closer, Alan's mother Glenice had none too gently awoken her two sons and urged them to get dressed in something warm. In the frantic dash to the shelter young David had taken a tumble and grazed his knee.

'Come on David, we'll be safe once we get to the shelter and I managed to grab some bread and butter and Mum's got some tea so we'll have a feast tonight,' Alan had encouraged the small lad who was now crying. The journey had seemed to take forever and in their desperation to reach safety they had taken a few wrong turns. Nothing looked familiar anymore and the billowing smoke was making it difficult to see through the small window of their gas masks. There were houses on fire, gaping gaps where buildings had stood, piles of rubble and destruction all around them. Screaming people were running in all directions like a swarm of ants calling frantically for loved ones as they tried to reach safety. Alan would always remember that his mum had tried to distract their fears by pretending that they were in the middle of a big adventure. This had worked until they had literally fallen over their neighbour Fred Cummings who lay burnt and dead on the ground adjacent to his burned out house. Even Glenice had screamed at that point and realising that there was nothing she could do had ushered her children away from the tragic sight. When they finally reached the shelter they were all exhausted and tearful.

Carefully stepping over dozens of other people who had sought refuge, they had struggled to find a space in the gloomy light.

'Over here Glen,' Breda Murphy their neighbour cheerily called. Breda lived in the flat below them with her husband and six children and Alan often played with the older boys Patrick and Declan. Mr Murphy who was also called Patrick was overseas fighting. Alan's father Alex had died last year at the Battle of Dunkirk, leaving only a few photographs to remember him by now. The boy sat down next to Breda's youngest daughter Sonia who was two years younger than him. She was sobbing into her mother's generous bosom and visibly shook each time the deathly thud of an exploding bomb could be heard. Alan had taken her dainty hand in his offering her a slice of bread and butter, and as she had looked up at him with her dark brown eyes, a bond was formed which would last for years.

Although everyone in that shelter had no idea if they would have a home to return to, they refused to let this dampen their spirits and the atmosphere was almost jovial. Vic Barritt had begun to play his mouth organ and Breda's sister Maggie had started to sing. Soon everyone was joining in and sharing whatever food that they had managed to grab from home.

In the dusky light of the early morning Glenice and Breda had companionably walked home together and had let out a sigh of relief to see that the large Victorian building that housed them and fifty other families had miraculously escaped Hitler's wrath. Later on that day Alan and Sonia had played for hours in the courtyard and a childhood friendship had begun that would eventually turn into love.

When Alan was seventeen and Sonia was fifteen they had begun courting much to the delight of their parents. Sonia was now a beauty. She was petite with a tiny waist and had a curtain of magnificent thick dark hair. She had come to the attention of some of the other local boys so Alan had made the relationship official and had given Sonia what he called a 'forever' ring. Alan had the sandy hair and faded blue eyes of his Scottish ancestors and was under no illusions that Sonia was the looker but liked to think that he was the brains and that they complimented each other perfectly. They shared a deep love and friendship born of nostalgia, trust, familiarity and lust which made them inseparable.

Sonia was nineteen when she had fallen pregnant. Their parents were pragmatic but Patrick Murphy Senior had insisted that the wedding be brought forward to spare his daughter's reputation and avoid any unwanted gossip. Alan had been only too happy to marry his soul mate and they had both been excited for the future.

The pregnancy had not been an easy one as Sonia had suffered from terrible morning sickness and her brother Declan had died in a motorcycle accident during her sixth month. Baby George Declan had been born in 1954 while Alan was listening to Vera Lynn singing My Son My Son on his transistor radio. Sonia had been in the bedroom with a kindly midwife and her mother and he had wept tears of joy when he had heard the first cry from his baby. Everyone fell in love with George who was docile and rarely cried. Alan and Sonia had taken to parenthood like ducks to water and were besotted with him. However, tragedy struck when George was four months old and Sonia had found him lifeless and cold in his crib. Her screams had echoed around the tenements and had alerted her mother who had been in the courtyard hanging out the sheets. Breda's heart broke as she tried to revive her unresponsive grandson and knowing the agony herself of losing a child she feared that her daughter would not survive the grief. Sonia's hysteria was replaced by anger and then silent tears which in turn had resulted into a depression that would plague her for the rest of her life. The image of her lifeless son would haunt her until the day she died. Alan shut away his grief in a box that he kept firmly at the back of his mind and tried to be strong for his fragile wife. On occasion, and when he had had a drink, his anger would surface and he had started to get into fights with local men so Sonia had been relieved when the council had allocated them a house in Tottenham. A new start was what they both needed.

Thirteen long years passed until confirmation came that Sonia was pregnant again with not one but two babies. At first she was terrified as the raw pain of losing George had never gone away but Alan had tried to convince her that they could finally move forward and try and accept the past. She was now looking forward to having two babies to love although she was still gripped with fear that they would die like George had. Doctor Dickson had tried to reassure her that the chances of losing another child in such an unexplained way would be very unusual but the fact that it was unexplained was what tormented her. Had she done something wrong, had she not been a good mother?

Alan was jolted back to the present by the clattering of the letter box. As he opened a letter advising him of a rent increase he was filled with a need to escape the poverty that was their daily life. His dream was to be a homeowner in a better part of North London like Crouch End or Muswell Hill. But he was a realist and knew that working in the local pub was never going to afford him his own home and especially in those areas that were considered well to do. It was unlikely that Sonia would return to work with two children to look after so it was up to him to go out and provide a better life for them all. The problem was that although he was bright, he had no formal education, the war had seen to that. His mother had refused to send her children away as evacuees and his school had closed during the blitz. So for the whole of the war many children who had stayed in London had received a very sparse education.

He had returned to school in 1945 but by then he was twelve and had missed so much learning that he no longer saw the point. His mum also needed money as she didn't earn much as a dressmaker and was bringing up two children on her own, therefore as the man of the family Alan had got a job at the local butchers. He had told the owner Mr Garvey that he was fifteen and he had worked there until they had moved to Tottenham. Once they had become settled in their new home, Alan had joined a local boxing club which helped to release his pent-up anger. One of the lads there had told him about a vacancy as a barman in a nearby pub and that is where Alan had worked ever since. But one thing that he wasn't short of was ambition, and he was soon managing the pub on a regular basis as the landlord Jim recognised that this capable young man was wasted serving pints.

Alan was determined to give Sonia the life that she deserved. He had watched his own mother struggle over the years. He had noticed when she had gone without food so that her sons ate, he had seen the look of despair on her face that had prematurely aged her. The poverty had given him fire in his belly to make something of himself and like many a man before him, he was determined that his children would have more than he had had. He wanted to give his wife the world as she had suffered from an all-consuming depression and an empty crib for long enough without having to worry about money as well.

It was still dark when Alan left the house to begin the two mile walk to work. Although his thin coat barely kept the cold out and his feet were freezing he enjoyed this time of day when he could do his thinking. He had a plan about his future thanks to his mum. Glenice had been wittering away the other day about bumping into an old friend Dolly McCardle at bingo. Alan was only half listening until she mentioned that Dolly had been showing off about how well her son Ron was doing and then it clicked that her son was THE Ron McCardle who was a well-known and respected face in North London and lived in a smart four bedroomed house near Enfield. Alan was aware that Ron earned some of his money through the protection rackets, an arrangement that was common these days between local businesses and racketeers. The pub that Alan worked in was protected by Ron's firm and Alan had handed over the money on more than one occasion. What Alan hadn't known was that his mum was an old friend of Dolly's. This gave him an idea as maybe he could use this as a way of opening up a conversation with Ron and just maybe that could lead to some sort of job if he played his cards right. Alan didn't really know how Ron came to employ his staff and assumed that it was a closed shop but he was hoping that the connection between Glenice and Dolly might help. Decision made, Alan decided to treat himself and jumped on a bus to take him the rest of the way to work.

Sonia woke up feeling happy and light for once. Usually she woke up in a flat mood that seemed to suffocate her. She knew that she would never get over losing her baby and brother so close together and in such awful circumstances but she did have great hope for the future and couldn't wait to be a mum again. Thinking of baby George she immediately felt her good mood deflating so she physically shook off her melancholy thoughts and went downstairs. She was grateful that Alan had put the fire on and sat warming her toes whilst she had her first cup of tea of the day. She mentally went through her to do list and decided to buy the Christmas tree and make the house all Christmassy. Sonia adored everything about Christmas, from the twinkly lights to the wrapping of the presents. This year she had bought Alan a new coat, the poor sod had been wearing the same one for four years now and it was threadbare. Her Mum had also chipped in as she would never have been able to afford it on her own. She was really looking forward to Christmas day, both their families were coming although her sister Bridget was with her in-laws this year and her Dad had died in 1960. She was grateful that her mother Breda had followed them to Tottenham as her mum was a great emotional support to her on her black days as she called them. She sometimes thought that Alan didn't understand her at all and that made her feel very alone. He refused to talk about George but her mum said that this was the way that men dealt with grief as her own father had been the same after losing her brother Declan.

She was painfully aware that she wasn't the carefree girl that she had once been and hoped she wasn't a burden on her husband who did assure her that he loved her dearly, even if she was a 'moody cow!' Alan had his boxing but what did she have to unburden herself? She was hoping that she would be so busy with the new arrivals that she wouldn't have time to dwell on her misery.

Finishing her cup of tea she decided to ring Breda and get the recipe for her famous Mince Pies and to ask her if she wanted to come with her to do a bit of last minute Christmas shopping. Her mother was permanently cheerful and that is just what Sonia could do with. She really didn't know what she would do without her mum who was always on hand to give advice and cuddles when needed.

Alan reached the pub at seven o'clock and let himself in with his set of keys. The landlord Jim Fleming trusted him to set up everything in time for opening which meant that he could have some extra time in bed with his wife Gloria which made him a happy man! Alan laid out the ashtrays on the tables and checked the stock. He noticed two envelopes on the bar, one with his name on it and one addressed to Ron McCardle which would be his weekly cut. Alan smirked as he put the envelope to one side. The one with his name on it contained a Christmas card and a small bonus. He let out a sigh of gratitude as it was more than he had expected and he could now buy Sonia a decent Christmas present.

Like his wife he was determined to have a good Christmas and in the New Year he hoped that he would be in a better job with more prospects. He just hoped that Ron was collecting tonight and not one of his men so that he could put his plan into action straight away.

Chapter 2

Ron McCardle was forty-eight years old, born in Deptford to an Irish mother Dolly and a Scottish father Angus who had died soon after his birth in 1919. His childhood had been loving but extremely poor. Ron had vivid memories of a groaning, empty belly and of having to wrap rags around his feet to substitute for the shoes that Dolly couldn't afford to buy for her son. To make ends meet she had worked with her brother Sid on his fruit and vegetable stall in East Street Market, in Walworth, South London. The cold winter months had played havoc with her arthritis so when Ron was thirteen he had left school and taken over working alongside his uncle. He had been relieved to leave the regimented confines of the strict boys' school that he had attended and Sid had been only too happy to take him on, as he himself had recurring bouts of malaria courtesy of the Great War.

Ron loved 'The Lane' and market life. He was a total natural and wasn't afraid of the hard work and long hours. His friendly disposition and gift of the gab endeared him to the locals and he soon became a real asset to Sid who looked upon him as a son.

When Ron turned fifteen he had come to the attention of James Taverner, a local receiver of stolen goods who needed someone who could sell the merchandise on. He set up Ron on a stall opposite his uncle's and it was there that Ron was officially introduced into the world of villainy.

He was ambitious and wanted to claw his way out of the squalor and poverty that he and his mother inhabited so he was thrilled to be earning a few more pennies. A few years later that stall had legitimately begun to sell ladies handbags as James had decided it was becoming too risky to blatantly sell stolen goods under the nose of the law. Behind the scenes was a different matter though, Ron was now making a good living and Dolly was grateful that she no longer had to scrimp. Even to this day Ron was still known affectionately by the locals of Walworth as Ronnie Handbags. His rise to the big time hadn't been plain sailing though. He always laughed when he recounted the story of the time he had raided a factory and stolen a dozen boxes of men's coats, only to discover that they hadn't had the arms stitched to them. Suffice to say, he hadn't made any money with that little venture!

James Taverner had never married and had no children so when a stroke claimed his life he had left everything to his protegee, and upon returning from the Second World War Ron had wisely invested in a small club. He was astute enough to know that the British public were more than ready to let their hair down and enjoy themselves after years of deprivation. There was a sizable room at the back of the club and this housed an illegal gambling den. Ron was climbing the career ladder and later on would own both legitimate and non-legitimate businesses. The secret to his success was that he wasn't greedy and he didn't tread on anyone's toes unless they stood on his, and then he would stamp them out without a second's thought.

Ron was a man who was respected and feared in equal measure and by 1967 he had amassed a small fortune.

Staring at the man before him, Ron felt nothing but contempt. He waited a full five minutes before he spoke as he knew that silence instilled more fear than a barrage of verbal. Studying the poor excuse of the man who was trembling and red faced he stifled the urge to laugh as the man's face was almost the same colour as his hair. Tom Bates or Ginger Tom as he was known locally had been trusted to work in the bookies and not only had he dipped his fingers in the till, he had been gossiping about Ron's personal life so needed to be taught a lesson. Ron cracked his knuckles and took a sip of his Scotch which was another deliberate move to delay the inevitable.

'You have seriously pissed me off Tom. I gave you a job when you were skint and not only have you thieved off me but you have been blabbing to all and sundry about my personal business.'

'No Boss, not me, I would never do that.'

Ron smashed his fist down on his desk and immediately regretted it as his hand was now throbbing. He couldn't stand liars, they were worse than thieves in his eyes. Further incensed he hissed, 'I am not letting this go, no one takes the piss out of me and I will not stand for idle gossip about me doing the rounds.'

Tom decided he needed to try and save his skin and tried a different tack.

'Look Boss, I may have mentioned to my old woman that I had seen you last week with some sort but I never told anyone else and as for the money, I was going to ask you for a sub but you haven't been near the bookies in weeks. I only borrowed the money, I promise.'

Unfortunately and not surprisingly Tom's pathetic admission of his version of events only enraged Ron further. The money he could just about swallow but calling his lady a 'sort' and discussing his private life was a betrayal that he was not going to overlook in a hurry.

'So you told your wife who has a gob bigger than the Grand Canyon? You may as well have rung up the local paper and they could have done a front cover.'

He called in his heavies, Rob and Doug Clarke, who had been waiting patiently outside the office and quietly said, 'number two.'

On hearing this Tom promptly started snivelling like a baby. It was a well-known fact that Ron graded his punishments on a scale of one to five (five being curtains) and whilst Tom was relieved that he may just get away with a few broken bones the prospect still terrified him. He could cheerfully kill his wife. Ron was right, she never knew when to button it and now he was paying the price. He conveniently forgot that he had eagerly given her this juicy nugget of gossip in the first place and had then stolen from this big man in front of him and Ron was a big man in both build and reputation. He certainly wasn't a man anyone crossed without being on a death wish.

Tom felt shame and fear as he inwardly admitted to himself that this wasn't his finest moment. It would have been wiser to take a beating from Kenny Latham who he owed money to in the first place because Ron McCardle's punishments were well known for being brutal whereas Kenny was a mate of sorts and may have been more lenient.

As Ginger Tom was dragged forcibly from the office Ron congratulated himself that another job on his to do list had been dealt with and made a mental note to be more careful in future with regards the women in his life: his wife Irene and his mistress Ebony. Although Irene was well aware of Ebony's existence in his bed, he loved her and would not have her disrespected. Being a somewhat self-centred man it did not occur to him to consider her feelings about his extra marital affair and he happily conducted both relationships with ease and no guilt whatsoever.

Ron had married Irene in 1947. They had rubbed along nicely for twenty years although they hadn't been blessed with children or any real passion. The first he could cope with, the second he couldn't. What they did have, however, was a great friendship and affection for each other. Irene had never had a high sex drive and was sensible enough to accept that Ron had his needs although she was hurt that Ebony appeared to be a permanent fixture. Ron assumed that his wife was happy to run his finances and the home in the knowledge that he would never leave her.

He was always careful to ensure that his two worlds didn't collide and couldn't believe that he had been clocked in Camden by someone who lived in Tottenham! Sighing he realised that he would have to be more discreet in the future.

Ebony Peters had had a long soak and was now applying her makeup. She smiled smugly at her beautiful reflection in the dressing table mirror. At twenty-four there was no denying that with her long auburn hair and doe like milk chocolate eyes, she was stunning and she knew it. With a five-feet-eight curvy frame, she had impossibly slim legs and a voluptuous bust. R affectionately called her tits on sticks which always made her laugh. She loved her gangster boyfriend and hoped that one day he would make their relationship official. He might be old enough to be her father but he was a reasonably attentive lover and more importantly he was loaded. Ebony could just picture herself as lady of the house and the lady on his arm permanently.

They had met in Pentonville prison of all places. Both had been visiting her father Gary who had been serving time for manslaughter. The visiting orders had been mixed up but they had both been allowed the visit and as their eyes had locked over their plastic cups of tea, they knew they would be seeing each other again. Ron saw a new bed companion whilst Ebony saw a meal ticket who was also sexy and dangerous. The following week Ron had called and taken her out to dinner at an exclusive restaurant in Mayfair.

He had been honest with her about his marital status and it hadn't bothered her at the time because just being with him filled her with excitement. However, a year on and she wanted more, even though Ron had made it clear from the start that he would never leave Irene. Why? She really did not know. She was beautiful and had youth on her side whereas to her way of thinking Irene was a dried up, old crow who hadn't even managed to give him any children. What Ebony didn't realise was that although Irene was well past her prime, Ron enjoyed her as a person. She was confident and had class. She was also intelligent and Ron could trust her like he could no other person. Ebony may have the looks but once they had finished making love she was more interested in reapplying her makeup and washing him away than having a meaningful conversation. So although Ron enjoyed her body he found her brain sorely lacking. Irene was known in the firm as Head Wife and the other wives and girlfriends looked up to her with respect. In turn she nurtured them and gave them a shoulder to cry on when needed. Ron couldn't imagine Ebony in the role that his wife carried out with ease and warmth.

Earlier on today, Ebony had been doing some Christmas shopping in Wood Green when she had accidentally almost knocked Irene off her feet. Irene had glared at the younger woman with a look of disdain. She was aware that Ebony meant nothing to her husband but she had a reputation to think of and was determined not to come across as a doormat. She was after all Mrs Ron McCardle and was respected in their world as such.

She wouldn't let this Barbie doll get the better of her. Ebony had had the grace to look away first mumbling an almost inaudible 'sorry Irene.'

'It's Mrs McCardle to you and there's no need to look caught out. I know all about you and my husband and do you know how? Well, I'll enlighten you, shall I? He told me because we don't have any secrets LOVE.'

Irene was sure that she had twisted her ankle but wouldn't give 'The Tart' as she referred to Ebony the satisfaction of knowing that. Ebony would have been enraged if she knew that Ron laughed when his wife referred to her as such. She was simply a means to an end and he had no real respect or depth of feeling for her, as he did his wife.

Ebony had stood with her mouth open, silently fuming with this little revelation and wasn't sure how to respond as the older woman pushed past her determined to have the last word.

'Out of my way, we're having a dinner party tonight and I still have shopping to do.'

Irene knew that this would wind up the tart and sniggered as she disappeared into the butchers to buy the last of the ingredients for her Beef Bourguignon. She was well aware that Ron would never leave her for this girl but it still stung a bit when she did bump into her, as there was no escaping the fact that Ebony was stunning. She had warned Ron that leaving Ebony wouldn't be easy because self-centred woman couldn't cope with rejection, but her husband was like most blokes in that he only worried about things when and if they were to happen.

It was getting cold in his office so Ron decided to call it a day and go home. They were having his bank manager over tonight for dinner and he didn't want to be late. Bob Manners was as crooked as he was and helped Ron to launder some of his wealth by supplying him with bank loans to invest in stocks and shares. The bank would provide some of the capital needed and Ron would use his own cash for the rest, which enabled him to clean dirty money. He wanted to discuss another loan tonight as he was branching into the property market and had found a large Victorian property in Crouch End which he wanted to convert into bedsits.

As he reached for his coat he received two phone calls in quick succession. Irene and Ebony had both let rip. Irene because she was now resting the beef for her Bourguignon on her swollen ankle and Ebony who was raging because he had told Irene all about them. Ebony liked to feel that she was in control of her life and at this moment felt that she was being used. Ron sighed and silently berated his wife. Sometimes his two lives were just too complicated and occasionally he asked himself if it was all worth it but he wasn't quite ready to lose the great sex that he had with his mistress, so he soothed Ebony with words of endearment and a promise of an expensive piece of jewellery to placate her. Irene was harder to manipulate but eventually calmed down because she was not usually a woman to make a fuss.

Ron had no intention of going straight home as the business with Ginger Tom and the fact that Ebony and Irene had just given him earache had put him in a bad mood. He was seriously in need of a drink but had just noticed that his bottle of Scotch was empty so decided to kill two birds with one stone and go and collect the weekly rents from the local pubs and have a drink while he was at it. He usually left this job to his collectors but liked to show his face occasionally especially as there were always wannabe firms out there waiting to take over. In his mind it was important to remind people that he was the boss and ran North London. As he buttoned up his warm sheepskin coat he wondered who he was going to replace Ginger Tom with. The bookies would be busy leading up to Christmas, especially so on Boxing Day with the races at Kempton Park. Ginger Tom had run the bookies with a middle-aged woman called Maureen Holmes but she was going home to Bristol next week for Christmas so he couldn't ask her. He had to find someone and quick but he was very choosey who he employed. Most of his workforce were handpicked or recommended to him by someone who he knew and trusted. They therefore came to him with good credentials. He vaguely remembered that the Clarke brothers had an older brother called Danny who had just been released from a stint inside, so that was an option, although all three brothers were more muscle than brawn and he needed someone who could at least count. Oh well, he would give it some more thought tomorrow. Making his way outside into the cold winter's night, he smiled at two of his men, John Webb and Greg Leeson, who were dutifully waiting for him beside his Rolls Royce.

'Where to Boss?' John asked as he stubbed out his cigarette.

'We're going to do the collections and have a Christmas drink Boys.'

John looked at Greg and smiled. They weren't usually allowed to drink on duty as Ron expected his men to always have their wits about them but if the boss was offering then who were they to refuse?

Chapter 3

Sonia had thoroughly enjoyed her shopping expedition with Breda who had insisted on treating her to lunch and some new Christmas decorations. She had walked her mother home and was now happily dressing the small tree which stood pride of place on the sideboard in her front room. When the phone rang she was happy for an excuse to sit down as her feet were aching. It was her friend Gina Davis who lived on the estate and was also pregnant. The two women were both due within weeks of each other and Gina was phoning to remind her that they had an appointment with the midwives at the clinic next week. After a quick catch up they said their goodbyes and Sonia went back to her Christmas decorations. Smiling, she carefully placed the shiny star on the top of the tree. She had felt so lonely last time as none of her friends had had children. Now she had Gina and Brenda Draper who lived in the next street. They were all due in December and couldn't wait to wheel their offspring proudly up the street together. Their men also got on well and the couples had spent lots of time together in the last few years, socialising and having fun.

As she thought of her friends she heard a hammering on the front door and waddling as fast as she could she yanked it open to find Brenda's boy Denny on the door step. He was eight years old and was jigging nervously from one foot to the other, 'The baby's coming, Mum is screaming, please help!' he pleaded.

'Where's your Dad Den?'

'He went out to see a dog.'

Sonia frowned until she suddenly remembered that when Geoff went for a swift half he always told his wife that he was going to see a man about a dog!

'Have you phoned for an ambulance?' she asked.

'No, I didn't know what to do.'

'Ok, listen to me, run back to your mum and I will follow you once I've phoned for help,' Sonia instructed the lad. Denny nodded in acknowledgement and ran back down her garden path.

Bloody men she thought, either under your feet or nowhere to be found when they were needed. Sonia quickly made two phone calls: one for an ambulance and one to the pub where she told her husband in no uncertain terms that she didn't care if Geoff had only just ordered a pint, he was needed home sharpish. She then gathered up some towels that had been airing by the fire and hastily made her way the short distance to Brenda's home. On the way she realised that she was still wearing her new, fluffy slippers and swore as they got wetter. Giggling she realised that she must look a right sight with her massive belly trying to run down the street in her now soaking slippers!

When she reached Brenda's, her poor friend was bathed in a film of sweat, beehive squew whiff and moaning in pain.

Denny was clearly overwhelmed as Sonia could see that he had wet himself and was now tearful at the sight of his mum who was clearly in agony. Sonia knew that the situation was going to become even more alarming for the boy and thought it would be best if he was distracted.

'Denny, be a good boy and go upstairs and change your trousers, then you can play with your toys. You must wait in your bedroom until I tell you to come back down, I am going to help Mummy.'

Denny nodded and left the front room and when she heard him trotting up the stairs she eased her bulk onto the floor next to Brenda and took her hand after reassuring her that both the ambulance and Geoff would be there in a minute.

'Oh my God. It's coming Son!' Brenda gasped through another contraction.

'Well it's not going to get very far, you've still got your drawers on!' Sonia dryly stated.

She gently eased them off for her friend and took a look down the business end.

'Bloody hell Bren, you're crowning!'

Panic began to build as Sonia knew from experience that the baby would come any minute and she didn't have a clue what to do and was terrified that something bad would happen to the baby or her friend without medical assistance. Was Brenda meant to push or pant at this point? She had no idea and silently prayed that help would come quickly.

Luckily her prayers were answered as it was at this minute that the ambulance men arrived and swiftly took over. Relieved, Sonia moved her cumbersome body onto the sofa and watched in awe as Brenda pushed her little girl into the world. Geoff arrived home in the middle of the commotion and Sonia cried as he cradled his baby girl.

'Blimey Bren, I only went out for a quick pint!' he chuckled. 'What are we going to call her?'

'How about a Christmas name like Christine or Carol?' Sonia suggested.

Brenda snorted and exclaimed, 'I'm not calling her after Crusty Christine and Angela Brown has just called her baby Carol.'

Sonia and Geoff both laughed. Crusty Christine lived on the estate with a gaggle of children all of whom looked like they needed a good wash, so Brenda had a point.

'I really thought that it was another boy and hadn't picked a girl's name. But I like Caroline, it's modern and classy. What do you think Love?'

Geoff looked at his wife fondly and said, 'Perfect, welcome to the world Caroline Draper.'

After the ambulance men had taken Brenda and Caroline to hospital, Geoff kindly walked Sonia home and she excitedly grabbed the telephone to call her mum and tell her the good news. Breda laughed when she heard about her daughter's adventure and said that she would come and visit Brenda and the baby once they were home again.

The pub was packed and full of Christmas cheer. Alan had been up since five-thirty that morning and was exhausted. Glancing at his watch he inwardly groaned as there were still another few hours before the pub shut and then the laborious task of clearing up would begin. Earlier on old Alfie Marks had just begun to play White Christmas on the ancient piano when Ron McCardle had walked in with two of his men, Greg Leeson and John Webb.

Geoff Draper had nearly knocked Ron flying upon his haste to get home but fortunately Ron had seen the funny side when Geoff had nervously explained that his wife had gone into labour. Chuckling, Ron had reached into his pocket and handed over a ten-pound note for the baby.

The atmosphere had, however, immediately changed when Ron and his men entered the pub. He was well known in Tottenham as the man in charge and most of the locals remembered only too well his altercation with Les Dwyer last year in this very pub. Ron liked to think of himself as a business-man (albeit not all of his enterprises were legal) and he only used violence when someone blatantly disrespected him. Les Dwyer had rather foolishly thought that he could set up his own firm and take over the protection rackets that Ron owned in the area. A well-aimed dart in the eye and a good beating by Ron had diminished any further ambitions from Les who had promptly had it away on his toes to Birmingham.

Most people were wary of Ron but the general feeling was that he was a fair man as long as he wasn't crossed and no one tried to take what he considered to be his. Relieving himself of his heavy sheepskin coat, Ron sat on a hastily vacated bar stool and ordered a large Scotch. Greg and John stood nearby ever watchful.

'How's it going Alan?' he asked.

'Not bad Mr McCardle, the twins will be here any day and then all hell will break lose!' Alan chuckled.

'Expensive business kids, eeh?'

'Not half, my Sonia is always up Wood Green buying something and the money that I earn in here just about covers the rent and bills and now the missus has gone and ordered one of those prams that the Queen had for all of her kids.'

Ron studied Alan closely. He was always respectful and Ron knew that he was discreet. When Les Dwyer had been dealt with, Alan had merely reached under the bar and had replaced the dart that had been used to shut the idiot up. He then had a drink ready for Ron when he had finished the beating. He was also impressed with the man's ability to quietly and swiftly deal with the brawls that often occurred in the pub.

'Are you happy working here Alan?'

'I am Mr McCardle but I'm ambitious and want my family to have a good life, the estate we live on is going downhill and I don't want my kids growing up there.'

'I can understand that, my old mum mentioned the other day that your mum had been keeping her updated about the impending birth. I had no idea that they had been mates for years.'

'Me either Mr McCardle, I never made the connection, small world eeh?'

Ron liked the fact that his mum Dolly spoke so highly of this man's mum, so throwing caution to the wind he made a decision.

'This is your lucky day Alan because as of today, I have a job going in the bookies and I will pay you more than you get in here,' Ron offered. 'Now it goes without saying that I demand total loyalty and discretion because as you may have gathered I am not exactly always kosher but the bookies is one of my legit businesses and I think you would do well in there.'

Alan couldn't believe that his plan had fallen so easily into place and didn't need to think twice. Anything was better than the pennies that he earned in here and he was hoping that the bookies would lead to better things.

'Thank you so much Mr McCardle, that would really help out. I'll do anything to earn more money.'

Ron liked the fire in the younger man's eyes and laughed, 'We'll see how it goes and go from there. My men have to prove themselves and earn my trust. Come and see me after Christmas for a chat and Alan for God's sake call me Ron, my old mum would clip me around the chops if she knew that I had you calling me Mr McCardle, mind you not in front of the other men,' Ron said with a wink.

Alan nodded while he poured Ron another Scotch. 'How is she Mr Mc sorry Ron? Mum said that her arthritis had been playing her up.'

'She is still driving me doolally with all her demands but your mum is your mum and she makes a mean roast dinner so I can't complain. Poor old dear has been a martyr to her arthritis for years but it doesn't stop her from her weekly bingo. She has been on at me to buy her a bingo hall!' Ron chuckled. 'Right, I'd best be off before the wife sends out a search party, we're having the bank manager over for dinner tonight and I am already late.'

As Ron downed his drink and nodded to his men, Alan remembered the envelope. Handing it over the two men wished each other a happy Christmas and Ron was just about to leave when Jim the landlord called out, 'Alan it's Sonia, she's having pains, you'd best get off home.'

'Oh my god, she isn't due for two weeks, will you be ok Jim? Where did I put my coat?'

Alan was in a flap and Ron being a decent bloke offered him a lift home as the buses were on a reduced service at this time of night.

As Alan sat in Ron's Rolls Royce, his mind was going into overdrive and his grief over the death of baby George was resurfacing. Wiping his eyes he turned and looked out of the window deep in thought. Now that the birth was imminent he was worried that something would go wrong and the short journey seemed to be taking an age. When they finally reached the estate he could see the doctor leaving his house and Breda stood at the front door waving him off. She then stared at Alan open mouthed as he got out of the car. It suddenly occurred to him that there had probably never been a Rolls Royce on this estate and he noticed next door's curtains twitching. Thanking Ron, he ran up the garden path and nearly knocked over his mother-in-law in his haste to get to his wife. Breda followed him in and informed him that the pains had been Braxton Hicks which was normal at this stage of pregnancy. Alan breathed a sigh of relief when he entered the front room and saw that his wife was well and eating a pickled egg.

looked up at him sheepishly, 'Sorry Al, I should have known that it wasn't labour.'

'Don't worry, you did me a favour as I got out of the clearing up!'

'What I want to know is whose car was that you were getting out of?' Breda asked.

was too tired to go into any detail and wanted to speak to Sonia first about his job offer, so quickly replied, 'Just the son of one of Mum's friends.'

'A very rich friend by the looks of it!' Breda exclaimed. 'Oh well, I'm off to bed,' she said and after kissing her daughter goodnight went upstairs.

Alan was grateful that his mother-in-law wasn't a nosey woman and had gone to bed because he needed to speak to Sonia.

'Who does your Mum know who is well off?' Sonia asked.

'Dolly McCardle, her son Ron is a local businessman and has offered me a job in his bookies. I've got to go and see him in the new year and he has assured me that I will be earning more money than what I'm on now, and let's face it we need it.'

'That sounds brilliant Al and you won't have to work nights. I'll need all the help that I can get with two babies to look after.'

Alan was relieved that Sonia was as excited as he was, although he knew that she may not have got the Baby Sham out in celebration if she had realised exactly who Ron McCardle was and what he stood for, because decent or not he was still a villain.

Later that night, with Sonia snoring softly beside him, Alan pondered over his day and couldn't believe his luck. His plan had worked and with little effort from himself, although he realised that Ron must be impressed with him because his firm was a closed shop. It stood to reason that it had to be. Alan was aware that Ron had his fingers in many pies. It was well known that he had opened up his own club in the late forties and rumour had it that the back room had been home to illegal gambling. He was clued up enough to know that you didn't have Ron's wealth without a bit of serious ducking and diving and now that Ron had offered him an opening he was determined to take full advantage of anything that was on offer. The thought both scared and excited him at the same time. This morning had looked so bleak but now he had real hope for their future. He was going to be a father again and he had a job with prospects. He wasn't worried about getting his hands dirty, he wanted a good life and would do anything to get one. He liked and admired Ron who, in Alan's mind, had earned his money fair and square and was family orientated like he was. Alan saw this as a good trait in a man. Luckily Sonia didn't really know who Ron McCardle was or what would be expected of her husband in the coming years because if she had, she wouldn't have approved. Sonia was as straight as a die and would have made him stay at the pub if she could have looked into the future and seen what was to come.

Unfortunately there would be many times over the next few years that Sonia wished that her husband hadn't cultivated a friendship with the local face of North London.

A few miles away, Ron McCardle was also in bed thinking of his day. All in all it had been a good one. The dinner party had been a success as Bob Manners had agreed to grant him a loan to help towards buying another property in Crouch End. Bob lent him part of the asking price and Ron used dirty money which he laundered to put towards the rest. If it all fell out of bed Bob would say that the bank had lent Ron the full price of the house. Ron liked the fact that he was building up a property portfolio. It made him feel more respectable and he was astute enough to know that all these Victorian properties that he was buying would be worth a fortune one day. He did sometimes wonder why he was risking his liberty on a daily basis as he had no children to take over from him or to leave his wealth to when he croaked it one day, but he loved the thrill of a serious earn and that is what kept him going. He was pleased that he had offered Alan the job in the bookies. He had watched him over the last couple of years and was impressed with him. Ron liked to think that he was a good judge of character and felt that he had made a wise choice. He had a strange feeling that Alan would be with him for a very long time. Satisfied, he turned over and went to sleep.

Chapter 4
December 1971

'Happy birthday to you, happy birthday to you, happy birthday dear Connie and Billy, happy birthday to you,' the small crowd in Sonia's kitchen sung merrily. Connie stood on a chair proudly wearing her long, frilly party dress lapping up all the attention whilst her brother Billy had promptly taken refuge under the kitchen table as soon as the singing had started.

Connie Eve and William Patrick Stewart had been born on December the 24th 1967. Two tiny scraps weighing less than eight pounds between them. Although Sonia had been a nervous mother to begin with, as the babies had thrived and become robust, chubby toddlers she had relaxed a bit and was now thoroughly enjoying everything that being a worn-out mother entailed. Her friends Brenda Draper and Gina Davis had also given birth that December to Caroline and Catherine respectively and the three girls spent a lot of time together. Sonia was grateful for her two best friends who helped to keep her grounded, and fortunately her earlier years of depression had lifted so much so that now she only suffered black days sporadically.

Although Connie and Billy were both pale skinned and shared an adorable flurry of freckles on their cute button noses, they couldn't have looked more different. Connie had almost black hair and dark brown eyes like Sonia whereas Billy had fair hair with a tinge of red and the pale blue eyes inherited from his father. Although his son was the image of him, it was Connie who shared Alan's determined nature and usually got what she wanted in life due to her stubborn streak and charismatic charm.

As Sonia watched her children, she was consumed with love and pride. Connie looked so bonny today and Billy was impossibly handsome in his matching sky blue, paisley shirt and tie. After devouring a slice of birthday cake and some orange squash the children were now all playing hide and seek whilst the mums enjoyed a cigarette and a glass of Mateus rose wine.

Alan was getting fed up. The old man who had been in the shop for nearly an hour was taking an age to place his bet and had already changed his mind twice. Alan needed to get home so he could spend at least some of the day with his children. It had been a quiet day at the bookies in that not many winnings had been paid out which would please Ron McCardle but it was sod's law that someone always seemed to walk in when he was about to close for the day and usually only to play on the newly installed fruit machine.

When the old man had finally shuffled off deflated that his horse had refused to jump the first fence, Alan picked up the keys and headed towards the door to lock up for the day. He was just about to turn the key when he was nearly knocked flying by a man in a balaclava forcing the door open. It took Alan all of two seconds to register the knife in the man's meaty left hand and locking eyes with him the man seemed to hesitate.

Alan used this opportunity to deliver an upper cut to the jaw followed by a knee in the groin. As the man dropped groaning to the floor clutching his crown jewels Alan noticed that he had no little finger on his right hand and it suddenly dawned on him who the man was.

'Stevie what the fuck do you think you're doing? You do know that Ron McCardle owns this place you moron?'

Stevie Baines slowly peeled off his balaclava and promptly burst into loud sobs.

'I didn't know what else to do Alan, I'm desperate. Doreen is up the duff again. We've already got four kids and I can't feed them. She sits on her fat arse all day and I'm out of work again. I wouldn't mind but she only opens her legs once in a blue moon and she's bloody in the club after one quick fumble a few weeks back.'

Alan could well sympathise. Doreen was a brash trappy cow whose only real interests in life were cheap wine, fags and the TV show *Coronation Street*. She churned out babies and had no real interest in them once they could answer her back.

Alan and Stevie lived on the same estate and had known each other growing up in the East End. Looking at his mate, Alan felt a surge of pity that he had had to stoop this low. Stevie had never had much luck in life. Born missing a little finger he had been bullied throughout his miserable childhood. His parents had been work shy and had spent their lives in the pub leaving their son to fend for himself. There had been many times that Alan's own mother Glenice had shared their own meagre meal so that the child would have food in his belly and the company of a loving family around him occasionally.

'Please don't grass me up Al, I would never have pulled a stunt like this if I had known that you worked here and that the place was owned by McCardle,' Stevie pleaded still snivelling.

Alan sighed, 'Look I'm no grass but I can guarantee you that Ron will have already heard, he has eyes and ears everywhere.'

'Oh my god, I'm a dead man, I've heard about his punishments, everyone has!' Stevie wailed.

Alan reached into his pocket and pulled out two one-pound notes. 'Take that, get some grub for the kids and I'll have a word with Ron and see if I can sort things out. I'm not making any promises though, as Ron will view this as a serious case of disrespect.'

Alan watched as his old mate dejectedly walked out of the bookies. Alan knew that he wasn't really a villain but desperation and hungry, crying children could make a man do anything Alan reasoned. When he had locked the front door, he managed to get hold of Ron on the telephone and pacify him for the moment promising that he would explain all tomorrow. Ron had been angry but was willing to hear what Alan had to say and was grateful that the situation had been dealt with.

'Where have you been?' Sonia demanded from the top of the stairs as soon as her husband stepped through the front door.

Alan bounded up the stairs into the bathroom where his wife had gone back to finish bathing the twins.

'Daddy!' they both yelled happily when they saw him.

'Sorry Love, I'll explain later,' Alan told his wife.

'Okay, well you can finish up here, I've still got some cleaning up to do from the party.'

While Alan was gently drying his children, he studied the bathroom with a critical eye. Since they had installed the new bathroom suite, it certainly looked better. The house had been redecorated top to bottom and the kitchen now boasted a twin tub, but Alan couldn't help feeling that he wanted more. The petty crime rate on their estate was on the increase and he didn't want his children growing up surrounded by low lifes. Only last week he had had to go to the aid of old Mrs Green when some delinquent had grabbed her handbag after knocking her to the pavement. Alan had kicked the bastard all the way down the street until he had begged for mercy, returned the handbag and apologised. Alan did not consider himself a violent man but like Ron McCardle he would use violence when necessary. He had been surprised at how much he had enjoyed the surge of adrenaline when he had been thumping the mugger. But as his mum often said: women, children and old folk should always be protected.

Ron McCardle was not having a good day. First, some toe rag had tried to rob the bookies and now he was feeling bored as he listened to the Grand Master of his masonic lodge drone on about local politics. As much as he knew that being a freemason was beneficial to him in many ways, all the Brother this and Master that and the endless speeches sent him to sleep. However he did take full advantage of the opportunity to network and had cultivated friendships with policemen, councillors, bankers and even a judge. He quite liked the 'you scratch my back and I'll scratch yours' arrangement and although most of the men whom he met were straight down the line, there was always the odd one who couldn't resist an extra payday. Thomas Turner was one such man. A policeman for fifteen years, he had built up many debts thanks to his demanding wife Janet who spent money like water. He had been only too happy to join Ron's ever expanding payroll and be his eyes and ears over the years so the alliance suited both men.

After the meal was over, Ron made his way over to Ray Briggs who owned a second hand car showroom and a scrap yard in St Albans. Ron had a bank job in mind which would be a nice little earner and he would need a car to use as the getaway vehicle. Ray had been supplying cars to Ron for years and then crushing them afterwards. Ray was as clean as a whistle, had never come to the attention of the police and was completely trustworthy because unbeknown to most people he was also Ron's second cousin.

Alan and Sonia were sat watching television but Alan wasn't paying much attention as he was still thinking about Stevie's botched attempt to rob the bookies. He was gutted that his old childhood friend had been brought so low. Apparently he had even flogged his grandad's war medals last week to pay the rent. A plan was forming in Alan's mind which if he could persuade Ron, would benefit not just Stevie but himself as well.

The next morning Sonia was making the children their porridge.

'Make if fluffy Mummy,' Connie demanded.

'I want lots of sugar,' Billy said.

'You'll get what you're given,' Sonia retorted.

She was feeling a bit jaded this morning and hadn't meant to snap at the twins. Last night she had finished the bottle of wine from earlier in the day as Alan had told her all about Stevie Baines and how he wanted to help him but needed Ron's approval. Her husband had then proceeded to toss and turn all night and consequently she hadn't slept well. This morning she felt anxious and didn't know why. Unfortunately unbeknown to her Sonia had every reason to be feeling troubled because Alan's kindness towards Stevie Baines would prove to have far reaching consequences that neither could ever have imagined.

Alan stood before Ron waiting for him to finish his phone call.

He was feeling a little nervous but was confident that Ron would understand once he had explained his idea because over the last couple of years the two men had grown close and Alan knew that Ron respected and trusted him.

Ron finished his call and cracked his knuckles before he spoke. 'So what exactly happened yesterday?'

Alan told him the sorry story of Stevie Baines and implored Ron to go easy on him.

'So what you're saying is that some cheeky fucker decided to take what is mine and disrespect me into the bargain but because his wife is having another kid that they can't feed, I should let it go?!'

Ron's eyes were screwed up in disbelief.

'I have known Stevie since we were kids, he had no idea that the bookies belonged to you and nearly shit himself when I told him. I gave him a good thump yesterday but what he really needs is a job and regular pay. He was desperate and we have all felt like that,' Alan explained.

'And what do you want me to do about it Alan? He has already shown that he is a thief and not to be trusted, you can't actually expect me to employ him?' Ron spat incredulously.

Alan could see that he was losing the battle but carried on determined to make Ron change his mind. 'Look Ron you got me out of a hole four years ago and I will always be grateful. I hope that you won't think that I am speaking out of turn but I am aware that you have other businesses and some are not strictly kosher. I am desperate to move up the ranks and to prove to you that I can be an asset. I am desperate to get my family off the shitty council estate that we live on and I am willing to do anything it takes to achieve that.'

Ron looked at the man before him who had become a friend and was impressed with his passionate speech. Over the years he had proved to be hardworking, loyal and he was handy with his fists when the need arose.

'What did you have in mind Alan?'

'Well I thought that maybe Stevie could take over from me in the bookies and I could work for you properly?' Alan stressed the last word so that Ron understood exactly what he meant.

Alan could feel that Ron was beginning to thaw towards the idea so hurriedly continued, 'Stevie will be my responsibility. I can show him the ropes and keep an eye on him.'

Ron thought for a moment, if Alan wanted an in then he would have to realise the risks involved. Big risks.

'Alan if I take you on as an active member of the firm you do understand what would be required of you, don't you? The job can be unpredictable and sometimes force is needed, if you want to earn a serious wedge then you will be stepping over to the other side and that means that you could end up in clink. Now with my contacts on the force, that doesn't happen very often but it could. I can't offer you job security and a pension Mate.'

Alan swallowed. There was no turning back. He didn't want a nine to five weekly wage packet anymore. He was willing to take the risk because he wanted more, much more.

'I'm ready Ron.'

'Okay, well for starters you can work the door of my club with Bill Smith and because the hours are unsociable you will be earning more than what you do now. I have a job coming up and if you prove yourself then I will think about getting you involved.'

Ron had faith in Alan but wanted to ease him in gently. When he saw the disappointed look on the other man's face he continued, 'You will need a day-to-day job to show the outside world and especially Sonia how you earn your money, otherwise people will get suspicious.'

Alan could see the sense in that and left the office feeling as he had when he had first been offered a job by Ron: scared but excited because he had just agreed to become a villain, which if he was honest with himself had always been the plan.

After he left Ron's office he went round to Stevie's flat to tell him the good news. Doreen answered the door in all of her seventeen stone glory.

'Alright Al, I guess you want the old man? Stevieeeeeeeeee,' she screeched into the darkened flat before padding back to her spot on the sofa to carry on watching the television.

'Bloody hell, your wife has got some lungs on her,' he chuckled when Stevie appeared.

'Don't remind me, imagine what it's like living with it,' Stevie said dejectedly.

Alan didn't have time for any small talk so explained to Stevie the upshot of his conversation with Ron.

Stevie understandably looked confused. 'So I try and rob his bookies but he has let it go AND he is giving me your job?'

'Look Stevie, I have gone out on a limb for you. Don't get me wrong, Ron was raging but I talked him down and he only listened because I assured him that you were sound and only made a grave error of judgement because you were desperate. He is a decent bloke as long as you don't cross him.'

Stevie was relieved but was still confused. 'I don't understand, if I am doing your job then what will you be doing?'

'Oh I am being promoted Mate, I'm moving on to better things. Now be in the bookies at nine o'clock tomorrow morning and I will show you what is what, it's a doddle and you were always good with numbers at school.'

Stevie suddenly smiled showing greying teeth and hugged Alan as hard as he could. 'Thanks Mate, I won't let you down.'

Alan looked him straight in the eyes and said, 'You'd better not because it won't just be Ron McCardle who comes for you if you do.'

Stevie looked shame faced and as he shut the front door couldn't help thinking that his old friend had changed. He was now speaking like a gangster and the thought unnerved him.

As Alan walked across the green towards his house he hoped that he had done the right thing asking Ron to give Stevie a job. He had a nagging feeling that he would live to regret it but it was done now. His next job was to convince his wife that working in a nightclub would benefit them. He had a sneaking suspicion that she wouldn't see it that way and he was right.

'I don't want you working in a night club Alan, no way!'

'But think of the extra money AND I will be around during the day to help with the kids.'

Sonia snorted, 'Get under my feet more like and anyway the kids start nursery soon. No I'm sorry but I don't like the thought of my husband fraternising with barely dressed women all night as I sit here like a lemon in my dressing gown and slippers.'

Alan had known this would be the real reason why his wife would object and was ready with his answer. 'I will be outside the club seeing off trouble, not that there will be much, all the women will be inside Love, and think of the money. We could get a new suite in no time.'

He could see that his wife was weighing it up in her mind and he gave her the time to digest what he had said. The secret was letting her think that she had made the decision.

'Well ok, I guess the extra money would come in handy but I am choosing the new suite.'

'That goes without saying Darling.'

He cuddled her close and said, 'Always remember that everything that I do is for you and the kids.'

In the years that followed Sonia would become sick of hearing this.

Chapter 5

1973

It was two-thirty in the morning and Ron was taking Ebony home in his new Mercedes. As they sat at the traffic lights in Green Lanes, he noticed a blue Capri pull up beside them. Ever vigilant, Ron glanced at the occupants and was incensed to realise that they were both hungrily leering at his mistress.

'Alright sexy?' one of them cheekily called over. The boy then turned to his friend and they both laughed before returning to drool over the beautiful woman with the impressive cleavage. Ebony who was busily filing her nails glanced up and being the friendly girl she was smiled in appreciation at their obvious admiration. Clocking the exchange, Ron hastily got out of his car but not before reaching for the tyre iron that he kept under the driver's seat for emergencies.

'How dare you disrespect me you little Fuckers,' he raged.

'Keep your wig on Grandad, there's no harm in looking,' the driver cockily stated.

Ron peered in at them with a dangerous glint in his eyes, his anger building. The two young men were now looking at him nervously, their eyes firmly fixed on the tyre iron.

Terry Sanders and Mick Latham were both eighteen and thought they were God's gift to women when in fact they were just two greasy haired, acne riddled idiots who spoke before they engaged their brains. They had also realised with frightening clarity that the angry man before them was none other than Ron McCardle. Suddenly they wished they were at home safely tucked up in their beds. With a swipe of the weapon Ron smashed the windscreen of their car and going round to the passenger side pulled out Mick Latham by his denim jacket and proceeded to give him a good hiding. On one level Ron knew that they were just kids but he could not and would not have anyone blatantly disrespect him. He had his reputation to uphold.

Terry Sanders sat rooted to his seat in fear as he watched his friend being beaten. Ron was brought back to his senses as Ebony was now screaming and had become hysterical. Throwing the boy onto the dirty pavement he got back into his car and drove off shouting, 'Let that be a lesson to you boys, oh and the hair is all natural you Tossers.'

Alan was having a quick cigarette break outside Ron's club in Tottenham before it emptied for the night. It had been a quiet night, no real trouble to speak of other than a couple of drunken oiks trying to get in and throwing a few air punches before being expertly removed from the doorway by Alan and the other doorman Bill Smith. As Alan smoked, he reflected on the last two years.

He was now earning a good, solid wage and had moved his family to a property in Crouch End courtesy of one of Ron's many rentals. It was a large Victorian house in Berkeley Road and he and Sonia occupied the ground and middle floors. It included a good sized garden and Sonia's mother Breda lived on the top floor which consisted of two attic rooms and a kitchenette. At first Sonia had been dubious coming out of the council system but Alan had assured her that Ron had promised him that with the way things were going, they would soon be in a position to buy the house and her mother had astutely pointed out to her daughter that the house would be worth a fortune one day. Alan was confident that Sonia didn't realise that all this would not be possible on a doorman's salary alone and that he was slowly but surely working up the ranks of Ron's ever-growing empire. In June 1972 Alan had been one of the drivers in the bank job that Ron had arranged and from that day on Alan had never looked back.

After Ron had dropped off Ebony and calmed her down, he had finally got home at four o'clock in the morning. As he entered the large entry hall of his Enfield home, he could hear the soft drone of the television. He walked into the front room and saw that Irene had fallen asleep on the sofa. Nudging her gently he said, 'Come on Love, time for bed.'

Irene blinked a few times and was soon awake.

Taking in her husband's dishevelled appearance she immediately sat up and exclaimed, 'What the hell happened to you, you've got blood on your shirt?'

'It's nothing that a bit of Daz won't sort out Girl,' he joked.

Sighing, Irene got up and with her arm out stretched told him to take it off so it could be soaked before she washed it. She knew from experience that he wouldn't elaborate and she had become an expert at not prying. In this life a wife had to learn when to turn a blind eye.

The next morning Irene answered the phone to Thomas Turner who she knew was on her husband's payroll. After enquiring after his wife Janet, she handed the receiver to Ron who signalled for her to close the door.

'Morning Ron,' Thomas's gruff voice came over the line. 'I understand that you had an eventful night last night, aren't you too old and well known to be brawling in the street?'

'Cut the crap Thomas, what's the news?'

He liked Thomas but the man could never quite grasp that he was merely an employee. He was his eyes and ears at the local nick and Ron could do without his opinions. In the cold light of day Ron realised that he had over reacted and truth be told, Ebony wasn't worth doing a stretch over.

'You do know that the boy you beat up is Kenny Latham's son?'

'I don't care if he is Al Capone's son, he deserved what he got.'

Ron was being belligerent but knew that he had to save face. There was a brief silence at the other end of the line, obvious confirmation that Thomas didn't agree before he assured Ron, 'It's all sorted, the other lad Terry Sanders has made a statement saying that they were jumped by a local gang of lads so the law side of it is taken care of. Unfortunately the boy you attacked is in hospital with concussion, broken ribs and a badly dislocated knee, he was a budding footballer apparently...' Turner left the last piece of information hanging in the air.

Ron thanked him and put the receiver back on the cradle. Kenny Latham was small fry, part of an amateur outfit from Finsbury Park so he wasn't overly bothered about what he thought. He had a more pressing matter to attend to and needed Alan to show him his true capabilities and loyalty in order to sort out the situation that had come to his attention.

Sonia had put the twins to bed and was having a cup of tea with her mum. As she took in the beauty of her spacious front room she smiled. She had been worried when Alan suggested that they rent privately but any reservations she might have had had disappeared as soon as she had walked through the front door and seen the potential of her new home. They had slowly redecorated and she particularly loved the pink and grey striped wallpaper she had chosen for the hallway and landings. It accompanied the rose red carpet perfectly.

Alan had allowed her to be in charge of the renovations and had only questioned her decision not to rip out the original marble fireplaces. Sonia thought that they were classy and was convinced that in time people would regret exchanging them for chunky York stone which was the fashion at the moment.

Although Sonia was grateful to be away from the old estate, she missed seeing Gina and Brenda every day and had begun to feel troubled, a feeling of anxiety that was growing daily. Alan must think that she was an idiot if he really thought that she believed their step up in the world had been achieved by his salary as a doorman. Her worries had started in late 1972 when she was packing up the loft in the old house in preparation for their move. Behind the water tank she had discovered a dusty bag full of cash. She had hastily put it back, instinctively knowing that she wasn't meant to find it. The following day she had mentioned to her husband that she had started sorting out the loft and unsurprisingly when she had next ventured up there the bag had gone. There were other things as well, such as the time when Alan had come home with blood on his coat and late night phone calls from Ron requesting her husband's presence for a 'bit of business.'

One Saturday Sonia had bumped into Elaine Smith in Wood Green. Elaine's husband Bill worked the door with Alan at Ron's club in Tottenham.

Sonia had complimented the other woman on her chunky gold necklace that she was wearing, to which Elaine had winked and said, 'Crime pays Love and I'm not complaining.'

Sonia hadn't really known what to say but it was starting to all add up. She had smiled politely and told Elaine that she must dash as she needed to pick up the twins from nursery school. Over the next few weeks she had done a bit of digging and discovered that Ron McCardle or 'Uncle' Ron as her children now called him was a well-known feature in North London and not for the right reasons! Her husband was working for a criminal and as the implications dawned on her so did her anxiety. She was now on medication to control the knot in her stomach and her brother-in-law David had given her something to help her sleep. On one hand she knew that her husband had always had ambition and wanted his family to enjoy a better standard of living than they would have had on the estate but at what cost? Some nights after she had put the children to bed, she sat on her own, her imagination going into overdrive. What if Alan ended up in prison or worse still, dead! She was ashamed to admit to herself that she enjoyed the benefits that whatever he was doing provided, and often tried to convince herself that what she didn't know couldn't hurt her. Therefore her coping strategy was to bury her head in the proverbial sand and not to ask any questions that she didn't want the answers to.

Ron was flushed and constantly refilling his glass as he told Alan the information that Maureen Holmes who worked in the bookies had given him.

'Your mate Stevie is stealing from me. He is pocketing the dosh from unplaced bets. Now I gave the prick a chance and he has royally taken the piss so I want you to sort it. I don't care what his excuse is this time, he's out and I want you to teach the ponce a lesson.'

Alan inwardly groaned and took a sip of his drink, furious that Stevie had put him in this awkward position. 'Don't worry Ron, I'll make sure that he is dealt with.'

Ron nodded, 'Make sure that you do.'

Alan nodded in agreement, there was no point arguing as Stevie had dropped a major bollock and deserved everything that he had coming to him.

Stevie sighed in relief as he watched the horse fall at the second fence. So far he had managed to get away with this little scam, however he had been in a complete state of terror these last few months but once again he had no choice. Doreen had racked up hundreds of pounds on her catalogues and she was up the spout again. Six bloody kids they would need to feed now and the fat slob had no intention to contributing to any of the poor little sods. The crux had come two months ago when his youngest Dawn had cried herself to sleep with a hungry belly.

It had been his brother-in-law Charlie who had come up with the suggestion of scamming the bookies and although Stevie knew that he was on seriously dangerous ground he was confident that he had been careful to cover his tracks.

Alan walked into the bookies with a heavy heart but a determined look on his face that didn't escape Stevie who looked horrified to see that his old mate was accompanied by Ron's two gorillas, Rob and Doug Clarke. With a sinking feeling somewhere in his bowels he realised that he had been rumbled.

Alan glared at him and said calmly, 'I can't help you this time Stevie, Ron knows you've been scamming him. You're out.'

Stevie felt his legs give way as Rob and Doug dragged him roughly into the back of the shop and pushed him onto the grubby carpet.

'Are you wired to the fucking moon Stevie? Ron hasn't got to where he is in life without knowing exactly what is going on around him,' Alan spat.

'I'm sorry Al, I was desperate, Dor is up the spout again and we can't feed the kids we already have.'

'The fact that you have impregnated that moose again is not my problem. You made the same excuse a few years back when you tried to rob the place and I took pity on you and asked Ron to give you a chance. You have just thrown that back in my face you disloyal cunt.'

Stevie knew that he had done wrong and couldn't help thinking that Alan had changed into a thug. He was now as hard as nails and this was confirmed when he was booted in the stomach by his old friend. Gasping for breath he tried to plead with Alan who just turned away as he instructed Rob and Doug Clarke to administer a number three punishment. Ron's grading system of punishments was legendary and Stevie knew that he was in for some broken bones and possibly a stint in hospital. The worse thing was that he had not only lost a mate who had helped him out but he probably wouldn't be fit to work again for months. As he felt self-pity overwhelm him he wept like a baby. 'Please Al, we're mates from way back.'

Alan bent down and grabbing Stevie by the hair snarled, 'Mates are loyal, I stuck my neck out for you, get him out of my sight Boys.'

Doug nodded and with his brother's help dragged the sobbing man out to the yard where he was flung into the boot of Rob's Cortina. He was then driven to the privacy of Ray Briggs's scrap yard where he would be punished and then dumped at the local hospital.

Once the shop was empty Alan sparked up a Rothmans and sighed. Stevie was a bloody fool and deserved a good kicking but even knowing this he still felt a twinge of guilt.

It was Irene's fiftieth birthday and Ron had pulled out all the stops and arranged a private party in the upstairs function room of his restaurant in Russell Square.

As the birthday girl came down the stairs in her floor-length lemon dress Ron let out an appreciative whistle, 'Blimey Girl, you look incredible.'

Irene brushed off the compliment but was secretly chuffed as she felt that sometimes Ron didn't see her as a woman. She knew that their lack of passion drove him into the arms of other women but was quietly confident that he would never leave her. They were soul mates for one thing and she knew far too much about him, she thought with a wry smile.

Alan had a similar reaction when he saw Sonia in her party attire. She had her beautiful, thick, dark hair piled on top of her head and her outfit of choice was a body skimming, red cat suit. Sonia felt a million dollars for once. Usually she lived in jeans and a t-shirt, so it had made a nice change to get glammed up tonight for Irene's party. She had a sneaking suspicion, however that the expensive looking necklace that Alan had given her earlier may have had something to do with a recent robbery she had read about that had occurred in Hatton Garden. But she was determined not to dwell on her worries and had pushed them firmly to the to the back of her mind where all her other worries lived.

Ron had really gone to town for the party. There was a disco, a live band, plenty of free drink and succulent food for all the guests to enjoy. Family and friends mixed happily with members of the underworld, some of whom had travelled from south of the river out of respect for Ron and because Irene was a well-liked wife.

The drink was flowing and Sonia was thoroughly enjoying herself. Her happiness soon evaporated though when she saw a serious looking Doug Clarke waving her husband over. He clearly had something important to tell him. Sonia discreetly followed and joined Doug's girlfriend Kimmy who was stood near to where the two men were animatedly talking. At one point Alan grabbed Doug by the shirt and as she strained to hear what was being said, she heard her husband angrily exclaim, 'For fuck's sake Doug, you were only meant to rough him up a bit.'

Sonia didn't hear what Doug's reply was because Kimmy had started talking to her. All she did know was that her once mild mannered husband was involved in someone being hurt. Picking up a glass of champagne from a passing waiter she made her excuses to Kimmy and walked away with a sinking feeling in the pit of her stomach.

Chapter 6

Alan woke the next morning with a stinking hangover and groaned. Stevie Baines was dead. According to Doug they hadn't even touched him. He had been slung into the boot of Rob's car and driven to Ray's scrap yard in St Albans. When they had opened the boot, Stevie was as dead as a doornail. The plan had been to teach the man a lesson. He had basically been a coward and Alan had believed that breaking a few bones would have been enough. Now he had a dead ex-friend on his conscience and he knew that Ron would be livid because although he could lose his rag on occasion, Ron liked to think that he was a gentleman villain who only used brute force when strictly necessary. He certainly wouldn't want a senseless death being connected to his firm. Ron was the boss, he was the only person with the authority to order a hit and that was a rare occurrence. Alan just couldn't understand why Stevie had croaked it. He had heard of people dying of fright, had that happened? Wearily he picked up the phone and rang his brother David who was a qualified doctor and now earning an extra income patching up villains who couldn't risk hospitals or questions. On rare occasions he was required to be economical with the truth on death certificates and, all in all, he was doing nicely. His wife Sandra was over the moon with all the extra cash coming in. In fact Sandra unlike her sister-in-law Sonia didn't have the brain power to ask questions or worry about how her husband could afford to drive a brand new car. She and their daughter Samantha thoroughly enjoyed the good life that the money afforded them and she had no intention of ever going back to a two up two down.

Sonia was sitting smoking and reading a magazine when her husband announced that he needed to pop out to sort out some business. She barely glanced up when he hastily kissed her on the cheek and then hurriedly left the house. After last night's revelations she had doubled up on her pills and although she appeared calm, inside she was screaming. Someone had been hurt, maybe they were dead and Alan was involved in hurting other people and could end up in prison. Although she had acknowledged to herself some time ago that Alan was working for a villain, her naivety had not allowed her to realise that violence could be a part of the life he now lived. Her mind was racing and going into overdrive so she tried to breathe like the doctor had advised her to when she felt anxious. It wasn't working, so she asked her mother Breda to mind the kids as she needed the total oblivion a sleeping pill would give her.

Breda was a hands-on Nan and only too happy to look after the twins but she was worried about her daughter who seemed permanently worried. In Breda's mind you had to deal with what life threw at you. She didn't hold much truck with talking about feelings or with pills to help a person escape reality. Breda came from an era where people kept themselves busy so that they had no time to dwell on all the sadness, misery and worries of life.

She wasn't stupid or oblivious to what was going on at home. She knew that Sonia was worried about Alan who worked for the local big man and who clearly didn't earn all of his money legally. Breda had heard the stories about him over the years but when she had met him she was relieved that he hadn't come across as some bully boy but instead appeared to be an articulate businessman who had taken her son-in-law under his wing and provided him with a decent wage which in turn meant that her daughter now lived a good life in a beautiful home. Breda could physically shake Sonia at times as she felt that she should be more grateful and just enjoy her life instead of battling with the notions that were in her head. Ron McCardle had never been arrested so surely that meant he wasn't doing anything too bad? He obviously didn't take unnecessary risks and neither would Alan. Hearing a door upstairs close, Breda sighed and called the children to the kitchen for their porridge.

As Alan and David looked at the pitiful body of Stevie Baines, they both felt a great sadness remembering the skinny, snotty nosed friend of their childhood. Knowing that time was of the essence they quickly set to work. Removing the body from the boot, they laid it gently onto the gravel and searched the man's pockets. They found a shopping list, three quid and an asthma pump. David looked at the inhaler and raised his eyebrows, 'Well it looks like he probably had an asthma attack, there wouldn't have been much air in this boot, the poor sod!'

'Thank fuck for that, at least it was natural causes,' Alan replied in relief. 'We'll take him back to the bookies, leave him there lying on the carpet, it will look believable. I will make out that I found him and call an ambulance. Pass us that inhaler.'

As Alan stamped on the inhaler, David was tempted to say that there was nothing natural about this little turn of events but knew when to keep schtum. Like his wife, he had learnt not to ask too many questions. He could see that Ron McCardle thought a lot of his brother and he was grateful that through this connection he was also reaping the benefits. Alan was now treated as Ron's number two and David felt certain that the older man was moulding his brother for the top spot when the time came. Their lives had changed dramatically from their lowly beginnings in the tenements. Both now lived in desirable areas, wore expensive clothes and drove decent cars. David could sense that Sonia had issues with Alan's chosen career. His brother had confided in him that she was struggling. She had recently stopped going to her own GP as she said that she felt embarrassed, so David was prescribing her sleeping pills and anti-depressants on a regular basis but in his opinion they weren't doing the trick. She often had a face like a slapped arse which was unfair on his brother who worked bloody hard to give his family a good life.

Sonia had slept for three hours and was now sitting in the garden with her mother trying to convince herself that whoever had been hurt had probably deserved it. Maybe this person had threatened her Alan? As she sipped at her cold drink she was filled with a feeling of foreboding. If her husband was giving orders to have someone roughed up then he had turned from a mild mannered man into a thug and the thought terrified her. She suddenly felt nostalgic for their old life back on the estate. Admittedly it had been a shit hole and money had been scarce, but they had been in the same boat as everyone around them and life had been so much simpler then. Her feelings were always at conflict because if she was honest with herself, she loved having more money and a lovely home but she hated the life that Alan had to lead to provide these luxuries. The constant fear that her husband would end up behind bars was all consuming and her anxiety was building with each day that passed. As the tears came, Breda turned to her and decided that a few home truths were in order. Not mincing her words she reminded her daughter that she was a very lucky woman. She had a husband who still only had eyes for her and worked hard to provide them all with a comfortable life which was more than she had ever had. What's more, he put up with her moods when most men would have sodded off down the pub or found someone else with a happier face.

Watching her children squealing with delight as they splashed in their paddling pool and realising that her mother was probably right, Sonia brushed her worries to where her other dark thoughts lived, firmly at the back of her mind and decided to cook her husband a lovely meal for when he finally got home.

Alan had had the day from Hell, after placing Stevie on the floor of the bookies, he had phoned for an ambulance and Stevie had been taken away. David had suggested that they go for a pint before going home but Alan had insisted that the least he could do was to let Doreen know that her husband had died. So getting into his car he drove back to their old estate to relay the bad news.

Doreen clung to Alan, her cumbersome body heaving with sobs.

'I don't understand, he always had his inhaler with him.'

Alan felt a twinge of guilt as he told her that they hadn't found anything on him other than the few quid and the shopping list.

'I thought that he had just gone on a bender when he didn't come home,' the distraught woman wailed. 'I even sent my brother Charlie round the bookies and it was all locked up.'

'Come on let's go inside and I'll make you a cuppa Dor,' Alan suggested.

Her wailing was becoming louder and his legs were beginning to buckle as she was hanging on to him for dear life.

He gently led her back into her flat and deposited her onto the shabby sofa while he went into the kitchen to make the tea. He was pleasantly surprised that the flat appeared clean and tidy. Give Doreen her due, she always stopped drinking when she was pregnant but soon went back to her slovenly ways once the child was born.

Now she would have six kids to bring up on her own. Ron always looked after the wives should an untimely death occur and Alan decided that he would do the same for Doreen on the quiet. Stevie had been an idiot but until now he had run the bookies and there had been no problems. He just wished that Stevie had come to him with his problems because everyone in their world knew that you didn't bite the hand that fed you.

When he came back into the front room, five children ranging from the ages of thirteen to two sat staring at him with suspicious eyes. Alan had to look away, the eldest boy Jason was the image of his Dad and it was at this point that Alan's eyes had momentarily filled with tears. When he turned back

Jason was staring at him with hate. Alan felt unnerved. The old saying 'don't shoot the messenger,' sprung to mind. Alan couldn't blame the lad who must be feeling confused and who would eventually be expected to step up as the man of the family.

'How am I going to feed my kids? We were only scraping by as it is and I'm due again in five months. I won't be able to work with six kiddies to look after.' Doreen was becoming hysterical again.

Alan lit a cigarette from his packet and passed it to her. He was tempted to point out that she had never worked but decided that this was not the time.

'Don't worry Dor, I will see you alright.'

'Why would you do that?' She looked at him suspiciously as did Jason who had put a protective arm around his mother.

'He was my mate and he would have done the same for me. We went back years Love.'

Alan was desperate to get out of this soulless flat with the accusing eyes of Stevie's family boring into him. Doreen eventually calmed down and Alan promised her that he would pop by in the week to see how they all were. Reaching into his pocket, he handed her twenty-five pounds which she greedily grabbed. Saying goodbye, he left the flat and ran away from his guilt as quickly as he could. Although he loved the business side of his new life and was happy to administer a kicking when it was necessary, a death was a whole different ball game and he wasn't sure that he was comfortable with it.

Ron had woken in a good mood. Irene had enjoyed a great birthday and they had actually made love last night. Ron realised that this had come about because she was pissed and grateful for all his efforts in making her birthday so special. On one hand these facts saddened him, but he had accepted a long time ago that this was how it was and these fleeting moments made him realise just how much he loved his wife. His mood had however been dampened when he took a phone call from Alan who had explained to him about the unexpected demise of Stevie Baines. Ron had been furious to begin with but had calmed down when he had assured Ron it had been sorted.

As he listened, he thanked his lucky stars that Alan had come into his life and his firm. There weren't many men in his life who he trusted and liked but in Alan he had found a kindred spirit and although there were only fourteen years that separated them, he now looked upon the younger man as the son he had never had. The son who would hopefully one day run the businesses while he enjoyed a well-earned retirement with his beloved wife in the country.

A few days later Sonia was on the phone to Brenda Draper having a good old natter. They were just about to say their goodbyes when Brenda suddenly exclaimed, 'Wasn't it terrible about Stevie Baines carking it like that? I bumped into Doreen today in the Co Op and she was in a terrible state, well you would be with five kids, another on the way and no man to support you wouldn't you?'

Sonia froze but was temporarily reassured when Brenda went on to explain that the death had been caused by an asthma attack when he was at work. As soon as Sonia put down the phone she ran into the kitchen where Alan was having a cup of tea and a cigarette.

'Why didn't you tell me about Stevie?'

Alan was taken by surprise at how fast the jungle drums had started and for a split second didn't know how to react. Sonia clocked her husband's discomfort and immediately guessed that Stevie was the person who her husband had been discussing with Doug Clarke at Irene's party. Suddenly it all made sense and she felt sick to her stomach.

Stevie had been a friend of her husband's, his children had visited their home when they had lived on the estate. Trying desperately to calm herself she urged Alan to be honest with her, 'Look Alan, I know there is stuff that goes on that I don't know about and maybe that is why I worry so much. I know that the other wives know far more than you tell me and I am beginning to resent you for treating me like a china doll who is too weak to be told the truth. Being kept in the dark is making me ill.'

Alan looked at his wife in surprise. He had realised that she was unhappy but he had always tried to protect her because, despite what she was saying, she suffered with her nerves and if she knew the truth of some of the stuff that really went on he knew that it would make her worse. Battling it out in his head he decided to be truthful to a point and try and alleviate her fears.

'Stevie Baines had been stealing from the bookies. Ron is a well-respected man and he couldn't be seen to let that go so he instructed his boys to give Stevie a slap, nothing heavy, just a message to anyone else with the same notions.'

Sonia was just about to interrupt but Alan held his hand up and carried on, 'Stevie had an asthma attack before the boys touched him so he died of natural causes Love.'

'Why wasn't he just sacked and why didn't the boys try and save him?'

'The only language that some people understand is some form of violence Son. Ron hasn't got to where he is in life without using his fists but that is very rare these days and as for saving Stevie, can you really see the Clarke brothers knowing what to do? They only possess about five brain cells between them! Ron is mainly legal these days and I know for a fact that he wants to be completely legit in a few years.'

Alan could see that his wife was trying to process what he had just told her. She would try and understand but in his hearts of hearts he knew that she would never be able to accept any violence. If he was honest, he didn't enjoy it but needs must at times. The other wives he had met were either oblivious or more interested in the money that their husbands brought home than the worry of where it had come from. He sighed. It was a bloody shame because Ron wanted him to take over one day but he was the one who had a wife with the inner strength of a new born baby!

Sonia wasn't sure what to think and although it suited her to believe that Stevie had died because his own body had let him down and was pleased to hear of Ron's plans to go legal she still couldn't help but think that Alan had just given her a load of old fanny to shut her up and to stop her worrying. It was clear that her husband was more than a club bouncer these days and what really bothered her was the close friendship that he shared with Ron who seemed to rely on Alan far too much for her liking.

Chapter 7

New Year's Eve 1977

Connie had woken up giddy with excitement. It was New Year's Eve and she was going to her first grown up party.

'Mummy can I put on my party dress?' she yelled down the stairs.

Sonia laughed, 'The party doesn't start for hours, now go and wake your brother while I make breakfast because Aunty Maggie will be here soon.'

Aunty Maggie was her mother's younger sister who was at this moment making her way from Kilburn and would be staying for a few days. The children adored her, although Sonia wasn't sure what Ron McCardle would think of her. She just hoped that her aunty wouldn't flash her knickers again like she had done at the Silver Jubilee party in the summer.

Sonia and Alan always spent New Year's Eve with their old friends from the estate: the Drapers (Brenda and Geoff, Gina and Nick) but this year they had extended the party list to include the nice Chinese couple from next door and the teacher and his wife from up the road who they had become friendly with. Alan's brother David and his wife Sandra were also coming with their daughter Samantha. Sonia had been a bit nervous when Alan had insisted they should invite Ron and Irene as well.

Alan was firmly established as Ron's second in command and oversaw a lot of the businesses. Despite his assurances all those years ago Sonia was more than aware that there was still a lot of illegal activities going on. She was very fond of Irene but Ron always made her feel anxious. He came across as a benevolent uncle but Sonia knew that he had blood on his hands and that her husband was in deeper than ever.

Connie had run back into the bedroom that she shared with Billy and had jumped on him.

'Get off me,' he squealed as his annoying sister began to tickle him.

Hearing the commotion Alan came into the bedroom and was soon tangled up with his children laughing his head off as they all rolled around the floor tickling each other. Sonia stood in the doorway smiling. It had been a long time since Alan had spent quality time with Billy and Connie. These days he was always out on business and in the last few years it had been Sonia and her mother who had raised them.

'Right you lot, break it up. Everyone has a job to do.'

Both children groaned but jumped up. They would clean the bathroom with a toothbrush if it meant that they could stay up late and see the New Year in with the adults.

Sonia turned to her husband, 'Will you go to the offie and get the booze Love? You can take Mum's shopping trolley.'

Alan looked at her in horror. No way was he traipsing down the road with an old lady's tartan shopping trolley! Seeing her husband's face Sonia snapped sarcastically, 'Sorry I forgot that it would ruin your street cred!'

Alan was getting fed up with his wife's snidey comments that had been building over the years. He worked damn hard and even if it wasn't all kosher, his wife hadn't complained when she had been presented with a solid gold bracelet on Christmas day. She had double standards and could be a pain in the pipe these days. None of her clothes came from C&A anymore. She wore the best that money could buy and was always happy to take the money that he generously gave her but would then mock how he made that same money. She had been delighted when they had bought the house but Alan could sense she still struggled with his line of work.

'Give me a break Son, I'm working my arse off for you and the kids. Do you want to be back on that shitty estate with the druggies?'

She didn't, so retreated to the kitchen to check on her sausage rolls. Sighing, Alan grabbed his car keys and went to buy the drink. Driving down the road he laughed, even Chinese Bob from next door wouldn't be seen dead with a shopping trolley and he was a bit of an anorak! When he got back, he went straight into the kitchen and hugged his wife because he knew that she still had cause to worry, and he hated it when they argued.

'Are you alright Son?'

'Yeah, everything is ready for tonight, I'm really looking forward to it.'

Alan leered at her and winked, 'Ooh does that mean that we have time for a quick fumble?'

'No we bloody haven't!' Sonia swiped her husband with her Silver Jubilee tea towel and chuckled, pleased that he wasn't cross with her anymore.

Ebony Peters was not a happy bunny. She was thirty-five now and her life was one big car crash. She had been the mistress of Ron McCardle for nearly eleven years and she could sense that he was cooling towards her. She was starting to feel insecure, a feeling that was new to her. Only last week he had cancelled a date and last night had been too tired to make love. Well she might not be in her prime anymore but he certainly wasn't Robert Redford. He had a distinct paunch these days that hung over his expensive y-fronts and his conversation bored her. Only the other day he had excitedly told her about a trellis that he had bought for his roses. A few years ago there would have been no idle chat, they would have been tearing at each other's clothes and spending the day in bed. If she was honest, she felt that the relationship had fizzled out. These days there was more fizz in a Lemon Sherbert sweet but she was too proud to be dumped, and miffed that Ron clearly no longer wanted her. Recently she had been having hot sex with a very handsome Turkish man who she had known for years.

The only problem was that he was married as well and she had realised over the years that these men never left the security of their wives. Ebony liked to be in control and call the shots but she had no control over her latest dilemma. She was pregnant and didn't know who the father was. She wasn't really a girl's girl and didn't have any close friends, so in desperation she had confided in her father Gary Peters who had been none too pleased with the news.

Gary Peters had been released from prison two years before after doing a stretch for manslaughter. He had been a well-known face in his time and was still liked and respected by the local criminal fraternity. He had been looked after in prison thanks to his best mate and childhood friend Deniz Mehmet who had contacts on the inside, namely a distant cousin who was a screw. As Gary sat in a pub in The Archway, he pondered over his daughter's news. He and Deniz had grown up together as orphans in Dr Barnardos and Ebony had known Deniz's son Kadir since they were kids. They had attended his wedding so why had the dense cow decided to jump into bed with him? Now she was in the family way by one of two married men, neither of whom he suspected would be leaving the family home anytime soon. But she was still his princess and help her he would. The question was which of her lovers would be receiving the news that they were about to become a father? One thing was for sure: He didn't want either man finding out about the other.

He had his daughter's reputation to consider, although a little voice in his head told him that that ship had long since sailed but he banished away such an unsavoury thought about his only child and tried to come up with a solution. An abortion was out of the question because she was already too far along. It was a ball ache alright and Gary couldn't see either man doing somersaults over the news. He wasn't scared of Ron McCardle. They had been casual friends for years and although Ron was known as 'The Man' by the locals, Gary knew that he was decent and fair and would hopefully do the right thing by his daughter. Also, he wanted an in with Deniz Mehmet who was now making a fortune importing and selling drugs. Furthemore, he was involved with arms trafficking and rumour had it that he had links with the Turkish Mafia, so he was definitely the right person to have on side. Gary also knew that the union of marriage was very important to Deniz who was very fond of his daughter-in-law Layla and adored his grandchildren. Gary realised there was no way he could bother the Mehmets with his daughter's pregnancy as too much was at stake. So that left Ron who had no kids. Maybe he would leave Irene and start a proper life with Ebony and the child. Gary was realistic enough to know that there was little chance of that. He loved his daughter dearly but was the first person to point out that an intellect she was not. She was merely a sexual distraction for Ron. Despite this reality, Gary decided that Ron was the best bet. He was a decent bloke and would support the child if nothing else.

Relieved that he had made a decision, Gary downed his pint, wished the landlord a Happy New Year and went to tell his daughter what was going to happen.

Sonia was putting the final touches to her buffet while Alan supervised the children's baths upstairs. Aunty Maggie had arrived at three o'clock with enough luggage for a month. She had bustled into the house leaving her familiar aroma of Rothman's cigarettes, humbugs and Tweed perfume trailing behind her. She was small and birdlike but had a booming voice which made her larger than life. Aunty Maggie walked into a room and commanded it with her joyful personality and Sonia loved her for it.

The two older women were now ensconced in Breda's flat upstairs, getting dolled up, and Sonia suspected that they had already started on the Gin as she could hear them giggling away like two school girls. Five minutes later they proudly appeared done up to the nines for the party.

'Well how do we look?' Breda asked.

Sonia had to stifle a laugh as her mother and aunty both looked like they had the whole makeup counter of Boots on their faces and the affect was alarming to say the least. She was saved from answering with the ring of the doorbell. The first guests had arrived.

Connie swooned when she spotted Denny Draper who was standing with his dad Geoff. She had seen him briefly in the summer but he had been a punk rocker then and had looked a bit scary.

Tonight he had toned down his look, the spiked blue hair and tight leather trousers had been replaced by a more natural look of soft, wavy, dark hair, black jeans and a white t-shirt. He was so much more handsome now and Connie decided there and then that she was going to marry him and not Donny Osmond after all.

As with most parties, the men stood chatting beer, in hand on one side of the room, while the women were scattered around gossiping. Alan was very fond of Denny who was his godson.

'So what happened to the spikes Den?' he chuckled, ruffling the boy's hair.

'Decided on a change, wasn't really attracting the ladies Al.'

Geoff laughed. 'Tell him the real reason Den, listen to this Al, bloody hilarious.'

Denny laughed too, 'Well I was in the pub a few weeks back minding my own business waiting for the pool table, when the button on my leather trousers popped off and landed on the table. The lads who were playing thought I'd thrown it at them, mods they were and let's just say that they weren't happy. Never legged it so quick I can tell you, they were built like tanks. Also the trousers were a bastard to get off and I was in real trouble if I needed a shit and had to peel them off!'

Alan was clutching his sides roaring with laughter. He noticed that Ron was doing the same. Denny was a good lad and a funny fucker to boot.

'Well I think that you made the right decision Den, you'd never have got a job in Barclays looking like that,' Alan pointed out.

'Sod that, I don't want a 9-5. I was going to ask you if you could set me up with a gig. You are my godfather after all,' Denny winked.

Alan saw Geoff's worried expression as did Ron.

'Don't worry Geoff, most of the rumours about me aren't true,' Ron said.

He knew that people were well aware that he was involved in some unscrupulous activities so he could understand Geoff not wanting his son to be involved in anything dangerous.

'Give Alan a bell in the week. I'm always looking for bar staff in the club,' Ron stated, nodding respectfully at the boy's father who still looked unsure.

'We're not the Corleones,' Alan laughed referring to the 1972 film *The Godfather*.

Geoff, like the others from Tottenham, wasn't stupid. They had all noticed that their old friend was far more self-assured these days and more suspiciously far better off financially. There had been plenty of speculation behind closed doors about Alan's association with the local gangster but they had all mixed with Ron socially over the years and liked him, so the general consensus was that what they didn't know couldn't hurt them. Geoff was a postman and led a simple life. He had no real aspirations other than paying the rent on time and having a pint on a Saturday night. He sensed that his boy wanted more out of life and, as he was nearly eighteen he didn't have much control over him anymore, so had no choice but to convince his Brenda that it was a good idea even if he himself had serious doubts.

Connie, Caroline Draper and Cath Davis were upstairs discussing what they had got for Christmas. They saw each other regularly and were close friends. Gina Davis had bought the three girls a diary each with a little padlock and they were thrilled that they could write their first entry in a few hours' time. When they heard the husky voice of Rod Stewart singing Maggie May they rushed downstairs because they knew that Aunty Maggie would have started the dancing. Sure enough when they walked into the front room Maggie and Breda were the centre of attention on the make-shift dance floor and soon everyone was up singing and cheering the two women on. Connie was beside herself as she was actually dancing with Denny Draper. She was petite and he had lifted her up and was swinging her around. She was in heaven and this really was the best night of her life she thought happily.

'Rod wrote that song for me you know Child,' Maggie confided in Connie when she finally sat down puffing from her exertions. Connie stared at her in awe. Breda rolled her eyes and laughed.

'You fell over his suitcase at that posh hotel up West years ago. If he had written a song about you it would have been called Clumsy Cow!'

Maggie huffed and winked at her great niece, 'Well I've never heard a song with the name Breda in it!'

Sonia, Gina, Brenda and Irene were sitting nearby listening to the two older women bantering when Brenda suddenly exclaimed, 'Guess who I saw the other day?'

'Rod Stewart?' Sonia replied dryly.

'Doreen Baines!'

'Who?' Gina asked.

'You know Stevie Baines's wife, died about four years ago, was found stiff as a door on the floor of the bookies, your Alan found him didn't he Son?'

Before Sonia could answer Brenda carried on, 'She was pregnant with the sixth kiddie at the time but she lost it.'

Sonia felt the colour drain from her cheeks but gathering herself she said, 'Yes, he had an asthma attack. How was Doreen?'

'I wouldn't have recognised her until she spoke, always had that voice that could cut glass, anyway she must have lost about four stone, looks like a bag lady now. She was sat on a bench in Ally Pally supping from a bottle of Voddie. I felt so sorry for her so I bunged her a few quid.'

Alan had been discreetly listening and silently cursed. He had regularly given Doreen money until one day he had gone to her flat and she had moved out. He had tried to find her but had given up in the end.

Sonia thought back to the time when Stevie had died. Alan had been on edge for weeks afterwards which had confirmed to her that there had been more to the so-called asthma attack story than he was letting on. Jumping up and plastering a smile on her face, she asked the other ladies if they needed more drinks. She needed to escape to the kitchen and have a moment to compose herself. Irene knew exactly what had happened to Stevie Baines and sensing Sonia's discomfort she followed the younger woman into the kitchen. Sonia was smoking, looking out of the window, deep in thought. She started when she felt the hand on her shoulder.

'Stevie did die of an asthma attack, I can promise you that,' Irene said.

Sonia didn't speak and Irene continued, 'Some wives find this life difficult. I was like that in the beginning and I didn't have children to distract me. As time went on I learnt not to ask too many questions and not to worry about what I couldn't control. What you can control is how you react. Most of the businesses are legal now and take it from me, our husbands don't take unnecessary risks, they aren't thugs. Enjoy what you have because most women can only dream about all the luxury.' Irene smiled and went back into the front room.

Sonia felt as if she had just been told to grow up and stop behaving like a self-indulgent brat, and Irene did have a point. She was just sick of hearing that one day the businesses would be legal but she decided that she would try and heed the sound advice and enjoy what 1978 had to offer. After all what other choice did she have?

Outside a scruffy woman stood on the pavement observing the party through the front room window. She felt nothing but contempt. She could see children running around, their faces lit up gleefully. She should be enjoying New Year's Eve with her children around her but her eldest was in Borstal, four of her children were in care and her baby was dead. Taking a swig from her bottle she grinned menacingly. When her boy was home they would hatch a plan. Revenge would be sweet. She had waited patiently and now the wait was nearly over. Satisfied, she trudged wearily down the street and back to the hostel where she lived.

Ron and Irene were in the car driving home discussing Irene's conversation with Sonia.

'I worry about her Ron. She always seems so nervous, she isn't cut out for this life. I gave her the speech that I have spouted over the years to some of the other wives but I'm not sure that she took it in. Remember Davey Mac's wife? Poor cow topped herself.'

'Yeah that could have been to do with the fact that she saw someone put a bullet in her old man.'

'I don't know Ron, there are some wives that thrive and some that don't survive.'

'Don't worry Love, we will keep an eye on her.'

Irene smiled but wasn't convinced and was even less so when five minutes later her husband announced that he was ending it with Ebony as he felt too old to be carrying on. Irene was a bit miffed that she wasn't the reason he was finally dumping 'the Tart', but like so many times before she kept her real feelings to herself.

Chapter 8

Gary Peters was holding his distraught daughter as she sobbed about her predicament. He had convinced her that she must tell Ron that the baby was his and that the Mehmet's were a no go. If Ron refused to accept account-ability then Gary would have no qualms about doing time again although he hoped that it didn't come to that, as Ebony would need him in the coming years. Naturally slim, she was just beginning to show, so he advised her to ask Ron to come and see her and get it over with. Picking up the phone she dialled his number.

Ron was just about to leave his club when Ebony rang and requested his presence tonight. He had promised Irene that he was ready to give her the elbow, so decided that tonight was the night. He was very fond of Ebony but eleven years was a long time to be with someone who had the brain capacity of a wet lettuce leaf, and truth be told he could no longer keep up with the sexual gymnastics that she enjoyed. So he decided it was best if he bit the bullet sooner rather than later although he had a sneaking suspicion that she wouldn't take the news very well.

Over the years Ron's empire had expanded and although he had had aspirations of going legal some years back, opportunities kept coming his way. He now owned two clubs, two restaurants, a car dealership based in Central London which sold high end cars and various properties around North London that he rented out.

His portfolio of legal assets enabled him to clean the earnings from some of his more criminal deeds and the fact that he had a number of local policemen on his payroll allowed him to go about his business without any bother. Although Ron had always been very careful in what he had got involved in, the thrill of a serious earn had always been too difficult to resist. He still remembered only too well the poverty of his childhood and he couldn't really see himself retiring and pruning his roses to keep himself busy. He had never regretted taking on Alan Stewart. He trusted the man with his life and was grateful that Alan had included him in social occasions as Irene had become like an aunt to Billy and Connie and it did his heart good to see her fussing over the children. He had sensed that Sonia had taken a while to warm to him and had always seemed nervous in his company but Irene had taken the younger woman under her wing and she had seemed more relaxed the last few times he had seen her. Alan had confided in him that Sonia was fragile and was on constant medication for her nerves. Ron just thought that she was spoilt and needed a kick up the arse but he hadn't shared his opinion with his friend. Alan was by nature fiercely loyal and Ron doubted that he would appreciate his input.

Sonia was still haunted by what she had heard about Doreen Baines on New Year's Eve, especially the loss of her baby. Sonia knew only too well how traumatic losing a child was and she felt a real need to help the woman which is why for the past week she had walked around Ally Pally hoping to 'accidently' bump into Doreen.

Today she was sat on a bench near the boating lake and was just about to go home when she spotted a shabby figure approaching her. Getting up from the bench she walked closer to see if it was Doreen but as the figure got closer she realised that it wasn't. As Sonia walked past the dilapidated woman she suddenly stopped and turning back asked her if she knew Doreen Baines.

'Who?'

'You might know her as Dor, she comes here sometimes.'

The figure looked at Sonia with blood shot eyes and shrugged. Realising that she wouldn't part with any information without an incentive Sonia reached into her purse and handed over ten pounds. The woman greedily snatched the money and studied it before saying, 'She don't come here much anymore, it's too far since she got moved to that hostel in King's Cross.'

'Do you know what the hostel is called?'

'Don't know but I know it's near the station.'

Thanking the woman, Sonia made her way to where she had parked her car. She would have to make some enquires and further her search. Alan wouldn't be happy if he knew what she was doing but she felt that they owed Doreen, although Sonia wasn't really sure why.

When she got home, the children were dancing around the front room with her mother and Aunty Maggie to Viva La Spania. Breda paused when she saw her daughter.

'You, my dear, are off to Spain.'

Sonia was confused, 'What do you mean Mum?'

'Alan has booked us all tickets to go on holiday, even Maggie.'

'Oh my god, I've never been abroad. Where is he?'

'Gone back to work, he said he will give you a tinkle later.'

Sonia was overjoyed, Alan rarely took time off work and a holiday was just what they needed. The excitement in her front room was infectious and soon they were all doing the Conga whilst happily singing and imagining sun, sea and fun.

Ebony had had a bath and washed her hair. She inwardly swore because her once luminous skin looked dull and her hair looked lifeless. All those magazines that went on about the glow of pregnancy were talking bollocks, because she had as much glow as a blown-out candle. She had wanted to remind Ron how lucky he was to have her as his girlfriend but at this moment she had no confidence that he would feel that way. Sighing, she stood up to put on her underwear and gasped as she caught sight of her bump. She had always had a tight stomach but in the last week it had popped out and she looked what she was: pregnant. She could have screamed with frustration. She had never been the maternal type and had no interest in children. Hearing Ron's key in the lock, she put a determined look on her face and went to greet her boyfriend. As soon as Ron entered the flat he handed her the door key.

For a moment Ebony was unsure what he was doing and then it clicked. The old bastard was dumping her!

'Look Ebony, it's been fun but let's face it, I'm getting on now, you're young, you don't want an old codger like me cramping your style.' He smiled trying to lighten the tension that had filled the room.

Ebony was lost for words, what did she do now? She wished she could ask her dad. He always had a solution to a problem. The baby suddenly moved inside her as if reminding her of what she had to do but one thing that Ebony did have going for her was pride. She wasn't going to beg.

'Actually I was going to finish it with you tonight, now fuck off Ron and go back to your shrivelled up old wife.'

Ron looked at the woman and saw the steely glint and bravado in her eyes. She was hurt and he couldn't blame her. He just hoped that he wouldn't get any grief from his old mate Gary Peters. In time he hoped that she would see that it was for the best. The last few times that they had had sex he had had to fantasise about the actress who played Wonder Woman just to get it up. It was at that point he knew the relationship was over.

Ebony was furious. How dare he finish with her! Who did he think he was? When he had left, she had felt a hot rage sweep over her and had thrown her shoe at the front door, smashed a mirror and finally collapsed sobbing on her bed, which is where she stayed for two days.

She had ignored the phone and had had a pity party whilst trying to figure out what she was going to do. Her ego had taken a serious bashing and she felt worse still when she had tried to arrange a rendezvous with her other lover Kadir Mehmet, only to be told by one of his minions that he was busy. She had hoped for one last session in the sack. Kadir was a professional when it came to sex and she missed the feel of his touch. Well sod the both of them. She would manage on her own. She cried when she realised that no one would want her now with someone else's kid in tow, and what the hell was this pregnancy going to do to her body? She had already discovered a stretch mark on her stomach and she still had three months to go. Luckily she hadn't put on much weight but her arse was looking decidedly saggy and this was a disaster for a girl who prided herself on her looks. She was so deep in thought that she almost didn't hear the door-bell when it rang. It was her father who was wild with fury when she told him what had happened. She could see the spittle from his mouth as he paced angrily up and down.

'What do you mean the prick dumped you?'

'He gave me the keys back before I got the chance to tell him about the baby.'

'You still should have told him.'

'I don't want a bloke staying out of guilt Dad. I'm not that desperate, I do have some pride,' Ebony tried to explain.

'You should have thought of that before you dropped your drawers for two married men.'

Ebony started crying because she knew her father was right, but at this moment she didn't need to hear it. Gary, however, was on a roll.

'I brought you up to have more respect for yourself, Girl.'

Ebony looked at him and sneered, 'You dumped me on Aunty Pat after

Mum died. You spent more time in nick than being a father and she was always pissed. I raised myself Mate,' she said jabbing her finger at her chest.

Gary had the grace to stare at the floor while he digested his daughter's outburst. He had spent her childhood in and out of prison and his sister had spent more time with her face in a bottle of booze than worrying about her young niece.

'I will go and see Ron, even if he doesn't want you, he bloody has a responsibility to his child.'

'But it may not be his Dad.'

'I don't give a flying fuck, he is the dad end of, and while we're about it, no contacting Kadir or going anywhere near Green Lanes. I might go way back with Deniz but he would disown us over this. I don't want any trouble from the Turks. Got it?'

When Gary had left, Ebony couldn't help but smile in satisfaction. Whatever way you looked at it, she was doing Ron over whether he was the biological dad or not.

Ron and Irene were having dinner when the phone rang. It was Nicos Akbay who was second-in command to Deniz Mehmet. Ron was on nodding terms with Deniz but was surprised that he wanted to meet with him. They had different business interests but Ron agreed as his curiosity was piqued.

'Who was that?' Irene asked when he sat back down.

'Apparently Deniz Mehmet wants a meet.'

'Isn't he into drugs and guns?' Irene was worried.

'I'm not stupid Irene but I am interested to hear what he has to say.'

Satisfied, Irene carried on with her meal. She knew that Ron hated anything to do with drugs and didn't really trust the Turks, so she doubted that he would be interested with anything that they had to say.

The Stewarts were enjoying fish and chips while they watched *Hawaii Five O*. Sonia had flung herself into Alan's arms when he got home. She was so excited about the holiday and for once felt completely content. She had temporarily forgotten about Doreen Baines and her quest to find her.

The young boy walked out of the bleak building and breathed in the fresh air.

'Over here Jason.'

He looked to where the voice had come from and was shocked to see the state of his mother. She looked like a bag lady and he was relieved that none of his friends could see her.

'Alright Mum.' It was a statement more than a question.

She hawked from deep within her lungs, oblivious to the shock on her son's face. 'The council came through, it's only a one-bedroom flat on the old estate but they've given me some money to do it up.'

Sensing her son's discomfort she said, 'I'll be going shopping for some new gear tomorrow. I know I look shit.'

'I am just shocked and angry at what has happened to you.'

'Well you can thank Alan Stewart for that. He killed your Dad and we are going to make sure he pays.'

Jason sighed. Ever since he had confided in his mother that he had heard his dad telling Uncle Charlie that he was scamming the bookies, his mother had got it into her head that Alan must have found out and got a bent doctor to say that he had died from an asthma attack. She was convinced that he had been killed and was hell bent on revenge. All Jason wanted was a hot bath, a good meal and a long sleep. As they entered their new flat, Jason looked around it in dismay. The floors were covered in peeling linoleum, the bath looked like it hadn't been cleaned in years and there was no cooker.

Seeing his disappointment, his mother said, 'I know it isn't much but we'll soon have it looking cosy. I'll go down the road and get in some chips and tins, celebrate you being home?'

As Jason shivered under a thin sheet that night, he thought about his dad. He had been a loser but Jason always remembered him being a decent enough dad. Maybe his mum had a point and his death did need avenging. As his eyes closed and sleep beckoned, his last thought was that he would think about it tomorrow.

Ron and Alan were in a restaurant in Green Lanes that belonged to a cousin of Deniz Mehmet. They had enjoyed a lovely meal of lamb on the bone and were now sipping expensive red wine. The conversation during the meal had been small talk but Ron knew that Deniz wanted something from him and was beginning to feel a little impatient.

'So as lovely as the grub was, I have a feeling that you have something on your mind Deniz.'

The Turk smiled, 'You are correct Ron. You and I have run our businesses independently and very successfully over the years. We have respected each other and not stood on each other's toes. Now I know that you have a favourable reputation as a trustworthy businessman and I like that. I have a proposition for you.'

Ron's heart sank because he knew that whatever this offer was, he was not going to give this man an answer that he was going to be happy with. He kept his face expressionless as Deniz continued.

'I want to offer you a chance to invest in my business and in return I would like the protection from the politicians that you are so friendly with.'

Ron stifled an urge to laugh, 'I don't know where you've got your information from but I don't have any politicians in my pocket. I am friendly with a couple but not in a business sense. Also whilst I appreciate you thinking of me, I have a strict rule to avoid drugs. I hate what they stand for.'

Alan noticed that Deniz was now looking at Ron through slitted eyes and realised that Ron had inadvertently disrespected him. The Turk let out a long sigh, 'I am very sorry to hear this, now I am a busy man and must bring this meeting to an end.'

The three men said their goodbyes and Deniz Mehmet almost stomped off, leaving Ron and Alan looking at each other in astonishment.

When they got outside the restaurant Ron spoke, 'Can you believe what just happened?'

'No I can't, but he wasn't happy. Where did he get the idea that you had the protection of politicians?'

'Fuck knows. I know the brother of one who is a member of my lodge and I have a cousin who is small fry in parliament but bloody hell he's got his facts wrong.'

Alan was worried, 'Do you think he will give us any grief?'

'Why should he?'

'Well it sounds like he was after dosh as well.'

Ron wasn't scared of anyone and especially not an immigrant who had done well for himself.

He had been approached by a few others over the years wanting him to get involved with the drugs trade and although he knew that it brought in a lot of money, he wasn't greedy and had already made a fortune. Every day he was reading about what heroin was doing to young people and he wanted no part of it. Deniz Mehmet didn't need his money, he just wanted protection which Ron couldn't provide anyway. As he drove away from the restaurant he put the whole business out of his mind.

Deniz Mehmet was on the phone to an associate in Turkey and after a heated conversation he slammed the phone down in frustration. His associate was not happy with the outcome of his meeting with Ron

McCardle. They needed his support if they were going to flood the local market with heroin and everyone knew that Ron ran the North London streets. They required protection and Deniz wasn't sure if he believed Ron's claim that he couldn't provide that. Deniz was used to getting his own way and was not happy at being turned down.

Chapter 9

The weather had been beautiful in Spain and Sonia had never seen sea that was so blue and transparent. The only sea she had ever swum in had been the murky cold water at Leigh on Sea and the two did not compare. Connie and Billy had had a ball and were already demanding to know when they could go back. Even Alan had relaxed and been his old laid back self. Sonia blushed as she remembered how attentive he had been during the humid nights in the privacy of their bedroom. But now they were home it seemed that his brain was again elsewhere and it was business as usual. This morning he had rushed out of the house barely brushing her cheek as he kissed her goodbye. Of course Ron had been on the telephone almost as soon as they had walked through the front door, and of course Alan had gone running. She sighed but reminded herself that obviously things wouldn't be the same when they got home, and being on holiday was almost like living in a fantasy world that always came to an end. Breda had mentioned more than once whilst on holiday that she was a very lucky girl but if this was the case, why was the knot in her stomach tightening and why couldn't she sleep? She decided to talk it over with her brother-in-law David. Maybe he could give her some stronger pills?

As she watched her children chasing each other in the garden, she suddenly remembered Doreen Baines and shivered. She must find the woman and see if she was alright.

Since Jason Baines had been released from Borstal he had tried to find work which was proving difficult. Apparently ex-Borstal inmates were not an employer's dream candidate! His frustration was growing by the day. His mother was in no fit state to earn and she had spent the money from the council on a load of crap. Some of it had been used to purchase a record player that was now playing Bob Marley on loop! If he heard No Woman, No Cry one more time, he was going to scream! Doreen had informed her son that his dad had loved the dreadlocked singer and that it made her feel closer to him, which was laughable because all they had ever done was tear strips out of each other. But he couldn't feel angry towards her. She had literally lost everything when his old man had died, not only him but her children and her home. She had always been a drinker but now the booze was her staple diet. The buxom, brash mum with the fog-horn of a voice had been replaced by a fragile, unkempt, bitter woman who often didn't know what day it was. She had worn Jason's ears down berating Alan Stewart and his role in his father's untimely death. Jason had discreetly asked around and had learned that the one-time bar man was now joined at the hip with the local villain Ron McCardle and, according to his mother, he was living the life of Riley in a big house in Crouch End. Crime was obviously the way to go and Jason was beginning to agree with Doreen that Alan Stewart owed them. So with that thought in mind he decided to pay the man a visit in the near future.

Brenda Draper's large bosoms heaved as she glared at her husband Geoff, 'I don't want our Denny working for Ron McCardle end of. You know as well as I do that he is the local gangster. Remember Les Dwyer? Ron blinded him in one eye, is that what you want for your son? I mean, I like to have a laugh with him and a sausage roll at a party but I don't want him as a permanent fixture in our lives.'

Brenda like her friend Gina Davis had noticed how nervous Sonia had become over the years and it was no coincidence in her mind that this had started when Alan had begun working for Ron. Brenda wasn't a jealous sort and was pleased that Sonia had climbed up the social ladder, but to what cost? She would much rather have her humble home and her Geoff who had the aspirations of a snail in a coma.

Geoff sighed. Once his wife got on her soap box, it was hard to shift her. This was going to be more difficult than he had envisaged. Thinking carefully he tried to reassure Brenda, who was now pacing up and down in fury and he conceded fear.

Thinking carefully and planning his response he tried to reassure her. 'Be realistic Bren, our son is eighteen now and didn't even hold down that Saturday job at the greengrocers. The boy needs a job. Do you want him lying in bed all day while you wash his dirty pants and socks?'

It wasn't what she wanted and Brenda was just about to open her mouth again as Geoff quickly continued, 'Think about it Love, Alan won't put him in any danger and Ron has only offered him a job at his club. What harm can that do? He needs to be paying us some keep now not dossing about all day like a hobo.'

'Yeah and Alan worked in the bookies and now what's he up to? Sonia is a bag of nerves these days. He and Ron are stuck together like a nun and her virginity.'

'I don't know what Alan is involved with and I don't want to know, but what I do know is that most of Ron's work force are just normal Joes like me and you. I mean Maureen Holmes has worked in the bookies for years and I can't see her robbing a bank can you?!'

Brenda couldn't help but chuckle. Maureen was a religious woman who lived for her cats, so Geoff did have a point.

Geoff felt her thawing, 'Bren face facts, Denny is never going to stick down a nine to five job. At least working in a club will suit his body clock.'

Brenda batted it out in her head, 'Okay but any sign of trouble and he leaves.'

Geoff nodded in agreement, 'That goes without saying Love.'

Denny who had been sitting listening on the stairs gave a silent 'whoop,' whilst his sister Caroline who was earwigging with him wrote it all down in her diary. Denny was home and dry if his mother had relented.

His dad was right, he didn't want a nine to five job, that would bore the pants off him. What his mother didn't realise was that over the years he had been watching his godfather Alan Stewart and he recognised a trait in him that he shared. Denny also had fire in his belly to earn some serious money and get him off of the crappy council estate that he called home, and he didn't care what he had to do to achieve his dreams. The mistake his parents had just made was to assume that he had no ambition.

Ron McCardle had been surprised to receive a phone call from Gary Peters this morning and somewhat wary when his ex-girlfriend's father had asked to meet him later on today. Surely Ebony hadn't got her father involved in their break up? The thought made him even more convinced that he had done the right thing in breaking up with the immature cow. Running to daddy was pathetic and there was nothing Gary Peters could say which would change his mind. He would meet with the other man and put him straight. Ebony was still young and attractive. She would soon have another sugar daddy in tow. Putting Ebony to the back of his mind he waited for Alan to arrive so that he could fill him in on his new money-making venture.

Throughout the years Ron had acquired a dozen or so large Victorian properties dotted over North London. They were all converted into bedsits and his old school friend Lily Jenson oversaw the running of them. She lived with her son Barry in the downstairs of one of the houses and the arrangement suited both her and Ron. They had grown up together in Deptford and had been occasional bed companions over the years, something that neither of them had ever made public. Ron trusted Lily implicitly which was why he had heard her out when she had come to him with an idea a few weeks ago.

He was now retelling this conversation to Alan who looked doubtful and exclaimed, 'A knocking shop Ron?'

'No, a high class establishment where people who want to unwind can do so in private. Lily will only take on classy girls and your brother can give them the once over to make sure that they are clean.'

Alan couldn't see his sister-in-law Sandra being happy with her husband giving pretty young girls the 'once over' and his Sonia definitely wouldn't be happy with this little scenario.

'What does Irene think?'

Ron had a steely glint in his eyes, 'Irene accepts my job and all it entails.'

It was a threat and Alan knew it. He also knew that a lot of firms dealt in prostitution to some degree. He just couldn't fathom why Ron would be comfortable with pimping young woman when he wouldn't touch drugs and the fortune that they could bring.

Ron could see the changing expressions on Alan's face and knew that he was struggling with his conscience.

'Look Al, Lily rumbled a tenant selling her fanny in one of the houses so it is going on anyway without my permission. This way, I will have control. It won't be seedy and we will be making a good earn for which you will receive a percentage. Lily told me all about swingers the other day. Apparently there are married people out there that like to go to parties and swap partners. They actually watch their other halves having sex AND they enjoy it. Imagine that!'

Alan couldn't but kept quiet as Ron continued, 'North London is full of money. Lily is going to rent out a few rooms and also have an area of the house for these swinging parties.'

Alan noted that Ron was excited and wasn't sure if it was the parties or the money that had got to him. Alan only hoped that it was the latter because he couldn't see Irene hopping with joy at the thought of joining the swinging community!

'Right, let's go and see Lily and she can explain it all to you in person but Alan this is happening, so take that worried look off your mush and just listen to what she has to say.'

Alan knew that the fact that Ron had run this past him was out of respect and he appreciated that. He also knew that he had no real choice in the matter so jumping up from his chair said, 'Come on then Ron, let's go.'

Ron smiled at his number two. He actually liked the fact that Alan had morals but in the end he was the boss and what he said went.

Lily Jenson was a faded blonde of fifty-five who liked wearing animal print and a big smile. She had a beautiful, welcoming face and the loveliest blue eyes that Alan had seen in a long time. Ron had confided in him that they had slept together over the years and Alan could see the attraction. What really impressed him about Lily was the strong bond that she shared with her twenty year old son Barry who had Downs Syndrome. When he had been born in the fifties people around her had been uncomfortable and she had often received 'the look of pity' as she called it. But Lily being the strong, confident woman that she was had brushed off any negative comments and merely told people, 'at least my kid will stand out in a crowd.'

Lily may have been naive about how hard it would be bringing up a child who was different but she had been right in that Barry did stand out and for all the right reasons. He was funny and quirky and Lily loved him with a fierce passion.

Sitting in her small front room with a cup of tea, Alan warmed to her even more, especially when she told the story of finding the tenant with the fat man (who Lily had recognised as a local plod) panting away on top the girl. Lily was a natural born comic and soon all three of them were roaring with laughter.

As Ron and Alan drove back to the office, Alan felt more at ease with the whole idea.

Somehow Lily had made it all sound respectable and as she explained, if local policemen were using the services of girls then that also meant Ron had more leverage with the law so it was win win. The one thing Alan was not happy about was the fact that if Sonia ever found out, it would tip her over the edge of the cliff that she was already dangerously close to. Hopefully he wouldn't have too many dealings with the house and all that it entailed, and he wasn't about to enlighten her about the new business anyway.

As they were driving down Green Lanes they spotted two people who unnerved Alan even further. The first was a young boy in his late teens who noticing them driving past had looked into the car with a strange expression on his face. He looked vaguely familiar and had carried on staring intently at them. Alan was reminded of Stevie Baines. Thinking of his old friend always made him feel uneasy. Maybe the boy was staring because they were in a flash motor which often attracted attention but Alan felt it was something else. The second person was a Mediterranean looking man who was stood outside Deniz Mehmet's cousin's restaurant. When they had stopped at the lights he made eye contact with Ron and slid his finger left to right across his throat.

'Is he fucking threatening me?' Ron spat.

He was just about to jump out of his car when the lights changed much to Alan's relief. The last thing they needed was a tear up with the Turks.

Alan had heard the rumours about Deniz Mehmet and knew that he was heavy duty. He certainly didn't want to go to war with him.

Alan turned to Ron, 'Should we be worried? Deniz wasn't happy that you turned him down over his business proposition.'

Ron chuckled, 'Fuck him. I am my own man. I don't want to get into a situation where I have to answer to anyone. I'm not interested in selling drugs, they fry people's brains. You're a dad, you can understand that.'

Alan could also understand as a father with a daughter that prostitution was unsavoury but he sensibly kept his opinion to himself. He could see that although Ron was reacting as if this little encounter meant nothing, the older man was in fact a little rattled and still had the meeting with Gary Peters looming over him.

Ron McCardle and Gary Peters had been casual friends for years and had always got on well, however as they sat in a pub in Highgate Ron could sense a chill in the air. Gary for all his cock sure promises to his daughter was feeling decidedly nervous now he was actually in front of Ron, who was a big man in every sense.

Taking a gulp of his pint Gary decided to bite the bullet, 'She's pregnant Ron, nearly six months.'

For a moment Ron didn't know how to react. This was not what he had expected and he was knocked for six.

He took a sip of his Scotch and said, 'She told me that she was on the pill, how could this have happened?'

Gary had the grace to look shame faced, 'These things happen Mate.'

'What do you want from me Gary? We're finished and there is no going back for me.'

Gary felt a twinge of guilt but there WAS a fifty percent chance that Ron was the father, 'She will need financial support Ron and you are the father…'

'Let me know when the kid is born and we'll talk then.'

Ron got up to leave. He needed to get away from Gary Peters and his revelation as quick as he could. Not much rattled Ron but he was feeling sick with worry about how this situation would affect his marriage. The only person who he had ever wanted kids with was his wife and despite her assurances over the years that their childless union didn't bother her, he knew full well that it did. He had heard her crying in the toilet over the years when another month went past and she wasn't pregnant. He kicked a dustbin over as he walked back to his car. Irene had put up with his bed hopping over the years but the impact of a child with another woman would destroy them. As he drove home, he decided that his wife must never know. Maybe he could set up Ebony and the child in a flat away from North London? What he really felt like doing was throttling Ebony and making her disappear, but he couldn't do that or could he?

Chapter 10

To say that Ron McCardle had not slept well was an understatement. He had tossed and turned all night until Irene had told him to go into the spare bedroom. He couldn't believe the situation that he now found himself in. Ebony had been so careless or maybe she had tried to trap him. He didn't really think that she had done it on purpose as she was certainly not the maternal type and her tight stomach was very important to her but that still didn't change the fact that he was tied to her whether he liked it or not. He could actually cry with frustration because he had every intention of now staying true to his Irene who he admitted deserved a medal for putting up with his roving eye for all these years. He was terrified that this little turn of events would cause the demise of his marriage, although if he was honest with himself he also had a feeling of excitement. To the outside world he had always portrayed the hard man who had no time for fatherhood. Children became your Achilles heel and there was no room in his mind for weakness in his line of business. But he knew he had been kidding himself. He had seen the love that Alan and other men shared with their offspring and occasionally he had experienced envy which he had learned to suppress over the years. He had been close to becoming a father once years ago when Lily Jenson had fallen pregnant. But being the good girl that she was, she had understood the impact it would have had on his marriage and had a back street abortion.

Lily, unlike Ebony, was selfless and Ron would always be in her debt, which was why to this day he still looked out for her. Although he had always been honest with Irene about his extra-marital activities, he had never confided in her about Lily because he had instinctively known that a pregnancy with another woman would have been too much for her to overlook.

This was a major ball ache of mammoth proportions. Ebony was nearly six months gone according to her father so an abortion was too risky. Ron knew damn well that she wouldn't have taken kindly to being dumped and would take him to the cleaners financially and he accepted that. The fear of Irene finding out far outweighed Ebony demanding the contents of his wallet though. His ex-mistress was not blessed with discretion and had already had a few run-ins with his wife over the years. He had to tread carefully. His first thought last night had been to arrange a fatal 'accident' for the mother of his child but he had since dismissed this notion because deep down he wasn't a murderer. He had only got blood on his hands in the past as a survival tactic. Also, Gary Peters was no fool and would be bound to put two and two together. Ron wasn't scared of him but in the world they inhabited women and children were a no go. You could torture a man but women and children were left alone. He had told Gary to contact him after the baby was born but realised that he would need to meet with her before that and try to persuade her to move away.

He would have to put his plan into action sooner rather than later, so wearily he picked up the telephone.

Ebony had been cool but secretly thrilled that Ron had called her. She instructed him to meet her at her flat later on today where they would have the privacy to talk. She didn't really want him back but was feeling smug that she now held all the cards as she was a girl who liked to be in control. Smiling she jumped up from the sofa and rushed into her bedroom to plan what she was going to wear.

Sonia, Brenda Draper and Gina Davis were in Brenda's garden drinking wine and putting the world to rights as the children played. Brenda had initially been frosty with Sonia when Denny had started working for Ron but had since thawed when Alan had reassured her that Denny would be working in a legitimate club serving legitimate drinks. Her worries had gradually disappeared as her son seemed to love his job and had even started paying her some much needed keep money. Sonia had been livid when Alan had offered the boy a job and had only stopped ranting when Alan had solemnly promised her that Denny was not part of anything dodgy and never would be, but she still worried. Brenda was one of her closest friends and she didn't want her to live with the same worries that she herself did. It had really upset her when Brenda had cooled towards her but now they were firmly back on track and Sonia was thoroughly enjoying the glorious summer weather with her friends and the kids.

Connie, Caroline and Cath were very close, being the same age, and Billy tagged along with them often joining in with their games as long as they weren't too girly.

The three mums looked up in alarm when they heard a scream followed by all four children charging towards them. Connie got to them first, 'Mum, Cath's upset because Billy has trod on a ladybird and killed it.'

Billy looked worried, 'I didn't mean to.'

'Well now it's dead and it's your fault,' Connie huffed.

Gina Davis looked at her daughter sympathetically, 'Come on now Love, it was an accident. The ladybird wouldn't have felt anything.'

Cath wasn't convinced, 'You don't know that. It might have been in pain.'

Brenda always good at diffusing uncomfortable situations looked at the kids and with a big grin announced, 'I've got some raspberry ripple ice cream in the fridge, who wants some?'

The untimely death of the ladybird was soon forgotten as the children charged indoors after Brenda who winked at her friends from her kitchen window. Sonia laughed. Cath was a compassionate girl and sometimes she wished that her Connie was the same, but as she got older it was becoming apparent she was becoming spoiled and sometimes only thought of her own needs. She would often have a hissy fit if she didn't get her own way.

Billy, in contrast, was placid like Alan had been in the old days. He was grateful for all his treats in life and would often ask, 'Is it ok if I have...' Whereas her daughter was more along the lines of, 'I want...' Sonia just hoped that Connie would one day meet a man who could keep her in the life to which she had become accustomed. As long as he wasn't a villain, then Sonia would be happy.

Ron and Irene were having lunch, 'I've got to pop out later Love to see Colin Yates about a new roof.'

Irene nodded knowingly. Colin Yates was the vicar of their local church and if he needed a new roof then Ron would lend him some 'dirty' money and that money would then be cleaned via the repayments from the church's cheque book.

Colin knew the score but needs must and Ron needed an alibi for tonight as he was planning to pop in to see the vicar and then go on to see Ebony.

When Ron knocked on Ebony's front door he was annoyed with himself that he was feeling nervous. Ebony opened the door with a flourish and immediately sensed Ron was agitated. Smiling demurely she let him in and poured him a Scotch. She had worn her tightest dress that showed off her growing bump and smirked when she saw him looking at it in distress.

'So how are you?' Ron was trying to play it calm but his insides were jumping about like a kid on acid. Seeing her pregnancy up close was unnerving.

'Cut the crap Ron, we both know you couldn't give a flying fuck so let's cut to the chase. I didn't plan this but it's happened. So what are you going to do about it?'

Ron gulped his drink and looked at his ex-mistress. He could tell she was enjoying this. She had a determined glint in her eyes and seemed relaxed and in control. Well there was no way he was going to give her the satisfaction of seeing him squirm.

'I will look after you and the kid financially but that's it Ebony.'

Ebony felt a little wounded but intent on not letting that show, 'I wouldn't have you and your ageing cock back even if you were gift wrapped, I just want what me and my child are entitled to.'

Ebony was beginning to seriously piss Ron off, 'I will give you a monthly allowance and set you up in a flat as long as you agree to move away and never tell anyone that the child is mine.'

'Oh no Ron, if you're the dad then I expect you to be in our child's life, not just at the end of a cheque book.'

There were only four words that Ron had just digested.

'What do you fucking mean if?'

Ebony realised her mistake and quickly gabbled, 'You know what I mean, so stop picking my words to bits and what do YOU mean move away?'

'You can't stay local Ebony, even you must know that.'

'Worried the old wife might find out? Well, if you don't give me what I want then she just might?'

For the second time Ebony realised her mistake as Ron jumped out of his seat and grabbed her slim throat with his meaty hand.

'If you ever talk disrespectfully about my wife ever again, I'll kill you. Got it?'

Ron knew he had gone too far and regretted his actions almost at once but Ebony had voiced his biggest fear. Realising he had to grovel, he gently sat her down and apologised.

'Look Ebony, this is getting us nowhere. I admit that I went too far but you cannot involve Irene in this and I won't have you threatening me. Now I will look after you and the baby but I can't be a permanent fixture. I will buy you a nice place to live and you won't go short. But if you keep on like this, I will deny that the kid is mine.'

When Ron left he was seething. The little cow had him over a barrel and she knew it. He had no alternative but to play it cool and hope that his offer would be accepted, although unfortunately he just knew that this problem was not going away and would only get worse. His mood was not improved when he got to his car and saw that someone had slashed his tyres.

Swearing loudly he traipsed up the road to a phone box and asked Alan to come and pick him up. He would have called one of the Clarke brothers but he needed to confide in someone and knew his number two was discreet and would take this secret to the grave with him. He would get one of his other men to come and collect his car.

Alan was quiet when Ron told him the whole sorry mess. It was obvious Ron was in a quandary and was genuinely upset at the thought of Irene finding out. He knew it would break her and probably his marriage. Alan was aware that Ron played away and although he didn't agree with it, he could understand. He couldn't imagine being in a sexless marriage and although Sonia was hard work at times he prided himself that he had never really looked at another woman.

'I think your offer is a good one Ron. She is all talk and tits that one but she won't bite the hand that feeds her.'

'I am not so sure Al, Ebony can be unstable. I am going to have to walk on eggshells for the rest of my life in case she opens up her trap and I am not looking forward to that. Bloody ironic, I had finally decided to be faithful and this happens. I mean a kid at my age!'

Alan didn't really know what to say and just let Ron vent as he clearly needed to.

'Tell you what, let's go and collect the weeklies from the pubs and get a drink while we're at it?' Alan suggested.

He knew that Sonia wouldn't be happy as he rushed out in the middle of *Hawaii Five O* and they always watched that together but his friend needed him. He would buy a bottle of wine and some chocolates to wheedle into his wife's good books again.

Irene looked at her watch and frowned. Ron had said he would only be an hour or so and that was four hours ago! She was just about to make another cup of tea when she heard a thud in the hallway. Going out to investigate she was shocked to see her husband in a crumpled heap on the carpet. He was clearly as pissed as a fart and looked up at her with bloodshot eyes, 'I love you Irene and I always have. I'm so sorry.'

It was at this point that he threw up all over her new carpet and while she gently helped him to bed berating him at the same time for his stupidity she wondered what he was apologising for. She felt uneasy as she took off his shoes. In her guts she felt that he had done something really wrong and it scared her because Ron could hold his drink. In all the years they had been together she had only seen him really boozed once or twice and that had been when he was younger. She would ask him tomorrow when he woke from his drunken stupor.

Sonia had given up watching *Hawaii Five 0* and had phoned Brenda for a chat and to ask if Caroline would like to come for a sleepover at the weekend.

'Yes she'd love to Son. I'll get them some sweets so that they can have a midnight feast. Oh I know what I meant to tell you today. Guess who has moved back into the flats on the estate?'

Sonia giggled. Brenda did love her 'guess who' games and she always played along, 'Hmmmm *The Bionic Man* ?!'

Brenda laughed down the line, 'I wish, I love my Geoff but would certainly put my slippers under Steve Austin's bed for the night! No, Doreen Baines and her eldest, think his name's Jason. He went to school with Denny.'

Sonia felt a surge of relief. This information saved her going on a wild goose chase and she was always visiting Brenda and Gina on the estate, so it wouldn't look odd if she casually bumped into Doreen.

'Tell Gina I'll pick up the girls on Saturday, I'll be at yours about sixish.'

The women said their goodbyes and Sonia had a smile on her face when Alan finally got home with her wine and chocolates.

Ron woke the following day with what felt like a stampeding herd of elephants in his head. Irene sat on their bed and after giving him a cup of tea and a plate of toast said, 'You were in a right state last night Ron. What made you drink so much?'

'I just got chatting with Alan and we got a bit carried away.'

Irene knew her husband was lying, whereas Pinocchio's nose grew, with Ron his top lip protruded like it was doing now.

'Are there any problems at work that I should be worried about? Have you heard anymore from Deniz Mehmet?'

'I swear to you there are no problems at work,' Ron answered truthfully.

'What then and don't lie to me because I haven't seen you in a state like that since my cousin Sue got engaged and she has been married twenty odd years.'

Ron sighed. He had always been truthful with his wife but how could he tell her that he had got bladdered because his ex-girlfriend was pregnant with his baby? Irene was watching him closely, 'Why did you say you were sorry?'

'Because I threw up over the carpet and I know that you love that carpet.'

'Bollocks, you said sorry before you ruined my carpet. Now just tell me Ron.'

Ron felt as cornered as a mouse that had a great big cat staring at it so decided to be economical with the truth, 'Ok, Ebony has been giving me grief about dumping her so I bunged her some cash. She wound me up and I needed a drink afterwards.'

Ron's explanation seemed lame even to him and he could see that his wife wasn't impressed. She glared at him with a malicious look in her eyes and spat, 'If I find out that you are lying or have been anywhere near that tart again, then it won't just be my carpet that needs replacing, it will be your balls as well.'

Irene walked out of the room with as much dignity as she could muster although the slamming of the bedroom door left him in no doubt that she was furious. Putting his sore head back on the pillow, he was just about to shut his eyes again when the telephone on his bedside table rang. Ron cursed as he picked it up. He was in no mood to talk to anyone. 'Yeah,' he gruffly greeted the caller. He inwardly groaned when he heard the voice of Gary Peters who sounded as angry as Irene had been not two minutes ago.

'Deniz Mehmet is not the only one who is pissed off with you MATE. How dare you manhandle my pregnant daughter, if you ever lay a finger on her again then you're a dead man.' And with that he hung up before Ron could summon up a response. Could this day or his life for that matter get any worse? he thought as he laid back down.

When he was feeling better, he would deal with Gary Peters and his bloody daughter.

Chapter 11

Denny Draper loved working at Ron's club. The hours suited his nocturnal nature and he was enjoying the company of all the scantily clad girls who frequented the place. He wasn't conventionally good looking as he had what his mother lovingly called 'a boxer's nose' but he was a natural born story teller and the girls seemed to hang off his every word, especially when he would, on occasion, let it slip that Alan Stewart was his godfather. Alan seemed to be as well-known as Ron McCardle these days and Denny's connection with him was certainly helping his pulling power. He had recently lost his virginity to a bubbly blonde called Lesley and now that he had finally dipped his wick, he was keen to try out as many girls as possible. He was however determined to create a good impression with Ron and Alan and wanted to be taken seriously, so he tried to be discreet. He had been mortified when last week Alan had caught him in the cellar with Lesley humping away like dogs. His godfather had taken in the scene that he had just walked into, chuckled and walked out. Much to Denny's relief Alan hadn't mentioned it again but he had realised that being caught with his y-fronts around his ankles was not going to create the right impression. Ron paid him a good wage but Denny wanted to be in a position whereby he could buy a decent car and move out from the claustrophobic council house that he lived in with his parents and little sister Caroline. He would just have to be patient and wait for an opportunity to prove himself. He hoped that he wouldn't have to wait too long.

Sonia arrived on the old estate at five o'clock. She had left the kids with her mother Breda so that she could look around for Doreen Baines before picking up Caroline and Cath for their sleepover. Carefully locking her car, she looked up at the imposing tower block where Doreen now lived. She could smell the urine and stale beer before she entered the concrete stairwell. Brenda had told her that Doreen and her son had a flat on the third floor and as there were only four flats on each one at least her mission to find the woman shouldn't take long.

As Sonia nervously knocked on the first door she jumped when it was opened almost immediately by a teenage girl who was wearing denim flares and an orange tie-dyed t-shirt. She looked at Sonia with curiosity and said hello as way of a question, more than a greeting.

'Hello Love, I just wondered if you knew what number Doreen Baines lives at, she has a teenage son about eighteen?'

The girl, screwed up her eyes thinking. 'Well if she's the woman who plays Bob Marley morning, noon and night, she has a son. They're next door.'

At that moment a male voice shouted from inside of the flat. 'Oi Angie, get back in here, I've lost me erection!'

The girl Angie, giggled, wished Sonia good luck and shut the door laughing. Sonia laughed too and turning around almost bumped into a young lad. As she looked at him, she knew this was Doreen's son as he was the image of his dead father Stevie Baines. 'Excuse me do you know Doreen Baines?'

Jason Baines eyed her suspiciously. Although Sonia had purposely dressed down she could still have been mistaken for someone of authority such as a social worker. She realised this boy was thinking the same thing. 'Who wants to know?' he asked cautiously.

'I'm Sonia Stewart. I'm an old friend of hers.'

Jason's ears pricked up. 'Alan Stewart's missus?'

Sonia nodded. 'Yes, I just wanted to see how she was.'

Jason couldn't believe his luck. He knew his mother would be very interested to hear what the wife of her nemesis had to say. 'I'm Jason Baines, come with me.'

He pointed to the flat next door and Sonia was surprised to see that the front door wasn't locked. He noticed the look on her face and smirked. 'Nothing worth nicking.'

As Sonia stepped into the narrow hallway, she was saddened to see the squalor of the place. The floral pattern on the wallpaper had long since faded and been replaced by brown grimy nicotine stains. There was no carpet and as Sonia walked into the front room she discovered that there were no curtains either although someone had improvised with a sheet. The only furniture in the room was a scruffy sofa which may have been green once, a small table and a record player. Sonia shuddered. She knew that Doreen and Stevie's previous flat hadn't exactly been Buckingham Palace but from what she remembered it had been reasonably homely. Their main problem had been too many mouths to feed and only Stevie working.

Jason had gone to get his mum and after a few minutes Sonia could hear slow shuffling coming down the hallway. She tried to hide her shock when she saw Doreen for the first time in years. Gone was the voluptuous brassy women with a voice that could wake the dead. Doreen was now a shadow of her former formidable self. She stood before Sonia in a tatty dirty dressing gown, waif like. Doreen still had a modicum of pride left and could see that this stuck up cow clearly felt pity for her. 'So what brings you here, not exactly your stomping ground anymore is it?' Her voice was now raspy from all the cigarettes and cheap booze.

Sonia felt nervous but was determined to make amends. 'I was in the area and Brenda Draper mentioned that you were now living on the estate, so I thought I would see how you were Dor?'

Doreen cackled like a witch and swept her right arm in front of her. 'Well as you can see, I'm just dandy, I bet your place is better than this shit hole.'

'Look Dor, I know that Alan looked after you after Stevie died but you moved from your old place and he didn't know where you'd gone.'

'Well he didn't look hard enough, did he? What do you want MRS Stewart?'

'I just want to make amends.'

Doreen sneered. 'And how are you going to do that? Resurrect my old man? Bring my kids back? Or MAYBE you're going to buy me and Jase somewhere half decent to live?'

Sonia felt out of her depth. 'Look I'm sorry that Stevie died but it was natural causes and my Al didn't have to help you out, but he did.'

Doreen's phlegmy cackle was back. 'Natural causes. If he died of natural causes then I'm Diana Dors. My Stevie's death stinks more than a pile of shit.'

Sonia was beginning to wish that she had left well alone. 'Do you need some money?'

'Take a look around you, what do you think?' Doreen was being sarcastic and Sonia felt that she was enjoying having the upper hand.

'I will get you some cash and give you a regular amount each week as Alan used to do. As I said before, we don't have to do this but Stevie was an employee.'

Doreen licked her lips. 'That will do for starters.'

'Ok, well I'll come back next week.'

'You got anything on you now?'

Sonia fished in her bag and gave the woman a ten-pound note and some change. 'That's all I've got on me, I'll see you next week.'

'I'm not going anywhere.'

After Sonia had hastily left, Doreen grinned at her son showing greying teeth. 'Well that was a bit of luck, her turning up out of the blue.'

Jason laughed but felt uneasy. He didn't really think his mother realised that Alan Stewart was in the big league now and wouldn't be too happy that his wife was being ripped off. Although he agreed with his mum that there was something dodgy about his dad's death, he had wanted to deal with it himself. He had wanted the man to give him a job and suss out the situation, then take revenge when he felt the time was right. Now there wasn't much chance of that because all his mother was interested in was a quick fix to the situation and he knew damn well that when Alan Stewart caught whiff of this financial arrangement, he would put a stop to it.

As Sonia was driving back to Crouch End with Caroline and Cath giggling in the back seat, she felt a feeling of dread. What had she done? Doreen would rinse her for every penny she had and she didn't have a never ending supply of money. Alan gave her a weekly allowance but that covered the food, bills and treats for the kids. He would become suspicious if she asked for more.

She had believed that helping Doreen would make her feel better but it had done the exact opposite. She had just not thought it through and now she had dug herself a hole that only her husband could get her out of. Sighing, she knew that a conversation with him was needed.

Later on that evening, once the kids were all settled Sonia sat on the sofa with Alan and snuggled into him. Alan responded.

'How was your day Al?'

'Quiet Love, I went into the club to pick up the takings. Denny is loving it. He is a natural behind the bar and the girls seem to love him.'

Sonia laughed. 'Yeah Brenda keeps saying that his shirts smell permanently of perfume.'

'I have high hopes for Denny, I reckon he will be head barman one day. He's certainly got the nous for it.'

Sonia really didn't have the patience for small talk this evening, so she poured her husband a beer and turning to face him told him in detail about her visit to Doreen. She knew he wasn't going to be happy but was surprised at how livid he was. He jumped off the sofa, accidentally knocking her onto the floor.

'You stupid cow! What did you think would happen? Doreen wasn't going to thank you for your concern and then ask if you wanted a cuppa!'

'I just wanted to see how she was. Brenda mentioned on New Year's Eve that she had fallen on hard times. I felt sorry for her.'

Alan none too gently pulled her face towards him and spat. 'You going round there has just confirmed to her that Stevie's death was suss. You never admit to anything in this life.'

Sonia started to cry and somewhere deep in Alan's heart he could understand that his wife was just being caring as what had befallen Doreen was her own worst nightmare. Maybe if he had been truthful and told her at the time the real circumstances behind Stevie's death, she could have accepted it and kept her beak out. Now Alan was going to have to sort it out himself. No way was Doreen Baines going to blackmail his wife. He would visit the lush and tell her the deal was off.

Ron McCardle was also having women problems. He had phoned Gary Peters to apologise for his outburst towards the man's daughter and had assured him that he would make it right with Ebony. He had then gone back to build some bridges with his ex-mistress but she had shut the door in his face! Knowing he needed to keep her onside, he had stood patiently outside her front door until finally she had let him in. He knew he would have to grovel as the last time he had seen her he had bullied her and been physical. He was ashamed to see that her neck was still red from when he had grabbed her.

Ron was a hard man, but never with women as a rule. He knew that he had some making up to do.

'Come on Ebony, we really do need to talk sensibly. I am heart sorry that I grabbed you but you were winding me up. You know I am married, you know that my wife can never find out about the child. I will buy you a lovely flat and I will give you a generous allowance but I can't be a part of your life anymore. You must see that?'

'All I see is a man who is running scared. I will move away on two conditions: One: that you buy me a HOUSE and two: that you come to see YOUR child at least once a month. Those are my terms Ron.'

Ron knew that he was cornered and would have to agree, so he did on the proviso that she moved away before the birth. At least then he would have some breathing space and the arrangement should please her father. Ron was feeling a little uneasy as Gary was well in with the Turks. The same Turks who were not happy with him at the moment.

When Ron left, Ebony thought about their conversation. A part of her realised that she didn't have much choice but to accept Ron's offer. She had heard that Essex was full of villains so maybe that was the place to move to! Who knows, she might just find herself another rich gangster boyfriend but this time without a wife in tow.

The next morning Alan Stewart banged on Doreen Baines's front door. He had brought Rob Clarke with him to add to the occasion and to ensure that Doreen knew exactly who she was dealing with. The door opened slowly and the two men easily pushed their way into the shabby flat. Doreen did not look overly worried. 'Wifey been telling tales has she?'

Alan pushed her onto the sofa and put his face about two inches from hers. 'No one takes the piss out of me or my wife. Now I was good to you for a good few years after Stevie died and do you know what Dor? He was fucking stealing from Ron McCardle so you're lucky that you got anything at all. Now I'm going to give you two hundred quid but that's the last that you will get out of me. Got it?'

Doreen just stared at him so Alan screamed in her face. 'I said have you got it?'

Doreen shrunk away from him. This was a different Alan Stewart to the one she had known as Stevie's friend. This man was scary. She shrank away from him and mutely nodded.

'Good girl, you know it makes sense.' With that he threw the money at her and strode confidently out of the flat, satisfied the situation had been sorted.

When Alan got home, he sat Sonia down and explained to her that he had paid Doreen Baines off. They then agreed to draw a line under the whole matter and never mention it again, both relieved that the situation had been dealt with.

However, unfortunately for them the death of Stevie Baines would have far reaching repercussions that neither of them could ever have imagined.

Chapter 12

Ebony Peters browsed through the housing brochures and sighed. She didn't have the energy to think about moving and all that it entailed. Throwing the glossy brochures onto her coffee table, she lay back and thought about the mess her life was. She was pregnant with a baby she didn't really want, she had no real friends and now she had no lover to keep her warm at night. Her father was supporting her as best that he could but he was working for the Turks and even he didn't have much time for her anymore. Gary Peters was a man's man and didn't really have the sensitivity to deal with his emotional daughter and her hormones. To him the situation had been dealt with and she just had to get on with it. She hadn't seen hide nor hair of Ron and she knew she had to keep away from her other lover Kadir Mehmet. Any previous notions of a Bon Voyage fuck had been abandoned because she could no longer conceal her pregnancy and her father had given her strict instructions to stay well clear as it was too risky.

As the baby moved inside of her, she winced. She had no real feelings for the life growing bigger as each day passed. She was only interested in the financial gain that she was determined to get from Ron. Feeling bored and lonely, she decided that a bit of retail therapy was in order. So slapping on some makeup, she got ready to take a trip to Wood Green to buy herself some jewellery.

She was vaguely aware that she should be buying some bits for her unborn child but, smirking to herself, she decided that Ron could traipse around Mothercare. The thought made her laugh as she left her flat.

Back in Crouch End, Sonia was feeling much better now that the Doreen Baines situation had been sorted. Alan had apologised for his reaction and things were firmly back on track. She smiled as she heard Connie, Caroline and Cath chasing each other upstairs. It made her so happy that they were still such good friends and hoped they always would be. Connie only had one friend locally, a little girl called Rosie who was the daughter of doctors.

Although Sonia was pleased that her daughter mixed with what she called respectable people, she was also aware that her family had to be careful with who they were friendly with. Although the Drapers and the Davis's were not part of anything remotely dodgy, Sonia knew they weren't stupid and because they had all known each other for years there was a mutual trust and Sonia could be herself. Overall, she was feeling much better than she had done and was gradually beginning to appreciate her life and, more importantly, how hard her husband worked to give her and the kids a good life.

Lily Jenson eyed the young woman stood in front of her with a critical eye and was pleased with what she saw. Vanessa Whelan was pretty and well-spoken which was a bonus.

She was studying to be a vet but having lost both her parents she didn't have the money to fund her education. She had previously worked in a high class establishment up West as a hostess who provided extras, so in Lily's mind had plenty of experience.

As they were concluding their interview, Lily's son Barry who had Downs Syndrome came bowling into the room minus his trousers. 'I'm hungry Mummy,' he announced.

Lily turned to Vanessa and said with a wry smile, 'Just be grateful that he has his pants on, last week he didn't when I interviewed one of the other girls.'

Vanessa who wasn't easily shocked just laughed. 'Would you like a sweet, I have some fudge in my bag?'

Barry smiled and hugged her. 'Yes please.'

When Vanessa left, Lily felt satisfied that she had made the right decision with the girls she had chosen and especially Vanessa who had been so lovely with Barry. The house was really coming together. Vanessa would work with two other girls: Melanie who was a beautiful redhead and Tian, a petite Chinese girl who had assured Lily that she had a few unusual sexual tricks up her sleeve. Lily felt confident that the three girls would pull in the punters and she already had a swingers' party booked for the following weekend so was sure Ron would be pleased with the progress she had made setting up the business. She sighed as she thought of Ron.

He had been her first love and unbeknown to him she still harboured feelings for him. Unfortunately their days of hopping into bed together were long gone. She was a realist and knew she could no longer compete with the younger women he chose to spend time with these days although she had heard a rumour that he was staying faithful to Irene. It would be interesting to see how long that lasted she thought with a chuckle.

Ebony Peters had had a very productive morning shopping but was now worn out. Carrying a large bump around was not easy with three bags of shopping so she decided to take a break and have a cup of coffee. Just as she was about to enter a café, she spotted Irene McCardle coming towards her. The two women made eye contact at the same time but the smug look on the older woman's face soon disappeared when she noticed that Ebony was clearly pregnant. Seeing the colour drain from Irene's face Ebony felt a moment of victorious joy which was quickly replaced by fear. This would cause ructions. As she tried to walk away Irene grabbed her roughly by the arm. 'Is that Ron's?' she asked her voice breaking.

'Of course it isn't, I haven't slept with Ron in ages.'

Ebony knew from the look on Irene's face that she wanted to believe her but didn't. Irene felt as if she had been kicked in the stomach and needed to get away and think, so without another word almost ran down the street.

Ron was having a cup of tea and a catch up with Lily blissfully unaware that his life was about to explode and that his wife was sitting at home sobbing into a cup of tea liberally laced with Brandy.

'So Lil, sounds like you have it all sown up. I must admit that I was a bit dubious at first about a knocking shop...'

Lily interrupted him. 'A high class sexual retreat if you don't mind. The girls are all upper class, clean and educated as will the clients be. I won't have any riff raff in here Ron. And as for the parties, the guests will also be the more affluent people in the area.'

Ron laughed. Lily had somehow made it all sound very respectable when at the end of the day it was a brothel where men would come to pay for sex and married couples would swap partners like kids swapping sweets. Mind you as long as it brought in money he wasn't really bothered and he knew that he was protected as some of the clientele would be policemen.

Lily had started to talk again and Ron could not believe what he was hearing. 'I have one bedroom left and I was thinking of taking on a young man who can cater for frustrated upper class women.'

Ron was no prude but this idea shocked him. In his old fashioned way of thinking it was men that craved sex not women.

Lily laughed when she saw the scandalised look on his face but after she explained to him that there was a market, he conceded that she could be right and that if she thought it was a good idea then he was happy for her to sort it out.

Getting up to leave, Barry came into the room. He loved Ron and the two men hugged. Lily smiled. She loved the fact that Ron accepted her boy and it melted her heart to see their genuine affection for each other. She wasn't sure if this would be true if Ron knew the truth. Lily had never gone through with that abortion. Barry was his son but she had always kept him in the dark to protect everyone concerned. As much as Ron was fond of the boy, she wasn't sure if he would ever have accepted her deception or their son's disability. She had always vowed to tell him and she would one day but somehow that day had never come and she didn't want to upset the apple cart when everything was going so well at the moment.

Irene McCardle was taking deep breaths, trying to calm herself down. When she had got home, she had broken down and wept with the hurt and frustration that was raging through her. Then she had cried for herself. It was clearly a problem with her why the marriage had never produced children. She was barren and the realisation was tearing her apart. Neither of them had ever been tested and the ignorance of not knowing which one could not produce children had been strangely comforting over the years but now she knew and the knowledge was devastating.

Her first instinct was to throttle both her husband and his mistress with her bare hands and that was still a possibility. She was that angry but she had to think about what this meant for her future with her husband.

Ebony Peters was back at her flat, not sure whether she should phone Ron or her father to inform them that Irene knew that she pregnant. She decided to try her father.

'I don't want you telling Ron Ebony. Irene may not even let on that she's seen you.'

Ebony doubted that very much. 'Come on Dad, she isn't going to keep this to herself.'

'Just sit tight Girl, she has too much to lose giving Ron earache. She isn't stupid. Her life is tied up with him. She isn't going to risk losing all that.'

Ebony wasn't so sure but promised Gary that she wouldn't say anything unless Ron mentioned it first. A little thought crept into her mind. If it was all out in the open, then maybe Ron and her could make a go of it but she dismissed this idea as she no longer wanted him as a lover and if she was honest, the feeling was mutual.

Irene was feeling calmer. She needed her wits about her to decide what to do about this revelation. It was ironic. Ron had been as good as gold lately and she had been sure that his relationship with Ebony had ended. He had been attentive and they had even started making love again and now this! The rotten bastard!

She could stomach and even understand to some degree his want of other women but fathering another woman's child was humiliating as far as she was concerned. 'The tart' had claimed that the baby wasn't his but Irene knew in her guts that it was. She wondered if her husband knew and how he would react to the situation. He had always said he wasn't bothered about having kids but she only had to watch him with other people's to know that was a kindly lie for her benefit. She and Ron were a team. She knew everything about the businesses, even his recent foray into the sex trade. He had always been upfront with her and he only trusted her with the books. But if he knew about the child, it meant that he had lied to her and their marriage was now a sham so what did that mean for her? Where exactly did she now fit in? She was confident enough to know that he wouldn't want a divorce but would he be able to resist the lure of an innocent baby? That was what was really troubling her. At this moment she wanted to kill her cheating husband for the fact that he had done the worst thing possible to her. He had made her feel inadequate and jealous. Although she couldn't imagine a life without him, she also didn't know if she could cope with this betrayal. She decided to sleep on it and not make any rash decisions. As her old mum used to say, 'tomorrow is another day.'

Unfortunately, Irene was only too aware that her troubles would still be there tomorrow. As she miserably climbed the stairs to bed, she heard a loud crash and the sound of glass shattering downstairs.

Gingerly she crept back down the stairs and quietly found the gun that Ron kept in a hallway cupboard.

'Who's there? I'm armed so I suggest that you piss off from where you came from.'

Irene's voice was loud and confident. She was still in a rage from earlier and in the mood to shoot someone. Her question however was met with silence and she knew instinctively that there was no one else in the house. Her suspicions were confirmed when she went into the front room. Her bay window was broken and lying in the middle of the room was a brick with a note wrapped around it, secured by an elastic band. She picked up the brick and looked at the note. It had one word written on it: Wanker! Irene began laughing hysterically. Whoever had thrown that brick had the measure of her husband and it would seem that he had pissed off someone else today, as well as her.

When Ron got home he was livid that someone had dared to put his wife in danger. He was surprised that Irene seemed strangely accepting considering the window was now in pieces all over her Persian rug.

'So who have you upset Ron?' she asked with a slightly sarcastic tone.

'Other than the Turks, no one.' Ron scratched his head. He genuinely didn't have a clue who would have done this. Most people he had to give a dig to knew the score and accepted it. Throwing a brick through the window was kid's stuff so he immediately dismissed that it was the Turks. They were a slick outfit and wouldn't resort to childish tit for tat. He momentarily thought of Ebony but again dismissed this idea as they had been ok when he had last seen her, and anyway she wouldn't jeopardise her weekly allowance that he was going to have to pay her. It was a mystery alright but when he found the scroat who had done it, he would give him a hiding that wouldn't be forgotten in a hurry.

Chapter 13

Irene woke up the following morning with a much clearer head. She decided to keep quiet until she had time to decide about her future. Knowledge was power and she would bide her time until she decided what to do about the whole sorry mess that her husband had created. She knew that being rash was not an option and now knew that the other week when Ron had come home drunk, he had been apologising for this unforgivable cockup but she needed time to think it through and plan. Satisfied with her decision to play her cards close to her chest, she phoned the local glazier to arrange for the front room window to be repaired and then went to wake her husband. They were going over to Alan and Sonia's today for lunch as it was Breda's birthday. Irene was dreading it as the whole family would be there and she would have to put on a brave face. She told herself that company may just be what she needed as if she was alone with Ron she wouldn't be able to trust herself and would blurt out her secret.

Sonia looked at the buffet for the birthday lunch and immediately started worrying that she hadn't made enough. The guest list in the last week had grown and now she was catering for thirty people. Not surprisingly, Alan had popped out on 'business' and she was at this minute trying to make a Quiche Lorraine whilst curling her hair.

She silently cursed her husband because she had asked him to lay out the drinks table and now she would have to do that as well. Hearing her children arguing upstairs, she was on her way to see what the fuss was about when the doorbell rang. It was their neighbour Su Lin, who was Chinese Bob's wife, carrying a container full of dumplings that she had made for the lunch.

'Ah thanks Love, I was worried that I hadn't made enough grub and these will go down a treat.'

'You're welcomes Sonia,' Su Lin said.

Thanking her, she closed the door and went upstairs to sort out the twins, who were now screaming at each other. When Connie noticed her mother stood in the doorway of her room she ran to her in tears.

'Look what Billy has done to my diary Mum,' she wailed handing her the small book that Gina Davis had given her for Christmas.

Sonia inspected the diary and glared at her son who was looking at her defiantly.

'Billy, why are half the pages glued together?'

'I was only leaning on the stupid book while I was gluing my plane, it was an accident.'

Sonia sighed, she didn't need this when she had thirty people on their way over and she still wasn't dressed.

'What have I told you about your air fix models? You do them at the kitchen table.'

'I can't cos you've put all that food on the table.'

'Oh just go and get dressed the both of you, Daddy will sort out your diary Connie, ok?'

The children could tell by the tone of their mother's voice that they needed to do as she said, so obediently went to get ready but not before Connie had slyly pinched her brother and stuck out her tongue at him.

Ron and Irene sat in silence on the drive over to the Stewart's.

'What's up Irene? You've had a face like a slapped arse ever since we left home. If we've had an argument then can you at least remind me what it was about?'

Irene pursed her lips. She would have to act normal but it was bloody hard work and they hadn't even got to the birthday celebration yet.

'I've just got one of my heads, I'll be fine once we get there.'

Ron nodded sympathetically, his Irene did suffer with her migraines and he just hoped they wouldn't have to leave early because he was looking forward to a good drink.

As they pulled into his mother's road to pick her up, Ron was just relieved that Irene wasn't cross with him about anything. She was a tough bird and would be ok after a Cinzano he reasoned.

Irene was anything but ok. The first thing she had spotted when they arrived was a bunch of guests cooing over a bundle wrapped in a pink shawl. Sonia's sister Sharon had recently given birth to a little girl called Lauren and the happy picture made Irene's eyes fill with tears. Realising that she had to compose herself she grabbed a bottle of Cinzano from the drinks table and poured herself a double measure.

Ron was thoroughly enjoying himself as he playfully sparred with Billy. Alan had recently started taking him to his old boxing club and the boy was showing real promise.

'You're getting a good right hook Billy,' Ron said impressed. Billy beamed at the man who he looked upon as an uncle. He knew that Ron McCardle was important although he didn't understand why but he did know that any praise given by the man was a reason to feel proud.

As Irene watched her husband playing with the lad she felt a fleeting moment of hate towards him. She wasn't a big drinker but felt the urge to blot out the pain so sat on the sofa steadily getting pissed. She realised she had had too much when she got up to go to the toilet and immediately fell back down again. Sonia who was sitting next to her chatting to her mother-in-law Glenice looked at her with concern.

Irene was usually in control and in all the years that she had known her she had only ever seen her a bit tipsy at her fiftieth.

'Are you ok Irene?'

Irene looked at the younger woman and knew she had to sort herself out. This was not the time or the place to make a show of herself. As Mrs McCardle she was expected to portray an impression of calm and be a good role model for the other wives and girlfriends.

'I'm ok Sonia, shouldn't drink on an empty stomach,' Irene laughed.

Breda had heard the exchange and immediately grabbed Irene and pulled her up off the sofa.

'Come on Girl, come and have a jive with me. If you can't get pickled at a party then when can you?'

The last thing Irene needed was to prance around on the dance floor but smiling she followed Sonia's mother and was soon quite enjoying herself, dancing to all the rock and roll hits of the fifties. Ron was watching his wife with interest as she flung her arms about and gyrated. Irene was not one for being in the middle of the action at a party and her antics today were very out of character. He had also clocked how much she was drinking and inst-inctively knew that something was wrong but he couldn't for the life of him think what it was. When she went arse over tit and landed on the Stewart's neighbour Su Lin, he knew it was time to make their excuses and leave.

'Come on Love, I think it's time to go home, you've had enough,' Ron urged his wife.

Irene glared at Ron. 'OH I've had enough alright,' she spat.

Ron was genuinely confused and was now feeling angry. His wife was making an exhibition of herself and showing him up. He hated seeing women drunk and especially his wife who he felt was making him look like a prize tit. Respect was everything to Ron and he could see that the other guests were now looking at them, some with shock on their faces. That did it for Ron, clutching tightly onto his wife's arm, he thanked Sonia for a lovely party and marched his wife out of the house and to their car.

'Oi how am I going to get home?' he heard his mother Dolly shouting.

He didn't actually give a flying fuck. He just wanted to get as far away as possible.

'Talk about over reacting,' Breda stated when they had gone. She was only enjoying herself.'

'Yeah but to be fair, she doesn't usually drink like that,' her sister Maggie pointed out.

Ron's mother Dolly was quiet. Maggie was right. Her daughter-in-law had always acted very lady like. Irene's erotic dancing had been very unlike her indeed.

Ron's mood was made worse when they reached the end of the street and Irene threw up all over herself. He was just about to let rip when she burst into tears and carried on sobbing all the way up the A10. Ron was at a loss what to do or say. Irene was a woman who was always in control. He loved that about her and as head wife it was important that the other wives looked up to her. When they pulled onto their drive, he opened the passenger door and gently carried her upstairs. By now she was just making a groaning noise. He undressed her and put her into the bath. As he bathed her and washed the vomit out of her hair she looked at him sadly.

'Sorry Ron, I couldn't help it.'

'Let's just get you into bed and we'll talk later Love.'

His anger had been replaced with worry but he knew she was in no fit state to talk to him about anything. After he dried her, he lovingly put her into bed, shut the curtains and went downstairs.

Nursing a large Scotch Ron thought over the day's events. Irene had no reason to be upset about anything. All the businesses were doing well and she had been fine about the house that Lily Jenson was running. Alan had kept the new venture from Sonia a secret as he knew that she would blow a fuse but Irene had been accepting like she was with everything else. Ron was stumped. He had even knocked his post marital affair on the head.

For one fleeting moment he wondered if Irene had found out about Ebony. He quickly dismissed that idea as Ebony was under strict instructions to keep away from anywhere where she may bump into his wife and it was in her best interests to do so. Refilling his glass, he decided he would talk to his wife in the morning. Maybe she had just let her hair down for once but Ron knew that was unlikely. He had known her for too many years and he knew when his soulmate was worried about something. He just hoped she wasn't ill. The thought that he might lose her was just too awful to contemplate.

Back in Crouch End the party was drawing to a close. As Sonia began to tidy up, her mind drifted to Irene. Her mother Breda had thought the whole thing was hilarious but, like Ron McCardle, Sonia was worried about her friend. Something had been off about her today. She seemed to have lost the spark in her eyes and hadn't been herself. This in turn had begun to worry Sonia. She just hoped that Ron wasn't in some sort of trouble because if he was that would impact her own husband. She had heard about the brick being thrown through their window but Ron had put that down to kids and even Sonia had to agree that it did seem more of a childish prank than retaliation for something big, but now she wasn't so sure.

'Penny for them,' Alan said as he came into the kitchen.

'Al, what do you reckon about Irene today? I've never seen her like that before. You could see that Ron was annoyed with her.'

Alan felt the same but wasn't about to admit as much. 'She just got pissed. It happens to all of us, now pass us a jug of water. Someone has puked into your cheese plant.'

'Bloody hell Al, this was meant to be a lunch party for a seventy-five-year-old woman…'

Alan chuckled. 'It was your mum who threw up, she's gone to bed.'

Sonia had to laugh, at least her mum had enjoyed herself.

Ebony Peters had spent the weekend dreading a phone call from Ron but as the hours passed she felt an overwhelming sense of relief. Clearly Irene had not told him that they had bumped into each other in Wood Green. Musing over her predicament she decided it would be best if she moved well away from North London, at least she could then go shopping in peace without the chance of running into the old crone. She also needed to keep Ron sweet as babies were expensive and she would need a lot of cash to keep her and the child in the life that she had become accustomed to.

Irene McCardle groaned as she opened her eyes. She may have been drunk earlier but she could remember every detail of her drunken behaviour. The images were floating around her head in glorious technicolour. She didn't really care what people thought if she was honest but she was annoyed with herself that she had let her guard down.

She needed to be very careful because she didn't know what she was going to do about Ebony most probably being pregnant with her husband's child. She would just have to apologise to Ron. Feeling parched she decided she might as well get it over with. So slipping out of bed, she found her dressing gown and padded downstairs.

Ron was sat in his favourite winged armchair watching *Chips*. When he saw his wife, he jumped up and went to cuddle her. Irene momentarily froze but knew that she must act normal.

'I'm so sorry about today Ron, I didn't eat enough and you know what Breda's like, wanting everyone to get up and dance. She and Maggie are so wild on the dance floor that I kind of just went along with it.'

Ron breathed a sigh of relief that it was nothing but over indulgence. 'Well you were going for it a bit Love.'

'Yeah I know, it won't happen again.'

'Good cos it's not a good look and we have an image to maintain. Can't have people thinking that my wife's a lush.'

Although Ron was joking, Irene was well aware that there was a subtle threat in his words. 'Bastard' she inwardly thought as she sat down on the sofa.

'Right I'll go and make a cuppa and we'll forget about today,' Ron offered.

Irene nodded but she was sure of one thing now. If that kid was her husband's, he wasn't getting away with it because he was right. She did have an image to maintain and being a mug wasn't part of that image.

Just as Ron returned from the kitchen with the tea, she heard laughter which seemed to be coming from their drive. Looking out of the window she spied three figures in dark clothing running back towards the pavement. One of them turned and gave a wanker sign then ran off into the night with the other two. Telling Ron, he immediately ran out of the front door to chase them. When he returned he was out of breath with the exertion and rage he was now feeling.

'They've fucking keyed the car, great long scratch.'

'Oh Ron, they looked like kids to me.'

'I don't fucking care who they are, first the brick and now this, tomorrow I'm getting someone to put in an iron gate, then let the fuckers try and get in.'

When Ron sat back down he wondered if the Turks were sending him a message. He knew through the grapevine that they were about to flood the market with heroin and he also knew that they had not been happy that he wouldn't come in with them. He ran North London and he just hoped they would respect that because if they didn't then he was ready for them. He just hoped that Alan was as well because until now his number two had not had to get his hands too bloody, but if they went to war with the Turks then they would all have to get involved.

Chapter 14

Deniz Mehmet had arrived as an immigrant into Great Britain at the age of four. His father Ediz had grown lemons back in Northern Cyprus but hadn't been able to afford to feed his large family of eight children. So he had decided that the more prosperous England was the place to make his fortune.

Unfortunately his wife Maria had died soon after arriving of Tuberculosis and he had succumbed to the same disease three weeks later having caught it from her. The children had ended up at the mercy of the state: the younger ones had been adopted by childless English couples but the older boys including Deniz had ended up living in Dr Barnardo's. His childhood had been lonely until a skinny boy called Gary Peters had moved into the home. They had forged a friendship which was still going strong today. Deniz grew up determined to make as much money as possible and to create a family home that was filled with the luxury and love that his childhood had lacked.

Today Deniz was like the cat who had got the cream. He had secured a good deal with his contact in Turkey and was about to supply London with high quality heroin. He would of course dilute it with talcum powder and baking soda. He had no qualms about doing this as all dealers used cutting agents to increase the weight for more profit. He was a businessman after all and had made a fortune over the last twenty-five years. He had a huge distaste for junkies but was also grateful for their existence.

He was now widely acknowledged as THE king drug baron in East London, but being greedy and ambitious wanted to branch out and increase his fortunes which is why his next project was widening his market into North London. He was more than aware that Ron McCardle ran this part of London and he was also aware that Ron did not deal in drugs. Therefore in Deniz's mind there was a huge gap in the market that he was going to fill whether Ron McCardle liked it or not. Being an arrogant man he wasn't worried about any repercussions. He had respectfully offered Ron a piece of the action and he had been foolish enough to decline. Ron's outfit was dated and some of his men had been with him for years and looked like they couldn't raise a pint never mind a fist, so all in all Deniz was confident that his plan would succeed even if Ron did decide to retaliate. Deniz had been insulted when his offer had been turned down and Ron had insisted that he could not provide protection, but in his heart he had always known that the other man wouldn't come in with him. He laughed when he had learnt that Ron was being targeted and laughed even harder when he found out that he thought it was Deniz. Did the man really think that the Turks had time to carry out childish pranks? Deniz's estimation of Ron had gone down after that. He knew full well who had a grudge against Ron McCardle and he would enjoy watching the situation play out. Since their meeting Deniz had increased his protection. He had policemen and even a high court judge in his pocket. Money certainly talked and Deniz had come to realise that was the only language people understood. He was looking forward to becoming even richer.

Irene McCardle was feeling better than she had done the previous week. Ron had not left her side and she was beginning to wonder if Ebony was telling the truth after all and that the baby was someone else's. There was obviously the chance that it was Ron's and that Ebony hadn't told him but she didn't believe for one second as Ebony wouldn't miss out on the chance of bleeding her husband dry for money. As she looked out of the window and surveyed the workmen putting in new railings, Ron came into the front room.

'I'm popping to Deptford for a few hours Love, John has invited me over for a pint and I haven't seen him in yonks.'

Irene smiled. She knew that her husband enjoyed going back to his old stomping ground and he was right, he hadn't seen his cousin John for ages. 'Ok Love, I'll have your dinner ready for you when you get back.'

Ron was grateful that his wife always believed his explanations and never asked questions, because he needed to see Ebony and sort out where she was moving to. He felt decidedly nervous that she only lived a few miles away and knew full well that she wouldn't stick to her promise of staying away from Wood Green which was where his wife often shopped. He had come up with a plan and hoped that she would agree. Unbeknown to Irene he owned a three bed semi in Brentwood which was in Essex. He had originally purchased it as a safe house for criminals on the run and although he had been paid handsomely for doing so over the years, he had now stopped as he didn't need the money or the hag so the house had stood idle for a few years.

Jason Baines looked at his motionless mother and his eyes filled with tears. The hospital room was eerily silent now that the heart monitor had stopped beeping, signalling the end for Doreen Baines. She seemed to have disappeared underneath the heavy hospital blanket. His once buxom loud mother was dead. A heroin overdose. The knowledge laid heavily on the lad. Doreen had taken the money Alan Stewart had given her and had promptly gone to the flat next door where that Angie bird and her long-haired boyfriend had welcomed her with open arms when she had flashed the cash at them. She had only been friendly with them for a few days but had wanted company to party with. The party had lasted four days. Four days of indulging in drink and cocaine and then finally trying heroin for the first and as it turned out, the last time. Doreen's six and a half stone body just couldn't cope and she had collapsed on the dirty carpet and suffered a fatal seizure.

As Jason left the hospital he was consumed by grief and anger. So instead of going straight home to the flat that he had shared with his mother, he had kicked Angie's front door down determined to kick the shit out of the two druggies who in his mind held some responsibility in his mother's overdose. Unsurprisingly the flat was empty.

Angie had been thoroughly traumatised by the whole event and had decided that London and drugs were not for her after all. She was now back with her middle class parents in Surrey who were relieved to have their seventeen-year-old, wayward daughter back home. The long haired boyfriend had had it away on his toes and was currently in Liverpool staying with a friend who had a very comfortable sofa, and even more importantly, a fridge full of beer and a coffee table topped full of cocaine.

Jason had wept when he took in the pitiful scene of used needles, silver foil and a rusty spoon. He broke down when he spotted his mother's Bob Marley LP which was lying forlornly on the carpet next to a half drunken tin of Tennents. In Jason's mind Alan Stewart was as much to blame for all of this as were the two scumbags who had done a moonlight flit. He was all alone in the world now except for his mother's brother Charlie but he hadn't seen him in years. He was just relieved that the rent book to the flat had been put in his name so at least he still had a roof over his head. Going back home he sat on the sofa sipping a cup of tea and thinking. His parents were dead and his brother and sisters were long gone. He hoped they had been adopted and were living in lovely homes because he wouldn't wish this scummy flat on anyone. He was pleased that they had been saved from this existence even if he did miss them all.

That night Jason had a vivid dream. They were all back in their old flat eating fish and chips. Doreen was laid on the sofa laughing as she watched *Coronation Street*. His dad Stevie was sat in the armchair with his sisters Dawn and Lisa who were sat on his lap feeding him chips as he pretended to be asleep. His other sister Michelle was sprawled on the carpet reading a magazine and his younger brother Peter was playing with a toy gun taking pot shots at them all. It was a happy, cosy scene although even in his slumber Jason knew that these family moments had been few and far between. Suddenly in the dream, there was an almighty crash and a devil came into the room. The scary man was Alan Stewart.

The next morning Jason woke with tears in his eyes. He had been crying in his sleep. The dream had confirmed one thing to him. The loss of his family started with Alan Stewart. He remembered the day that Alan had come round to the flat to tell them that Stevie was dead. Jason was only a boy at the time but he clearly remembered sensing the man's guilt. He had struggled to look them in the eye and had scarpered as soon as the deed was done. Jason was now more determined to plan his revenge. It could take years but one day he would make sure that Alan Stewart suffered as he had been suffering for the last five years.

Ron McCardle drove home from Ebony's flat satisfied that they had reached an amicable agreement. Ebony hadn't initially been too enthusiastic about the house until Ron assured her that it would be decorated top to bottom and that she could pick out some nice furnishings. They had also discussed what room would be the baby's nursery and Ron had suppressed the excitement that he couldn't help feeling as Ebony had prattled on about cots and Winnie the Pooh wallpaper. One thing Ebony had insisted upon was that Ron visited the child once a month and if he was honest he was glad that he would get to see his baby. Despite what he had first said, he was overwhelmed with the thought of becoming a father and he didn't actually feel that he could stay away. A little voice in his head said that he was dicing with danger because if Irene ever found out, he was sure that his marriage would be over. However the pull of his little baby overpowered his worries about his marriage. He would take his chances and hope for the best.

When Ebony had started discussing baby names he had made his excuses and left as he didn't want to appear too keen. Looking at his watch he realised that he had been longer than he had intended. He had stayed close to home in the last week as he was worried about the fact that someone had been targeting him and he was also worried about his wife. She hadn't been right since the party and he had a strong feeling that her behaviour was more than the over indulgence of alcohol. His Irene had always been a lady. She had never once let him down in company and she had always been the perfect role model to the other halves of his employees. It was a real mystery and although she kept insisting that she was fine, Ron knew her well enough to know that she wasn't. He was however relieved that she had seemed more herself today. Maybe it was just due to the change of life that she kept harping on about. He didn't really know what that all entailed and being a man's man didn't really want to know.

Irene was also checking her watch and wondering where her husband was. She was tempted to ring his cousin John but quickly changed her mind. She had never in the whole of their marriage checked up on him and she wasn't about to start.

Although Jason Baines had promised himself that he would wait to take his revenge on Alan Stewart, he was too angry and bitter not to do anything. This morning he had visited a local firm of undertakers and had quickly realised that he could never afford to pay for a funeral. The funeral assistant had been kind as he had explained that the council would arrange everything. So his mother would have what amounted to a pauper's funeral. Jason was seething with anger and embarrassment as he walked home and his mood had gotten worse as the day wore on, which was why he was now stood outside the home of Alan Stewart with a petrol can and a box of matches.

He had waited until it was dark so that he wouldn't be seen and bided his time until he was sure that no one was at home. He didn't want to hurt anyone just cause some damage so he was relieved when he saw Alan, his wife and two kids all pile into their car at eight o'clock. Waiting five minutes he crossed the road, poured some petrol through the letter box and lit a match.

Breda had had a bath and was enjoying a cup of tea with a nip of whisky in bed. She had a cold and was hoping that the hot toddy would help her to sleep. Alan and Sonia had taken the children to the Wimpy as a treat and although they had asked her to join them, she hadn't felt well enough. Picking up her Mills and Boon book, she decided that a quick read and a long sleep was what the doctor ordered.

Chinese Bob and his wife Su Lin were walking home from his sister's house and as they walked passed the Stewart's home there was a loud shattering of glass as the front room window blew. Chinese Bob immediately dived on top of his petite wife to protect her. Neighbours had started to gather and it was the teacher from number thirty who took control. 'Bob go and phone the fire brigade, does anyone know if there is anyone inside?'

'Soniaaa say that they all go Wimpy tonight,' Su Lin confirmed before bursting into tears.

'Well thank God no one is at home,' the teacher said relieved.

Five minutes later they could all hear the wail of fire engines.

Breda woke up coughing. She couldn't see properly and her eyes had started stinging. She tried to sit up but she had a pain in her chest which was crushing her and travelling down her arms. She then realised with fright that her bedroom was full of smoke. Needing to find the strength to get up and call for help she tried to ignore the pain shooting through her body and tried to ease herself up again. The effort was too much and she fell back down onto her pillows. The last thought she had before she died was that she would soon be with her deceased loved ones and that it had been so long since she had held her boy Declan in her arms.

Alan had driven a mile or so and then realised he had forgotten his wallet so they had had to turn around again. As they pulled into their road they could see there was a fire engine outside of their house. Alan had barely stopped the car before Sonia had opened the passenger door and jumped out. 'My mum is in there,' she screamed.

The fireman in charge immediately turned to his colleagues. 'There's someone in there.'

He then turned back to Sonia who was now hysterical. 'Where would she be in the house?'

'Right at the top.'

The fireman wasn't hopeful, there was fire raging through the downstairs of the house and he couldn't put his men in danger at that moment. Sonia saw his hesitation and made a run towards her burning home. Alan grabbed her and pulled her back.

'Let the men do their jobs Darling, they'll get your mum out.'

The children were shaking and started crying when they saw their mum collapse on to the pavement. Su Lin took them by the hands and ushered them up the road to the teacher's house. Sonia had fainted just as the ambulance crew arrived. They immediately put her into the ambulance and when she had come to howling like a wounded animal she had promptly been sedated.

Ten minutes later the fire was out and two firemen entered the house. Alan's heart was beating heavily in his chest as he prayed that his mother-in-law would be saved.

His worst fears were confirmed when the two firemen emerged and one of them shook his head. They were carrying Breda and although the ambulance men tried to revive her she was pronounced dead at eight-thirty five. Alan cried like a baby. He had known and loved Breda nearly his whole life. She had been the beating heart of their home and he had always been grateful that she had been in the house with his family when he was out working. He would miss her terribly and he really didn't know how his wife would cope without her mum by her side. He tried to compose himself as the chief fireman approached him.

'I can't say officially but my men could smell petrol when they went in, the police will need to take a statement as I'm afraid that it looks like arson.'

The words winded Alan as the realisation hit him. Someone had done this on purpose. Someone had killed his mother-in-law. But who? Alan didn't have any enemies as far as he knew.

Suddenly a little voice in his head reminded him that he didn't lead a normal life. He worked with villains. He WAS a villain. But even knowing these facts, he was still confused as to why someone would have it in for him. He knew one thing for sure, Sonia would never forgive him if she ever found out. She had struggled for years with his foray into a criminal life and had never really accepted it. It was ironic that what she had always been worried about was him getting a capture because at this minute that option would have been a lot easier to bear. Thanking the firemen for all of their hard work he trudged up the road to the teacher's house and asked Su Lin to take the children to her home where he would pick them up later. He then got back in his car and drove to the hospital to tell his wife that her beloved mum had died.

Chapter 15

Alan held Sonia's hand as he gently explained to her what had happened to her mother. As she looked up at him with her big brown eyes he was reminded of the little girl that she had been back in 1941 in the air raid shelter in Bethnal Green. Sonia was feeling groggy after the sedation and trying to process the enormity of what she was being told. As the sickening realisation dawned that she was never going to see her beloved mother again she began shaking uncontrollably and let out a piercing scream like an animal who had been caught in a painful trap. Her screams echoed around the walls of the small hospital room alerting two nurses who came running in. Sonia was thrashing around and accidentally kicked one of them in the stomach. 'Get Doctor Williams,' one nurse urged her colleague. 'This woman is in severe shock and needs sedating.'

The other nurse ran out of the room to summon the doctor while Alan helped to restrain his hysterical wife. Doctor Grey arrived five minutes later and expertly administered the sedation which would send Sonia to a place of oblivion. Once the medical staff had left the room satisfied that their patient would sleep for a good few hours Alan once again took his wife's hand and stroked it. 'We'll get through this Darling, I'm heart sorry about your mum, she was a legend, but you still have me and the kids and we all love you so much. Don't worry about the house, it's only bricks. I will find you another house. I promise that I will make it up to you.'

Sonia briefly opened her eyes and just stared at him before falling back to sleep.

Even as Alan whispered comforting words to his wife he was acutely aware that he would never be able to make it up to her and realised that she must never find out that the fire had been arson. Sonia would never forgive him. He was worried that she would never recover from tonight's events. She had suffered with depression ever since they had lost their first child George and her brother Declan in 1954, and she had been popping pills ever since and even more so since he had started working for Ron. She just couldn't deal with loss and Alan wasn't hopeful that she would cope with the huge void losing her mother would create. Breda had been Sonia's touchstone, she had always been on hand with her love and wise words. Sighing, he kissed her on the forehead and quietly left the room. Connie and Billy would be feeling confused and upset and needed him.

The Stewart's neighbour Su Lin had kindly made the children some dinner but they just pushed it around their plates. Usually they loved her dumplings but understandably had no appetite. Billy had been softly crying on and off for the last hour and Connie was staring blankly at the television screen. Su Lin's heart went out to them. The nice teacher from up the road had informed her about Breda and she was just grateful that the children hadn't had to witness the firemen carrying her lifeless body out of the house. Su Lin would miss Sonia's mother walking up the road with her tartan shopping trolley. She would miss the cheerful woman very much but not as much as her family would. Glancing out of her front room window Su Lin was relieved to see Alan walking up her garden path. She rushed to open her door before he had time to ring the bell and offered her condolences and a cup of tea. Her poor neighbour looked totally devastated.

'No thanks Love, I just need to borrow your telephone please?'

'Of course,' she replied pointing to the phone that sat on a small table.

Alan phoned Ron and explained in detail what had happened. The older man listened in shock and urged Alan to bring the kids round to his house and told him that they could stay as long as they needed to. Unbeknown to Alan, Connie had been eavesdropping on the conversation and upon hearing the words 'Breda' and 'dead' had charged into her father's arms quickly followed by her brother. Alan tightly held on to his children as he once again had to gently break the news that Breda had died. He then explained that they would be staying with Uncle Ron and Aunty Irene tonight for a sleep over. Once the children had stopped crying they naturally had a barrage of questions.

'But where will we live Dad?' Billy sniffed.

'Don't worry Billy, it will all be sorted,' Alan tried to reassure his son.

'But I don't want to move away from Rosie, we're starting Brownies next week,' Connie stated. Rosie was Connie's little friend who lived around the corner.

'I said I will sort everything out,' Alan replied.

'Where's Mum?' Connie demanded. 'And will my Sindy dolls be burnt?'

'I want Nanny,' Billy started to cry again.

Alan looked at his children's desperate faces and crumbled. He had tried to hold it together for three hours but he could no longer stop the tears that had been building up. Holding his children, they all wept instinctively knowing that life was never going to be the same again. Connie and Billy had always accepted that their father was the stronger parent and were alarmed that their big, strong dad was crying. Wanting to comfort him, they temporarily forgot about their own pain.

'Don't cry Dad, we will look after you and Mum,' Billy solemnly promised.

His son's words broke Alan's heart. It was his job to look after his family. He hadn't protected them although he didn't know what he had meant to be protecting them from.

'Come on kids, time to go. I will explain about Mum in the car.'

Alan thanked Su Lin and her husband Bob and drove towards Ron's house deep in thought. He had needed to release his emotions but now he needed a clear head to think about the events of tonight and to try and work out who could have done such a despicable thing.

It was an occupational hazard having enemies in his line of business but women and children were generally safe and left out of business dealings and feuds.

Jason Baines was enjoying a joint and a can of lager. He chuckled to himself as he thought about what he had done. He had felt a sense of calm and satisfaction as he saw the first flame take hold of the Stewart's home. He hadn't hung around for long as he didn't want to be spotted but just long enough to see his revenge being served. He had then casually walked down Berkeley Road and on to the bus stop near The Clock Tower to wait for the number forty-one bus which would take him back home to Tottenham.

Alan Stewart sat in Ron McCardle's study nursing a tumbler of whisky. Irene had been a diamond with the kids. They had needed a woman's love and care tonight and obediently drank some hot chocolate and eaten some beans on toast. They were safely tucked up in bed and Irene had just confirmed that they were asleep. Alan hoped that the reprieve of sleep would help them cope with tomorrow. Ron studied his friend and his heart went out to him. He looked done in, the poor man and, like Alan, wondered who could have deliberately set fire to a home where children lived. Like Alan, Ron also feared for Sonia who, in his opinion, was not the most stable of people and who had been popping pills for years to help her to cope with life.

Ron cleared his throat, 'What are you thinking Al?'

'I just don't get it Ron, we haven't stepped on anyone's toes lately. I mean who would do something like this? I know you've had a bit of aggro but that was kid's stuff. This is heavy duty. This is like a warning.'

Ron agreed but he had a strong suspicion that it must be related. It was just too much of a coincidence not to be.

'I'll round up my men on the streets and see if anyone has heard anything and then we'll call a meeting. I've got a lodge meeting tomorrow night so I'll ask around there as well.'

'Ron you know as well as I do that the only person who has anything vaguely resembling a grudge is Deniz Mehmet, remember that bloke outside the restaurant a few weeks back and you said yourself that Gary Peters told you that the bloke wasn't a happy bunny.'

'I agree Al but it won't hurt to ask around before we act, I still can't see this as being his style but you're right I can't think of anyone else either. You look knackered Mate, why don't you try and get a bit of shut eye and we'll talk again tomorrow.'

Alan suddenly jumped up. 'Shit I haven't told the family about Breda, can I use your phone?'

'Of course you can, help yourself to anything that you need Al. I'll leave the whisky.'

Ron get up and went to find his wife leaving Alan with the sad task of informing his wife's family.

He phoned Sonia's older brother Patrick Junior who promised he would let his brother Noel and sisters Bridget and Sharon know. His brother-in-law had been in bits. Then Alan phoned Breda's sister Maggie. They had been very close and the woman had broken down crying. She had never married and lived alone and Alan felt sorry that she would have to bear the burden of this awful news on her own.

'I can't believe this Child, I was only talking to her on the phone last night. She was rotten with the cold and said that she was getting an early night, my poor sister and sweet Jesus, how will Sonia cope? That child and her mother were as close as could be.'

As Maggie started crying again, Alan politely assured her that he would look after Sonia and that he would ring her again tomorrow. After he had put the phone down, he poured himself another drink and sunk back into one of Ron's comfortable leather armchairs. Irene found him sound asleep two hours later and gently released his fingers from around the whisky tumbler that he was still clutching. She covered him with a blanket and went upstairs to bed where she found Ron on the telephone. When he finally put down the receiver he turned to his wife. 'I don't get any of this, I've spoken to all the guys on the street and nothing. Petrol being put through a letterbox is personal and if Alan has got any enemies then they would be my enemies as well and all we've had done is minor shit.'

'Do I need to be worried Ron?'

'I'll let you know when I know Love but in the meantime I'm going to get the Clarke brothers to stay close to you. I'm not taking any chances until I have sorted this.'

Irene really didn't need all of this. She was still trying to decide what to do about Ebony Peters and her pregnancy and she really wasn't looking forward to being followed around by Doug and Rob Clarke. Their very presence would make her worry and last time Ron had trouble and the brothers had been dispatched to 'mind' her, they had eaten her out of house and home! She just hoped that the culprit of all the bother was found and dealt with as soon as possible but deep down she prayed that it wasn't the Turks because if it was there could be a bloodbath and her husband was too old for all of that.

Sonia Stewart gingerly opened her heavy eyes and immediately felt distress-ed. For a moment she didn't know where she was but as she took in her surroundings she remembered that she was in hospital and that her beautiful mother had died in a fire at their home. As the tears fell down her cheeks she could feel herself beginning to panic. She couldn't catch her breath so quickly rang the button to summon a nurse. Lucy Sprig was on the night shift and coming into the room said brightly, 'Ah you poor pet, here take deep breaths into this,' she urged Sonia handing her a brown paper bag. Sonia did as she was told and soon felt her breathing returning to normal.

'Good girl, now I bet you could do with a cuppa and some toast?' the kind nurse said.

Sonia's stomach recoiled at the mention of food but she agreed that she would love a cup of tea. Lucy Sprig went to make the tea and Sonia laid her head back down on the pillow. She felt totally alone and bereft. The thought of her mother being frightened and burnt alive was tormenting her. They should never have gone out because if they had stayed at home, Sonia was sure that the fire would have been put out. Her mother had lived at the top of the house so she hadn't stood a chance. Sonia couldn't understand how it happened because she always unplugged every plug in the house before she went out and before they all went to bed. She suddenly started to panic that it could have been caused by a cigarette but she'd her last smoke in the garden and had trampled that cigarette out and Alan was only a social smoker these days. As the tears started to fall again Lucy Sprig came back into the room and sat on the bed. Sonia sipped at her tea. The lovely nurse stayed with her all night holding her hand as she spoke about her beloved mother Breda.

The next morning Connie and Billy were also waking up in strange surroundings and were just about to get up to find their father when Irene breezed into the room trying to be as cheerful as possible. 'Morning kids, now who wants waffles and Maple Syrup?'

The children briefly forgot their grief as they bounded down the stairs after Aunty Irene and followed her into the kitchen. Their dad was sitting at the table with Uncle Ron having a cup of coffee and some toast and the kids immediately went to him for a cuddle. Irene was reminded that a child's love for their parents was like no other and vice versa and fleetingly remembered that her husband may be about to become a father. She brushed these thoughts aside because these two children and their parents needed her at the moment and Irene admitted to herself that although the circumstances were tragic, she liked the feeling.

Ron had called an urgent meeting with his team and they were all holed up at his Cousin Ray Briggs's scrapyard in St Albans. As he explained the turn of events he could see the changing expressions on the men's faces alternating between curiosity, anger, pity, and worry. Most of them had wives and children and if their firm had enemies that could affect all of them. Greg Leeson was the first to speak. 'So what do we do Ron?'

Ron liked the fact that Greg had used the word 'we.' It showed loyalty. 'I've contacted all my men on the street and even Larry the limp hasn't heard a dickie bird.'

Larry Duggan known locally as Larry the limp due to having one leg shorter than the other had been Ron's eyes and ears on the pavement for many years. If he didn't know anything then no one did, which posed a problem.

As the men started talking at once Ron raised his hand to indicate that they needed to listen. 'We stay vigilant and we wait, I can't be sure it's the Turks and I don't want to start a war with them unless I have to.'

Alan Stewart immediately jumped up. 'With respect Ron, my mother-in-law has just been murdered, what the fuck are we waiting for?'

'Alan, we don't have anything to go on.'

'You sound like fucking old bill, my home has gone up in flames, my wife will probably end up in the nut house and I have two kids who have lost their Nan and have no bloody clothes to wear.'

Ron knew that his friend was on the edge so chose to overlook the fact that Alan was questioning his judgement in front of the workforce.

'Don't you worry Al, if that Turkish prick has had anything to do with this then he's a dead man, I promise you that.'

Alan knew his outburst showed a sign of disrespect and remained silent.

As Ron's men discussed the situation they now found themselves in and the possible involvement of the Turks, the man in question was currently enjoying a glass of champagne on a flight back from Turkey where he had finalised the drugs deal with his business associate. Sighing contentedly, he almost rubbed his hands with glee. He loved money and he was about to have a lot more of it.

As the plane took off he hoped he would be home in time for dinner with his family. His son Kadir and daughter-in-law Layla had just had a baby boy who they had named Jem and the family were gathering tonight to welcome him into the family. There was nothing more important than family and money he thought as he finished his drink and settled down for a nap.

Chapter 16

The next day Alan drove Sonia and the children to Aunty Maggie's in Kilburn. Breda's sister had insisted that they come and stay with her and Alan had agreed as he believed that it would be safer. He just didn't know how this was going to play out. He did know that he had to distance his family from Crouch End. Sonia was very close to her aunty and the two women would be a comfort to each other, he hoped. Also Maggie like her sister was a cheerful person who he knew would put her own heartbreak to one side to care for her fragile niece.

As soon as they arrived at her smart terraced house, she was already standing on her doorstep, arms wide ready to embrace them. Sonia and the children leapt out of the car and held on to her for five minutes before she gently disentangled herself. 'Well if hugs were worth money, I would be a very rich woman indeed, now come inside I have some jam donuts waiting for you.'

Connie and Billy needed no persuading, jam donuts were their absolute favourite. As they all trundled into the house, Maggie turned to Alan and winked. A gesture that said, 'I will look after them, don't worry.'

Alan smiled in gratitude. Bless her heart, he thought. She must be in bits over Breda but like her sister, always put other's needs before her own. The donuts were devoured within minutes and the children were soon chasing around the front room with Maggie's terrier Winston.

When Maggie's china tea pot was knocked off her coffee table she good naturedly shooed the three offenders into the garden. Sonia felt as if she was in a foggy haze. She couldn't think straight and needed to be alone. Excusing herself she told them that she was going to the toilet. Maggie immediately turned to Alan. 'So what happened and don't give me any old flannel. How did the fire start?'

Alan had always been aware that his mother-in-law had been more clued up about his career and what it entailed than she had ever let on to her daughter. He also knew that being so close to her sister meant that Maggie would be in the know, so taking a deep breath he told her what he knew which to be fair wasn't much. Maggie looked at him in horror as she digested the fact that her beloved sister had been murdered. 'Are Sonia and the kids in danger Child?' she worriedly asked.

'To my knowledge I don't have any enemies. The truth is, I just don't know but if Son and the kids could stay here for a few weeks, that will give me time to try and find out who did this.'

'Well when you do, God forgive me but get justice for my sister.'

'Don't you worry Maggie, when I find the culprit I will personally break every bone in his body.' And Alan meant it. He wasn't a violent man but at this moment felt like he could commit murder.

For all Maggie's insistence that she wanted revenge for her sister, she was only an old aged pensioner from Kilburn, she wasn't violent and she suddenly regretted her outburst. She was worried for the future. She had an awful premonition that this was only the start and that life was going to change in a bad way for all of them. Alan sensed her fear and tried to back track on what he had just said. 'Look, for all we know it could have been kids. Don't worry Maggie.'

Maggie smiled in fake agreement but silently thought he must think her an idiot if he thought she believed that. But like her old mum used to say, there was no point in worrying because it didn't change anything and she needed to be strong for her niece who was looking on the verge of collapse. When Sonia came back into the room Alan cuddled her. 'Ok I'm going to go now, I need to go back to the house and see what the damage is. A bloke from the Fire Brigade phoned me earlier and he reckons it is only smoke damage.'

When they had moved in, Sonia had painstakingly spent hours stripping wood, painting, choosing colour schemes and furnishings. She had been so proud of their home. Now she didn't know if she could ever step foot in it again. Nodding she kissed her husband on the cheek and Maggie saw him to the front door. 'Don't worry Alan, they can stay as long as they want to. It will be company for me and Winston,' she reassured him.

Alan took her tiny frame in his arms and lovingly hugged the old lady.

Handing her a wad of cash he urged her to try and persuade Sonia to go on a shopping trip and buy them all some new clothes and toys for the kids.

On his drive home Alan felt comforted that his family would be well looked after. Maggie had refused to accept any money for the extra food she would have to buy but Alan would treat her at a later date he promised himself.

Sonia was in the bedroom that she would be sharing with Connie and Billy and tried to muster a smile as she looked out of the window and watched them playing with Winston in the small back garden. She felt dead inside, a numbness that felt like it was physically dragging her soul out of her body. It had taken years and a lot of medication for her to be able to cope with the loss of her baby George and her brother Declan. On top of these tragedies she had suffered from extreme anxiety due to the worries that her husband's job gave her. Her mother had been her touchstone, her voice of reason, her comfort blanket and she didn't know if she would be able to endure the intense grief that she was feeling and the fact that she felt so alone now. She had two brothers and two sisters but she had always been closer to their mother and none of them lived local to her anyway. Breda had always made her feel safe, her warm embrace had always been close by. Sonia knew that she had to carry on for her children but she really didn't know if she had the strength. Deep in thought she didn't hear Maggie come into the room.

'Sharon is on the phone Child, she sounds upset.'

Sharon was Sonia's older sister and Sonia really couldn't deal with her own grief at the moment let alone anyone else's. She just wanted to be left alone. 'Can you tell her that I'll call her back later please?'

'I can, but remember that you have four brothers and sisters who have all lost their mother too,' Maggie stated gently.

Sonia just turned back to watching her children as a black cloud descended upon her and felt like it was suffocating the life out of her.

Alan was back at the house to inspect the damage. He was meeting with a helpful member of the Fire Brigade who introduced himself as Martin Potts. As they entered the hallway Alan was relieved that although there was some fire damage, the structure was still intact. There was however a film of black soot covering the walls and all the furniture and the smell of smoke and petrol was overwhelming. Martin Potts explained that the removal of the soot would have to be dealt with professionally and that it would take some weeks perhaps months before the family could move back in. As they made their way upstairs various possessions lay strewn around, blackened by the soot eerily reminding Alan of their owners who had escaped the same fate. Finally reaching the top floor where his mother-in-law had perished, Alan gently opened the door that led to her bedroom. Martin Potts kept a respectful distance as Alan picked up Breda's Mills and Boon book that she had been reading. He had always taken the piss out of her slushy choice of books and right now the book looked as he felt: lonely. Spotting her fluffy pink slippers that were laid neatly under her bed, he stifled a sob. He had seen enough. He had shed enough tears and needed to take control.

'Have you seen enough Mr Stewart? The house has been passed off as safe so our job is done. We will send you a report in the next few days,' Martin Potts said.

'Yeah, thanks Mate, I'll be staying a while as I have a glazier coming about the window and a bloke coming to fit a new front door.'

As he drove back to Ron's house he racked his brains trying to fathom out who had tried to destroy his home and in the process and more importantly had killed his mother-in-law. None of it made any sense, but he would find the person and when he did he would kill him stone dead.

Jason Baines was in his local nursing the only pint that he could afford when Denny Draper walked in with his new squeeze Julie. The boys had gone to the same school and were casual acquaintances so when Denny spotted him, he immediately shouted over. 'Alright Mate? What you doing sitting over there on your own? Come and join us.'

After a stint in a crowded Borstal, Jason rather liked his own company these days but knew that it would look weird if he refused, so picking up his pint walked over to where Denny was stood with his girlfriend. Julie was not at all impressed. It had taken her weeks to snare Denny and now she had, she didn't want to share his company and especially not with this trampy looking bloke who looked like he needed a good wash. 'Go and grab that table over there Doll and I'll get the drinks in,' Denny urged her.

Once they were all seated with a drink in front of them the two lads chatted amiably while Julie sat with a face that could curdle cream. This was definitely not the romantic evening she had envisaged and she kept getting a distinctive waft of body odour every time that Jason raised his arm to drink his pint.

'So what are you up to these days Jason?' Denny pleasantly enquired.

'Not much, trying to find work is not easy when you're an ex-borstal boy, I heard you're doing alright though.'

'Yeah I work for my godfather Alan Stewart and his business partner. They're top blokes and the pay's not too shabby.'

Jason nodded his head and smirked. Alan Stewart was a cunt. He momentarily switched off as he thought about his dead parents and was so deep in thought that he only just caught the tail end of what Denny was saying. 'Such a shame about Breda dying like that, apparently someone poured petrol through the letterbox. She was like a nan to me, my mum hasn't stopped crying...'

Jason felt the colour drain from his face and he went cold. He had only meant to cause damage, he hadn't meant anyone to get hurt.

He remembered Breda from years back. She had made him a jam sandwich once when his dad Stevie had taken him to Alan's old house. He hadn't known that the old bird had moved in with them. Trying to compose himself he made his excuses and fled to the gents where he promptly threw up his pint and the fry-up he had eaten earlier. If Alan Stewart ever found out what he had done he would come for him and unlike when he had come for his mother Doreen, it wouldn't just be a barrage of threats that he would get. He knew that Alan was a face these days and with sickening realisation it dawned on him that he had just signed his own death warrant. After splashing some cold water on his face he went back into the bar area where Denny and Julie were sat cuddling. 'I'm going to make a move, dodgy guts. Nice to see you Den, bye Julie.'

'He's a fucking weirdo Den,' Julie exclaimed as Jason made a hasty retreat. 'He kept looking at my boobs.'

'Oh he's alright, just had a hard time of it Doll and you've got a great pair of knockers. Poor bloke was locked up for ages so he's probably frustrated,' Denny chuckled as he fondly squeezed Julie's left breast. Giggling she responded by sticking her tongue halfway down Denny's throat, all thoughts of Jason Baines gone.

Two days later Ron and Alan sat in Ron's study discussing recent events. They were no further forward in establishing a culprit. Most of the local nick who were on Ron's payroll had been told to keep their ears to the ground but no one had heard a dickie bird.

Ron had asked around at his Lodge but again had drawn a blank. It was a real mystery. As they spoke in hushed voices Irene came into the room. 'Denny's on the phone Ron, some sort of trouble at the club in Tottenham.'

Ron and Alan looked at each other both worried that they had once again been targeted. Alan poured himself a drink as Ron went to take the call. When Ron returned he explained that a girl had overdosed in the toilets.

'Bloody hell Ron, we need this like a fucking hole in the head,' Alan stated.

'Come on, get your coat, this needs sorting pronto,' Ron urged.

For the first time in years Alan agreed with his wife. Life had been much easier back in the old days when he was a barman. He may have been piss poor but at least he hadn't had to deal with arson and dead bodies.

As Alan and Ron drove to Tottenham to deal with the latest crisis, Sonia was trying to pull herself together for the sake of her children. She had taken to her bed for a few hours earlier and after doubling up on her pills was feeling a little more human. Maggie was pleased to see her niece smile as she played Snakes and Ladders with the twins. This was going to take time, the old lady thought, but they would get through it together.

Having no children herself she had always been like a second mum to her sister's children and another nan to all the grandchildren so she was determined to be there for them all for as long as they needed her. 'Who wants some tea and crumpets?' she asked brightly.

'Me, me,' both children shouted in unison.

'Ok my Lovelies, I will be back in a jiffy,' Maggie said getting up from her armchair to make her way into the kitchen.

When she had gone Connie looked up at her mum and asked innocently. 'What is arson?'

'What did you just say?' Sonia demanded, her voice rising.

Connie didn't understand why her mum seemed angry and now wished she had kept her mouth shut. 'I heard Dad on the phone and he was talking about the fire and he said that word.'

Sonia began shaking as the implications became clear to her. When her aunty came back into the room she barged past her to the phone and dialled Ron's number wanting to confront her husband. The bastard had lied to her. She had been so worried that it had been one of her cigarettes or a faulty plug socket and all the time someone else had done this. Her daughter may not understand what arson was but she bloody did! She was almost hyperventilating by the time Irene answered the phone. Ignoring the other woman's news that the children's clothes that had been ordered from the catalogue had arrived, she bluntly demanded to speak to Alan.

'They've had to go to the club Sonia. Whatever is the matter?'

'Just tell him to call me when he gets back.' And with that she slammed down the telephone receiver. She knew that she had just been very rude but she didn't care. Falling to the floor she began sobbing loudly which is where Maggie found her five minutes later. As she gabbled hysterically Maggie heard the word arson and her heart sunk. It had shaken her the other day when she had realised that her sister had been murdered but Sonia would never get over this fact and more importantly she would never forgive her husband because whatever way you looked at it, his job had most probably caused this. The same job that Sonia had always feared and never been able to accept. Cuddling her niece, she gently led her upstairs and sat with her while she sobbed herself to sleep. She then went back downstairs and explained to the bewildered children that Mum was having a sad moment because she missed Nanny so much and not knowing what else to do challenged them to a game of Twister. The children readily agreed as last time they had played with Aunty Maggie, they had caught a glimpse of her knickers which had been so funny.

Alan returned his wife's call two hours later and listened in distress as Maggie explained what had happened. He asked to speak to Sonia but Maggie felt it was better to let her sleep as nothing would be resolved with her in the state she was in. Alan agreed but unlike Maggie he didn't think this revelation would ever be resolved.

He knew his wife and with a sinking feeling knew she would never forgive him.

Chapter 17

As Alan lay in a hot bath back at Ron and Irene's home he was beginning to feel seriously stressed out. He had phoned Aunty Maggie's again and his wife was flatly refusing to speak to him. When he had spoken to Aunty Maggie Sonia had been screaming in the background incoherently. In desperation he had called his brother David and asked him to drive to Kilburn and prescribe his wife something that would calm her down, but he was extremely worried. His wife had been unstable for years and he feared that the revelation of their home being deliberately torched resulting in her mother Breda's death had finally tipped her over the edge. He also couldn't get the image of the dead junkie who had been found in the club out of his head. She had been lying motionless on the cold toilet floor. The poor kid couldn't have been more than eighteen years old. Her long blonde hair had been caked in vomit and she had a syringe sticking out of her left arm. Ron was enraged. A dead young girl on his premises was not good for business. They had both been impressed with the efficient way that Denny Draper had helped them to move the body out to the back of the club. He had then been instructed to telephone Thomas Turner, a local plod who had been on Ron's payroll for years. This was his patch and Ron was confident that he would deal with the situation discreetly.

Ron had still been seething when they had reached his home and had explained to Alan that this was one of the reasons why he refused to be involved with the seedy world of drugs. That and family loyalty, as his cousin John had lost a son to an overdose some years ago. Ron had seen first-hand the grief that his cousin had suffered and had vowed never to sell the stuff even if it was a serious earn. He was aware that Deniz Mehmet wanted to flood the market with heroin but the man was taking the piss if he thought he could do it on Ron's turf. Ron would retaliate if it came to light that was what was happening.

David Stewart had driven over to Kilburn. He was alarmed that his sister-in-law was in such a bad way. She was crying uncontrollably and in his opinion had suffered a nervous breakdown. He would have to speak to his brother about the situation as he was running out of options to treat her. She needed to be in hospital. The children were confused and tearful and he could see that Maggie was struggling to deal with her niece. When he left he had been satisfied that at least the sleeping tablets that he had given her would help her to sleep and the tranquilisers would calm her down. Once he got home, he telephoned Alan and gave him the name of a private hospital in Surrey that dealt with patients with mental health issues.

'She's not going in a nuthouse David, no way. She's grieving. You know how close she was to her mother.'

'She's seriously ill Al and has been for years, me dosing her up with tranqs is only masking the real problems that she has. She needs professional help Mate,' David urged his brother.

Alan sighed but agreed to at least think about it. Deep down he knew that his brother was right. Sonia hadn't been right for years. She had good days but they were helped along by all the pills that she shoved down her throat otherwise she couldn't function. He loved his Sonia passionately and sadly realised that if he had never gone into this life, she would have eventually coped with her sadness's and they would have lived a peaceful life with their twins. But he wanted more. He wanted to provide his family with the good things that life could offer. He didn't want to scrimp from one pay packet to the next. He wanted to be a someone but at what cost he now asked himself? His home and possessions were ruined, someone was after him, his wife was heading towards a straight jacket and Breda was dead. No wonder Sonia always craved for normal.

He suddenly remembered a Saturday night years ago when they had just married. They had moved into their new home in Tottenham and hadn't even owned a cooker. Alan had come home from a busy shift at the pub and when he had walked into the front room, Sonia had been sitting on a blanket on the bare floor proudly pointing to a plate of fish paste sandwiches.

She had given him the biggest smile and he remembered thinking at the time that everything was going to be alright. That night they had chatted amiably as they devoured the sandwiches and had later spent the night making love. Alan smiled as he remembered the sweet memory but shaking himself he reminded himself that the past was the past, he had to find a way to sort out the mess that he was currently in and, more importantly, he had to find a way for his wife to forgive him.

Jason Baines was feeling on edge. He wasn't a bad lad and certainly not a violent one but now he had a death on his conscience and was struggling to accept what he had caused. He had only intended to avenge the tragedy which had befallen his family. He had meant to create some aggro but now he was looking at serious time if he was caught or, worse still, the wrath of Alan Stewart if he ever found out. Alan would never let this go, he was sure of that and the thought immediately made him rush to the toilet again.

Sonia lay in bed fixating on a large crack in the ceiling above. It reminded her of her life: perfect apart from a gaping void that would only get bigger in time. She was feeling a lot calmer now, thanks to whatever the pills were that her brother-in-law had given her but inside she was screaming.

She would miss her mother with a vengeance and she desperately needed her husband to help her through her crushing grief as he had done when her brother died and when they lost baby George but her best friend was now her enemy, even if she still loved him with all her being. If the fire had been caused by arson then it was something to do with him or more probably Ron McCardle and she would never forgive either of them.

The following day Deniz Mehmet was sitting in his cousin's restaurant with his number two Nikos Akbay and his friend Gary Peters. The two Turks were having a good chuckle about the recent misfortunes of Ron McCardle and his side kick Alan Stewart.

'So someone has it in for Big Ron,' Deniz laughed.

'I wonder if the old woman was cooked medium rare or well done?' Nicos enquired, looking at the steak on his plate.

Gary laughed along but felt undecidedly uncomfortable. His daughter Ebony was only one month away from her due date and he needed Ron onside to provide for her and the baby financially. What he didn't need was any bother between Ron's camp and his friend who he now worked for.

'Have you any idea who is targeting them Den? I mean if it isn't you, then who?' Gary asked.

'The attacks on Ron are kid's pranks and I know who is responsible for them but the fire, well that is a mystery.'

'But do you think they will think it's you Den?' Gary asked worriedly.

Deniz tapped his old friend on the shoulder. 'You worry too much Gary, If I had a grievance with Ron McCardle then believe me he would know about it and give me some credit. Frying old ladies is not my style. Now who wants some more wine?'

Gary knew that Deniz was bored of the topic of conversation so accepted another glass of wine. Deep down though he felt troubled.

Ebony Peters was feeling fat and fed up. She had tried unsuccessfully to get in contact with Ron for two days. She was due to move next week and the least he could do was stay in some sort of contact. He had sent one of his goons yesterday with a van to start moving her but the idiot hadn't been willing to discuss his boss so she had no clue as to his whereabouts. This really wasn't good enough and she had a sneaking suspicion that she would end up in Essex on her tod with only a screaming brat for company. Well if Ron McCardle thought that is what would happen, he had another thing coming! Trying him one more time on the telephone, she angrily slammed the phone down when it went unanswered. As she got up to make a cup of coffee a pain shot through her stomach. Gasping she sat back on her chaise shaking. Ten minutes passed and she was just about to get up again when a similar pain made her cry out.

Ebony Peters was in labour and unlike most women who were going to give birth early, her concerns were not for her unborn child but the fact that she hadn't had a chance to have a trim down below! Picking up the phone again, she quickly dialled for an ambulance and then phoned her father who she knew was in Green Lanes with Deniz Mehmet.

Gary Peters was pleasantly pissed on fine red wine when his hysterical daughter rang him and told him to meet her at the Whittington hospital pronto. Downing the dregs of his drink he explained that he had to go. Deniz laughed as he said, 'Whoever heard of the Grandad being at the birth? Where's the father?'

'It's complicated Mate but I need to go.'

Deniz nodded and wished him luck. In his mind it was a father's job to raise his daughter with respect and he had always thought that Ebony was very flighty and now, an unmarried mother! What was the world coming to? He was just grateful that all his children were respectfully married because if one of his daughters had come home pregnant he would have whipped her to within an inch of her life.

Gary Peters didn't realise how drunk he was until he tried to put his car key in the lock and dropped it twice. Fumbling around with it for a third time, he finally unlocked the car and drove off as fast as he could towards Highgate and the hospital. He loudly swore as each traffic light turned red as he approached it.

Bloody typical he thought as he drove down Highgate Hill. He didn't know how long a woman was in labour before the baby came but he knew that he had to get to his daughter's side sharpish because she had sounded so frightened on the phone. Accelerating, he was just about to overtake a bus when a woman with a pushchair suddenly appeared from nowhere. Slamming on the breaks Gary was alarmed that the car wasn't stopping, he tried again, nothing. Seeing the woman getting closer he abruptly swerved and smashed into a nearby tree. Barely conscious, his last thought before he died was that his daughter would never forgive him for this.

Ebony was in agony, her insides felt that they were being ripped apart.

'Just push as if you are doing a poo,' the jolly West Indian midwife urged her.

Ebony looked up at her in disgust. There was no way that she was taking the chance of crapping herself. She did have her dignity. Unfortunately no one had told her that childbirth was an undignified business and soon her body took over as she pushed her daughter very loudly into the world. As she looked down at her daughter she felt a flicker of pride and also a strong inkling of who the baby's father was. But what she wanted to know at that moment was where her father was. She had phoned him three hours ago and the bastard hadn't shown up. Feeling sorry for herself, she began to cry as the nurse took the child from her.

'Hush now, the baby needs to be checked over as she is early but she is a good size,' the midwife said softly. 'Now the doctor is on his way and will stitch you up.'

Ebony looked up at her in distress.' What do you mean?'

'You have a slight tear but you will be as good as new. Dr Mcallister is very good.'

Ebony didn't doubt that but was mortified when he arrived and shining a big lamp at her lady bits set to work.

Deniz Mehmet took the call at eight o'clock that evening. One of his men had been driving home when he had spotted Gary's crushed car which had been taped off and was being guarded by a policeman who had explained to him what had happened. Deniz was distraught as they had grown up together in Dr Barnados but he needed to sort this out. Ebony was in hospital having a baby and would be wondering where her father was. She needed to be told. His son Kadir had always been close to the girl so he phoned him and told him to go to the hospital and give her the bad news. Kadir was immediately on edge. He hadn't even known that his ex-mistress was pregnant and had tried to keep a distance from her in the last six months.

'Do I have to go Dad, I told Layla that I would take her out for dinner?'

'It is not a request Kadir, now explain to Layla. She is a good girl. She will understand that it's business.'

Kadir knew that when his father gave an order, he expected it to be followed with the minimum of fuss so putting the phone down, he went into the kitchen to tell his wife that he had to go out.

Ebony was having a snooze when she heard the curtain around her bed being opened. As she opened her eyes, she was more than surprised to see her ex-lover approaching her bed. He took her hand and told her as gently as he could that her father had died. Ebony was by nature a dramatic woman but she was in so much shock that she was speechless. Her only reaction being a solitary tear that ran down her face. It was at this moment that a midwife came into the ward pushing the new baby who was sleeping in a small cot on wheels.

'Aaw how lovely, Daddy has arrived. You will be pleased to know that the baby is fine. The doctor thinks that you got your dates mixed up.'

Ebony stared at the other woman. All she could think about was her father and the fact that she was now all alone in the world because having to rely on Ron was like relying on a prostitute not opening her legs! As the baby whimpered Kadir looked at the tiny scrape and froze. She was the image of his new son Jem. His eyes locked with Ebony's and at that moment they both knew. Feeling faint he made his excuses and hastily ran from the ward, much to the midwife's surprise. 'It takes time to sink in sometimes,' she kindly said.

Ebony just nodded and started crying as it dawned on her that she would never see her Dad again and Ron would take one look at the baby and realise that he was not her father. If that happened Ebony was in real trouble because Deniz Mehmet was not a man who would take kindly to an illegitimate grandchild or any scandal surrounding his precious family.

Chapter 18

Sonia was having a heart to heart with her Aunty Maggie who was desperately trying to persuade her to keep quiet about the real truth of the fire. 'I'm as upset as you Child, I have lost not only my sister but also my best friend, but if the truth comes out your brothers and sisters will probably turn against you and where will that leave you?'

Sonia tried to digest this piece of logic. She wasn't overly close to her siblings but the last thing she needed was them blaming her for their mother's death. 'But how do I go back and live with Alan like nothing has happened? If he hadn't met Ron McCardle then my mother would still be alive. How can I share a life with someone who is responsible for her murder? And what about me and the children? I don't feel safe,' Sonia's voice was rising as the panic enveloped her in a tight grip.

Maggie could understand her niece's fears but she had to be tough with the girl, who in her opinion needed to get a grip. She was devastated herself but had no room in her life for self-pity or resentment. She knew that Alan was a good man who had worked hard to provide his family with a life others could only dream about. She wasn't naive, she was well aware that he was what was probably termed a criminal but, according to her sister, so were half the local police force who enjoyed the benefits of being on Ron's payroll.

They all needed to try and pick up the shattered pieces of their lives and move on. 'Now listen to me Child, we are all assuming that the fire had something to do with grievance, revenge, whatever you want to call it but do we have any proof? Do we actually know that to be a fact?'

Sonia opened her mouth to reply but Maggie was on a mission to make her see sense. 'It could have been kids. Didn't you tell me a few weeks ago that kids had been setting fires to letter boxes in your area? What if it was a prank that got out of hand and you are ripping your family apart by automatically blaming your husband? A husband I might add who loves the bones of you and works all the hours to provide you and the kids with the very best? And let me tell you something else, Alan and Ron may not be strictly law abiding citizens but neither are the policemen and legal people that take their money regularly.'

The old woman seemed exhausted after her tirade and taking a sip of her tea, searched Sonia's face for a sign that her words had struck a chord but the girl just stared back at her blankly. Maggie silently cursed David Stewart who in her mind needed to stop supplying Sonia with all these drugs because the girl's brain seemed to have turned to cotton wool. After a few minutes Sonia began nodding her head gently and Maggie immediately felt gratified that she must at least agree with some what she had said so quickly continued her crusade. 'What has happened is a tragedy but we have to all pull together Child. I just want you to have a long think about what I've said.'

Sonia suddenly got up from her seat and went over to her aunty and like a child threw her arms around her. 'I will Aunty Maggie, I love you.'

Maggie stroked Sonia's long dark hair and comforted her as she had seen her sister do hundreds of times over the years. 'We will grieve together and then we will live the rest of our lives which is what your mother would have wanted and that I do know.'

Even though Maggie knew her possible explanation of the fire being started by kids seemed far-fetched she was gratified that Sonia seemed to have calmed down and would possibly rather believe that it had been a dangerous prank that had gone wrong.

A few moments later the children bounded into the room. They had heard the ice cream van and were demanding a ninety nine each. Sonia smiled and for the first time in days realised that Connie and Billy needed her. She had been so caught up with her own grief and bitterness that she had shamefully let her aunty care for them when she was also hurting. She felt guilty and ashamed and decided that from now on her precious children needed to come first. She would cut down on the pills and be more present. Aunty Maggie was a shrewd woman and she was right. They didn't actually know what had happened on that fatal night and what if her Alan was innocent?

A tiny voice inside her head reminded her that her husband's job put them all at risk on a daily basis but she mentally pushed this thought away as she was desperate to get back to some sort of normal and, if she was honest, she needed her husband's strength to get through the loss of her mother. Her brothers and sisters were coming over this evening to discuss the funeral arrangements so on impulse she phoned Alan and asked him to join them.

Alan was thrilled for the invitation. He had loved Breda like a second Mother and although he wouldn't feel her loss as acutely as Sonia, he would still miss his mother-in-law very much. Sonia had seemed brighter on the phone and although his brother felt that she had had a breakdown he wasn't so sure. His wife had depended on Breda and had been mollycoddled to a degree being the baby of the family so it stood to reason that she would take the bereavement the hardest. He had been over the moon when Sonia had declared that she wanted to reduce the pills. She hadn't wanted to talk about the house but he could understand that. He just wanted his family back. He was very grateful to Ron for putting him up but Irene still wasn't herself and he didn't need anyone else's domestics on top of his own.

Sonia was reading *The Hobbit* to the children when Maggie came running into their bedroom in a flap. Gesticulating for her to come downstairs Sonia urged Connie to continue reading and followed her aunty.

'The Coroner has just been on the phone, she died from a massive heart attack. She wasn't burnt alive and the smoke didn't kill her. It was her ticker Child. It could have happened at any time.' Maggie wiped her eyes with a handkerchief. She felt a huge sense of relief and convinced herself that her beloved sister probably hadn't even known about the fire. As the significance of the Coroner's findings sunk in, Sonia didn't really know how to feel. Her mother was still dead and her beautiful home was still ruined but she consoled herself with the fact that at least she would be able to look her brothers and sisters in the eye now.

Dolly McCardle and Glenice Stewart were sat in the pub sipping sherry and toasting their friend Breda Murphy. Dolly had told her son that they couldn't wait for the funeral as both of them felt they needed to do something to mark her passing so Ron had kindly laid on a car and one of his men. Rob Clarke was waiting patiently on the other side of the pub to ensure their safety and to get them home. As Glenice was regaling Dolly with stories of their lives in the tenements and the Blitz a young dishevelled man walked in. He was already two sheets to the wind as they noticed he was unable to walk straight. As he passed their table he stumbled into it knocking Dolly's drink flying. Rob immediately bounded over and grabbed the boy's arm roughly. 'You want to be careful,' he shouted.

Dolly waved Rob away. 'Oh leave him be, he's only a kid, now go and get me another drink and we'll each have a bag of pork scratchings.'

Dolly quite liked being the mother of an important man as she felt that it gave her the right to boss people around although she clocked that Rob Clarke didn't look impressed! Chuckling, she looked at the young lad. He looked familiar but she couldn't place him. Shame that these youngsters couldn't hold their drink she thought.

Jason Baines slumped down at the table behind the old biddies and pulled out a battered hip flask from his jacket pocket. He had been steadily drinking all day. Before the fire he hadn't really been a drinker. His mother Doreen's antics had put him right off but these days he needed to get off his face to help him cope with what he had done and his mounting fear that Alan Stewart would find out.

Dolly and Glenice continued their own personal wake in honour of their friend but had stopped reminiscing when the odd looking boy who had bumped into their table began talking to himself. At first he was mumbling but as his voice got louder they could hear odd snippets of what he was saying.

'I didn't mean to, would never kill anyone, my poor Dad.'

Dolly and Glenice were becoming more alarmed as they strained to hear.

'Bloody Alan Stewart, hate him, it's his fault that the lady died.'

As these words penetrated Dolly's brain, she immediately jumped up and pushed the boy onto the floor.

'You fecking bastard, you killed my friend, it was you!' she screeched which brought Rob Clarke running over.

Glenice was a faster drinker than Dolly so hadn't realised what was going on at first as she was feeling a little bit woolly-headed. When Dolly angrily explained to her she hit the shaking boy over the head with her umbrella as Rob Clarke put him into a head lock and marched him unceremoniously out of the pub. When they were outside he slapped him about the face and threw him roughly into the boot of his car, as he had his father Stevie six years before.

When Ron got the call half an hour later he felt relief that it wasn't the Turks who had caused all the aggro and amused that it had been two pensioners who had cracked the case! He told Rob to take the boy to his cousin Ray Briggs's scrap yard in St Albans and wait until he got there. Alan was at Maggie's sorting the funeral so he would call him there and give him the good news.

Although the evening had been sad, Alan had been thrilled when his wife and children had run out to greet him earlier. Sonia had cried but seemed less vacant and the funeral would be in two weeks. Alan said that he would foot the bill if everyone agreed and that it would be the best send-off ever. Sonia's brothers and sisters were only too happy with the arrangement as none of them had much money. All in all the get together had been productive and congenial. He had been even happier when Ron called and told him the latest developments.

He was shocked and saddened that it had been Jason Baines all along but at least he could be honest with his wife and report back that it had been kids, well one kid anyway, although he would lie and wouldn't reveal the boy's identity. Alan was relieved and nervous because he knew that it would only ever be over once he had killed the toe rag and he had never taken someone's life before but his mother-in-law was dead and even if she had died of a heart attack she could still have easily of been burnt alive. Jason Baines needed obliterating and as the adrenaline started flowing, Alan knew that he was the only man for the job.

Chapter 19

Jason Baines had never felt such acute terror as he did at this precise moment. He had had a very uncomfortable ride in the boot of that gorilla's car. The journey had seemed to take forever although he wasn't exactly sure if that was a good thing or not. The smell of petrol had been sickly and he had had to use all his strength not to chuck up in the confines of his prison cell. When they reached their destination he had been dragged from the boot of the car and beaten. His assailant was at least nineteen stone and with his glistening, bald head and angry face looked menacing. As he had rained punches on the boy, Jason had known there was no point in fighting back. He was only ten stone and felt as weak as a kitten. As a blow connected with his nose, he knew it had been broken. The pain was intense and he cried out. The big man had suddenly stopped and with one final kick to Jason's head once again had him in a head lock and marched him towards a large metal container. As Jason gingerly looked around him, he realised he was in a motor scrap yard and that it must be out of London because he could see lots of trees and green fields. All around him were dozens of old cars piled on top of each other. The panic began to build and he just hoped and prayed he wasn't going into the jaws of the big crusher that seemed to be mocking him as he glanced nervously at it.

The big man rummaged in his pocket for some keys and when the door of a container flew open, he booted Jason up the arse and onto the damp floor. He then went to work tying the boy up and binding his eyes with an oily rag. As Jason heard the door bang shut he stifled down the urge to sob. He could feel his heart beating heavily in his chest and droplets of sweat dripping down his sore body. He was trying desperately to breathe through his mouth as his nose was clogged with blood but this was difficult as the gag was bound tight. He had never believed in God but like many a condemned man before him realised that if there was a saintly man in the sky then he was his last hope. He began praying and begging that when Alan Stewart came, he would be lenient, although deep in his heart he knew that he had fucked up and there was no way out of this mess.

Ron was just about to leave home to drive to St Albans when he received a call from Denny Draper, also now managed his club in Tottenham.

Apparently there had been an attempted arson attack in the foyer of the club and as Denny relayed all the details Ron swore loudly and ran out the house.

Denny Draper was confident he had dealt with the situation efficiently thus avoiding any alarm. Earlier in the evening the club had been packed with happy customers enjoying a night out and dancing to the latest hits. He had been working for four hours so had decided to go out front for some air and have a well-earned cigarette. As he had walked into the foyer he had been surprised that Helen Price who manned the cloakroom was not at her post and nor was the doorman Bill Smith. He had turned towards Paula Jones who was sitting in the ticket booth to ask why half the staff were missing when he felt something hot fly past his left ear. It took about five seconds to realise that a bottle containing a burning rag had been thrown into the foyer. Leaping into action Denny had no option but to quickly put the fire out with the nearest fire extinguisher to prevent the flames from causing any more damage, so had been unable to see who the assailant was. As the flames died down Bill Smith had casually sauntered back into the foyer followed not long after by Helen Price, who Denny noted was hastily buttoning up her blouse! Taking in the scene Bill immediately realised that he was in for a bollocking for leaving his post and he was right.

'Well I don't need to ask you why you weren't here when some wanker just tried to torch the place,' Denny sneered.

Bill didn't appreciate being spoken down to by a slip of a kid. 'I went to take a piss,' he said belligerently, his eyes challenging Denny to make more of it.

'Oh is Helen's bladder now in sync with yours?' Denny sarcastically snapped back.

It was at this moment that Ron arrived and angrily demanded to know what had happened.

Listening intently to Denny Draper he grabbed Bill Smith around the throat and pushed him onto the carpet. Leaning over him he shouted, 'Next time you decide you need a shag, you do it in your own time, got it? The only reason I'm not firing you is because up till now you have always had a brain in your head but you can take this as a warning, if anything like this ever happens again then you're out and I will be the one to tell your wife Elaine why.'

Bill had the grace to look ashamed and admitted to himself that Ron

McCardle may be getting on a bit but he was certainly still a force to be reckoned with. He was a good and fair boss but tonight had shown that he would turn on you if you didn't comply with his rules.

As Ron drove away at speed he was seething with anger and frustration. He would not stand for a sloppy workforce. Bill Smith had always been dependable but had recently had his head turned by the delectable Helen on coats. Well she would be looking for another job tomorrow. Most of his team had been with him for years and he trusted them. The females at the club could easily be replaced. He made a mental note to employ someone else on coats who didn't have such an impressive pair of knockers. As he made his way to Epping, he realised that someone other than Jason Baines was targeting them, unless the boy had been working alongside someone but he didn't believe that. You needed money to build a team and the Baines family didn't have that or any connections that he knew of.

So that meant there was still someone out there who bore a grudge. It had to be the Turks even though Ron conceded that this latest bit of grief would still be classed as a childish prank. Maybe the Turks wanted to throw him off the scent? It was really grinding his gears because they were still no further forward although at least they had Jason Baines bang to rights. He had asked Paula Jones the ticket girl if she had got a good look at tonight's culprit but all she could say was that he was white, wore a hood and may have had a slight limp. Well that didn't tell him anything but Ron was seriously pissed off and would find whoever was behind all this and personally kick the granny out of them!

Alan Stewart reached the scrapyard before Ron and gratefully accepted a large Scotch from Rob Clarke. Sitting down he quietly sipped the drink and thought about what he was about to do tonight. It had started to rain and the sound of it hitting the windows had a strange calming effect on him. He had always known this day might come. It stood to reason in their line of work. There were always plastic gangsters who arrogantly believed they could step in and take what you had worked so hard for but he had never imagined in a thousand years that he would be murdering a young boy because he had a warped sense of revenge. It was ironic really because the boy's father had died of natural causes but his family had been too stupid to accept this fact, and now Alan had no choice but to wipe out a life to protect his own family.

Alan's thoughts were interrupted as Ron entered the porta cabin with a face like thunder. 'You'll never guess what's happened tonight? Some toe rag tried to torch the club! Luckily young Denny sorted it but we still have a problem.'

Alan listened and his heart sank. He had truly believed that after tonight they would be able to get back to some sort of normality but the implications of what Ron told him meant they still had trouble with a capital T. He had hoped he could've sorted out Jason Baines without having to have a conversation with him but now they would have to question the boy and find out if he had been working with someone else.

Jason was shivering with fright and the cold that was seeping into his weary bones. He must have been in the container for over an hour and with each passing moment his fear was mounting. He had already pissed himself and his nose was in agony. He just wished he would quickly slip away because that would have been preferable than waiting to be killed. As he painfully tried to move to a more comfortable position he heard the door clanging open and footsteps approaching him. Not being able to see was pure torture and as the footsteps got closer he began to cry. 'I'm sorry Alan, I didn't know that the old woman was in the house, I swear I didn't. I just wanted to cause you some agg.'

Alan bit his lip, he didn't want to hear an apology, and he wanted this over. Ron handed him a gun and he could feel his hand sweating as he clutched hold of it.

If the boy started begging, Alan didn't know if he would be able to carry out his task. Rob Clarke pulled the weeping boy onto his feet and pushed him roughly on to a nearby chair. Ron could see that Alan was slightly shaken at the state of Jason. He would have words with Rob Clarke later who shouldn't have taken it upon himself to rough him up, although Ron could understand why he had. They had all been fond of Breda Murphy who had always been so welcoming to anyone who visited the Stewart home. She had treated all his men's children as she had her own grandchildren and her cheery smile would be sorely missed. Taking the lead, he pulled up a chair opposite Jason's. 'Right Lad, I promise you that we will make this quick but I need to know who you were working with.'

Jason was confused, what did this man mean? He desperately wanted to tell him what he wanted to hear and instinctively knew that if he gave him a name his death would be quick and his terrifying ordeal would be over. He racked his brains thinking of a name and suddenly remembered that when he was a kid he had knocked around with this Turkish kid called Ali Mustafa. 'It was Ali Mustafa, he approached me a while back, said he wanted to take over Tottenham with drugs, I was skint so I agreed to cause you some bother because he said that you would be against it and I had my own reasons as well.' Jason's voice was stronger than he felt but he smirked as he finished his speech. Ali Mustafa had died in a car crash when he was thirteen and his family had left the area to return to their native Turkey.

Let these animals waste their time looking for a dead boy. Jason was feeling quite proud of himself in the minute before Alan Stewart blew his brains all over the dirty floor.

'I bloody knew it was the Turks all along,' Ron said as they drove home. He noted that Alan didn't answer him and respected that he was a bit shaken after tonight's events. He had felt the same with his first murder years ago but you had to get used to it. Sometimes it was a case of kill or be killed and only the strongest men survived in this world. Alan would be alright once he got his family back with him.

Deniz Mehmet was in one of his famous rages. He had grown up with Gary Peters in Dr Barnados and had treated and loved him as a brother. Now it had come to his attention that his friend's car had been tampered with. The brakes had been cut causing the car to career into a tree and Gary Peters was dead. Deniz had gone into his study when he had heard the news and cried bitter tears. He had told his wife that under no circumstances was he to be disturbed. He was a proud man and would not allow anyone to witness this weakness but he was bereft and angry. This had Ron McCardle's name all over it and the stupid man had now started a war. He would wait until after the funeral which he would pay for and then he would strike and get revenge for his dear friend.

Deniz's son Kadir was in a quandary. His father had already announced tonight that with Gary dying they would have to look after his daughter Ebony and her baby as she had no other family.

At the hospital, Kadir had taken one look at the child and known that she was the product of his affair. Gary had never told them who the father was but it was obvious to him that after producing three sons with his wife Layla, he now had a daughter. Most men in their world craved sons but he had always secretly yearned for a little girl. He had finished the affair with Ebony because it was just too dangerous and his father would have blown a fuse. Despite his ruthless reputation he was at heart a family man and looked down his nose at men who disrespected their wives in such a fashion. Kadir didn't know what to do. He loved his wife but Ebony had given him the sex that excited him. He wished now they had just stayed friends because if anyone ever found out about the baby he would lose his family, and his father would disown him. But even with these fears he wasn't sure if he could stay away from his daughter who was his flesh and blood.

Chapter 20

Ron had kept away from the funeral of Gary Peters. He knew full well that the Turks would be out in force and feeling as he did about them he couldn't trust himself. He also hadn't wanted to draw any undue attention. He had known Gary for years but they had never been close so he felt that his absence wouldn't be missed, and if he was honest Ebony hadn't been too keen on him attending when he had mentioned it to her anyway. She had however insisted on taking the new baby Chantelle, which Ron hadn't agreed with but as she had pointed out, he was the part-time parent so didn't get a say.

Ebony had settled in the house in Brentwood and Ron had managed to visit her twice. The baby was enchanting with her shock of black hair and olive skin and Ron already loved her with a passion. Surprisingly, Ebony was becoming a decent enough mother although she didn't stop complaining about sore nipples and sleepless nights. He did feel that she left the baby in her cot for long periods of time but reasoned with himself that he had never had kids, so what did he know?

Ebony stood by her father's final resting place clutching her baby to her chest. She was wearing a large black hat and dark sunglasses and felt confident that she had pulled off the grieving daughter look to perfection.

She would miss her father but in truth he had been in and out of her life like a boomerang, what with his regular stays in prison, so she was used to being on her own. She had been relieved and grateful when Deniz Mehmet had insisted on paying for the funeral and earlier on today he had discreetly shoved an envelope in her hands full of cash. He had tears in his eyes as he told her that she was family now and that he would always look out for her. Ebony had secretly smirked to herself as she thought that the old boy was indeed family without even realising it.

Back at the wake, Kadir Mehmet looked at Ebony. She caught his gaze and half smiled. She was beginning to feel jittery as his wife Layla had fussed over Chantelle at the church and Ebony was terrified that other woman would see the similarities between her son and Chantelle. But fortunately Layla had simply cooed over the child as people do and then joined her husband, who was sitting a few rows behind. Ebony knew that she had to be careful and that the baby's paternity had to be kept a secret because Deniz Mehmet would drop the hand of friendship like a diseased bollock if he ever found out the truth and would think of her as a whore. No, it was best that she stuck to her story and she was on to a good thing with Ron who was already besotted with the child. Last week she had had to stop herself from laughing out loud when he had declared that the olive skin and dark looks that Chantelle possessed must have been passed down from his Romany ancestors.

As Kadir looked at his ex-lover, cradling their daughter, he physically had to stop himself from going over and snatching the pink bundle. But he also realised that if he avoided Ebony, it would look suspicious as they had been friends since they could walk and talk.

An hour and three drinks later he walked over to the other side of the hall and stood beside Ebony. 'Hey, how are you doing?'

'Alright, you?' It was a challenge and they both knew it. He didn't answer and Kadir was saddened that his easy relationship with her was now gone. They had always been able to have a laugh and she had been his first crush. Now they stood in an awkward silence. Ebony put the baby in her carry cot and was surveying the mourners. She didn't know half of them but was pleased that her father had received a good turnout. His sister, her Aunty Pat, had been the only other family member. She had turned up half pissed and had had to be put into a cab back to Islington halfway through the proceedings. As she stood next to Kadir, Ebony felt the magnetic allure of him. He was so damn handsome and sexy and she was suddenly having a flashback to all the things they had done in bed. The sex had been electric and his body had fulfilled her like no other man ever had. The same sex had produced a problem that was now lying sound asleep not three feet away. She loved her daughter in her own way but could kick herself for being so stupid and getting pregnant. She wished things could be different but she didn't want to be cut adrift from the Mehmets who were the closest thing to a real family that she had. She knew that if the affair was exposed, it would cause untold murders so she had no choice. Turning to Kadir, she said as calmly as she could, 'The baby isn't yours.' With that she picked up the carry cot and confidently left the wake leaving him feeling confused and angry. He was certain the child was his but if there was a slim chance that she wasn't then the bitch had been sleeping with someone else at the same time as him. A little voice in his head was telling him to leave well alone. She had given him an out but he knew he wouldn't rest until he knew for sure.

Ron McCardle and Alan Stewart had agreed to discuss their next move after the funeral of Breda Murphy as a mark of respect to the much loved woman. Ron had however asked around if anyone knew of an Ali Mustapha but his inquires had drawn a blank. Ron knew all the main villains in London and had concluded that this one must be small time or working for a bigger fish in the pool of villainy. It stood to reason as Jason Baines wasn't exactly the sort of person to have any worthwhile connections. This Ali Mustapha must be something to do with Deniz Mehmet and Ron realised with a sinking heart that retaliation was needed in order to show his strength and send a message that he would not stand for any more attacks.

A few days later Sonia Stewart woke up and momentarily forgot what day it was. As she stretched and yawned, a black mist descended over her. Today was the day they buried her beloved mother and she didn't know how she was going to get through it. The last few days had been a blur as she had doubled up on her pills, but Aunty Maggie had urged her last night not to take any today so that she could have a clear head. At least she was feeling friendlier towards her husband because she was going to need him. He had been a bit detached recently which worried her but she knew that he still felt some guilt over what had happened, although she didn't blame him anymore. He assured her that the fire had been a childish prank which unfortunately resulted in tragic consequences and she accepted this explanation. What else could she do? Alan was her best friend and she couldn't lose him as well. As she looked at her smart black dress she braced herself for the day ahead.

Rob and Doug Clarke were in their local having a pint. They had been minding Irene McCardle since all the recent trouble, but Ron had told them he was taking Greg Leeson and John Webb to the funeral so they could have a well-deserved day off. As they sat discussing the football scores Doug saw a large dark-haired man enter the pub and walk to the other side of the bar.

This was the sort of place where everyone knew everyone so unknown characters were always noticed with interest. As Doug looked up the unknown man, who now had a pint, smiled as he raised his glass in a friendly gesture.

Doug, who was not the friendliest of men, just scowled back. 'Right, I'm off for a piss, then we'll get round Mum's for dinner,' he told his brother.

Rob just grunted in acknowledgement without looking up from the newspaper that he was reading. Unfortunately if he had looked up he would have seen the large man follow his brother into the toilet and could have prevented what happened next.

Sonia Stewart held on to her husband's hand as her mother's coffin was lowered into the ground. She was gratified that all her friends were there to support her. Even her neighbour Su Lin was there with her husband Bob and some of the other neighbours as well. Sonia had felt numb in the church although inside she was screaming. She was trying hard to be dignified but when her Aunty Maggie started wailing with grief she couldn't hold her overwhelming feelings in any longer and began crying hysterically, which set off the children. Even little Cath Davis was crying and had to be led away by her parents. As Alan comforted his wife, he had a vision of Jason Baines lying dead with his brains splattered all over the dirty floor of the container in St Albans and wondered, not for the first time, how his life had come to this.

Doug Clarke heard the door of the toilet open but didn't pay any attention until he sensed someone stood behind him. As he was still in the middle of urinating, he didn't realise at first what was happening until he felt a sharp movement across his throat.

As he collapsed onto the floor and saw all the blood, he realised his throat had been slit. As he died on the cold floor of a pub toilet his last thought was that his John Thomas was still hanging out of his trousers.

Rob was wondering where his brother had got to when the large man from earlier swept passed him. 'Deniz Mehmet says hello,' he sniggered before hastily walking out the door.

Registering the man's words Rob felt the colour drain from his face and rushed to the men's toilets as fast as his nineteen stone frame would allow him to. The sight that greeted him broke his heart. His brother was lying in a pool of blood with his eyes wide open in a look of surprise. Blood was still seeping from his throat. Rob took off his t-shirt to try and stem the flow although he knew it was too late. His brother was dead and he didn't know how he was going to break the news to their mother.

As the house in Crouch End was still being repaired, Ron and Irene had kindly offered to have the wake at their home. Sonia had calmed down and as they all sat in the front room reminiscing about Breda, Alan felt himself relax, until Ron came into the room looking like he had seen a ghost. Alan immediately got up from his seat and followed Ron into his study. 'Deniz fucking Mehmet has had Doug Clarke done, he's dead.'

It took a few minutes for Alan to digest the enormity of Ron's news.

'You do know that we are going to have to retaliate, don't you Al? This has gone way too far now. I am bloody gutted, I have worked hard all of my life and rarely had to use any real violence and now at my age I'm in the middle of a fucking war!'

All Alan could do was nod mutely. He hadn't signed up for this. For a moment he felt he was out of his depth. He had always known he would sometimes have to give someone a dig but this was a whole different league and he could now fully understand his wife Sonia's worries over the years. They had been regular people before all of this and, now, somehow, even the wealth that this life brought them seemed meaningless. He was still having nightmares over Jason Baines and now there would be more murders literally but he was in too deep. He loved Ron like family so even with his fears he knew that he couldn't abandon him. 'Let's get today over with Ron and then we can talk about it Mate.'

Ron nodded in agreement but inside he was seething, and to be honest he was worried as well. Deniz Mehmet was heavy duty and he didn't know where this would all end.

When the men went back into the front room Maggie, Dolly and Glenice were all singing and their kitchen sink voices had at least lifted the spirits of the other mourners. Sonia was sitting with her sisters, Sharon and Bridget, and Alan was pleased that the women seemed to be bonding over their loss.

He didn't know how much he would be around in the coming weeks, what with all the troubles they were having and Sonia would need her friends and family. He had already asked Maggie if she would like to live with them in their new home in Crouch Hall Road which was just around the corner from their old home. He had been relieved when she had readily agreed so at least

Sonia would have her aunty to keep her company. Maggie had been thrilled with the invitation as she didn't like her new neighbours who played their 'booming music all fricking night long.' So everyone would be happy with the arrangement. He just hoped that Sonia liked the new house which he had spent a fortune doing up.

Deniz Mehmet was satisfied that he had sent a clear message to Ron McCardle and had avenged his friend Gary's death. In his world it was an eye for an eye and now that he had evened the score he hoped that would be an end to all the unpleasantness. After all he had a business to run, as did Ron. He conceded that the deaths were unfortunate but he now needed to focus on his growing drugs empire. Unfortunately for him, however, Ron McCardle was at this moment sat at home planning how he would retaliate and show Deniz Mehmet that there were consequences to anyone who disrespected him on such a grand scale.

Chapter 21

Three days later, Ron called an urgent meet with all the men on his firm and they were now sat in the plush upstairs office of his car dealership in West London. Ron had thought long and hard about their next move. He didn't really want any more bloodshed but Deniz Mehmet needed to realise that his atrocious actions would not be tolerated. Ron was determined to show his strength. They were all still reeling over the death of Doug Clarke and were listening in respectful silence as he informed them of his plans. 'Mehmet owns an industrial estate off the M4 in Staines. It's in the name of one of his distant cousins, some bloke called Ahmet Adin, who imports carpets from Turkey. But a little bird has told me that it's a holding place for some of the drugs that Mehmet is bringing into the country. Apparently he has sites like this all over and I am planning to blow up the one in Staines to send the bastard a clear message.'

Ron noted that most of the men looked impressed, although it was hard to tell what Rob Clarke and his brother Danny were thinking as their faces were devoid of any emotion. He understood they were grieving. He'd had a private word with them both instructing them not to take matters into their own hands and had made assurances that Doug's death would be avenged. They weren't the brightest lights on the Christmas tree so he hoped they heeded his orders and didn't muck this operation up.

As Alan listened to Ron, his nerves got the better of him and he had to excuse himself to go to the toilet. Inside the cubicle he let out a loud sigh. Sonia was not doing well. After her mother's funeral she had been inconsolable and wouldn't stop crying. In the end he had taken his brother's advice and sent her to a hospital in Surrey where they had swiftly diagnosed a breakdown. The children and Aunty Maggie had moved into one of Ron's rentals in Crouch End until the new house was finished. Alan thought that being in familiar surroundings might help them. They also needed their friends and to go back to school as they had become bored and restless staying at Aunty Maggie's in Kilburn. Alan could have cried, he had enough on his plate and now on top of everything he found himself in the middle of a gang war, which worried the life out of him. When they retaliated, so would the Turks and where would it end? All he had ever wanted was to provide his family with a good standard of living. Until now he had been comfortable with the path he had chosen. He enjoyed the business side of things even if it wasn't all legal and he was happy to apply his physical abilities when the need arose, but this was a whole new level of villainy. This was what amounted to a war and wars meant death and destruction. There was only ever one victorious side and he really wasn't sure that it would be them. Deniz Mehmet was not the sort of man that you went into battle with. He was hardly going to sit back and declare a truce. What really worried Alan was what this meant for his precious family.

Sonia Stewart sat on the pretty veranda staring out at the lush, green gardens that surrounded the hospital in Surrey. Although she was broken after losing her beloved mother Breda, she felt at peace for the first time in years. Being amongst nature could do that she mused, and this private facility was in a remote location ten miles from the nearest village. It helped that she only had herself to consider. She didn't have to cope with the daily grind of running a home and keeping two children entertained. Alan had been busy overseeing the new house and it looked lovely in the photographs he had shown her. But she had no real excitement, how could she? She just went along with him and tried to muster some enthusiasm and gratitude. Inside she just felt numb. Her doctor had explained to her that there were stages of grieving and that she must go through all of them before she would be able to carry on. Before the funeral she had stopped taking her medication but apparently that had been detrimental because a person had to wean themselves off, especially as she had been shoving pills down her throat for years. So when she had been hospitalised she had been put on some new meds but at a lower dose.

This hospital worked alongside the natural approach so she had found herself in yoga classes and group therapy. During the therapy session she had just sat and listened as other women described regular domestic violence, infidelity and sexual abuse. She had nothing to contribute. She could hardly be truthful and share with everyone that her husband was a well-known face in North London who was involved in organised crime and that she couldn't cope with this life that had been thrust upon her. As the other women tearfully told their stories of degradation and humiliation she had had moments of feeling that at least her husband loved and cared for her. She knew in her heart that he had only ever wanted to remove them from a life of poverty and she was proud of him for succeeding. But she also knew she was not cut out for a life of constant worry. Sometimes she envied her friends Brenda Draper and Gina Davis for the simplicity of their lives. They may not have much money but they were content with what they did have. It seemed to Sonia that when a person had ambition, it brought nothing but heartache. What was the expression that her father used to quote? The grass is never greener on the other side. Well, he did have a point. As she sat thinking, she heard someone sit down beside her and was pleased to see who it was. Kerry Watts was a beautiful blonde with the biggest brown eyes that Sonia had ever seen. She had been married to a well-known South London face, Sid Watts, for twenty years.

Kerry had been seduced by the glamour and wealth of being a villain's wife but, like Sonia, as the years had rolled on she had become disillusioned and nervous that her husband would end up with a capture. Unfortunately her worries had come true as Sid was now serving a long stretch at Her Majesty's pleasure for a botched gold bullion heist. He would most probably die in prison as he was already well into his sixties. Kerry had gone to pieces but had been sensible enough to check herself into the hospital that had helped keep her sane over the years. At last Sonia had someone who understood, who got her, and the two women were fast becoming close friends.

Irene McCardle had decided to get her husband's suits dry cleaned so she was looking through the pockets in case he had left anything in them. As she absentmindedly put her hand inside some trouser pockets she felt a small box. Pulling it out she frowned as she opened it and looked inside. Her frown soon turned to fury as she looked at the solid silver baby bangle. As she inspected it she saw that it bore the name Chantelle. Throwing it across their bedroom she collapsed onto the bed and wept bitter tears. The dirty bastard. The baby that Ebony had been carrying was clearly his. He had done the worst thing possible to her. She had turned a blind eye to all the affairs over the years but this is something she would never be able to live with. Going downstairs she made a quick phone call and then opened the hall cupboard and placed the gun into her handbag before swiftly leaving the house.

Ron McCardle was back in his offices at the club in Tottenham. He had just had a call from his wife suggesting lunch and had readily agreed as he was starving. He hadn't given her much attention in the last few weeks and it would be great to share a bottle of red and have a natter. He was feeling decidedly on edge about all the trouble with the Turks but he knew that if he didn't show his hand then he would lose the respect he had built up over the years and he could never allow that to happen.

Lily Jenson who ran the house in Crouch End was sitting enjoying a cup of tea, pleased with herself at how well the business was going. The three girls, Vanessa, Tian and Melanie, got on really well in more ways than one and had over the last few months built up an impressive clientele. She had employed a handsome young man called Joseph for the spare room and had been surprised at how popular he had become to the well off, sexually frustrated housewives of North London. The house ran like clockwork and all her employees had become like family to her and her son Barry. She was especially grateful at how much they loved her boy and one of them always sat with him in their flat downstairs when the swingers' parties were taking place.

Vanessa Whelan had just finished with one of her clients, Mr Smith, and was showing him to the front door.

She knew how to make a man feel important and cheekily gave his bottom a squeeze as she thanked him and sent him on his way back to his wife and three kids. As she turned to go back inside the house she heard the man scream in pain and turning around saw him on the garden path clutching his stomach. Confused, she went to see if he was alright feeling slightly conscious that she was wearing a see-through negligee. The man had gone quiet and Vanessa started shaking when she saw the growing pool of blood on his white shirt. Although she was in shock she instinctively knew that she mustn't draw attention to the situation and quickly went into the house to alert Lily.

Irene had arrived at Ron's offices and he was dismayed to notice that she wasn't herself. She was definitely on edge and seemed almost hyper. They were just about to leave to have lunch at a local restaurant that he owned in Muswell Hill when the phone rang and Lily Jenson explained that they had trouble at the house in Crouch End. Ron slammed the phone back onto its cradle and swore. Looking at his wife he informed her that lunch would have to wait as they needed to take a detour due to more trouble. Irene secretly smiled to herself. Serves him right she thought as they hastily got into his car and drove off.

Lily was a calm woman by nature and had asked young Joseph to help her take the man inside the house. The last thing she needed was old Mr Chatsworth from next door sticking his beak in. Mr Smith was now a dead weight and it was a struggle to get him through the house.

As they gently laid him onto the kitchen floor Ron arrived with Irene. Ron quickly felt for a pulse. There was none. The man had bled to death. 'For fuck's sake, what the hell happened?' he shouted angrily.

Vanessa who had swapped her work attire for a Marks and Spencer's dressing gown tried to explain through her tears. Ron was listening intently. 'So didn't you see anyone?'

Vanessa shook her head. 'No Mr McCardle, I had my back to him and whoever did it was gone by the time that I turned back.'

Ron nodded but was silently seething. Another attack and he hadn't even had the chance to retaliate for the murder of Doug Clarke yet. Well, any doubts he might have had, had just evaporated. He was now convinced that this was the work of the Turks. He had been careful not to lay the blame at their door when all the troubles had started but they had admitted to the death of one of his men and now it looked like he had another knifing to contend with, and a dead civilian to deal with. Turning to Lily he instructed her to cover the man and asked Vanessa and Joseph to give them some privacy. 'I'll send some of the boys round to take the body Lil. In the meantime Rob and Danny Clarke will stay close to make sure that you're protected.'

Lily looked worried. 'Ron what about Barry?'

'Oh come on Love, he won't understand what's going on now will he?'

Lily was hurt that Ron was dismissing her son as some sort of imbecile who didn't matter. He had confided in her about Chantelle after too much Scotch one evening and she doubted that he would leave her in the firing line of a gang war. She felt tempted to blurt out the truth there and then. Barry was as much his child as Chantelle was, but she didn't want to hurt Irene who was stood listening and didn't deserve such a revelation at a time like this. So smiling she said that she would make up a room for the Clarke brothers.

As Ron and Irene drove off they decided to go home as neither of them had much of an appetite for lunch. Irene was deep in thought. Maybe Deniz Mehmet would do her a favour and kill her low life, cheating husband and she wouldn't have to get her hands dirty after all she joked with herself. Ron had updated his will recently and she knew that he had left everything to her. Most of the businesses were in her name anyway as he trusted her more than he trusted anyone. Well she had done her bit of being the dutiful and supportive wife while behind her back he had been creating a family with someone else. Oh, she knew that the pregnancy had probably been an accident but that thought didn't make her feel any better. There was a living child now. A baby girl who he was clearly already soppy over if the bangle was anything to go by. What if he changed his will again and cut her off without a bean? She didn't really think that would happen but she didn't know about anything anymore. It was a possibility. She had looked after Ron's finances, provided countless alibis over the years and had given him a loving home. There was no way she was going to be cut adrift without a penny because he now had a bastard heir. Irene was a proud woman and she was raging. She had intended to shoot him today but could she really do that? She was certainly angry enough but maybe she had to be one step ahead. Maybe she had to be as devious as he had been. She had a plan forming in her mind but would bide her time and really think things through. She had to be clever. She couldn't be seen to be the person who brought her husband down. No, it had to look as if someone else had done that. The thought scared her as much as it thrilled her. He had destroyed her emotionally and had broken her heart. He had underestimated her and assumed she was accepting of all of his affairs over the years. He had thought that by being honest with her, he wasn't really cheating. But every time that he had announced he had a new bed companion, the feeling of betrayal and resentment had grown like a malignant tumour. Now she had had enough. A child was a living reminder of what she would never have and it was a slap in the face. Oh she knew that some women accepted outside children but she was no one's fool. Her husband bleated on about respect but didn't he realise how much he had disrespected her over the years? Everyone had their limits and Irene had reached hers. She had no alternative but to protect herself from any further heartache and if she played her cards right she would be a very rich woman and would be able to start again somewhere where no one knew her or had ever heard of Ron McCardle.

Satisfied that she had made a concrete decision, she turned to her husband and putting on a smile asked him if he would prefer a tuna or ham sandwich for his lunch. He smiled back thinking to himself what a diamond his wife was. She had remained calm at the house and was now thinking about feeding him, not at all phased that their lunch date had been cancelled. She always put him first he thought, feeling very lucky and she never moaned or made a fuss unlike some of the other wives in their world. He vowed to himself that when all the trouble was over, he would treat her to a lovely holiday in the Caribbean.

Chapter 22

Ron had driven to Staines a few times to suss out the industrial estate that housed Turkish carpets and thousands of pounds worth of heroin. The location was relatively remote which was perfect in Ron's mind as he didn't really want any innocent casualties if he could avoid it. At the entrance of the site there were two locked iron gates which were automatically opened by a security guard who stood guard at all times. Ron had, in the last few weeks, cultivated a friendly exchange with the guard and as luck would have it had discovered that Frank Tennent hailed from Deptford and they knew some of the same people. After a few conversations it had become evident that Frank was not happy working for the Turks who paid him a pittance and expected him to work unsociable hours including Christmas day. Ron was an expert in the art of persuasion and it hadn't taken long for Frank to agree to switch his allegiances, especially after Ron had promised him a position in the firm and a much healthier wage packet.

Everything was falling nicely into place. Ron's cousin John who had served with a bomb disposal unit during the war was making a bomb and they had access to the industrial site courtesy of Frank Tennent who was only too happy to see the Turks taken down a peg or two. Soon Deniz Mehmet would realise that Ron McCardle was not a man to take liberties with. He had tried to give the man the benefit of the doubt but as soon as Jason Baines had given up the name of his Turkish accomplice Ali Mustapha, any doubts had disappeared. He hadn't been able to find out anything about the man but Ron was convinced he must be another of Deniz Mehmet's minions who had got to the son of Stevie Baines and that all the attacks lay firmly at the Turk's door.

Irene McCardle was also doing some plotting of her own. She had arranged the opening of some off-shore bank accounts in her name and would slowly siphon small chunks of Ron's considerable wealth until she bled him dry. She had access to all the money and was his unofficial accountant as he didn't trust anyone else. It wouldn't be difficult. If Ron noticed, she would simply tell him that she was helping to make money less accessible to the tax man, which he wouldn't question. He never looked at the accounts anyway. For a man who had built an empire from nothing, Irene thought that he was a fool but she wasn't and she would show him! She would bide her time and take as much money as she could and see how the situation with the Turks played out. If Ron got himself killed then she was home and dry, although in truth she didn't really know how she would feel if he died. She still loved him but he had slowly destroyed her self-esteem over the years and he had been arrogant enough to assume that she was accepting of all his marital betrayals. That he loved her, she was in no doubt, but it wasn't enough anymore. He had humiliated her and she was no longer willing to share him with anybody else. In fact she would rather be a widow than a door mat. Ron was a selfish husband and she had reached the end of the line with being the dutiful wife who overlooked every humiliation that was thrown at her.

Ebony Peters sighed as she heard the baby crying. Getting up from the sofa, she put down her glass of wine and trudged up the stairs. She did love her little daughter but was the first to admit that motherhood was not her strong point. A baby wreaked havoc with a woman's waistline and then drained you dry. Chantelle had colic and as Ebony looked at her expensive watch, she saw that it was the 'witching hour' as she called it. The baby would now scream solidly for the next few hours while Ebony tried to soothe her whilst getting through a bottle of wine to calm her rattling nerves. She was aware she shouldn't be drinking so much and vaguely worried that she would end up a lush like her Aunty Pat but the wine helped to dull the relentless crying and the loneliness that Ebony was feeling. It didn't help that she was in a strange area and knew no one. The lady next door also had a baby and had tried to be friendly but Ebony only generally befriended people who could make her life better and she doubted that the overweight mother next door with the home perm fell into that category, so she had tried to avoid her. Ron only rocked up as and when he felt like it, usually laden down with gifts for the baby. Probably to ease his guilt she thought. Last week he had turned up with a silver bangle for Chantelle but she hadn't seen him since and was becoming more frustrated and angry with the situation that she now found herself in. She had a growing feeling that she should have come clean to Kadir Mehmet and admit that the baby was his. Maybe he would set her up in a house somewhere? She had felt the sexual tension between them at her father's funeral so she knew that if Kadir was in her life regularly they would probably end up in bed together. Ron was more like an uncle these days. There was no longer any chemistry between them and she was a girl who enjoyed sex. She needed to feel desired and beautiful. She missed the touch of a strong and vibrant man. Admittedly, she wasn't as confident with her body after child birth but she was dutifully doing exercises to put her pelvic floor back in place and at least she hadn't let her body go to pot like Mrs Home Perm from next door. She should never have listened to her father and his stupid plan to dupe Ron because at this moment she felt Kadir would have been the better choice.

Alan listened to Ron as the older man explained their next plan of action. It was all systems go and the bomb would be planted next week. Alan was uneasy about the whole thing but as Ron's number two had no option but to go through the motions of readily agreeing. He wanted revenge but was worried of the ramifications, especially to his own family who were only just beginning to get back to some sort of normal.

He nodded as Ron spoke.

'So we plant the bomb next Tuesday. They get a delivery of carpets at ten o'clock in the morning except it won't be the usual driver if you get my drift. The bomb will be concealed in a roll of carpet. It's only small so they shouldn't notice a thing. I know for a fact that once the delivery is made the carpets are immediately unloaded and stored in the same warehouse as the drugs. The kosher delivery is on a Tuesday whereas the hidden drugs come in on a Wednesday.'

Ron could see from the unsure look on Alan's face that he had doubts. 'What's the problem Al? I've done my homework and this plan is fool proof.'

Alan had to choose his words carefully as he didn't want to come across as a pussy. As Ron's second-in-command he was expected to agree with his boss and more importantly to have the ability to expect the unexpected and to protect their reputations whatever the cost might be. 'I agree that we have to show our hand, but what do we do if they retaliate? We've already lost Breda and Doug, not to mention that bloke who got knifed at the house. I can't see Deniz Mehmet just swallowing a bomb attack.'

Ron could understand Alan's concerns but felt this needed to be done. Deniz Mehmet was responsible for three people being murdered. Breda Murphy may have had a heart attack in the end but she could just have easily have been burnt alive or died from smoke inhalation.

'Look Al, we haven't murdered anyone, all of this trouble started with that flash prick just because I wouldn't go into business with him. Mark my words, this is just the start of it. I can see him trying to take over everything we have worked bloody hard for. He is known for being greedy and wanting to be the main man. In the past we have worked reasonably well respecting each other from a distance but he wants it all. I can feel it. I will ask for a meet in due course and hopefully appeal to him that enough is enough. But he has to be sent a clear message. Now if you don't mind, I need to get home to Irene, she's not herself so I'm going to take her out to lunch as last week's date was cancelled for obvious reasons.'

Alan knew better than to question Ron any further. He just had to trust that Ron knew what he was doing. After all, this wasn't the first battle that he had gone into and Alan doubted it would be the last. Smiling he picked up his coat and told Ron that he would see him tomorrow. He was going to show the children and Aunty Maggie the house for the first time and was excited to see their reactions. He was then meeting Geoff Draper and Nick Davis from the estate for a much needed pint. It would do him good to be in the company of his old pals who were regular people and who he could pass the night away discussing football and ordinary things. Brenda Draper had kindly offered him a bed for the night and he was grateful as he felt the need to distance himself from Ron and all the talk about bombs and revenge for at least one night.

Maggie walked into the house in Crouch Hall Road and whistled, 'This is even more gorgeous than the first house if that is even possible.'

Alan was very proud of the finished result. He had paid an arm and a leg for an interior designer and she had been worth every penny. He knew that Sonia didn't go for all the bold patterns that were fashionable so had chosen soft cosy colours throughout. The front room and the other reception room had been knocked through and led out into a Victorian conservatory which overlooked a beautiful garden which was full of colour. The kitchen, although modern, had a real family feel to it and he knew that his wife would love the big print on the wall of them all with Breda. It had been drawn from a photograph that had been taken when they had holidayed in Spain. He was pleased that it captured his mother-in-law's sunny personality perfectly. The children had bedrooms the same size next door to each other and each child had gasped when they had seen them. He had even thought to fill them with toys. Connie cried when she spotted the Sindy dolls. 'Oh Dad, I love them, did you get me the Sindy car and wardrobe?'

Alan had to laugh to himself, trust his daughter to want more! 'No Darling but we can visit the toyshop tomorrow. Do you like your little dressing table?'

Connie nodded in awe. She had never had anything so grown up before and it matched the one that Mum had in her bedroom.

She noticed that her father had also bought her a diary to replace her old one. 'Sorry Dad but I don't want this, I don't think it's good to write everything down.'

Alan laughed again, typical of Connie! She just didn't want to risk getting into trouble. A few months ago she had written about stealing some pick and mix sweets from Woolworths and Sonia had made her go back to the shop to apologise!

Billy was also thrilled with his room. This was the only room in the house that had bold colours of green and orange on the walls and the woodwork was a navy blue. He especially loved the little table and chair that his dad had bought so that he could do his airfix modelling and he even had a little punch bag so that he could practise his boxing. Alan had purposely had a room downstairs decorated for Maggie and she had smiled her thanks. All in all everyone was happy. She particularly loved the chaise lounge by the window in her bedroom. 'Ooh I'm going to feel like Sophia Loren lying on that!' she declared. He just hoped that Sonia would love the house as much as everyone else did although he knew it would be a while before she finally came home.

Sonia was actually laughing and it felt so good. She had attended a yoga class with her new friend Kerry and some woman had inadvertently broken wind whilst attempting one of the positions. The two women were now rolling about the bed in Sonia's room giggling like two school girls.

'Did you see her scraping her foot on the floor so everyone would think that it was her shoe that had made the noise?' Sonia was gasping for air she was laughing so hard and soon tears were rolling down her cheeks. She suddenly remembered her mother and began crying harder but this time with pain in her heart. 'Oh my god, what am I doing laughing over a fart when my mum has just died?'

Kerry looked at her with sympathy and said deadpan, 'Sonia, you really needed that fart, look how much it has helped you to laugh again!'

Sonia looked up suddenly howling with laughter. She really had needed some light relief in her life. Her mother would have told her to live her life and get a grip. She felt safe with Kerry in the hospital. There was no pressure to pretend to be happy. That had probably been the hardest task over the years and so exhausting. She had no responsibilities and it was liberating. She didn't have to be on constant tender hooks wondering what the day would bring. Being at the hospital was like being in a womb, all safe and cosy. She knew her family were moving into the new house in the next few days and she knew that she should be missing them but she didn't. They complicated her thoughts, they made her worry and resentful at times because someone always needed something, and she had been running on empty for years. The lovely doctors here had made her realise that she had been mentally ill for a long time. They called it post-traumatic stress which caused severe anxiety. They had also diagnosed her with depression. She could swing for her brother-in-law David who had been supplying her with tranquillisers and sleeping tablets for years. They had just made her feel worse. She had only felt half alive and had often been trying to function whilst in a trance. Her current prescription was not as potent and conse-quently she was beginning to feel more alert and stronger than she had in years. The thought of going back to her responsibilities filled her with dread. The doctors said she would know when she was ready to go back home but at this moment she felt she never wanted to leave this haven or to leave Kerry who was the only person in the world who understood her.

Alan sat on the smart leather sofa in his new home and sighed contentedly for the first time in months. Once this business with the Turks was sorted he was determined to spend more time with the family. Sonia, although fragile, seemed to be making progress at the hospital in Surrey and he was pleased that she had made a friend. He had gently asked her when she might be home but she had brushed his question off with a deep sigh, so he hadn't pushed the point. The doctors had told him that if she came home too soon, she would most likely end up being readmitted at some point. Apparently it was crucial to get to the crux of her problems and then they would be able to treat them accordingly. Alan was grateful she had palled up with another lag's wife because she could hardly discuss protection rackets, robberies and arson during this group therapy that she went to!

Sonia was close to Brenda and Gina from the estate but she couldn't really speak to them either so he guessed that she had been bottling up a lot of feelings over the years which had overwhelmed her. He didn't really understand all this talk about mental health but he was determined to try and, more importantly, get his little family back together living under one roof.

Chapter 23

Deniz Mehmet lived in a luxurious six bedroomed house in Ongar, Essex. He was enjoying a hearty breakfast which had been lovingly prepared by his wife Emine when he received a phone call from his number two, Nicos Akbay. Listening intently to what he was being told, Emine watched the changing expressions on her husband's face. As his eyes began twitching she knew from experience that whoever was on the phone had just delivered some bad news and unfortunately she was right. She watched as he slammed down the phone, roughly pushed his plate away and promptly left the house whilst cursing loudly in his native tongue. Sighing, Emine wondered what had caused all the upset. She had been married to her husband for over thirty years and had seen him this angry many times but was confident that as in the past he would sort it out and would get back to normal very soon. Sitting down in his now empty chair, she absentmindedly picked at the rest of the breakfast and decided to pay her son Kadir a visit and see if he knew what had happened.

Alan, the children, Aunty Maggie and Winston the terrier were settled into the new house and were settling in nicely. Alan thanked God every day that he had Maggie who had taken over the running of the house and caring for the children with a kind but firm hand. It also helped that she was so much fun and, like her sister Breda, had the knack of cheering them all up when required. She was just what the children needed and provided the love and security that was now missing from Breda and Sonia, who was still recuperating in the hospital in Surrey. It was early November and Sonia had agreed to come home in time for Christmas. Alan felt that this was ideal as his wife had always loved this time of year and wouldn't want to miss out on the family festivities. He and the children had recently visited her and she had seemed like the old Sonia before all the sadness and worry. He had felt his heart burst with love as he had watched her playing and laughing with the twins. When all the trouble with the Turks was over he was going to step down as Ron's number two and concentrate on the legal businesses so that his wife could have some peace of mind. He believed this was the least he could do for her. He was shamefully aware that he had inadvertently brought about most of her misery over the years, being so heavily involved with organised crime. He really didn't know if Ron would accept his decision, he may feel like it was a slap in the face. Without Ron he would never have achieved the wealth that he had made over the years but his family had to come first. He would sound out Ron in the New Year when things had hopefully settled down. Humming along to the song being played on the car radio Alan drove across London to meet Ron, feeling happier about the future blissfully unaware that the trouble was far from over.

Irene McCardle ate her breakfast deep in thought. She was slowly amassing a decent amount of money in her name and would soon be able to put her plan into action and leave her cheating bastard of a husband for good. The future scared her as much as it exhilarated her. She was on the wrong side of fifty and starting again but, start again, she would. In her mind she would rather be on her own than be with someone who treated her like a mug. She had turned a blind eye to his various affairs but having a baby with another woman was a step too far. Irene was a resilient woman, it stood to reason that she had had to be over the years and would rise again somewhere far from

North London and Ron bloody McCardle. When she had enough money and had dented his bank accounts enough to impact him, she would pack a small suitcase and leave for good. She quite fancied America. It was vast and she felt confident that Ron would never find her. As she raised her mug to take a sip of her morning coffee she heard the intercom go from the front gate where a male voice informed her that he had a package for her. She thought nothing of it as she had recently ordered a gold watch for herself. She had never really been a materialistic woman but was enjoying draining her husband's bank accounts and frittering away his money on crap. Getting up from her chair, she buzzed the driver in and waited for him at the front door.

The young man walked quickly up the pebbly drive as quickly as his gammy leg would allow him to. It was a cold morning and his leg always gave him more pain when the weather turned. The doctor said it was arthritis. Fucking arthritis! His Nan had that and she was eighty! He was only twenty-three and it wound him up on a daily basis. Clutching the small knife in his sweaty hand he now wasn't sure if he could carry out his father's instructions.

The men in Ron's office were laughing and celebrating with top notch champagne. The bomb had caused as much destruction as one of Adolf Hitler's during the Blitz. The security guard Frank Tennent had played a blinder and Ron had been impressed with his part in the operation to retaliate for the deaths and aggro caused by the Turks. He would ensure that Frank was given a good earn to repay him for his loyalty. As Ron cracked open another bottle, the telephone rang. It was Denny Draper calling from the club in Tottenham. Apparently Deniz Mehmet wanted a meet. Putting the receiver down he turned to his team smiling. 'What did I tell you boys? He now wants to talk.'

Alan still felt uneasy but Ron had been in the business for years so he had to trust that his boss and mentor knew what he was doing. He just couldn't believe that a cosy chat would be the end of all this.

Irene knew that Ron would be annoyed and alarmed that she had opened the front door to a stranger, what with all the aggravation that was going on at the moment.

Rob Clarke had been standing guard over her for weeks and quite frankly she had had enough. He was a nice enough bloke but not exactly an intellect and if she had to hear his noisy eating for much longer, she was going to scream! Anyway, he was at the meet with Ron so what was she supposed to do?! She was sick of feeling like a prisoner in her own home and like everybody else wanted to get back to normal. As she opened her front door the first thing she noticed was that the delivery driver was not wearing a uniform and was not carrying a package. She quickly scanned him and was shocked to see he was carrying a knife in his right hand which was shaking. Irene instinctively knew this young man didn't have the bottle to hurt her. 'Put the knife away Son, my bastard of a husband isn't here anyway and I take it that you wanted him?'

To prove her point she shouted Ron's name as loudly as she could and when her calls went unanswered she could see the man visibly relax. She could sense his anxiety and regret seeping out of him. 'Look, why don't you come in for a chat?'

He was standing not five feet away from her holding a weapon but Irene felt calm and strangely smug that Ron's little plan to blow up his rival had perhaps not worked, or maybe it had because the man before her didn't look Turkish and Deniz Mehmet was known for only employing his own kind with the exception of Gary Peters. This fact could mean that another firm had a grudge against her arrogant husband and the thought pleased her. Smiling, she opened the door wider and welcomed the stranger into her home. She was grateful when he put the knife in the back pocket of his jeans pocket and followed her inside.

Deniz Mehmet was in Staines inspecting the damage to his warehouse. It was completely destroyed, along with a quarter of a million pounds worth of heroin. Miraculously no one had been hurt although at this moment that would have been preferable. He had an excellent reputation in Turkey and his suppliers trusted him implicitly. Now he was going to have to dig into his own fortune to pay them back because they would not be impressed with this turn of events. He was seething with anger but the only thing that was sensible was to end this which is why he had decided to arrange a meet with Ron McCardle. As he swallowed an indigestion tablet he was aware he was getting too old to be playing what amounted to Cowboys and Indians and decided there and then that he would transfer most of the responsibility to his son Kadir and sit back to enjoy the profits.

As Irene listened to the young man's story she could understand why he had a grievance against her husband. Ron had gone too far when the man was a lad, just because he had been flirting with her husband's tart. Trust her to be the cause of this she thought as she listened.

Five years ago Mick Latham had been a promising professional footballer with the world at his feet when Ron had beaten him senseless with a tyre iron. He had woken from the brutal beating the following day in a hospital bed. His body was battered, he had a leg that would never work properly again and his future was in tatters. He had suffered from headaches and depression for years and had endured countless operations on his leg. His father Kenny had bided his time as he had been a small time villain in those days and was sensible enough to know that he couldn't win a war with Ron McCardle who had always been the main man in North London. It had broken his heart to witness his son's suffering but he had always known that patience was a virtue and that one day Ron would pay for what he had done and what he had taken from his boy. When Mick had admitted to keying Ron's car, throwing a brick through his window and trying to torch the club, Kenny hadn't blamed him but had explained that these acts were childish and would not make an impact. They had to think of the bigger picture. Luckily, it soon became known in their world that Ron and his firm were at odds with the Turks and that Mick had inadvertently caused a lot of the mayhem while each side blamed the other and retaliated.

Kenny's idea to take out Gary Peters had been genius because Deniz Mehmet had automatically blamed Ron McCardle and had taken revenge. Kenny Latham had sat back and enjoyed the repercussions of his clever plan because now they were at pistols drawn, and he sincerely hoped that the Turk would kill the man who had ruined his son's life.

Irene couldn't help but feel impressed with what she was being told. Apparently Mick Latham had come here today to harm HER because his father knew this would intensify the ongoing battle with the Turks as Ron would automatically blame them. As Mick finished his story he said in a small voice, 'I just couldn't do it, you remind me of my mum and I'm not really like my dad. All I ever wanted to do was play for Spurs.'

Irene knew Kenny Latham of old. He was a small man in height with a massive temper and a tendency to be a bully. She doudln't really blame him for wanting to hurt Ron. It was the natural animal instinct to protect your child. She wondered briefly if Ron felt this way about Chantelle but she knew that he would. Ron could be a teddy bear at times and especially around children. She only had to look at the way he was with the Stewart twins to know that. Brushing her sorrow to one side, she carried on listening to this young man who she found herself feeling sorry for and, more surprisingly, liking.

Irene's mind was whirring with all the information that he had given her but she had a master plan. She was going today and this nice young man was going to help her. She had enough money sitting in an off-shore bank account which would provide her with the life she had become accustomed to. She didn't really need to wait. This young man who had come to hurt her had given her a brilliant idea. Ron would never find her because Ron would think that she was dead!

The meet between Ron McCardle and Deniz Mehmet was arranged for next Thursday at a pub in Soho which neither of them had any links to. Ron was feeling confident that they would be able to negotiate a truce and then keep their distance from each other. He was however going to insist that drugs be kept away from his manor. Ron felt it was the least he could do seeing as the brute had had three people killed and in Ron's opinion got away lightly.

As Ron reached his house he noticed the gates were open and as he neared the property he could see the front door was ajar. Warily he reached for his gun and called out for his wife. The house was silent and as his fear grew so did the knowledge that she clearly wasn't there. When he entered the front room he was incensed to see it was in disarray. The small tables that the lamps usually sat on had been knocked to the floor and the coffee table was broken. He gasped as he saw a pool of blood on the carpet.

Someone had hurt his Irene. Falling to the carpet he let out a cry of anguish and then hastily got up and searched the rest of the house. She was nowhere to be seen which meant someone had taken her after they had hurt her. He was enraged and frightened for his wife. That treacherous Turk obviously didn't have any intentions of smoothing things over. Well, he would find him and when he did he would kill him very slowly.

Alan and the children were watching a film at home when they were interrupted by a phone call from Ron. Alan couldn't believe what he was hearing and felt a coldness sweep over him. He told Ron to come over to the new house but Ron had insisted on rounding up all the men. He would not leave Irene at the mercy of that bastard any longer than he had to. They were going to get her back immediately.

Alan's heart was racing. He had installed some men to discreetly mind his family and he was now on his way to Ray Briggs's scrapyard to meet with

Ron. He was worn out. The last few months had been exhausting mentally and physically and he had two children to care for in the absence of their mother. But he was also seriously scared. Women and children were always left out of feuds. Deniz Mehmet was a family man and was known to stick to this unwritten rule as well. Something felt off to Alan but he put these thoughts to the back of his mind because the most important thing was getting Irene McCardle home in one piece.

Chapter 24

Irene McCardle smiled to herself as Mick Latham drove her to a safe house in Berkshire. He didn't owe her any favours but after hearing her story he wanted to help her. He had telephoned his father Kenny who had been only too happy to assist Irene in escaping, as he knew only too well that Ron McCardle would be having kittens fearing for his wife. Yes, this little plan would be the ultimate revenge and the beauty of it was that he hadn't really had to lift a finger. As Irene and Mick drove up the M4 they chatted companionably. Irene would be on a flight out of Heathrow Airport tomorrow morning bound for her new life in Boston, America, and her husband would be a broken man waiting for a phone call from her 'abductors' that would never come. In time he would believe that she had been murdered. All in all it wasn't a bad day's work Mick thought as he whistled along to the radio. For the first time in five years he finally felt at peace.

Kenny Latham was laughing as he regaled his men with the latest news. Justice had been served and Ron McCardle would never suspect him because he wasn't even on his radar. The arrogant prick had brutally beaten up his boy and then forgotten about it while his son had endured years of operations, pain and bitter disappointment that his promising football career had been ruined. Ron McCardle would automatically blame the Turks for Irene's disappearance, just as the Turks had blamed him for the killing of Gary Peters. Kenny Latham was impressed with his own brilliance and happily poured himself a large measure of his favourite brandy.

Ron McCardle was beside himself. He was insanely angry with himself that he had trusted Deniz Mehmet's olive branch but, above all, the growing feeling of fear for his wife's safety was almost crippling him. Like Alan, he strongly felt that harming and kidnapping an innocent wife was not

Mehmet's style but obviously the man was more devious than they had
believed. As he paced angrily up and down his office willing the phone to ring
his men exchanged worried glances and Alan spoke. 'So what do we do now
Ron? It's been two hours and we haven't had any contact. Surely they would
have shown their hand by now and stated their demands?'

Ron ran his fingers through his thinning hair. This was the first time in his
adult life that he felt totally helpless and wasn't sure what the best course of
action was. Sitting down wearily in a nearby chair his mind whirred with
scenarios. Deniz Mehmet went everywhere with an entourage of heavies so
grabbing him wouldn't be easy. The only other option was to go after a
member of his family, maybe one of his precious sons. Ron knew that
making a rash decision could put his wife in more danger. He needed to
think. 'Give me a few hours to come up with our next move. I want every
phone manned in every business while we wait for news. I also want you to
instruct your wives and families to make themselves scarce until this is sorted.
Stick together and make sure that you're all tooled up. I'm not taking any
more chances.'

The men nodded in agreement, each wondering how this would all pan out.
They just hoped that Irene McCardle would be found safe and sound because
if she wasn't there would be more than one hysterical wife to contend with.

As Ron got into his car, he decided to pay Ebony and his daughter a visit.
He didn't really know where else to go and needed to distract himself. He also
needed to smell the innocence of his baby as she had a knack of calming
him. On the drive over to Brentwood he thought about how he was going to
get his wife back home where she belonged.

Layla Mehmet had taken the children to Cyprus to visit with her relatives who
hadn't yet met the new baby so Kadir decided to drive over to Ebony's house
and confront her about the baby. He had tried to put it to the back of his
mind but he didn't believe her cock and ball story that he wasn't the child's
father. Chantelle was the image of his sons and especially baby Jem with her
olive skin and jet-black curls. She looked like a Turkish baby and he was
determined to find out the truth. Kadir was a family man like his father,
although admittedly his morals were not as scrupulous. His father thought
that men who had affairs were scum but like his father Kadir was passionate
about his children and if he had a daughter then he wanted to know.

Ebony Peters smiled smugly when she answered the telephone to her ex-lover Kadir. His deep sexy voice had asked her politely if he could come and drop off some money from his father who had promised to look after her financially. Ebony had given the family her home telephone number at the funeral but hadn't expected a call so soon. Ron would have a fit if he knew that she had told anyone where she was now living but he hardly ever visited so what harm could it do? After checking on her daughter who was sound asleep in her cot she ran gleefully into her luxury bathroom where she hurriedly spent twenty minutes plucking, shaving and moisturising her body. Well a girl had to be prepared, didn't she?

Irene was impressed with the safe house. It was an eighteenth-century quaint cottage set in three acres of beautiful land near the market town of Wokingham. She was even more impressed that Kenny Latham had driven down to welcome her. She was astute enough to know that he was doing this to see if she could be trusted and she was happy to alleviate any doubts that he might have. Smiling broadly he ushered her inside and made them both a cup of coffee. Mick understood he was no longer required and said his good-byes. Irene had only known the lad for about four hours but had grown very fond of him in that short time. Hugging him, she thanked him and watched as he limped back to his car. Feeling sad she turned to his father. 'I'm sorry.'

Kenny nodded. 'I'm not going to lie Irene, can I call you Irene...'

'Of course.'

'Because of your husband, my boy's life has been ruined. As a father I had to help. He has never been the same since that night. Do you know what it's like watching your child suffer? He tried to top himself when they told him he would never play football again. Broke my heart that did.'

Irene had never met Kenny Latham before but she had heard the rumours that he was a small time villain, a bully who hurt people if they didn't do what he wanted. Ron had always said that he had little man syndrome and had to use these traits to compensate for his lack of height. As Irene listened to the man all she saw was a father who loved his child, and she even forgave him for instructing his son to come to her home to hurt her. He was a father who was spilling his guts to her with a tear in his eye and was not ashamed to do so. Ron had always said that loving a child made you weak but Irene could now see that it made you human and that it must be a beautiful feeling. 'Kenny I do understand and I don't blame you for the way that you feel. I have never been blessed with children but I do know that if I had and anyone had hurt them, then I would have killed for them.'

She went on to confide in him why she hated Ron so much now. Kenny listened respectfully all the time shaking his head. Ron McCardle was a fool in his opinion.

Irene was a good looking intelligent woman who was full of love and empathy. She had helped to run the businesses over the years and had been a shoulder to cry on for the other wives. A one-off in Kenny's eyes and her prat of a husband had totally taken her for granted and then fathered a child with another woman. He himself had been married for twenty-five years to a similar lady and he had never cheated on his Barbara. Oh he had the chance over the years. There were always air heads throwing themselves at you in this life but they were only after the brand, not the person. His wife had known and loved the real him and he had loved her fiercely until the day that she had died of cancer. He still did, but the raw pain of losing her had eased over the years.

As Irene and Kenny chatted into the night, they laughed and shared stories and for the first time in months Irene felt excited for the future. She also rather liked this man who she found to be articulate and good company. She would never forget his kindness and would always be grateful that he had helped her. When he had gone home and she was in the bath she had a feeling that she had just made a new friend.

Kadir Mehmet knocked tentatively at Ebony's front door. He shook off his nerves, feeling a tad annoyed with himself that he felt excited. When Ebony opened the door in a tight mini dress that left nothing to the imagination, he felt like a horny fifteen-year-old again.

All her voluptuous curves were on show and it was evident that she wasn't wearing a bra as her nipples which he had always enjoyed sucking on were standing to attention as was his penis that he could feel straining through his trousers. Both drank in the other knowing where this reunion would end. As he followed her inside and surveyed her pert little arse wiggling in the confines of her tight dress, he grabbed her and pulled her towards him. Ebony was elated. Kadir always smelt of expensive aftershave and a lemony soap. As he kissed her passionately she felt like she had come home. Her whole body was on fire with expectation and desire and the feeling was mutual. He took her on the stairs and although it was a bit uncomfortable she didn't care. She savoured his touch and as he entered her she gasped. She had almost forgotten what a big boy he was! They were both in a temporary ecstasy each realising that it had never been so good or so carnal with anyone else. Kadir's wife was a strictly lights out, nighty up sort of girl and Ron wouldn't know what to do with his tongue if his life depended on it! He hadn't been a selfish lover but had certainly not been as imaginative as Kadir. As they writhed in a natural rhythm nothing else mattered, only this moment of pure lust and need. It was over in a matter of minutes and they both laughed when they heard the baby crying and demanding some attention. Leaping up they hastily rearranged their clothes and bounded up the stairs, aware that they were going to tend to their daughter.

Ron McCardle rang the same doorbell Kadir Mehmet had rung twenty-five minutes before him and waited impatiently for Ebony to let him in. He hadn't used his key as even he knew it would be a piss take as he hadn't visited in over two weeks. Ebony pulled back the heavy front room curtains. 'Fuck, it's Ron.'

Ron could see that Ebony was flustered when she opened the door. Her hair wasn't as groomed as it usually was and he was confused as to why she was wearing such a provocative dress. It suddenly occurred to him that she must have a bloke inside and his anger mounted. A small voice inside his head reminded him that they weren't a couple so it was none of his business anymore, but he still felt a pang of jealousy and annoyance that she might be entertaining with his precious daughter in the house. When he walked into the front room he was greeted with a scene that tore at his heart strings. The baby, his baby was sat on Kadir Mehmet's lap and as he looked at them both he froze. He noticed the same skin tone, the same black, curly hair and the same profile. As the truth smacked him in the face he lunged at Ebony who was nervously watching everyone in the room and who had realised that her lie had been exposed.

'You fucking whore,' Ron spat as he grabbed her by her throat.

Kadir immediately sprang into action. Placing the baby gently into her playpen he took out a knife and pulled Ron off of Ebony who was spluttering and trying desperately to catch her breath. Ron had almost forgotten that the other man was in the room so intense was his fury and heartbreak at Ebony's deceit. As he spun round to confront Kadir he suddenly felt a sharp pain in his head. He tried to lift his arm but it felt like a dead weight. He tried to speak but no words would come. Ebony and Kadir then watched in fascination and confusion as he slumped to the floor. 'I hardly touched him!' Kadir exclaimed.

Ebony stood glued to the spot shaking as Kadir felt for a pulse and then shook his head.

Ebony fell back on to the sofa in shock as Kadir telephoned his father.

Deniz Mehmet was in his study reading the newspaper when he received the call from his son. As he listened, he silently rejoiced that all his troubles were over. Ron McCardle was dead and he could now get back to running his businesses. He instructed his son to go home. He would send some of his men over to drive the body back in Ron's car and then dump it where it could be found.

When Kadir finished the call with his father he turned to Ebony and asked the question that had been niggling him. 'What was he doing here and why was he so angry? What is he to you?'

Ebony was thrown for a moment but decided to be truthful so she started at the beginning leaving out the fact that she had been sleeping with both men at the same time. She lied and said that she had only started an affair with Ron a few weeks after Kadir had ended it with her. Kadir was shocked. Ron was old enough to be her father and he was in the middle of a turf war with his own father! As he digested all the information he sighed. He could understand that Ebony had been trying to protect his wife and family and felt some compassion for the dilemma that she had found herself in.

'Layla and my family must never find out. I will support you and our daughter but you must keep quiet about who her father is because my family would disown me if they ever found out and I must protect my sons,' Kadir stated.

Ebony nodded but deep down a misery overwhelmed her as she realised that she had swapped one secret for another and would always effectively be in hiding. Oh she knew that Kadir would visit, like she knew that they would probably carry on having sex when he did, but she also knew that he would never countenance her starting a relationship with another man. Turkish men were proud like that. He would see her and the baby as his property while he lived a cosy life with his real family. As she opened a bottle of wine later that evening she wept with frustration because she was aware that she was trapped.

Donald Bryne had enjoyed an evening at his local pub and was whistling as he walked the short distance home to his flat in Enfield. As he walked past a flash motor he was alarmed to see a man slumped over the steering wheel. At first he assumed the man was drunk and had fallen asleep but on closer inspection he was shocked to see that he was dead! Donald was a retired doctor and one look at the man's twisted face told him that the poor sod had probably died of a stroke. Thank God he had seen fit to pull over Donald thought, as he walked to the telephone box to phone for an ambulance and the police.

Alan and the children had been to visit Sonia for the day which is why he only heard of his friend's demise as he was getting into bed at twelve-thirty. Putting his dressing gown and slippers back on he went into the Victorian conservatory with a large glass of Scotch and cried like a baby. Ron had given him the opportunity to make something of himself. He had been his mentor and a great friend and Alan had loved him like a father. It was almost too much to bear coming so soon after losing his mother-in-law Breda. He was however comforted by the fact that it looked like he had died from natural causes and hadn't been harmed by Deniz Mehmet. Ron had apparently died from a massive stroke and his death would have been instant. As it was a sudden death there would have to be an autopsy although the doctor who had telephoned Alan had been confident with the suspected diagnosis and assured him that his friend wouldn't have suffered. Alan was always dubious when a doctor said that because how could they possibly know?

Although he had always felt this was only said to comfort grieving relatives, he now desperately needed to believe that Ron had passed away peacefully. Mind you there was no escaping the fact that he had died with the knowledge that someone had taken his beloved wife through no fault of her own and Alan was aware that it would now be his job to find out what had happened to her.

Chapter 25

The following morning Irene McCardle snapped shut her small vanity case and smiled at her reflection in the mirror. Now that she had made her decision to leave Ron and her life behind in England, she felt calm and in control. She had had a lovely evening with Kenny Latham who had managed to take her mind off all the troubles that had been dragging her down for so long and she was feeling very positive about her future. Kenny had respectfully left her at ten o'clock and had insisted on coming back this morning to drive her to the airport. As she went downstairs she was surprised to see he had arrived earlier than expected. Noticing the serious expression on his face she asked him what the matter was.

'I'm sorry Irene but I have some bad news. I heard this morning on the grape vine that Ron is dead. Apparently he had a stroke. Some bloke found him in his car last night.'

Irene said nothing for what seemed like ages and then suddenly let out a small, desperate sound followed by tears that slid silently down her freshly rouged cheeks. As she cried, Kenny felt like he was intruding on her pain but he also knew from personal experience that his presence would be a comfort. As she wept, he went into the kitchen and made her a cup of sweet tea. His old mum had always said that tea laced with lots of sugar helped in a crisis and there wasn't much more that he could do.

Irene was in deep shock over the news and was feeling a mixture of emotions. It didn't escape her notice that one of those feelings was relief but she had loved Ron deeply for years and, although he had betrayed her, the sadness and grief that she was experiencing was far greater than anything else. 'Kenny could you arrange for someone to take me home please? I'm not going anywhere now and there will be people looking for me and that's not fair. I need to see Alan Stewart as soon as possible.'

Kenny was strangely pleased she wasn't going to America because, like Irene, he had also felt he'd found a friend and hoped he would see her again once things had settled down. 'I will drive you to the West End. I own a cab firm up there so will get one of the lads to then drop you off in Crouch End as it's probably not a good idea that we are seen together.'

Irene agreed, nodding her thanks and as she sipped at her tea she realised that Ron's death changed everything. She would be respected as the grieving widow thus giving her back some of her self-esteem which had gone on holiday recently. She would also be very wealthy and would be able to live her life as she chose and without worrying about what her husband was getting up to and with whom. She no longer cared about his child or its tart of a mother because she had her life back and the knowledge was liberating.

Alan Stewart couldn't face the children today and was relieved when his old

friends Brenda Draper and Gina Davis offered to take them to the funfair at
Ally Pally.

Irene was still missing and he had to figure out the next move. It had always
been Ron's intention that he took over the running of the businesses should
anything happen to him and he didn't want to let him down, especially at this
crucial time. As he sat at the kitchen table Maggie plonked a full English in
front of him. 'Now get that down you before it turns to shite. You need a full
stomach to do your thinking.'

Alan gratefully grabbed her hand and kissed it. 'I bloody love you Aunty
Maggie.'

Maggie puffed out her cheeks and did a little dance out of the kitchen
pleased she was helping her beloved sister's family. As Alan tucked into his
breakfast he was becoming more and more anxious about Irene's safety. So
far no one had contacted them which was very odd. It was like she had disappeared into thin air. He had telephoned Larry the limp who was their eyes
and ears on the street and even he had heard nothing. It was a real mystery.

Irene was impressed with the new house that Alan had bought. It was
magnificent but homely looking, standing three storeys high. She walked up
the garden path and nervously rang the doorbell not knowing how Alan
would react to her deceitful plan to let them all think she had been abducted
and possibly murdered.

Alan stood with his mouth wide open in surprise when he saw who his
visitor was. He was so relieved that he grabbed Irene in a bear hug not
wanting to let her go.

Soon they were both crying for the man whom they had both loved so
much. 'Come on in before someone thinks that I've gone soft,' Alan laughed.

As they sat by the fire in the front room, Irene tried to articulate what had
driven her to do what she had. Alan allowed her to put into words all her
years of hurt, finally admitting that the baby was the last straw. Alan had the
grace to look ashamed.

'You knew didn't you?' she said sadly.

'I did, but I can assure you that it wasn't common knowledge and what
could I do?'

Although Irene was aware that Alan had been put in an impossible situation she still felt hurt. Alan sympathised with this lady and she was a lady. She
had put up with Ron's affairs with grace and dignity but even he could see

that having a baby and not telling her would be too much for any woman to accept. If it had been him, he knew for a fact that his Sonia would have strung him up by the balls using barbed wire.

Irene felt relieved that she had come clean. Her admissions had been surprisingly cathartic. She sensibly left out the Latham involvement. That family had suffered enough in her opinion and she didn't want any further repercussions. Ron was dead and the Turks could do what they wanted with North London as far as she was concerned. Her plan was to legalise most of the business. She knew in her heart that Alan would jump at the chance.

He was a businessman at heart, not a thug, and the past few years had almost cost him his marriage so she wasn't surprised when he readily agreed with her when she told him of her plans. They talked for hours and before they knew it, it was six o'clock and they both realised they were starving hungry. Maggie kindly made them some food and as they were eating Alan suddenly had a thought. 'Irene, where did all that blood come from that Ron found on the carpet at your house?'

Irene chuckled, 'I had defrosted a joint of beef which was swimming in blood so I used that!'

Hearing her explanation Alan nearly choked on his food. Seeing the scandalous look on his face, Irene laughed, 'Ron wasn't the only devious McCardle Alan.'

Raising her glass of wine she raised a toast to her husband who despite everything she would always love, 'To Ron and the future.'

'I'll drink to that,' Alan agreed.

It was at this moment that the children returned home. They were delighted to see her and enveloped her in warm hugs and love which was just what she needed.

Chapter 26

Lily Jenson was heartbroken at the news of Ron's death. They had slept together periodically over the years and had produced a wonderful son, a fact that she had kept from Ron. She so wished she had told him now but it was too late. Barry had been born with Downs Syndrome and was loved by everyone. Ron especially had had a great relationship with him and had shown him love and acceptance, so why hadn't she just bitten the bullet and admitted the truth? But she had kept his parentage a closely guarded secret when by rights her Barry now had a claim to Ron's fortunes. Lily wasn't a money grabber but facts were facts. As she puffed on her cigarette she worried for the future. Rumour had it that Irene and Alan Stewart wanted to legalise the businesses so where did that leave her and Barry? She had spent the last year building up the house and it had paid off. Well she would soon find out she thought as Irene McCardle was popping over today to 'discuss' things.

Deniz Mehmet had only agreed to meet with Irene McCardle out of curiosity. Personally he felt that women should stay out of business and only belonged in the kitchen or the bedroom but he was interested to see what the widow of Ron McCardle had to say which was why she now sat opposite him. 'I am so sorry for your loss Mrs McCardle…'

'Cut the crap Mr Mehmet because we both know that you and Ron were at each other's throats, I'm here to talk business, no more no less.'

Deniz Mehmet was taken aback as he wasn't used to being spoken to in such a disrespectful manner and especially by a woman but, despite that, he was mildly struck with this one. She had spunk and he liked that.

'I am going legal so I am here to offer you the protection list for a price of course. I am doing this as a gesture of good will and I also want to assure you that going forward, I have no interest in anything that you do. We have all been through enough trouble lately and I hope that you will agree with me that we need to call a truce?'

Deniz was impressed. She had come to have her say and hadn't waffled and flapped like most women he had ever met. 'I will happily take on the lists IF I am happy with your asking price and in future we will respect each other from a distance.'

Irene stood up, shook his hand and mentally ticked this job off of her to do list. Her next stop was the undertakers. She had a busy day and rather liked it as it took her mind off her grief.

Sonia Stewart was in the day room at the hospital with her new friend Kerry Watts. 'Bloody hell Kerry, I feel like a kid again making these paper chains. Next they'll be making sure that we write to Santa! Mind you it's relaxing isn't it?'

'Yeah it is Sonia, I'm quite looking forward to going home now although I'm really going to miss you.'

The two women had been each other's rocks and had helped each other to recover from their mental distress. It had helped having similar lives as they could fully understand why the other hadn't been able to cope. Sonia would miss Kerry but she knew they were friends for life now and she wanted to get back to being a wife and mother. The doctors had slowly weaned her off her medication and she was now feeling sharper and more importantly happier than she had in a long time. She had been sad to hear of Ron's death because although she had always been slightly nervous around him, he had become like an uncle to her and she in turn had grown fond of him. But her life had really only turned to shit when he had come into it in 1967. Oh she knew that she would probably still be living in her council house back on the estate scrimping by, but she also knew that she wouldn't have become ill with all the worry and ended up in what amounted to the nut house! When Irene had told her of her plans to go legal, she had almost jumped for joy with relief because now she wouldn't live with the threat of Alan being sent to prison or worse still being murdered. In a few weeks and after the funeral she was going to surprise her family and go home for good. She could hardly wait!

Irene was at the undertakers with her mother-in-law Dolly making the final arrangements for her husband's funeral. He would receive a lavish send-off that befitted a man of his status. Dolly who was usually as hard as nails sat beside her softly crying. The poor old girl had taken the death of her only son very badly but Irene loved her dearly and would take care of her for the rest of her life. 'It's not right, I should have gone to the Pearly Gates first,' she kept repeating through her tears.

Irene lovingly patted her hand and asked the undertaker if he would be kind enough to get her mother-in-law another cup of tea. The funeral was booked for two weeks' time on the tenth of December. Alan had explained to her that Sonia wouldn't be attending as it was too soon after losing Breda and the doctors felt that it could set back her progress. Sonia had however sent Irene a heartfelt note of condolence insisting that she was a part of their family and as such must come to them on Christmas Day. Irene had been really touched by the kind words and grateful that she would have somewhere to go as she hadn't relished being on her own. Dolly had been invited as well. After Christmas Irene was going to sell the house and get somewhere smaller for herself, perhaps in Hampstead or Highgate. Her home was too big for her to be rattling around in on her own and she needed a fresh start. After she had taken Dolly home she drove to Crouch End to see Lily Jenson. As she drove past Alan and Sonia's old home she saw their neighbour Su Lin who waved at her.

She really liked Crouch End, it was a good area but not snooty like some and had an almost urban village feel to it. She might move Dolly here so that she could be closer to Maggie and Glenice she thought as she pulled up outside the house that she called Pervert's Paradise. Lily opened the door and hugged her with real affection. The two women were of a similar age and had always liked each other. 'Come in Love, it's bloody freezing out there.'

Once they were settled in the front room Irene decided to get the matter in hand out of the way. 'I'll get straight to the point Lily, I don't want the hag of illegal businesses and I certainly don't need the money. I am in the process of negotiating a price for the protection list and that only leaves this place. I appreciate all your hard work but I want to turn this house back into a rental. You will of course be able to continue living here if you want to as I would love you to run it along with the other rentals for me. I can offer the girls and Joseph jobs in one of the clubs or restaurants and they can carry on living here as well. I can't say fairer than that.'

'To be honest trade has fallen off a bit anyway Irene since that punter was knifed. Obviously word got around and Vanessa was so traumatised that she left the week after it happened.' Lily admitted. 'I think that Melanie and Joseph would bite your hand off for a job but I'm not sure about Tian. She seems to have a lot of job satisfaction if you know what I mean. I don't know what she gets up to in her room but let's just say that I have to turn my telly up when she is entertaining!'

Irene was laughing when Barry plodded into the room clutching his tatty toy dog. 'Where's Ron?' he innocently enquired when he saw Irene.

Lily couldn't help herself and burst into tears and in that moment Irene took one look at them both and somehow knew. Both women were a good judge of a situation and as Lily noisily blew her nose she looked at Irene and said 'I'm so sorry.'

'Don't be Love, I have come to terms with everything and admit that I am partially to blame. I have never been a swinging from the chandeliers sort of woman and Ron had his needs. I accept that. I also know that I should have been more vocal over the years about my true feelings because he hurt me so badly but my silence made him think that I was ok with him dropping his pants for anyone who took his fancy.'

Lily had always admired Irene but her estimation of her just shot up. It took guts to admit when you were wrong and integrity to take ownership for your faults. 'Thank you Irene, he always adored you, no woman ever came close, and I know that because he was always telling me.'

Irene nodded in the direction of Barry who was happily munching on a packet of crisps.' Did he know about him?'

'No, I never told him.'

Lily's words comforted Irene because if Ron had known then that would have been two children he had not told her about and she had enough hurt to deal with already. Lily had protected her and she was grateful to her for that fact. It can't have been easy bringing up a disabled child as a single mother and Irene respected Lily for keeping the truth to herself. When she got up to leave the women warmly hugged again and as Irene said goodbye to Barry she noticed that his hair colour was the same as his father's. Her husband Ron. She turned to Lily before she reached the door. 'Oh and Lily, I will make sure that Barry is remembered when it comes to Ron's money.'

Lily didn't say anything, she was too choked. Irene McCardle was the most decent woman she had ever met and Ron McCardle had been a very lucky man indeed.

The day of the funeral was bitterly cold and there was a hint of snow in the air. The wake was being held at the Stewart's home which had taken the pressure off Irene. Aunty Maggie and Alan's mother Glenice were quietly moving around the kitchen preparing the food for later when Glenice suddenly said, 'Ron McCardle...'

Maggie was confused. 'What about him?'

'You know.'

'No I don't so you will have to enlighten me.'

'Well he was a fine looking specimen of a man, if I was twenty years younger I would have...'

'You need to get out more and don't let Dolly hear you talking like that.' Maggie was now laughing, glad that the sombre mood had been lifted.

Irene had chosen a smart black jacket and skirt and had accompanied it with a crimson blouse for the funeral. Ron had always insisted that should he croak it, he didn't want everyone wearing black as it would depress him so she had followed his instructions and asked the other mourners to do the same and add a splash of colour to their attire. As she studied herself in the full-length mirror she was satisfied with her reflection. Not bad for a meno-pausal old bird she thought as she applied her lipstick. The last few months had been tough but she was determined to try and put that behind her and remember her husband when she had still been happy with him and before all the resentment had built up.

Ebony Peters had swallowed her pride and had asked Mrs Bad Perm from next door to mind Chantelle and was now debating whether to go to the funeral. In the end she decided she would sit at the back. After all she had been with Ron for years and had loved him once upon a time.

The church was packed to the rafters with family and friends. Ron McCardle had been a well-liked and respected man and some of his contem-poraries had travelled from as far away as Spain to attend the proceedings. As Colin Yates the vicar spoke about Ron there was not a dry eye in the house.

Dolly had wept loudly when the choir boy sang Amazing Grace. She had sung that very song to her son when he was a baby. She was standing next to Alan who held her up and comforted her throughout the service. When it was his turn to say a few words, he wasn't sure if he would be able to speak without breaking down. But he knew he had to try. He spoke about his friend lovingly and told everyone how the man had become a father figure to him. He then read a poem that Connie had written about her Uncle Ron which made everyone smile and weep some more. Alan concluded his reading by saying that Ron had been a legend and would ensure that his name lived on. There was cheering and clapping as Alan made his way back to his place in the front pew.

Ebony watched from the back of the church confident that no one had spotted her. She was wearing a large black floppy hat which partly obscured her face but unfortunately just as she was about to get up and leave, the old biddy next to her had a coughing fit and Irene turned around and spotted her. Ebony could see her old rival was fuming and saw her quickly say something to a big bald bloke who immediately got up and began walking towards her. When Rob Clarke reached her, he grabbed her none too gently by the arm and escorted her outside into the cold December air. 'Mrs McCardle told me to tell you that if you don't leave then she will shove that stupid hat up your skinny arse.'

Ebony got the message and hastily did as she had been asked, knowing full well that she had got away lightly.

The funeral had gone well apart from that stupid bitch turning up. Irene couldn't believe the audacity of her but was confident that no one had noticed her being walked out of the church. The wake was in full swing and she was enjoying hearing all of the old stories about Ron. As the drinks flowed everyone relaxed and began to shake off the sadness of the day and Irene felt that Ron would have approved. She raised her glass and said a silent toast to her husband. He was gone but life went on and so would she.

Part Two

Chapter 27

Summer 1986

Connie Stewart sighed as the video ended. She had watched the film *Officer and a Gentleman* at least five times and loved the main character Zack Mayo who had been played by the hunky actor Richard Gear. Her friend Cath Davis was still drying her eyes. She always sobbed when Gear's character carried his woman off into the sunset. Connie, Cath and Caroline Draper had been born within weeks of each other in 1967 and were now approaching nineteen. Their parents had always been great friends and the girls had remained close over the years. Caroline had even lived with the Stewarts for a few years after her parents Brenda and Geoff had been killed in a car accident in 1982. She was now back home living with her brother Denny on the estate because she always remarked, 'that someone had to make sure that he had clean pants to wear each day.'

'Shall we start getting ready then?' Connie asked switching off the telly.

Caroline looked up from scribbling in her diary. 'Sounds good to me, just let me finish this entry.'

The two other girls laughed. Cath's mother Gina had given them all a diary for Christmas 1977 and they had only written in theirs a handful of times.

Connie now had a posh filo fax which helped her to timetable her life. She had worked for her father since leaving school and had taken over from Lily Jenson overseeing the rentals this year. Lily had retired to Hartlepool to live with her brother. Caroline had enjoyed annotating her days and still did. After her parents had died, her diary had been a life saver because she could pour out all her thoughts onto the pages and this had been therapeutic in the grieving process. Closing the book shut she smiled. 'Connie will you do my makeup please and can I borrow your black lycra dress?'

'Yeah of course you can as long as I can wear your white canvas boots.'

'It's a deal.'

All three girls were pretty but Connie was glamorous. She was an expert with makeup and always wore some even when she was at home. Her brother

Billy used to joke that she wouldn't answer the phone without applying her lipstick first! It was therefore her job to help Cath and Caroline with theirs and she was happy to do so. As the three friends got ready they drank a bottle of wine and discussed the night ahead.

'Soooo are you going to make Wayne a happy bloke tonight?' Connie teased Caroline.

Caroline had been seeing Wayne Stubbs for two months but because they were both shy nothing sexual had happened although Caroline was now eager to change that. Both Connie and Cath had lost their virginity ages ago and she felt a bit left behind. They'd had a little fumble but she didn't feel the need to tell her friends that. Caroline was quite a private person and it was between her and Wayne anyway. 'Mind your own business, Nosey,' she laughed.

The girls were heading to the West End to a club called Hombres. They didn't really like going into the local clubs because Connie's father owned most of them and Caroline's brother Denny ran the one in Tottenham. When they were out they liked to let their hair down without the worry of prying eyes. They giggled as they got ready and sang along to the song Lady in Red by Chris De Burgh which was playing on Connie's stack system, each looking forward to the night ahead.

Sonia Stewart tutted as she heard the music blaring from her daughter's bedroom. Bounding up the stairs she threw open the bedroom door. 'Bloody turn that down before you wake up the dead in Highgate Cemetery.'

Connie stuck her middle finger up at her mother's retreating back. She was getting fed up living at home. Her mother was always miserable and moaning, and Connie was seriously considering moving out.

Sonia silently berated herself now and regretted her outburst. 'Bloody menopause,' she thought as she stomped back into the kitchen. She impatiently started to make a cup of tea and felt the urge to cry. Things had been alright when she had first come home but unfortunately the honeymoon period had not lasted. She felt as if she and Alan had drifted apart and didn't really know when this had happened but it had and she now felt lonely. She missed her mother and her friend Kerry who had also died. Alan was always working and she was worried that his drinking was becoming a problem. When she mentioned it to him he just brushed off her concerns. Her fluctuating moods had not helped either and she realised that her husband had begun to avoid her which she couldn't really blame him for as she didn't like her own company much these days either.

Denny Draper was twenty-seven and still an eligible bachelor. He'd had a string of girlfriends over the years but had never felt the urge to settle down. He was married to his job but he still had a burning desire to make it in the world of villainy as he knew that he would never make a big earn being Mr Sensible. As he sat with his godfather Alan Stewart, he eloquently pitched his idea.

Denny reminded Alan of himself at that age: full of ambition and drive and as he listened to his godson he felt something stirring in him that he hadn't felt in a long time: excitement.

'I'll fund you on one condition that you only get involved with coke and puff and nothing that is mixed with shit.'

'That goes without saying Al. I have a trusted supplier. I've known him for years and he is as sound as a pound. All these yuppie sorts love the magic powder and I have loads of contacts in the city so we'll make a killing.'

Alan nodded. 'I'm in but I'm a sleeping partner, this is your baby and I'll expect you to do all the leg work.'

Denny jumped up and hugged his godfather. His happiness reminded Alan of when he had bought the lad a top notch action man one Christmas.

When Denny left, Alan thought about their conversation. If he was being truthful with himself, he needed this deal as much as Denny did. When his great friend and mentor Ron McCardle had died in 1978 from a stroke, his wife Irene had sold off all the dodgy businesses and made them legal. Alan had been relieved at the time because the run in with the Turks had cost them all dearly. Irene had retired three years ago to Spain with Kenny Latham which had certainly been a topic of gossip for a while. She had been closed lipped about the details of how they had met and Alan hadn't pried as he felt she deserved a fresh start. He had therefore been left to manage everything at home but spoke to Irene regularly on the phone. He had done a great job and was making good money but it had turned into a salary as opposed to an earn. Alan missed the adrenaline of a successful negotiation, he missed the thrill. Somewhere along the line he had lost his zest for life although he was acutely aware that the problems at home hadn't helped. Sonia had loved the new house when she had come home from hospital for Christmas 1978 and, like him, had been full of positivity for the future.

Their lives had never been better until one night when her friend Kerry Watts had appeared in a dreadful state on their doorstep with the news that her husband Sid had been fatally stabbed in Parkhurst. She had stayed with them for a few weeks and had then insisted on going home where she would be looked after by her mother who was moving in with her. Four days later Kerry took her own life, having overdosed on a cocktail of sleeping tablets and vodka. Sonia had been distraught. She had finally found a kindred spirit, a friend who had understood her and now she was gone. She had refused to go back on her tablets and from that day on had lost any sparkle that she had left. Now she was what she called menopausal as well and Alan, like most men, didn't understand that. All he did know was that it was like a beast that couldn't be tamed and his wife was bloody hard work. If she wasn't snapping at her family she was crying. His brother David who was a doctor had given them the name of a woman's hospital in London but she had point blank refused to go. She was adamant that she didn't want to be pumped full of hormones because they were probably full of 'horse shit.' Therefore, home was not a happy place. Aunty Maggie, bless her, tried her best to gee up her niece but even she was losing patience. Alan felt like they were leading separate lives and the knowledge made him sad. Their sex life was non-existent and Sonia had announced one day that her libido had disappeared and it was too uncomfortable 'down there' anyway so he was living like a monk these days.

Sonia's mood was also not helped by the fact that the children didn't need her anymore. Connie was a grown woman who was out gallivanting all the time and Billy was currently serving in the British army. He had joined the Parachute regiment and was in Northern Ireland which didn't help Sonia's already shattered nerves because she now worried about his safety.

As Alan poured himself another drink, he was aware that he was pouring himself rather too many drinks these days. He didn't want to go home yet and wondered whether he should visit the club in Tottenham. Last time he had been there he had got talking to a more mature customer. Rachel was thirty-two, slim with long dark hair. She had reminded Alan of Sonia years before and he had enjoyed talking to her. She was intelligent and worked in a bank. Alan knew that his status as a successful businessman and his shady past meant that he was attractive to women but he had really felt a connection with this one. He had never cheated on his wife and had always loved her but a marriage needed love and intimacy and he wasn't getting that at home and the way things were going probably never would again. Putting his car keys into his pocket he made up his mind. She probably wouldn't be there anyway.

Sonia swore loudly. The dinner she had made was ruined. After she had angrily thrown it into the bin, she sat down and absentmindedly opened one of Maggie's Humbugs.

As she sucked on it she realised that Alan used to always phone her when he was going to be late but just lately he came and went as he pleased. The thought depressed her. She knew she wasn't good company and she worried that he might look elsewhere if she didn't buck up her ideas. As she tidied up the kitchen Maggie came in as cheerful as ever. 'What the hecky pecky is wrong with you? You look as miserable as a wet weekend in Bognor.'

As Sonia poured out her heart to her aunty she was surprised and a tad annoyed when she didn't receive the usual sympathy. 'You need to take a long and hard look at yourself Child,' Maggie stated. 'You're always miserable about something and you are as snappy as a crocodile. We all walk on egg shells and it's exhausting. We've all lost people and half of us will go through the change because we're women. You just have to get through it with a smile on your face.'

Sonia knew that her aunty was speaking the truth and felt ashamed. She looked down at her legs that she hadn't shaved in a week and resolved to do something about her appearance at least. Maggie noticed her staring at her hairy legs and offered to run her a bath and urged her to make herself look nice for her husband who worked so hard for them all.

It was ten o'clock and Alan decided to leave the club and go home when the delectable Rachel tapped him on the shoulder. 'Hi there, have you got time for another?'

Alan knew he should get home but he needed female company tonight. Sonia had probably already gone to bed anyway so he accepted a drink which turned into three. Rachel was great company. She was articulate and listened when he spoke. She knew that he was married but didn't care. When she put a slim, manicured hand on his thigh and suggested a nightcap back at hers he readily agreed and couldn't get there quick enough.

Connie and her friends had danced the night away and were pleasantly tipsy. Caroline had spent most of the night snogging Wayne in a dark corner of the club and Cath had enjoyed getting to know his friend Paul. Connie had stood on the side lines happily watching the unfolding love stories. She was a beautiful girl who got a lot of attention but boys her own age didn't really do it for her. There was only one man for her and he hadn't danced with her since her parent's New Year's Eve party in 1977 when she had been ten years old.

Alan's hands were shaking on the steering wheel as he drove home at midnight towards his home. He had just enjoyed the best sex of his life but now felt grubby. Rachel had certainly been an eye opener. He was almost blushing remembering some of her antics! She was certainly no wall flower when it came to letting herself go! But as much as it had been a much needed respite, Alan wouldn't see her again. He recalled only too well all the trouble that Ron's affair with Ebony had caused and briefly wondered what had become of her.

Rumour had it that she had moved to Scotland of all places. Well he didn't need the aggro of a full blown affair but now he had broken the seal, he would definitely be embarking on some more light relief as he wasn't getting any at home.

Sonia had a bath, washed her hair and even put on a sexy negligee. She felt a mixture of disappointment and relief when Alan hadn't arrived home. She was mildly worried about where he could be but sleep soon beckoned and she drifted off, not hearing him come in.

Alan got undressed and spotted his wife's negligee. As realisation dawned on him, he felt an overwhelming sadness that his marriage had come to this. On the night that he had broken his marriage vows, his wife had decided to end the draught on their sex life. Bloody typical he thought, as he drifted off to sleep. He was soon awake when the phone by their bed rang. It was Connie. Apparently they couldn't get a cab and needed a lift home. Wearily he got dressed again and went to pick up the girls, vaguely aware that he was probably over the drink driving limit.

Chapter 28

Denny Draper was buzzing with excitement. He had just negotiated his first deal and was confident it would put him on the road to riches. Always ambitious, he had eagerly devoured all the stories passed down to him from

Ron McCardle and had been inspired by how both Ron and Alan had climbed up the criminal career ladder and had become respected faces in North London. When Ron's wife Irene had sold off the protection rackets and the sex house Denny had been disappointed. He had just started carving out a name for himself collecting the rents and had been earning a serious good wedge doing so. For the last six years he had been managing the various clubs but was hungry to make it on his own and was thrilled that his god-father Alan had agreed to his new venture. Denny thought that drugs were for mugs but he had done his homework and there were plenty of mugs out there. They were slap bang in the middle of the Yuppie era and many of these city workers consumed cocaine like children ate sweets. There was definitely a market and he was determined to take advantage of that fact. It suited him that Alan had insisted on being a sleeping partner as he wanted to prove himself and build up his credentials. The Turkish mob from Green Lanes headed up by Deniz Mehmet tended to stick to North London and dealt more in heroin whereas Denny was aiming on a more upper class market in West London and the City so he wouldn't be treading on their toes.

He remembered only too well the feud that Ron and Alan had with them six years before and certainly didn't want a repeat. Denny Draper was deter-mined to be the next big face, just as Ron McCardle had been in his time.

Sonia was aware that her husband was being unusually attentive this morning. He had made her breakfast in bed and was now sitting on the corner of their bed chatting to her as she ate it. Tucking into a crisp bit of bacon she was suddenly overwhelmed with a sense of sadness realising that they hadn't spent any real time in each other's company for months. She knew she was partly to blame and hated herself for her moods which she seemed unable to control, so she was touched that he had made an effort.

Alan had woken up with a vivid flashback of Rachel's pert tits and had immediately felt guilty and a little ashamed. He always prided himself that he was a faithful husband and secretly thought that men who cheated were just behaving like born again randy teenage boys, but he now understood how an infidelity could happen. Sonia's moods were out of control and had drained him over the years until he was running on empty. The lack of intimacy was also a big problem that he was now unwilling to overlook. When they had last had sex which was months ago it had been a bitter disappointment. His once eager wife had lain there as stiff as a plank of wood and with about as much enthusiasm as one.

He hadn't bothered to instigate anything since but he was only fifty-three and in his opinion was too young to retire from sex! Thinking of Ron he could now condone his extra marital affairs as Irene hadn't been a keen participant either according to Ron and, although he had adored her, this issue had driven him into the arms of other women. Women were always bleating on about the fact that they needed a man to make them feel special and wanted but what about the needs of the man? It was all double standards as far as Alan was concerned. As he sat on his marital bed it dawned on him that although he felt love for his wife, he would never understand her and was ashamed to admit to himself that he didn't actually like her anymore. The thought made him depressed but it was a fact. Putting on a smile he held out his hand for the empty breakfast plate. 'Blimey Son, you must have been hungry, you gobbled that down sharpish.'

'Well last night's dinner went in the bin.'

Alan wasn't sure if her comment was a dig but chose to ignore it. 'Right I'll take this plate downstairs and then I'm going out as I've got a bit of business.'

Sonia immediately looked up at him in alarm. Since the businesses had been legalised he hadn't used that turn of phrase anymore. He always said he was going to work these days. 'You're not doing anything dodgy are you? I can't live like that anymore Alan. For God's sake look what happened last time, I…'

As she carried on ranting Alan switched off. For nearly seven years Alan had been as straight as a die. He hadn't been involved with anything remotely shady. He had been Mr Boring. Although he had recurring nightmares about the death of Jason Baines, he missed being where the action was. It really annoyed him that his wife was still suspicious as he had gone out of his way to ensure that she had nothing to worry about. He had even turned down lucrative deals which could have made him a lot of money just to keep her happy and she was still miserable. It bloody rankled. He turned to Sonia who was still droning on. 'Drink your tea before it goes cold.' And with that he went downstairs.

Sonia cursed herself, why did she not know when to shut her mouth? Alan had made her a lovely breakfast and she had just ruined his kind gesture. She so wished she still had her great friend Kerry to confide in because they had really understood each other. These days Sonia was feeling detached from her family and knew she was losing control of her thoughts again. Lying back on her pillow she decided to spend the day in bed and try and keep out of her husband's way.

Aunty Maggie was washing up when Alan came into the kitchen. 'Bloody hell you look happy,' she said sarcastically.

Alan sat down at the dinner table and sparked up a cigarette from Maggie's packet of Rothmans.

'As bad as that?' she commented.

Alan had given up smoking years ago but as he inhaled the nicotine deep into his lungs he admitted that he needed the respite. 'I've really tried Maggie but nothing I do or say helps her and I'm fed up with it. I feel completely exhausted with her moods and do you know what? I don't think that I care anymore.'

Aunty Maggie patiently listened and could sympathise with Alan as she also didn't know what to do or how to help. Now that the children were grown and there was no longer any childish laughter running through the house, the place had become soul less. Her niece drifted through the rooms like a lost and tormented spirit. She often didn't even bother to get dressed and her mood swings and depression were hard to live with. Maggie clasped Alan's hand. 'So what are we going to do Child?'

Alan always found it highly amusing that Maggie still referred to them as a child even though they were now middle-aged but he found the term of endearment strangely comforting all the same and he needed comfort. 'I don't know Maggie but what I do know is that I can't live like this.'

Maggie nodded. 'I think she takes after my old grandmother Nora. She was another batty one, always in and out of the nut house. She'd come home and be alright for a few months and then would get carted off again. My grandfather Francis left her in the hospital one day and never picked her up again. She died there when she was only sixty-five. It's an illness. They can't help it. Sonia can't help it.'

Alan sharply pulled away his hand from Maggie's grasp. 'Your story about Nutty Grandmother Nora is not really helping Maggie. I can't live like this anymore.'

'Do you still love her Child?' Maggie asked in a small voice.

A year ago Alan would have answered straight away and said that of course he still loved his wife but his hesitant pause told her all she needed to know. Alan had had enough not because he didn't care but because he didn't know how to make his wife better. He was worn down by her illness just as

Grandfather Francis had been worn down by her grandmother's all those years ago. History was repeating itself and the fact frightened Maggie who had vowed to take care of her sister Breda's family. She felt she had let them down and the knowledge broke her heart.

Alan carried on smoking deep in thought. 'You're right Maggie, she is ill. Losing her mate Kerry has tipped her over the edge. I think she needs to go back into hospital again, it really helped her last time. I'm going to call her doctor this afternoon and get the ball rolling.'

Maggie was saddened but knew that Alan's suggestion was probably their only option.

Connie, Cath and Caroline had decided to stay local and had gone to the club in Tottenham that Alan had inherited in Ron's will.

Connie was sitting at the bar while the other two girls strutted their stuff on the dance floor with Caroline's boyfriend Wayne and his friend Paul, who was trying to get with Cath. As Connie sipped at her Malibu and pineapple she noticed that Denny Draper had suddenly appeared behind the bar. Noticing her he came bounding over with a big grin on his handsome face. 'Hey Titch, how's it going?'

Every time that Connie was in his company she found herself lost for words and feeling all jittery. It annoyed her because as a rule she always had the upper hand when it came to men. Taking a sip of her drink she smiled at him alluringly. 'Will you quit calling me Titch, I'm five foot six and a half now.'

Denny laughed. 'Yeah mustn't forget that HALF an inch, makes all the difference!'

'It certainly does. You should know that every inch counts.' Connie bantered back.

Cheeky cow, Denny thought as he looked her over and really saw her for the first time. She had certainly grown into a beautiful woman with her perfect curvy figure and long dark hair that flowed over her slim shoulders. He was glad she hadn't succumbed to the awful poodle perms that most girls sported. Tonight she was wearing tight black trousers, a boob tube and a black leather jacket with red lapels. As Denny looked at her he wondered why he had never really noticed her beauty before. She dressed and looked different to all the other girls as she wasn't a follower of fashion trends.

Connie Stewart had a style of her own and she had class. 'Cat got your tongue?' she teased fully aware that he was checking her out.

'The cat never gets my tongue, young lady.'

'So I've heard Den.'

Was it his imagination or was she flirting with him, he wondered. He suddenly felt nervous. This was an alien feeling to him due to his success with woman but Connie was different. She was so damned beautiful, almost like an exotic bird with her dark colouring. He liked the fact that she didn't hang off his every word but she was his little sister's best friend and Alan's daughter. He had watched her grow up from a baby so he really didn't want to be feeling like this. As she licked her luscious lips he decided it was time to steer the conversation in another direction and asked where Caroline was. Connie pointed in the direction of the dance floor where Caroline and Wayne were trying to recreate the moves to the final song 'We go together' from the movie *Grease*. Wayne was certainly no Danny Zuko who was the character played by John Travolta in the film. He was a big lad and had the grace of a startled elephant but he was certainly giving it his all. Denny laughed as he watched their antics. 'He's not exactly God's gift but he makes my sister happy. It's good to see her laughing again.'

Connie nodded in agreement. Understandably Caroline had taken the death of her mum and dad Brenda and Geoff badly.

She had come to live with the Stewarts and had spent months in her bedroom listening to her parents' Elvis Presley record collection and writing in her precious diary. Sonia had been brilliant with her and very understanding, telling everyone that she needed time to grieve as losing someone you loved was the worst thing to happen to a person. When Caroline had finally emerged from the sanctity of her room she had destroyed all the records saying that they bought back too many memories. Connie had been thrilled when her friend had met Wayne. He seemed kind and gentle and she knew that he would look after Caroline. As she watched them kissing, she smiled. Wayne may not be the best looking bloke on the planet but he had made Caroline smile again and for that reason alone Connie would always be grateful to him. She was a bit disappointed when she saw Denny checking the time on his watch. 'You got to be somewhere?' she asked trying to sound nonchalant.

'Yeah got a bit of business going down and need to meet someone in a bit.'

Connie was relieved that he hadn't mentioned he had to meet a girl but still felt deflated when he made his excuses and left. What she didn't know was that he had felt the exact same as he had walked away from her.

When the slow music started, or the Erection Section as it was lovingly referred to, Connie was just about to go to the toilet when a dark-haired guy about her age tapped her on the shoulder and asked her if she would like to dance.

Connie subtly looked him up and down and was pleasantly pleased with what she saw. He was smartly dressed in beige jumbo cords and a black Fred Perry polo shirt. He had lovely dark brown wavy hair worn in a buzz cut (Connie wouldn't be seen dead with anyone who favoured a curtains hairstyle). When he smiled at her she saw that he had nice straight teeth and his eyes were a sparkling hazel. He was a seven out of ten, so she accepted his invitation. It would distract her mind from images of Denny Draper if nothing else. As they got onto the dance floor Cath looked at her in mock surprise as Connie had high standards where men were concerned and hardly ever spoke to the men who frequented this place, let alone danced with them.

Soon the dance floor was filled with couples swaying to the soulful tones of Marvin Gaye. Girls were dreamily wondering if they had found love whilst most of the boys were drunkenly hoping they would get lucky and end up with a shag. As Connie's partner pulled her closer she was impressed that he could actually dance and hadn't trodden on her feet once. He had rhythm which was unusual for men in her opinion. She smirked as she remembered the expression about men being good in bed if they could dance and decided that she was due a sexual interlude. When the record ended, the lights went on and people started leaving to get their coats. Cath, Caroline, Wayne and Paul were going to a burger restaurant in Muswell Hill. 'Are you coming with us Connie?' Cath asked. Before Connie could answer Caroline was all questions. 'And who was THAT and what's his name?' she enquired.

'In answer to your questions, no I am not coming for a burger and I don't know his name. He is just a random who asked me for a dance.'

'Aaaw well, good for you, I'll call you tomorrow,' Cath said kissing Connie goodbye.

As her friends walked away Connie felt annoyed that everyone always made a big deal if she pulled. In a way she could understand it because she rarely gave guys the time of day but it still frustrated her. Her love life was very much private and if she ever bagged Denny Draper it would have to stay that way as she wasn't sure how Caroline, her best friend, would react to her dating her brother. She walked through to the foyer and was just about to leave the club when she felt a tap on her shoulder. It was the guy from earlier. 'Hey do you fancy getting a bite to eat?' he asked.

Connie liked the fact that he didn't sound too keen and was even more impressed that he was still appealing on the eye in the lit up foyer. 'Yeah I'm a bit peckish as it goes.'

He smiled and held out his right hand. 'Great, pleased to meet you properly, what's your name?'

'Connie, Connie Stewart.'

'Nice name and makes a change from all the Traceys and Sharons that I usually meet,' he laughed. 'My name's Peter, Peter Baines, now let's go and get some food.'

When Connie finally got home and went to bed that night she had a smile on her face. They had gone to an all-night café in Bethnal Green and feasted on a massive fry up before he drove her home. He was great company: funny, articulate and surprisingly candid about his life. He admitted that he had grown up in care and had lost touch with all his family. His father was dead but he had no idea what had happened to his mother, brother and sisters. Connie had listened, feeling grateful that although her mother was a bit of a fruit loop at least she herself was loved and cared for. She respected the fact that Peter had made his own way in life. Apparently he was a trainee accountant and had a rented flat in Palmers Green. When he kissed her goodnight she had eagerly responded and had decided she would like to see him again.

Chapter 29

The next morning Alan was on the phone speaking to his wife's doctor at the hospital in Surrey when she came into the room, gently took the receiver from him and ended the call. 'Sit down Al, we need to talk.'

They both settled themselves into the winged armchairs facing each other and Sonia spoke. 'I am not going back to hospital. I know that I've been a pain in the arse lately but I'm not crazy, not like I was when Mum died. I'll admit that I am depressed though.'

Alan looked at her properly for the first time in months. The weight had dropped off her and her eyes looked lifeless but they still held a determined glint that told him that maybe she was in control. In his heart he knew she was just unhappy but that thought was almost worse, because he felt that it was his fault and didn't know how to put it right. 'I can't live like this anymore Son, you're miserable all the time, we're all walking on egg shells and you suck the joy out of everything.'

Sonia was hurt by his words but knew he was right. She was unhappy and had been for years. 'When we lost Baby George I thought that I would never recover. I was so young and didn't know what to do with my grief and that got worse when Declan died so soon afterwards. But we had the twins and I could look forward again. When you started working for Ron I had no idea who he was and you certainly didn't enlighten me. I just thought he had given you a decent job with a secure wage and was grateful that we could get off the estate. But I'm not stupid Al, even I realised early on that Ron McCardle was dodgy and had his fingers in lots of illegal pies. That's when the worry started. I was terrified that I would end up as a single mum bringing our children to the Scrubs to visit their father every month. That's when your brother started giving me pills. I didn't even ask what they were, I was just grateful for a decent night's sleep. Then when Stevie Baines died I realised that you were involved in violence. Oh, I know that the story is that he died from an asthma attack but you and I know full well that there was more to it. I was in such a mental state that David started giving me tranquilisers and for the next few years I was walking around half alive. Thank God that I had Mum to help with the kids and then she died.'

Sonia was now crying, Breda had meant the world to her. Blowing her nose she continued baring her soul. 'I never fully believed that her death didn't have something to do with all that bother with the Turks, but once again you tried to convince me otherwise so I have shouldered the guilt for years that YOUR lifestyle killed my beautiful mother. My mate Kerry understood me completely because she had lived with the same fears. Neither of us were mad. We were just two housewives who had a life of crime and its consequences thrown at us. Kerry topped herself because she couldn't cope with the fact that Sid was murdered by a rival gang member in prison. This lifestyle may bring wealth but it also brings heartache and death and I want no part of it anymore.'

Kerry's death had been the final nail in the coffin as far as Sonia was concerned. She felt angry and after months of thinking and playing it out in her mind, she had made a decision. 'I want to leave Alan. I do love you but I don't always respect your choices. We've lost that connection that always held us together and when I look at you all I see is what I've lost: my mother, all the years wasted worrying and at times, I'll admit, my sanity.'

Alan was thrown because although his wife spoke the truth, he hadn't expected this. 'What do you mean that you want to leave? I can't go anywhere, I need to be here, what with Irene being in Spain.'

Sonia looked him in the eye and took a deep breath. 'I want to leave you Alan. I need a simple life which is drama free. I want to live by the sea. Even you must see that our marriage has died?'

Alan felt his eyes well up because at that moment he realised he did still love her. 'But I love you, I always have. I don't want you to go.'

Sonia felt sorry for him. She had loved him almost all her life, ever since he had been so kind to her at Bethnal Green air raid shelter back in 1941.

He was as much a part of her as her arms and legs were but she knew that their marriage couldn't limp along in a haze of misery any longer.

As Alan started to cry, she got up from her chair and went to him, embracing him tightly.

'Where will you go?' he sobbed.

'I have rented a small cottage in Cornwall in a place called Carbis Bay. I leave tomorrow with Aunty Maggie.'

Alan pulled away from her. 'You've got it all planned out then?' he said bitterly. 'What about the kids?'

Sonia laughed. 'Billy is away with the army and Connie is never here. They are all grown up now. They don't need me anymore. I have already spoken to Billy and he understands my decision. I will talk to Connie later.'

'But Son, surely we can work things out?'

Alan was fast realising that he didn't want to lose her, he loved her but he also knew he was clutching at straws.

'My mind was made up when I found a condom wrapper in your trouser pocket and when I heard you talking to Denny on the phone about a drugs deal.'

Alan opened his mouth to protest but Sonia held up her hand. 'I admit I was hurt when I realised that you had been playing away but I knew that you would never have gone anywhere else if things had been ok between us. I admit that I have let that side of things slide and the bloody menopause hasn't helped but I knew then that we were over.'

'I'm so sorry Son, I was just so lonely.'

'As I have been for years Alan. I'm not angry. I am more upset about what

I heard you talking about on the phone to Denny and the fact that you are clearly being sucked in again to a life of crime. I can't live that life anymore and I am saddened that Denny is now a part of it. Geoff and Brenda would be turning in their graves if they knew.'

Alan tried to find the words to dissuade his wife but was unable to do so. He had always known in his heart that she wasn't cut out to be a villain's wife. She was too decent and straight. He had tried to ignore her suffering over the years and blame it on everything other than his chosen career path but he now had to admit defeat. She wanted no part of this life while he was tired of being Mr Straight. They were on different pages. Denny Draper's drug deal had got his adrenaline pumping again. Admittedly, he had been relieved when Irene had made the businesses legal after Ron had died but he had become increasingly bored as the years had passed.

'I'm going to really miss you Son.'

Sonia gently kissed him on the lips and they both cried.

Connie was sat on her bed thinking. Her mother had just informed her that she was leaving and had explained why. She had said that Connie was old enough to be told the truth (although Sonia had been economical about the violence and had left out names). Connie was grateful that her mother was treating her as an adult. Growing up she had known that her mother was fragile. Nanny Breda had always said that Mummy was having a sad day when she took to her bed or when she had appeared spaced out. Connie and her brother Billy had always accepted the explanation but had never really had any real comprehension of the situation. Now she did and although it made her sad, she was glad for her mother who would at last find some peace and quiet. Personally she did think that Sonia worried too much. Connie herself would only marry a man who could provide her with the wealth that she had become accustomed to and she didn't really care how that wealth was achieved, but her mother was different and she loved her. They had hugged and cried and as she had helped her mother to pack she had secretly felt that life would be easier for them all now as the tension would be gone from the house. She was busily painting her toenails, excited for the evening ahead. Peter Baines was taking her for a meal in Soho and then they were going clubbing. She was amazed that he had been on her mind constantly since they had met, as usually men only held her attention for a few days. But they had enjoyed some long telephone conversations and Connie really enjoyed his banter. He was intelligent, witty and pleasing on the eye and she hadn't thought of her major crush Denny Draper all week. She was enjoying being with a man for the first time in her life and it felt good.

The next morning dawned bright and warm. Sonia and Maggie had packed and were ready to leave. Alan had kindly arranged for a car to take them to their new lives in Cornwall. As he hovered next to their suitcases in the hallway, he looked at his wife and thought that she looked better than she had in months. She was wearing a white cotton summer dress covered in red poppies, her hair had been freshly washed and she had put it in a smart up do. Alan was overwhelmed with a feeling of loss and sadness and wondered if this was the same feeling his wife had experienced over the years. If it was then he could understand why she wanted to get away from it, because it was suffocating him. When the driver had taken the last of the suitcases to the car and Maggie had discreetly followed him, Sonia turned to her husband. 'Goodbye Alan, I wish you well. I only have one request and that is keep an eye on Connie. She is more like you than you realise with her ambitions and wanting. Please don't let her get too involved.'

Alan simply nodded. He was too choked to speak. They hugged and then she was gone. Alan felt his heart had been torn out and cried as he sat at the kitchen table with a large glass of Scotch in front of him. The walls of the kitchen seemed to close in on him and he felt like a lifeboat without a paddle. His world had just become smaller and loneliness engulfed him as he drank his drink and wondered at a future without his soul mate by his side.

Connie was in Peter's bed and stretched lazily as she ran though in her mind the events of last night. They had enjoyed a delicious meal at a little Italian restaurant near Soho Square and had then danced until two in the morning at a local club. Even though it was just the two of them they had both thoroughly enjoyed each other's company and had laughed into the small hours. Peter was a gentleman and it had been Connie who had instigated going back to his flat. When they had arrived she had literally pounced on him and their love making had been everything she had hoped it would be. The first time was frantic but they had taken their time after that savouring getting to know each other's bodies. Peter shared Connie's adventurous spirit in bed and they were both surprised at how well they fitted together sexually. Connie felt like the cat who had got the cream. She genuinely liked Peter and couldn't wait until he returned home with their breakfast because she was up for another round if he was!

Sonia felt a sense of peace and calm as the car left the busy London streets and the scenery changed to the lush colours of the countryside. As her Aunty Maggie dozed beside her, with her little dog Winston on her lap, Sonia felt for the first time in years that a huge weight had been lifted from her shoulders and that she had some control of her life. She lit a cigarette and smiled, excited for her future that didn't involve crime and pain.

Denny Draper had had a very productive meet with his trusted supplier Wesley Pritchard, who lived in South London. He was now pulling into Crouch Hall Road to keep Alan up to speed on the progress of the deal when he spotted Connie waving at a bloke in a Saab. She was still wearing her going out clothes so clearly hadn't been home and if the smile on her face was anything to go by he could just imagine what she had been up to. He was surprised to realise that he felt gutted at the thought of her being with another man. He waited until she had gone into the house and the Saab had driven off, then wearily got out of his own car and went to knock on the door.

Alan greeted him half-heartedly and Denny was shocked at the man's appearance. He was normally dressed immaculately but although it was nearly midday he was still in his pyjamas, needed a shave and had been drinking. Denny immediately realised that Sonia had left and that his godfather must be taking it badly. 'Come on Mate, let's make you a cuppa and we can have a chat.'

Denny settled him in the Victorian conservatory and went into the kitchen where he observed an empty bottle of Scotch. Sighing, he put the kettle on and hoped that Alan wasn't going to fall apart just as his new venture was taking off, because although his godfather was a silent partner he still needed to have his wits about him.

Alan sat and gazed out into the garden. He had a beautiful home but it meant nothing now that he didn't have anyone to enjoy it with anymore. He had only wanted to provide a good life for his family but in doing so he had pushed his wife to her limits. Billy was away on tour with the army and although Connie worked for him she was out and about all the time with her new man. Alan had never felt so alone. He even missed Aunty Maggie and her little dog Winston padding around the house. Aunty Maggie, like her sister Breda, had held them together and now he was alone in a six bed-roomed house with no one to fill the rooms. Maybe he would ask his mother

Glenice to move in. She lived locally anyway and had only been complaining the other day about the fact that her street had gone downhill and that she was wary about going out at night. When Denny brought in the tea he mustered a smile knowing that he had to pull himself together. 'Sorry Den, bad day. Sonia has gone and I'm feeling sorry for myself.'

Denny was alarmed when the older man started to cry and feeling embarrassed didn't really know what to do. Putting down his mug of tea he grasped Alan's hand. 'It will be ok Al. You have to keep moving forward. Life changes and you have to change with it. Maybe give Sonia a few weeks and then go and see her?'

'No Den, she made it perfectly clear, she has never been able to cope with this life and all the worry. She's had enough and I don't really blame her. I have been realising lately that this life is where I fit. She doesn't, so she's made the right decision. We were making each other miserable but I'll tell you one thing, I will always love the bones of that woman.'

Denny nodded, silently agreeing. Anyone with half a brain could see that Sonia had struggled over the years. He had often heard his parents commenting on it. Hopefully this drugs deal would distract Alan and give him a new lease of life because Denny was raring to go!

Chapter 30

Three Months Later

Ebony Peters woke up to her daughter Chantelle roughly pulling on the sleeve of her blouse. 'What is it?' she hissed impatiently.

'I'm hungry, I want some crisps,' her daughter whined.

Ebony sighed. She loved the child in her own way but there was no escaping the fact that she was a spoilt brat with no manners and Ebony secretly knew that this was her fault. She was never going to win a mother of the year award anytime soon.

Ebony reflected on the last few years with a frown on her attractive face. After Ron had keeled over and died in 1978 her daughter's real father had promised her that he would take care of them both but only on the condition that they move out of the country. He had told her about a villa he owned in Turkey. He had purchased it for a song from a man with a gambling problem and an accumulation of debts owed to Kadir thanks to his addiction to cocaine. The man had been only too happy at the time to hand over the keys to his beautiful villa because being homeless seemed more preferable to owing a Mehmet family member any money.

Kadir had gladly done the deal keeping the transaction a secret from his overbearing family which was just as well, as it was the perfect place to hide away his second family. His father had vowed to look after the daughter and granddaughter of his deceased lifelong friend Gary Peters but the child, even as a baby, had resembled what she was: a Turkish baby and that was worrying as she also looked like his other children, especially his youngest boy Jem. Kadir told his father that he had found Ebony and her child a home in Scotland and that he would deal with sending them the money that Deniz Mehmet generously provided each month. Deniz had been a bit surprised that Ebony wanted to move so far away but had understood a change would do her good and he hadn't seen her since.

At first the arrangement worked. Ebony had loved the villa with its white-washed walls and kidney-shaped swimming pool. She had handed over her parental duties to a local woman who had loved Chantelle as she did her other four children and Ebony had spent her days sunbathing and shopping. Kadir had dutifully visited twice a month but just recently his trips to see them had dwindled. He told her that his father had had a heart attack and that he had to step up and take over running the businesses. Ebony was not impressed but Kadir had told her that they were having some trouble with a firm from Brixton who were trying to muscle in on their territory.

The last time he had visited had been eight weeks before and she hadn't heard from him since. More alarmingly, the money that had been wired once a month for the last seven years had stopped. One day Ebony had been sitting by the pool worrying where their next meal was coming from and even the cute young man with the tight arse who came in to attend to the pool couldn't distract her fears. She had known for a long time that Kadir had been growing bored. He loved his daughter but she couldn't compete with the love that he had for his children who lived in the United Kingdom and especially not with his new daughter who his wife Layla had given birth to last year. Ebony was feeling lonely, worried and extremely annoyed. She had toyed with the idea of telephoning Deniz but how could she do that when she hadn't spoken to the man in years? No, what she needed was a miracle, and as she applied sun tan cream the woman who looked after Chantelle ran out of the house and handed her a telegram from England. It was from a firm of solicitors in Highgate. When she phoned them and they explained the situation she let out a whoop of relief. Her prayers had been answered and her saviour had come from a very unlikely source. Her old Aunty Pat. A well-spoken male voice had informed her that her aunt had died six months previously and had left her a two bed-roomed flat in Islington and some cash. It wasn't a fortune but it would help Ebony to be able to relocate back to England and the cash would tide her over.

Pat had been a drunk and had shamefully neglected her niece when she had been her guardian growing up but she'd come good in the end, Ebony thought as she hurriedly booked two fights back to good old Blighty.

As Chantelle munched happily on her crisps and drank her cola, Ebony surveyed her and felt a touch of pride. She really was a good looking child with her thick black hair, bright green eyes and olive skin. She felt confident they would make a new life for themselves. She was sick of hiding away in a foreign country and wanted to confront Kadir and find out what the hell was going on. She knew he would be angry that she had come back to England but that was tough shit, he owed her an explanation and she was determined to get one.

Two hours later the captain announced over the tannoy that they would be landing soon. It couldn't come quick enough for Ebony. She had been seriously annoyed that they had flown economy and the old man next to her stunk of garlic and had snored for the entire journey. Her mood was made worse when Chantelle had spilt cola all over her white blouse and then had the audacity to scream the place down and demand another drink. When they were able to disembark Ebony had dragged the child off of the plane and marched her through the airport like a woman on a mission.

Alan woke with a throbbing head and a desperate need to pee. He'd had a bad week feeling sorry for himself and wondered if he had depression. He couldn't be bothered to wash or change his clothes and was drinking too much. Sonia, it seemed though, was thoroughly enjoying her new life in Cornwall and had taken up painting and pottery. She phoned him once a week and as she had prattled on about her new hobbies and about how happy she was, he had felt the urge to tell her to piss off but hadn't. He was only grateful that they were still friends and that she hadn't mentioned anything about divorce again. When he had enquired about Aunty Maggie Sonia had laughed as she told him that her aunt had a man friend called Malcolm and that she had even given up smoking as she wanted to keep her breath fresh 'just in case!' Alan had wondered how he would feel if Sonia got a 'man friend' and knew it would kill him but he had to put those thoughts to the back of his mind. He was just about to shut his eyes again when his mother Glenice bustled in. He was aware that she wrinkled up her nose as she opened up the heavy curtains.

'It smells like a tramp's armpit in here. Now get yourself up and washed. There's a fry up waiting for you downstairs,' she told him.

Alan groaned. His stomach was doing somersaults after coping with a bottle of Scotch last night and a fry up was the last thing it needed. But despite that he was grateful that Glenice had moved in and taken over the running of the house as he wasn't up to it and he would rather have her doing it than a stranger. He was glad of the company as well. Glenice had been thrilled to leave her own home and live in this beautiful house. She happily divided her time between her sons' homes and after years of being on her own was pleased to feel that she was needed again, even if she was worried about her eldest son and his drinking. She was busily picking up his dirty pants and socks that lay discarded on the carpet when Alan spoke to her in a croaky voice. 'Thanks Mum, I really appreciate it. What are you up to today?'

'Well after I have done the laundry, I'm going to the hairdressers. Samantha said that she is going to do my hair the same as Lady Diana's.'

Samantha was Alan's brother David's daughter and she worked in a local salon. The poor girl was always being asked by her Nan to copy a celebrity's hair style and had confided to her uncle that it wasn't always an easy task. Only last month Glenice had insisted on a hair do like the character Frenchy from the film *Grease* but unfortunately she had ended up looking more like Emily Bishop from *Coronation Street*! They all had a good laugh and Glenice had good naturedly berated her granddaughter for making her look like a grandmother. Sometimes Alan thought that his mother didn't realise how old she was, or maybe she did and chose to ignore it. Good on her, he thought as he slowly lifted his throbbing head off of his pillow.

'I'm going to see Dolly later, I know she appreciates all my hair dos,' Glenice winked.

Dolly McCardle was Ron's mum, and she and Glenice had been friends for years. She was eighty-five now and had never really gotten over the death of her only son. Her health had gone downhill and two years ago it had become evident that she had sadly developed dementia. Glenice had dutifully done what she could to look after her, but even she had admitted defeat when Dolly had been found wondering down her street in her nighty. She had been knocking on her neighbours' front doors aggressively asking them if they had kidnapped her son. She now lived in a plush nursing home in Hampstead and Glenice went to see her weekly, often smuggling in a bottle of spirits in her shopping bag.

Alan had loved Ron like a father and he and Dolly had become family. Alan suddenly felt nostalgic, wishing for the old days. 'How is the old girl?'

'Ruling the roost, she even set up an illegal card game one Thursday night, invited everyone then forgot to show up! It's sad though Al, watching someone's mind become like cotton wool. Sometimes she is the old Dolly, laughing, joking and regaling the residents with stories and other days she sits there like a mute, dribbling into her tea. It's a cruel disease. It makes you appreciate life.'

Alan knew this was a subtle dig at him and the way he was behaving. He decided to knock the booze on the head. He knew that Denny was worried about the new business. He relied on Alan's experience and wisdom and at the moment he was being as helpful as tits on a bull!

As Glenice was about to levae the bedroom, she turned and reminded her son that Connie was bringing her new boyfriend to meet him today. 'I've made a Dundee cake that is in the cake tin next to the tea caddy.'

Alan did a thumbs up. He had forgotten about Connie bringing her bloke home but was curious as to who could have wiggled their way into his daughter's heart as this was definitely a first. He had been fully aware over the years about her crush on Denny Draper because although she thought that she had hidden her adoration, she had always gone all soppy when his godson was around. Although Alan adored Denny like a son, he didn't really want his daughter caught up in his life especially as he was becoming a bit of a face. Alan knew only too well the strain that it put on the wives and he didn't want that life for his daughter. Apparently this Peter was a regular guy. An accountant or something so hopefully this relationship would prosper and his daughter would lead a normal life just like her mother had yearned for. A little voice inside his head reminded him that Connie was just like him, she wanted wealth. She knew what her father had been and it didn't faze her. Billy however, had no interest.

Alan felt the love from his son but had a sneaking suspicion that the boy didn't respect him and his choices. The thought saddened him but he was proud that Billy had chosen such an admired career path as a soldier and he respected his boy's determination to protect his country.

As Denny Draper pumped away on top of his new girlfriend Nikki, it was Connie Stewart's face that he saw as he shot his load. When her boyfriend rolled off her on to his back she smiled at him adoringly. 'That was amazing Den.'

Denny simply nodded and got up to go to the bathroom. He felt like an arse hole because Nikki was a lovely girl. She had it all: intelligence, a gorgeous face and a cracking pair of tits, but she wasn't Connie and there lay the problem. He knew that Nikki was in love with him but the feeling just wasn't mutual because ever since Connie had taken up with her new boyfriend Denny couldn't stop thinking and fantasising about her. She was the first person he thought of when he woke up in the morning and the last person he thought about before he shut his eyes at night. He was annoyed with himself because he had never felt jealousy in his life and he didn't like the feeling one little bit. He was jealous. He wanted Connie Stewart more than he had ever wanted any woman.

Ebony and Chantelle had finally arrived at their new home. As they entered, their nostrils were assailed by a smell like rotting cabbage. Chantelle wrinkled up her cute button nose and said in disgust, 'It stinks.'

Ebony agreed with her daughter and entering the front room they took in the untidiness of the place. There were old magazines strewn everywhere, empty vodka bottles on every surface and the carpet was filthy and sticky through years of spilt drink. Ebony plastered on a false smile and opened the dirty curtains. The solicitor had advised her that the money would be in her account tomorrow and when it arrived she was going to hire a Mrs Mop to come and clean the place. Unfortunately, until then they would have to brave this dump. The thought appalled her but she had no choice, so she did something that she hadn't done ever in her adult life. She rolled up her sleeves and began cleaning. It didn't escape her notice that her daughter was looking at her in awe and it annoyed her. 'Well aren't you going to help me?' she snapped.

Chantelle hesitated but decided it might be fun to play a cleaning game with her mummy because it wasn't often that she played with her.

Alan had made an effort to tidy himself up, ready to meet his daughter's boyfriend because he knew how much it meant to her. He had cheered up after receiving a phone call from Billy who told him that he would be home on leave in a few weeks' time. Alan was thrilled at the news because he hadn't seen his boy in nearly a year and couldn't wait to spend some time with him. As he was putting out the cups and saucers on the dining room table he heard Connie come in. She bowled into the room. He had never seen her looking so beautiful.

She was glowing with happiness. He looked at the young man next to her and took in his smart clothes and genuine smile and decided that he liked the look of him. Holding out his hand he was impressed that the boy had a tight grip as he returned the handshake. Ron had always warned him to be careful of men with a limp handshake but this boy oozed an understated confidence so he immediately felt at ease with him. 'Pleased to meet you, I'm Connie's old Dad.'

The boy grinned. 'I'm Peter, Peter Baines and it's great to meet you at last.'

Alan felt the colour drain from his face and as he looked at the boy, the resemblance was staring him in the face. The same build, the same eyes and the same bloody surname. But he couldn't be sure. He discreetly asked some questions, as any dad would, about his daughter's boyfriend's family and upon hearing the answers he had no doubt in his mind. The nightmares had only recently stopped. The nightmares of his old friend lying dead in the boot of a car, the nightmares where a young lad lay on a dirty floor dying as the blood seeped out of him. Dying because he had murdered him as revenge for Breda. Pouring a large measure of Scotch he inwardly cried, all thoughts of giving up the booze forgotten because Stevie and Jason Baines had just come back to haunt him and as he looked at his daughter's radiant face he knew he could never tell her. He would have to live with his demons in silence.

Chapter 31

December 1986

No one was more surprised than Connie that her relationship with Peter was flourishing and as they decorated the Christmas tree in the Victorian conservatory she sighed with happiness. Her mother had always loved

Christmas and that had rubbed off on herself and Billy. As she thought of her twin she sighed. He had come home a few months before on leave and hadn't enjoyed being dragged around numerous pubs with their father whose sole purpose these days was to drink morning, noon and night. He was coming home in a state and she and her Nanny Glenice had put him to bed more than once. Billy had confided in her that they had gone to one pub and a shady character had approached Alan to discuss 'the drugs.' Billy had realised there and then that his father was involved in something that he wanted no part of and had made his excuses and cut his leave short. Connie herself had been surprised but was more concerned that he was using the businesses that were now legal to launder the proceeds of drugs deals. Alan had always been a careful businessman with integrity, but he was acting like a fool because if Connie was right then he was also using the businesses in Irene McCardle's name and she would blow a fuse when she found out.

Irene had entrusted Alan to look after her investments and the way he was going he was going to end up in with a capture! Connie knew that he had taken the departure of her mother badly but there was something else which wasn't right with him. He had always been a man who had been in control but his drinking was escalating. He was clearly having blackouts and for a man who had always prided himself on his appearance, he now looked shabby and unkempt. She had also heard him calling out in his sleep and knew her Nanny Glenice was also worried.

Connie had been managing the rental properties for a while but now found herself having to check in on the clubs, restaurants and car dealership as she no longer felt her father was capable of managing them. It meant she was always chasing her tail but she had risen to the challenge. She knew that Irene was grateful. Irene had been sympathetic when Connie had explained that her father had had a bit of a breakdown due to Sonia leaving but in this life men had to be strong and Irene was already beginning to ask awkward questions.

Alan could hear Connie and the boy as he thought of Peter laughing and joking in the back of the house. As he sipped his Scotch, he closed his eyes as he felt like crying again. Feeling guilty about so many things was tearing him apart. He couldn't sleep or eat very much and he knew that he looked like a pile of shit but couldn't muster the strength to do anything about it. Every time the boy was in the house all he saw was his dead brother Jason.

Alan had never felt comfortable having his death on his conscience. He had pushed it to the back of his mind and had finally felt his unease disappearing, but his own daughter had unknowingly brought it all back to haunt him again. He was sure that Peter didn't have a clue about what had happened to his family but he was so like Jason that Alan was reminded about the callous murder every time that he saw him. The guilt was crippling him. He could only just about function with a drink inside him to numb the pain. It was ironic really, because in all the years that Sonia had been bad with her nerves, it had irritated him in the end and he was now acutely aware that his family felt the same about him. He had been mortified when Billy had cut short his leave and could have cheerfully strung up Dexter Bryant for approaching him in the pub, even though he knew it was his fault for not being on his guard. Knocking back his drink he reached for the half empty bottle hoping that if he drank enough, he would be able to sleep.

Ebony Peters was looking at her bank statement in disgust. The money left to her in Aunty Pat's will was almost gone and she had no alternative but to contact her daughter's father Kadir Mehmet. When she had come home to England a few months before, she had decided to get settled and live off her inheritance while deciding what her next move would be. Unfortunately the sum of money had only been a modest amount and Ebony, who had never been savvy with money, had spent the bulk of it decorating the flat and buying top of the range furniture.

Consequently, she now lived in a beautiful home but hardly had any money in her designer purse so she would have to go cap in hand to Kadir. He owed her anyway, she reasoned as she picked up the telephone.

Emine Mehmet shuffled towards the hallway when she heard the phone ringing. Her lumbago was playing her up and her heart was heavy with sadness so she didn't really want to speak to anyone but was pleased to hear the familiar voice at the other end of the line. 'Ebony it's so good to hear from you, it's been too long!'

'Hi Emine, I've just got back from Scotland. How are you all? I'm living in London again.'

Ebony heard a muffled sob as Deniz Mehmet's wife replied. 'Oh Ebony, my heart is broken my darling husband had another heart attack three weeks ago and died. I am going to live with my sister in Turkey after Christmas.'

Ebony felt a moment's sorrow but needed to find out about Kadir. 'I am so sorry to hear about that, Deniz was always good to me and my dad.'

'He loved your father like a brother Darling, I don't know how I am going to live without him.'

'Oh I'm sure the boys will look after you, how are they all?'

As Emine started to sob, Ebony knew that the next piece of news was not what she was going to want to hear and she was right.

'My Kadir was killed six weeks ago. Some low life stabbed him. His father died of a broken heart.'

As Ebony digested what she was being told, she felt her legs buckle and slumped onto her new Habitat sofa. Emine explained that the whole family were in mourning and would be following her to Turkey once the businesses were sold.

When Ebony politely ended the call, she realised with horror that she would have to get a job which was something she had never had to do before.

Denny Draper was having a good day. His finances were growing and he had just had a Christmas drink with the Barker brothers, Frankie and Graham, who were drugs barons from South West London. Although Denny knew that the invitation had been an excuse to sound out his intentions, he had been treated with respect and gratitude when he had informed them that he wouldn't be treading on their toes. He was doing nicely supplying to West London and the City and they had agreed he could take over North London now that the Mehmets seemed to be out of the picture. Frankie and Graham had other fish to fry in East London so everyone was happy that they knew where each other stood. The meeting had been a success.

Denny was singing along to Bing Crosby's White Christmas very badly as he headed towards Crouch End. Connie had contacted him saying she needed to have a chat with him. Denny felt sure it was about her father's behaviour and he would have to tread carefully. He loved his godfather and would always be loyal to him but he too was getting seriously concerned. Alan had invested in the business and had promised he would only be a silent partner which had suited Denny, but now he was becoming a bit of a liability shouting his mouth off and even had people approaching him in pubs asking to score! Denny had wanted transactions to be discreet for obvious reasons. He had people on the street to take care of the selling. He certainly didn't need a drunk middle-aged man walking around with drugs in his pocket ready to sell to the highest bidder! Denny had known for a while that he was going to have to have words with Alan so he would pacify Connie and assure her he would sort it.

Peter had been gone an hour and Connie was getting ready for her Christmas night out with Caroline and Cath when the doorbell rang. Running down the stairs with her towel wrapped tightly around her, she opened the front door and as she looked at Denny Draper she saw him blatantly give her the once over. She suddenly felt vulnerable standing before him in just a towel, all thoughts of Peter suddenly gone. She took in the manliness of him and inwardly shuddered.

'Well hello you,' Denny said saucily.

Connie regained her composure and ushered him in. 'Put your tongue away.'

'I can think of better places for it!'

'Oh shut up and come into the front room, I'll just run upstairs and put some clothes on.'

'I'd rather you didn't, you look positively delicious in that towel,' Denny leered, putting on a posh voice.

The flirting had gone up a gear since Connie had last seen him and it unnerved her because she was happy with Peter or she thought she was until she clapped eyes on the man whom she'd had a crush on since she was ten years old.

'And how is your girlfriend, Nikki, isn't it?'

'Stop trying to change the subject.'

Connie laughed as she left him sitting on his own and went up to her bedroom to change. When she sat on her bed to pull on some socks she saw a note from Peter saying 'Love you Baby.' Usually the little notes he left her to find made her happy but she was confused. Today, it made her feel unsure and troubled. Damn bloody Denny Draper and his wondering groin she thought as she hurriedly pulled on a track suit.

When she went back downstairs Denny was in the kitchen making a pot of tea and munching on one of Glenice's mince pies.

'One sugar, isn't it?'

Connie felt more comfortable now she had some clothes on and sat down at the kitchen table. She had checked in on Alan and he was sound asleep sprawled on his bed.

'Denny, I am worried about Dad. Something is really bothering him and I don't think it is just Mum going. He has these nightmares and shouts out in the night. I went in to him last week and he was tossing and turning and calling out the words "no" and "sorry". Do you know what is wrong? And don't bullshit me.'

Denny sat opposite her and spoke softly. 'I really don't know Connie. But what I do know is that the drinking has to stop.'

Connie sipped at her cup of tea and looked Denny in the eye. 'He's involved with drugs as well. I don't get it because surely he has enough money and Uncle Ron would be spinning in his grave. I know for a fact that he never got involved with that side of things.'

Denny deliberated with himself and decided to be truthful about her father's investment in his business. Connie was already heavily involved with the other business and she was aware that Ron McCardle and her father had been well known faces. As she listened, she was surprised that she wasn't shocked. But then again, she had grown up with wealth and had always known that her father didn't work for a bank. She was worried about the money laundering though and explained to Denny what she had found out. He listened and knew he was going to have to put the hard word on his godfather before it all fell out of bed. He loved Alan but he wouldn't have him putting them all at risk.

Alan had assured him he would deal with cleaning the proceeds but Denny hadn't thought he would be stupid enough to use Irene's businesses as well! Irene who was currently coupled up with Kenny Latham who would not take too kindly at Alan's audacity! Sighing, he promised Connie it would be sorted and he would keep an eye on her father. He was touched when she smiled in relief. It reminded him of the little girl she had been when she had danced with him at a New Year's Eve party years ago.

When she hugged him goodbye, he savoured her clean smell. Her hair smelt of strawberries and even without makeup he thought she was the most beautiful girl he had ever seen. He hugged her back tightly, knowing that one day she would be his.

Connie, Caroline and Cath had had a fantastic night. Although they were all loved up, they still made a point of having a night out every couple of weeks and had thoroughly let their hair down and danced to every Christmas tune that the DJ in the pub had played. Caroline was particularly excited for Christmas as she had confided to her friends that she thought Wayne was going to propose. Personally, Connie thought she was too young but if Caroline was happy, then so was she. When they left the pub, the street was heaving with people wanting a cab. It was a cold night so Connie rang Alan to see if he could pick them up. His words sounded a bit slurred on the phone but at least he had appeared lucid.

'Let's go for some chips. At least we can then keep warm while we wait for Dad,' Connie urged pointing to the chip shop.

'Great idea,' Cath said happily.

Alan looked into the rear view mirror and wiped his nose on the back of his sleeve. Earlier on he had done something he had always promised himself he would never do. He had sampled the merchandise and was pleased it had sobered him up and put him in a better mood. Maybe cocaine was the way to go he thought as he spotted the girls waiting for him. They all looked like sisters with their dark hair, the same dark hair that his wife had. He quickly banished any thought of Sonia from his mind and smiled at his daughter when she waved at him. He felt a moment's shame that he was really in no fit state to drive and that he had sniffed a line before he had gotten into the car, but he needed medicating just as Sonia had for all those years. He had just what he needed on tap. Luckily, none of the girls noticed his huge pupils as they were all sitting in the back of the car. Connie wanted dropping off first as she needed the toilet and as Alan drove the other two girls home to the estate in Tottenham he began to feel a bit drunk again and was finding it hard to concentrate. He felt alone when he drove past his old home that he had shared with Sonia many years before and quickly took a crafty swig from his hip flask when he felt the girls weren't looking.

When Cath got out, he chatted amiably to Caroline as he drove down the narrow roads that led to the home that she shared with her brother Denny. As a Christmas song came on the radio he felt an urge to cry. Caroline looked at his face and felt sorry for him. He was like an uncle and it saddened her that he was in such a bad place. She felt a little alarmed when she realised he was drunk. When they reached her house she decided to invite him in for a coffee to sober him up. She would regret her decision for the rest of her life.

Chapter 32

Three Months Later

Alan rolled up a twenty-pound note and sniffed the white powder that was helping him to get through each day. Within a few minutes he felt alert. Although he felt shame that he had become a user he reasoned with himself that at least now he could remember what he had done yesterday, unlike when he had been drinking heavily and had lost whole days in a drunken stupor. He couldn't recall much of Christmas but he did know that it hadn't been a happy one like the previous ones. Sonia and Aunty Maggie had travelled up from Cornwall and had spent Boxing Day at the house with him, his mother and Connie but it had been strained. Maggie had taken one look at him and had declared that he looked like Worzel Gummidge with his scruffy hair, that needed a trim, and his creased clothes. Sonia had taken him aside and tried to talk to him but her very presence made him feel even more depressed. She was looking healthy and happy which just reminded him of why she had left, making his feelings of guilt stronger. For years she had struggled with the worry of his job. She had sleepless nights and taken medication in order to cope. Losing her mother Breda had broken her and although she didn't know that it had been Jason Baines who had started the fire, he did and that knowledge was just another thing to beat himself up about.

Sonia and Aunty Maggie had tried to make the festivities fun but had seen that Alan was in a state and that his mother and daughter were worried about him. Sonia felt guilty about her relief when she got in the car to drive home. As far as she was concerned, Alan had brought this on himself. He had thrived being part of the shady world of organised crime whereas it had nearly destroyed her. As she drove away from her old home, she wondered if they would have been happier if they had stayed on the estate and if Alan had never met Ron McCardle. She knew her husband better than anyone else did and had always known that he had never really been cut out for life as a criminal. He had always been a decent family man but as he had got in deeper with Ron's empire, he had changed. He had become obsessed with the money that could be earned. He had liked his status as a North London face. He had not thought of how it had affected her and ultimately his children.

Oh she knew that Connie enjoyed the luxury and didn't really have a problem with crime but Billy didn't want anything to do with it. Like her, he wanted to lead a decent life. If Alan carried on as he was then he would lose his boy. Maybe he already knew this. Billy had confided in her that his father was dealing in drugs and this revelation had shocked her. Alan, like Ron before him, had always been so anti-drugs but once again the money had clouded his judgement.

She was glad she had left. She had peace of mind and the freedom to live her life as she wanted. She had wasted so many years in turmoil and spaced out on tranquilisers. As she had driven away she realised that Alan had swapped places with her because it was obvious he was now struggling with demons that were preventing him from sleeping and functioning.

Alan had watched from an upstairs window as his wife and Aunty Maggie drove away. He felt an urge to cry. Sonia had looked so well and carefree which made him happy but also gave him a sense of acute failure. He closed the curtains to block out the world and went into his wardrobe and pulled out a shoebox containing dozens of plastic bags full of cocaine. Over the next few hours he had shoved as much of it up his nose as he could. He had drank half a bottle of Scotch and passed out on his bed.

Connie found him there an hour later and seeing the state of him, in disgust, had gone to see Cath back on the estate. Her parents Gina and Nick were having a small party tonight and Connie desperately needed to be around some normal, regular people. Her father was turning into a pitiful caricature of his former self and it was depressing her. Her mother had suggested she should spend a few days with her in Cornwall and she had taken up the offer the week after Christmas. She could understand why they loved the place with its beautiful coastal towns and quaint villages, but after a week she had been pleased to get back to the hustle and bustle of London.

Alan had woken to a darkened bedroom. A street light was shining through a crack in the curtain so he knew it was now evening. He felt awful, his head was pounding and his mouth was as dry as toast. He knew he was out of control but his guilt and shame over some of his wrongdoings was overwhelming. Every time he closed his eyes at night he saw the face of Jason Baines. Sometimes it was Stevie Baines, and sometimes their faces merged into one. They were taunting him, shouting at him, calling him a murderer. Alan needed the drink and more importantly the drugs to help blot out these images that were plaguing him. Getting up he padded downstairs through the dark empty house. He went into the kitchen and saw that his mother had left him a plateful of stew and dumplings. He briefly wondered where she was but remembered she was spending the night at David's house. He sat at the kitchen table and picked at the stew feeling lonelier than ever.

Connie and Cath had spent a few hours at Cath's house where Gina had laid on a buffet and they had dutifully played some party games. They were now sat in a pub in Tottenham planning what they were going to do that weekend. Cath had telephoned Caroline but she had a sickness bug and was staying in.

As they sipped at their wine Cath asked Connie how her father was doing. She knew her parents were worried about him.

Connie was embarrassed as there was no hiding the fact that her father's life had turned into a car crash. 'He's getting worse Cath. He never goes to work anymore and has been wearing the same pyjamas for a week. I've asked Uncle David to give him a call and try and talk some sense into him. He took Mum's leaving really hard but I feel there's more to it than that.'

Cath nodded sympathetically but didn't really know what else to say so changed the subject. 'So how are things going with Peter? Anyone can see he's crazy about you!'

'I like him a lot Cath but I just want some fun.'

Cath looked at her friend and decided to bite the bullet. 'Is it because of Denny?'

Connie stared at Cath open mouthed. She had always thought that she had been discreet about her feelings.

Cath laughed. 'It's always been obvious to me. When you were little you always looked at him with puppy dog eyes and now you're older I can just sense the electricity between the two of you.'

'Oh my god, does Caroline know?'

Cath laughed again. 'Well if she does, she has never mentioned it to me. Connie, look, you know that I love you and I love Denny too. We have all grown up together but he is a player and I've heard on the grape vine that he is into some real illegal stuff these days. Stick with Peter. He is kind, devoted to you and won't be getting his collar felt anytime soon. Denny is bad news as nice as he is. Look at how your dad's life affected your mum.'

Connie agreed with Cath but wondered if she wanted a normal, regular guy because there was a part of her that craved excitement, and as lovely as Peter was, she realised that she was becoming bored. Their relationship had become a comfortable routine and as good as he was in bed he didn't make her tingle all over as Denny Draper did when he was within two feet of her. Downing her drink she steered the conversation in a different direction.

'Have you seen much of Caroline? I haven't seen hide nor hair of her since we went out at Christmas.'

Cath nodded in agreement. 'I know what you mean, since she got engaged to Wayne I haven't seen much of her either. Mind you she has been ill quite a bit what with that chest infection and now this sickness bug.'

'Let's sort something out, a night out when she's better,' Connie suggested.

'Good idea, I quite fancy a trip up to the West End,' Cath replied.

Ebony Peters tried to hide her boredom as Charlie West humped away on top of her. As he groaned and shuddered to a stop he looked at her and grinned. 'Did you come Love?'

Ebony felt an urge to say, 'If you have to bloody well ask then clearly not,' but instead purred like a cat and stroked his hairy back which seemed to satisfy him. Rolling off her, Charlie farted like a pig and was asleep in minutes. Ebony pursed her lips in disgust and inwardly screamed at how the last few months had panned out.

After her telephone call with Emine Mehmet she had realised that with the deaths of Deniz and Kadir, her money supply had stopped. She had no alternative but to look for a job. The problem was that she had no experience and was lazy. Ebony had always been a kept woman: firstly by her father Gary and then Ron McCardle and Kadir Mehmat. She had always felt that going out and earning her own money was beneath her, now she had no other option. She had reluctantly gone for an interview as a classroom assistant at a local school but when the snooty woman conducting the interview had asked her if she liked children, she had been unimpressed when Ebony jokingly said she didn't particularly like her own, let alone anyone else's. The woman had got up and suggested that perhaps working in a school was not the right career choice after all! Ebony had left the interview feeling both annoyed and relieved.

The thought of working with thirty little people day in and day out with all their snot and demands hadn't really appealed to her. It was only the school holidays that had attracted her anyway. When she got home she knocked at the flat below hers to pick up Chantelle who was being minded by a young single mother called Cassie. Cassie had a son called Micky who was mixed race. His father Errol had gone on the trot when he was three and Cassie worked in a hostess club in Russell Square to make ends meet. As Ebony moaned to her about her money situation the younger woman had looked her over and said, 'Why don't I see if I can get you a job at the club,? You're not bad for your age and the owner Charlie was only saying the other day that he needed some more girls.'

Ebony had been irritated by the reference to her age but decided to give it a go as, apparently, the money was good and Cassie was sure that old Mrs Daws who lived in the basement flat would look after Chantelle as she did Micky, when Cassie was working.

So that is how Ebony had met Charlie West. She had taken great care to look good for her interview and had used some of her dwindling funds to get a professional blow dry. As she walked into the club she had been disappointed that in the cold light of day it looked dingy and tired. She noticed that the burgundy wallpaper was peeling in places and the carpet was sticky. It smelt of stale smoke and beer and she almost turned around and walked out until she reminded herself that her child needed to eat.

As she stood taking in her surroundings a bald, stout man who was about five-foot-eight bounded out of a side room and loudly introduced himself as the owner. He looked her over critically and rather rudely declared that she was a bit past it to be a hostess but that he could offer her a job on reception. Ebony had been secretly livid with his bluntness but had been pacified when he had told her what her wages would be and that it would be cash in hand.

She had only been working there for two months and was already fed up with the travelling and having to work, so had begun flirting with Charlie. She didn't fancy him but he was wealthy and she needed another man to fund her expensive tastes. He was a means to an end. She knew he was married to a woman called Denise but a wife had never stopped Ebony before and it certainly wasn't going to stop her now. The first time they had gone to bed had been a huge disappointment. Ebony was used to lovers who cared about her enjoyment but Charlie just sweated away on top of her and clearly had never heard of foreplay. However he had fallen for her charms, hook line and sinker and it had been his idea for her to stop working as he would now look after her. Chantelle had taken an instant dislike to the little man with the big voice but enjoyed all the treats that he bought her, so the arrangement worked. Ebony would go with it until something better came along. She had a plan to boost her bank balance but potentially needed Charlie's help so she would keep him onside until she had decided what to do.

Alan was feeling marginally better after eating half a plate of stew. He was now sat in the front room watching an old western when he heard the doorbell ring. It was Denny. As he looked into his godson's face he realised the boy was here to talk about his recent behaviour. Wearily he let him in and showed him into the front room.

Denny looked uneasy so Alan made it easier for him. 'Look, I know Denny, you don't have to say anything. I've taken my eye off the ball. I'll knock the drinking on the head and get back on track.'

The younger man looked him in the eye and said, 'But it's not just the drink Al, is it? Your pupils are more dilated than a dinner plate, you are bang on the gear and that has made you sloppy. You have even taken to doing private transactions.'

Alan was annoyed and it showed. 'Who are you to tell me what is what? If it wasn't for me, you would still be pulling pints.'

Denny had expected this kind of response and was ready for it. He knew Alan was embarrassed that he had been caught out. 'Look Al, I will always be grateful to you and Ron too for giving me a leg up but I have worked too bloody hard the last few years to get a capture because you're being careless. You may not care how people perceive you but I bloody care how they perceive me. Irene knows you have been laundering money through her accounts and she is not happy. She has told me to tell you that if you don't stop pronto, she will put someone else in charge.'

Alan merely grunted so Denny continued in a softer voice. 'What's going on Al? I know you are cut up about Sonia but I feel something else is up.'

'In truth I don't know Den, I have always loved the wheeling and dealing but there is other stuff that haunts me you know, that's in my head.'

Denny wasn't really sure what he was talking about but guessed that at some point Alan had hurt someone and could understand why he felt the way he did. Butt he had to realise that it went with the territory and he told him so. 'I'm not trying to patronise you but we have all done things that we aren't proud of. We have to accept them and move on. In this life everyone knows there is a risk of being hurt.'

Alan appreciated his words but it didn't make him feel any better. He did however plaster a smile onto his face and promised Denny that he would get himself together. When Denny left he telephoned Irene and apologised for his shortcomings. She had been curt at first and he could hear Kenny Latham mouthing off in the background. Irene had told Kenny to shut up and then threatened Alan in no uncertain terms that if he ever laundered money through her businesses again she would cut off his balls and hang them from the Town Christmas tree.

Alan took on board what Denny and Irene both said to him, grateful he had been given another chance. He was feeling a slight glimmer of positivity and his brother David was pleased to hear it when he telephoned him the next day to see how he was.

Chapter 33

Connie and Cath stared at Caroline open mouthed as she told them her news and then Cath started crying tears of joy.

'Oh my god, you're going to have a baby!' Connie exclaimed in shock.

Caroline nodded. 'Yes it's due in September. Wayne is over the moon.'

Connie took in her friend's miserable face and was not sharing the excitement that Cath was feeling. 'Are you happy about it?'

Caroline looked at her and Connie could sense she was trying to muster some enthusiasm. 'Yeah of course I am, I have just felt really ill and anyway there's not much I can do about it now.'

Connie studied her closely. Caroline's face was drawn and pale but she was hardly showing so maybe she had her dates wrong?

'Well there is another option if you're not ready.'

Caroline fiercely shook her head. 'No, like I said, Wayne is really happy about becoming a dad and anyway I don't believe in abortion. It's not the baby's fault this has been pushed upon me.'

Connie nodded and suddenly grinned. 'Well that little baby is going to be the most loved and spoilt child in North London and me and Cath are going to be the best aunties ever, aren't we?'

Connie looked over at Cath who agreed with her. 'Oh I just love babies, I'm so excited!'

Caroline burst into tears and soon all three girls were hugging and crying. They had grown up together, gone through every stage of their lives together and now one of them was going to become a mother which was another milestone in their friendship.

Later on in the sanctuary of her bedroom, Caroline manically wrote down her private thoughts in her diary. It was the only place where she could pour out how she was really feeling because no one could ever know the truth. Three months ago her best friend's father had raped her and now she was carrying his baby. This knowledge and the awful images of that night haunted her daily.

When she had come back out of the kitchen with the coffees she saw that Alan had fallen asleep on the sofa. Turning off the lights from the Christmas tree she had bent over to cover him with a blanket when his eyes had suddenly opened and he had pulled her towards him but he wasn't seeing her, Caroline, he was seeing Sonia in his drunk fuddled state. 'Darling, I've missed you,' he whispered in a voice thick with emotion.

Caroline gently tried to explain but he wasn't hearing her. It was as if he was in another place.

As he pulled her on top of him she struggled but they ended up rolling on to the carpet and as he quickly unzipped his trousers she froze in terror, mute, unable to move or scream. He lay heavy on top of her and she was trapped underneath him as he went about his task. He was gentle and murmuring endearments into her ear and as she lay there paralysed she willed her mind to travel somewhere else. When he had finished. He kissed her gently on the lips and started to cry. 'I'm sorry Son, I should never have done that but I miss you so much.'

He then left and as she heard his car engine drive off into the night she curled up into a ball and cried. In the morning she was still lying on the carpet her eyes fixed firmly on a photo of her beloved parents Geoff and Brenda.

Alan had managed to pull himself together. The night that he had picked up Connie and her friends after their night out was a blur. He had come home and carried on drinking before passing out. When his mother had found him slumped in an armchair the next morning she had told him in no uncertain terms that he was an embarrassment to his children and needed to sort himself out. Finally her words had penetrated. For a few weeks he had completely laid off the booze and only had a toot in the mornings to give him a boost and to enable him to face the day ahead. He was sleeping better as well, thanks to the pills that his brother David had given him and although he still had nightmares they weren't as vivid and he no longer saw the faces of Stevie and Jason Baines.

It probably helped that Connie's boyfriend Peter Baines didn't seem to come to the house as much anymore, as his familiar face had tormented Alan. Recently his dreams had been about a struggle between himself and a faceless person. David said this dream was a sign that subconsciously he was fighting with himself which made sense, because he had been in turmoil with the past for months. He missed Sonia desperately but was trying to keep busy so that he didn't dwell on his feelings or his loneliness. He had even phoned Billy and apologised for his behaviour. He was proud of his son and wanted his son to be proud of him. Every day he went to work and was back on track with Irene who he had always respected almost as much as Ron. He certainly didn't want her to think that he was a weak link.

The drugs business that he had invested in with Denny was making lots of money and he was due to meet with him and their supplier Wesley Pritchard today. As he towel dried his hair he felt that at last he had taken back control and it felt good. He was just about to put on his trousers when his mum burst into the room.

Genice smiled as she saw the alarm on his face and said, 'I've had a husband and two sons. You've got nothing that I haven't seen before. Now there's a lady downstairs asking for you. Have you got something to tell me?'

'No I haven't! Now, do me a favour and find out who it is please.'

Alan hadn't been expecting anyone and was curious as to who his visitor might be.

'It's someone called Ebony,' his mother informed him when she returned to his bedroom. 'What sort of a name is that and who is she?'

Alan was even more curious now. What could Ebony want after all these years? Oh well, he would soon find out he thought as he padded down the stairs.

Ebony Peters took in her surroundings and felt the jealousy welling up inside her. Alan Stewart had certainly done alright for himself and Ron had been the reason for that. The house was beautifully decorated in pale greys and pinks. The furniture was classy but homely and the marble fireplaces were adorned with fresh flowers. Now this is the type of house that I should be living in she thought, as Alan entered the room with a confused look on his face. She had never really been into ginger men but decided that he wasn't at all bad on the eye, even if his hair was thinning and he now sported bags under his blue eyes.

'Blimey Ebony, you were the last person I expected to see, what brings you here?'

Ebony knew she had to put on a show and licked her lips demurely, an action that immediately rang alarm bells with Alan. She was obviously after something he thought warily as she started her story.

'As you know Alan, I went to Scotland after Ron died. I needed to escape from all of the painful memories.'

Ebony saw Alan nodding sympathetically and carried on with her tale of woe. 'I was devastated when Ron died. I know we weren't together at the time but we had a lot of history and a child together. We had even spoken about getting back together.'

This was news to Alan but he politely let her continue. 'I took our child and made a new life for ourselves up North. It was tough Alan. I had to work long hours as I had no one to support us. When my Aunty Pat died she left me her flat so I decided to come home. I realised that home is where the heart is.'

Ebony hoped she hadn't sounded too corny and almost giggled as her lies came tumbling out. She inwardly congratulated herself for being such a good actress as she watched the changing expressions on Alan's face.

Glenice came into the room eyeing Ebony with suspicion and put out a tray of tea and some dainty cakes which gave Alan time to think.

'So what can I do for you Ebony? And more importantly, what are you after?'

Ron had told him enough stories about his ex-mistress and had often described her as being a ponse so Alan was on his guard.

Ebony looked at Alan and realised that he wasn't as gullible as she had hoped so she decided to cut the crap and get to the point. 'Look Alan, Chantelle is Ron's child and I need money to support her. For obvious reasons she wasn't named in the will but as his only child she is entitled to some of his estate.'

Alan could see her point but all of Ron's money had gone to Irene and he wasn't about to bother her with all of this.

'I don't really know what this has to do with me. Ron left the bulk of his money and businesses to his wife.'

Ebony smirked, 'Yes and he didn't leave you out did he? I know that you did alright and you weren't even family, like my Chantelle is. My daughter, Ron's daughter, deserves a slice of the pie.'

Alan stood up signalling that this meeting was over.

'Let me have a think about it and I'll get back to you.'

Ebony uncrossed her slim legs and smiled. 'Thank you Alan and I'LL be in touch with you, you have one week.'

Alan laughed. 'You have more front than Blackpool and I'm not talking about your tits. Now I said I'll think about it and I will, but until then be patient otherwise you won't get a bean.'

Ebony knew when to retreat and picking up her coat left the house feeling quietly confident that she would suck Alan Stewart dry one way or another.

Later, when Alan was driving to his meeting he couldn't get over the audacity of the woman. Turning up and demanding money when she had been on the missing list for years. Why hadn't she made a fuss when Ron had died, when everything was still fresh? In all honesty he had forgotten about her over the years but the reality was that Ron had fathered a child and like it or not he wouldn't have wanted his daughter to go without. Alan could still remember the joy in his friend's voice when he had spoken about the little girl. He just couldn't understand why Ron hadn't secretly made some sort of provision for her. He assumed it was because at the time they had had all that trouble with the Turks and Ron had been very worried about Irene who had been acting strangely, so his mind must have been distracted.

Irene had confided in Alan a few months after the funeral that Ron had a child but it was Barry, the son of Lily Jenson, who had run the sex house in Crouch End. Alan had been shocked but after thinking about it he hadn't been surprised. Ron and Lily had always had a special friendship and he had caught her looking at him sadly over the years, so it had all made sense. Irene had told him that she had respected the fact that the other woman had kept it quiet over the years and hadn't asked for any money when Ron had died, although Irene had sent the other woman a lump sum out of Ron's estate as she had said to Alan that it was the right thing to do. Alan knew though without a doubt that Irene McCardle would not look so kindly on Ebony's plight.

In his mind she didn't know about Chantelle so how could he dump it on her seven years later? He would have to have a good think about it. He had to be in control of this situation because if he wasn't Ebony would be the type of woman to keep coming back for more. One thing he was sure about was that Irene must never know. Ron would not want her to be hurt and she had been good to Alan and his family over the years, especially recently when she had given him a second chance.

Ebony was telling her boyfriend Charlie West about her meeting with Alan. She had told him last week that Ron was her daughter's father and he had been impressed. Everyone in their world knew that the late great Ron McCardle had been a legend. Charlie had known both him and Alan by reputation and knew they had both made fortunes over the years. He had readily agreed with Ebony's plan to use her daughter as a means of getting her slice of Ron's wealth. He assured her that if Alan Stewart didn't play ball then he would make his life very difficult. He had the clout and, being a greedy man like his girlfriend, he was also seeing the pound signs that could also benefit him. They both felt Alan would cough up. She just hoped he didn't take the piss and insult her with a small amount to keep her quiet. She wanted what she was owed. After all, Ron had believed that Chantelle was his so there was no reason for Alan to think otherwise and with Charlie onside she now had an ally. He may not be in Ron's league or even Alan's but he had cockily informed her that if Plan A didn't work, he had a Plan B up his sleeve.

Chapter 34

Alan had mulled over Ebony's demands and decided that Ron would have expected him to help his daughter. After all he had been a true friend, had been good to him over the years giving him the opportunity to earn decent money which had enabled him to provide well for his family. He had introduced him to a way of life that paid huge dividends. Admittedly, that very same way of life had ruined his marriage and the violence had given him nightmares but it didn't change the fact that Ron McCardle had been loyal and had always had his back. Alan therefore believed it was now his duty to ensure that Chantelle was looked after.

The problem was how much money was he going to have to part with? Most of his money was tied up in his house and the club that Ron had bequeathed him. He had some cash stashed away thanks to his involvement with Denny's drugs empire that was flourishing but he needed to be in total control of this situation because otherwise Ebony would try and fleece him dry. Deciding on a sum that should satisfy her and not put too much of a dent in his assets, he phoned her and told her to meet him in a restaurant in Holborn later on that day so that they could discuss the terms of the arrangement.

Peter Baines was feeling dejected and confused. He felt that he had met the girl of his dreams and had fallen deeply in love with her during the last few months but he could sense she was going cold on him. She was cancelling dates and appeared distracted. He just couldn't understand it because they got on really well and had a great connection in bed. He understood she was worried about her dad and was busy with the businesses and especially the rentals, but surely she could make some sort of an effort?

As Peter worried about their relationship, Connie was doing exactly the same thing. The truth was that although she was fond of Peter, she was in love with Denny Draper and always had been. Unlike her mother, she loved the thought of being the partner of a well-known face. She didn't want Mr 9 to 5. She knew that Denny's growing notoriety was part of the attraction but she had loved him since she was ten years old so it was more than that. She was confident that he fancied her but wasn't sure how he actually felt. Denny had had a string of women over the years and although he was now seeing Nikki she just knew she could give him more. They were bound by history and had a deep bond. She would never have that with another man. Nervously she picked up the telephone. She knew what she had to do.

Ebony walked into the restaurant like she owned the place. She may be in her forties but she still looked good. As she sashayed towards Alan her beautiful auburn hair swayed and her pert cleavage caused more than one male diner to give her a second glance. Alan smirked as he watched her work the room. She certainly had confidence and he conceded that she was a good looking woman, but Ron had often confided in him that she was as interesting as watching paint dry. Ron once told him that Ebony only loved one person and that was herself but Alan could see what had attracted his friend all the same. His Sonia was beautiful but intelligent as well and he felt an overwhelming sense of loss as Ebony sat down opposite him.

As she settled herself, he decided to get down to business. 'So I have given it a lot of thought Ebony and have decided to give you a lump sum of £10,000 as a one off payment.'

Ebony screwed up her brown eyes. She had wanted at least £20,000. 'That's a rather disappointing sum Alan I have a child to bring up and bills to pay.'

Alan knew Ebony was a greedy bitch and he wasn't parting with a penny more. 'Look Love,' he said sarcastically, 'you and your daughter are not my responsibility. It's not my fault the way things turned out. It's not my problem that Ron didn't make provisions for the kid but out of respect for him I am willing to help you out this once. I don't have to, so take it or leave it.'

Ebony battled it out with herself and decided to accept the offer as £10,000 was not to be sniffed at. She would discuss the matter later with Charlie and see what he had to say.

'Okay I'll take it,' she said grudgingly.

'Good girl, you know it makes sense,' Alan replied getting up.

'Oh and do you have a photo of the girl? I'd like to see a picture of Ron's daughter.'

Ebony was suddenly nervous. She did have a photo of Chantelle in her purse but wasn't about to show him as she didn't want to arouse any suspicions. The child was olive skinned, dark and looked nothing like her or Ron. She had to keep her daughter well away from Alan who was no fool, unlike Charlie who had believed her when she told him that Ron was the father.

'No I haven't, sorry. She looks like her dad though,' she told him whilst suppressing a giggle.

Alan nodded as he put on his coat. 'Fair enough, lunch is on me.'

Ebony was miffed that he hadn't stayed to have lunch leaving her to dine alone. So clicking her fingers she summoned a young waiter over and ordered the most expensive champagne on the menu.

Later on that evening she told Charlie about Alan's offer. Like her, he wasn't impressed and as he angrily paced up and down the carpet of her small front room, she thought that he reminded her of father Gary when he had been in a rage about something.

'What a wanker, you are owed more than that. Ron was worth a small fortune and £10,000 doesn't even touch the sides. Well don't worry, there are more ways to skin a cat. Leave it with me.'

Ebony didn't particularly like Charlie West or his hairy chubby body but she was a user and if he could get her more money then who was she to argue? Ebony always prided herself with knowing how to play the game so licking her lips she gracefully parted her long legs and said in a husky voice, 'Come here Big Boy, you deserve a treat.'

It was early evening and as Peter watched Connie walking up the road from his flat and out of his life, he felt an urge to cry. She had dumped him, given him some old cods about being too busy for a relationship. He had said nothing, what was the point? She had clearly made up her mind and he had his pride. The worst part was that he felt so lonely. He had grown up for most of his life without a family around him. His mother, brother and sisters were strangers to him and he had no idea how to find them anyway as no one who he had asked on the old estate had heard of them. He had become used to being on his own until Connie came along and given him the human connection that only someone you love can give. Now she was gone. He was alone again. Going into his fridge, he pulled out a six pack of lager and decided to get pissed. He opened the first can and was greedily gulping at it when he heard a loud knock at the door. Jumping up quickly he knocked over the can.

He wasn't expecting company and felt sure that it must be Connie back to tell him that she had made a mistake. As he flung open the door his happiness turned to confusion as he looked at the man stood on his doorstep.

'Hello Son, it's been a long time. Have you got a drink for your old Uncle Charlie?'

Chapter 35

Peter and his Uncle Charlie sat drinking and reminiscing about the past and it had taken Peter's mind off his heartbreak over losing Connie. He was gutted to hear that his mother Doreen and brother Jason were dead but he wasn't surprised about his mother as she had always been a drinker and hadn't coped after his father Stevie had died. As Charlie spoke, Peter was assailed with long forgotten memories that he had buried over the years. He could now clearly remember the day when he and his sisters Michelle, Lisa and Dawn had been taken away by two middle aged women wearing smart skirt suits. They had turned up at the front door and kindly telling the children that their mummy could no longer take care of them. As they forlornly walked down the narrow corridor of their flat towards the front door Peter had turned back to look at his mum who lay on the thread bare sofa crying. Even at his tender age he had instinctively known that she had given up on life. They had muddled though after his dad had died but that was mainly due to his older brother Jason, who had got a job as a fly pitcher which had helped to put food on the table. Peter had idolised his brother who had been determined to try and look after his younger siblings. Doreen always seemed to have the money for booze and lay around the flat all day, devoid of any real maternal instinct.

Her neglected children had drifted in and out of the flat almost unseen by the self-consumed woman until the neighbours started talking amongst themselves and started 'sticking their noses in.' It was at this point when Doreen finally moved her bulk from the sofa to angrily berate the people who were only trying to look out for the children. Things got steadily worse when Jason was arrested for injuring a policeman and sent to a borstal for boys with behavioural issues. Michelle, the oldest girl, tried her best but there was little money coming in and the dirty unkempt children soon come to the attention of Social Services.

Peter remembered his childish belief as they were ushered out of their home that they would be going to live in a nice house with an abundance of food and clean clothes. Although he felt frightened, this thought had cheered him because even as a small boy he had known that these basic necessities were a child's right. However, his hopes were crushed when he and his sisters were placed in separate cars and this was the last time he had ever seen them. He was driven to a large Victorian building that housed forty other children and that is where he had stayed. He now realised that he had suppressed these memories as dwelling on them would have been too traumatic.

As Charlie told him all that he knew, Peter felt the loss all over again and was upset to learn that Doreen had miscarried the baby that she had been carrying at the time, although it had probably been for the best. Apparently Doreen had disappeared for a while and then turned back up onto the estate with Jason in tow. She had died from a drugs overdose shortly afterwards and his brother had disappeared, and Charlie said that he had heard a whisper that he was now dead as well. Michelle, like himself, had been placed into a children's home and was now thought to be in London but Charlie had no more details. The younger girls, Lisa and Dawn, had been adopted by a professional couple who had then immigrated to Australia. Peter was grateful that at least they had escaped the care system and hoped they had had a good life.

As he opened another can of lager, he slumped back on the sofa with an overwhelming feeling that what had happened to his family was tragic. They had hardly been The Waltons but they were bound by blood, and they had been a family once.

Charlie looked at the boy and could only imagine the thoughts that were going through his mind. He'd been close to his sister and would have taken the kids on if it had been up to him, but his wife Denise had flatly refused. She had always looked down her nose at his 'slovenly' sister and her 'feral' offspring, stating that they would be a bad influence on their own two daughters, and maybe they would have.

Charlie had dropped the subject pretty quickly as they didn't really have the room anyway for four more children but he always made a point of keeping tabs on his sister's family.

Peter's mind was whirring and he was overcome with sadness with what had befallen his family after his dad had died. 'So did you look for Jason. How do you know he's dead?'

Charlie bit his bottom lip (a sign his wife knew only too well which meant he was lying). 'He was on the drugs as well and then he vanished, a good source told me that he had died the same way like your mum.'

He felt uncomfortable lying but the time wasn't right for the truth. He needed to rebuild his relationship with his nephew and see how things panned out with Ebony's quest for getting money out of Alan Stewart before he involved the boy. He would, however, involve him if his girlfriend didn't get what was owed to her. He had heard that Peter was seeing Connie Stewart and was disappointed to discover that they had broken up as he could have got to Alan through her, but he was still confident that if he spilled the beans to Peter then the boy would want to retaliate.

After leaving Peter's flat earlier, Connie had needed cheering up so had gone into the hair salon where her cousin Samantha was a stylist and had her hair washed and blow dried. She felt sad about Peter but there would only ever be one man who could push all her buttons and she was determined to do something about it. Sod what anyone else might think, her mum had gone off to find a happier life and she was determined to do the same. As she checked herself out in the full length mirror in her bedroom she was satisfied with her reflection. Samantha had done a great job and her dark hair fell in a curtain of soft curls below her shapely shoulders. Connie didn't really favour the current bright makeup look and had opted for smoky eyes which she had created with soft browns and black mascara. Her clothes were classy but sexy and she felt that the bright red lipstick completed the ensemble. She laughed when her dad whistled his admiration as he saw his beautiful daughter leaving the house. 'Seeing Peter tonight Love?'

'No we finished, I'm off to the club to meet the girls.'

As the front door closed, Alan let out a sigh of relief. Thank God, he thought. The whole situation with Peter Baines had literally given him nightmares. Every time he looked at the lad, he had seen Stevie and Jason and each night he would be haunted by dreams. He had been a mess for months but had recently cleaned up his act. He only drank in the evenings now and had recently knocked the gear on its head. Hopefully now that Peter was off the scene he could get back to some sort of normal.

Denny's drugs empire was booming and he had just negotiated another lucrative deal. He used the office in the club for his meeting and as he walked towards the main bar she walked in and took his breath away.

Connie was wearing a knee length red leather skirt, black basque and a short black leather jacket. On her head sat a black roll up brim fedora bowler hat which most girls in his view wouldn't be able to get away with. The whole look was stunning and so was Connie who wasn't a follower of fashion which just made her stand out from everyone else. As he looked over to the table where his girlfriend Nikki was sat giggling with her friends, he knew there was no comparison. Nikki was a nice girl with great tits but wasn't a patch on Connie. She loved Madonna and had tried to emulate her idol tonight. Her hair was shaggy and she was wearing a tutu type skirt and a white cropped t-shirt. Although she looked cute, Connie was all woman and he could feel his heart beating in his chest as the vision that was Connie Stewart glided towards him. 'I'm in trouble,' he thought as he nervously glanced at his girlfriend.

Cath had persuaded Caroline that what she needed was a night out at the club. Caroline hadn't been keen. She was still trying to come to terms with being pregnant and didn't know how she would feel seeing the daughter of the man who had raped her. It was exhausting trying to pretend to everyone and especially to her boyfriend Wayne that she was alright. But she had no choice because if her brother found out there would be murders and although she hated Alan for what he had done she didn't want him killed. He had been out of his box when he had violated her. She could tell that he had actually thought she was Sonia.

He had never got over his wife leaving and had turned to drink and god knows what else to numb the pain although Cath admitted to her recently that he seemed a lot more like the old Alan.

Caroline didn't really care. She just wanted to avoid him and try and look forward to the baby which was coming. She turned her attention to Cath who was wondering where Connie had got to.

'There she is,' Cath stated as she clocked Connie approaching them from the direction of the private office. She froze as she saw Denny behind her with his hand on her arm. He looked at her friend in a way that told Cath that IT had finally happened. She nervously glanced at Caroline who looked livid.

As Connie reached their table Caroline got up to leave. 'You have got to be fucking joking Connie, so like you to just take what you want without a thought for anyone else.'

With that she hastily gathered up her things and stormed off. Connie sat down deflated. She had just spent the best forty-five minutes of her entire life and was surprised at Caroline's reaction. Cath kindly patted her hand.

'Well it was never going to be easy was it?'

'I just don't see the problem Cath, we are both adults and it's not like we're related or anything.'

'You know how moral Caroline is and he does have a girlfriend. He's been with her months.'

'I know, but we have always had strong feelings for each other. There is no one else for me Cath and I think that he feels the same.'

'Well I would usually ask you for all the details but as it's Denny I think I'll pass as I don't want to know the measurements of someone who is like my brother!' Cath laughed.

'But that's the thing Cath, he doesn't feel like my brother, he hasn't for years but what am I going to do about Caroline?'

'Don't worry Connie, she just has to get used to it. I think you have more of a problem with his bird,' Cath said as she nodded in the direction of the dance floor where Nikki was trying to get Denny to dance with her. Connie wasn't bothered as although they hadn't spoken, their bodies had communicated a thousand words and Connie knew that Nikki was history.

The next morning Connie dialled Caroline's number but the phone just rang. Connie shrugged, made a cup of tea and took it back to bed with her. She wanted to be on her own to digest what had happened last night.

When she had walked over to Denny, he had simply took hold of her hand

and guided her into the office and locked the door. They had looked at each other for at least a minute and he had stroked her face as if it was a precious jewel.

The next minute they were tearing each other's clothes off and Denny gasped when Connie stood before him naked. He went to her then and just held her, skin to skin. He sat her down in his office chair and gently began kissing her, starting at her feet and working his way up. As he stroked and administered soft kisses Connie felt she was in ecstasy. He treated her like she was a work of art and appreciated every part of her. Connie merely sat there and moaned as his tongue reached her clitoris and he began sucking it. It was at this point where Connie could hold it in no longer and she had the best climax of her life. Denny smiled but it wasn't his usual self-assured smirk. He needed to know that she had enjoyed it and as he looked at her with a question in his eyes she simply nodded and stood up. Once again they drew their bodies together but this time she took charge. As she began licking his nipples he groaned and as she pushed him on to the chair that she had just vacated he laughed. She stood up and brushed her own nipples against his mouth and then crouched back down and took him in her mouth gently sucking whilst using her hand to move the skin up and down. Denny thought that he was about to explode but she kept stopping as she reigned kisses on to his muscular chest, wanting this moment to last as long as possible for him. When he finally came, he felt like he had never felt before. The experience had been exquisite. Afterwards, he silently poured them both a drink and when Connie had finished hers he took the glass and put it on the desk. Then he picked her up and positioned her against the office wall.

His thrusts were gentle at first and built in momentum as they each began to feel the tidal wave of their orgasms. Connie cried out as they began rhythmically to move faster until they both collapsed, secure in the knowledge that this was what making love was all about. As Connie got dressed, she realised that the reason why so many women could take or leave sex was because not enough time was spent touching and loving. She had always known that it wouldn't be like this with Denny and she had been right.

Connie wasn't the only person mulling over the events of last night. Back home in Tottenham, Caroline was feeling overwhelmed with anxiety. Things were not going well with Wayne which she knew was her fault as she wouldn't let him within five feet of her so it was to her brother Denny she turned to for comfort and support. She knew that her thoughts were childish, but she now felt that Connie had taken him away from her. She also needed to discreetly distance herself from the Stewarts which was going to be difficult if Denny and Connie became a fixed item so when the phone rang she purposely ignored it as she knew who it would be.

As Connie drank the last of the tea wondering whether she should have a shower there was a ring at the front door. She knew Nanny Glenice was out and her dad was having a bath so she padded down the stairs to see who it was. Stood on the doorstep was a short man she didn't recognise asking for Alan.

She showed him into the front room and went to tell her dad there was a man called Charlie West to see him. Then she went back to bed to day dream about Denny Draper, all thoughts of having a shower forgotten.

Chapter 36

Alan didn't recognise the man sitting in his favourite winged armchair until he started talking. He had the same booming voice as his sister Doreen and Alan sighed as the man told him in no uncertain terms that his 'friend' Ebony Peters was entitled to more money than the paltry ten thousand pounds Alan had offered her. By the time he had taken breath, Alan was seriously wound up by the pure cheek of the man.

'Look MATE, Ebony and her kid have sod all to do with me. I didn't have to give her anything out of my own pocket but I did.'

Charlie stood up and wagged a pudgy finger at Alan. 'But you did all right when Ron snuffed it didn't you, as did that wife of his. Ron owned a lot of properties and businesses and was loaded so it's only right that his only child is taken care of.'

Alan had heard enough. How dare this wanker come into his home with his ridiculous demands so without answering Charlie he picked up the phone and began dialling? As the call connected he pressed the loudspeaker button and a woman could be heard saying hello.

'Hi Irene, it's Alan. I have an unwelcome visitor in my home, Charlie West brother of Doreen Baines. Apparently he has got himself involved with Ebony Peters who seems to think that she has a claim on Ron's estate. Now

I've already weighed out ten k for the kid but she wants more. What do you think to that Darling?'

There was a silence at the end of the line followed by sarcastic laughter until Irene McCardle spoke. 'You can tell him from me that the tart is entitled to nothing and will get not a penny more. I am not responsible for her bastard child and if Ron didn't see fit to provide for them then it's jack shit to do with me or you for that matter.'

Alan ended the call and looked into Charlie's small beady eyes. 'That clear enough for you? Now piss off out of my house and pass on the news to your "friend", I'm bored now.'

Charlie was not a man to be fobbed off and glared at Alan in contempt. 'You haven't heard the last of this Stewart, I know things that could wipe that smile of off your face.'

Alan laughed. 'Just fuck off and don't come back because you have wound me up and you don't want to see me lose my rag. You have no idea what I'm capable of.'

Charlie held his gaze and said smugly, 'Oh but I do Alan so watch your back.'

Alan only used violence when it was necessary but feeling that this was such an occasion he threw his right arm back and delivered a well-aimed punch to Charlie's face. He laughed as the other man squealed like a girl as he immediately put his hand up to his nose which was now bleeding. Deciding that there were more ways to skin a cat and also because he was a coward who knew that Alan Stewart could handle himself, Charlie picked up his discarded coat and looking at Alan with menace in his eyes made a hasty retreat.

Connie had been in her room listening to George Benson on her Walkman and hadn't heard a thing so was alarmed when she came downstairs, walked into the kitchen and found her dad washing blood from his hands. Not asking any questions she quietly went back upstairs because unlike her mother she knew when not to make a fuss and how to play the game.

Charlie West was annoyed that when he got back to Ebony's flat she was more concerned that he didn't bleed all over her new cream carpet than she was about his injury, which wound him up further. As she sat painting her nails he silently seethed. He had gone out of his way for her and the selfish bitch wasn't even grateful! Well maybe he would forget about her and her bratty kid and just rinse Alan for his own gains.

Denny Draper was waiting outside the clinic for his sister Caroline who had an appointment with the doctor. As she climbed back into the car he grinned at her. 'Everything alright Sis?'

'Yeah everything is fine with the baby,' she said with a glum expression on her face.

'Why the moody boat then?'

Denny would never understand his sister. She had always been quite reserved, always with her head in a book or that stupid diary that she wrote in but in the last few months she had withdrawn into herself like she had when their parents Geoff and Brenda had died. Turning off the engine he turned and looked at her and was sad to see that she looked pasty and miserable. Caroline clocked him studying her and sighed.

'I'm only nineteen Den, I'm not ready for all of this. I know Wayne is as happy as when Spurs score but I'm scared.'

Taking his sister into his arms (as best as he could with a gear stick in the way) Denny cuddled Caroline. 'Please don't worry Sis, you've got me and the girls. Connie and Cath will help you and Wayne adores you, you know he does.'

She did know this but wasn't sure that she still felt the same about her fiancé. He was a decent enough bloke but she had gone right off sex and she knew that he was getting fed up with the situation. But she reasoned with herself that now she had a baby on the way, she would have to just get on with it. She could even hear her mother's voice in her ear telling her the same thing. Pushing her brother away she looked at him. 'I'm also really pissed off about you and Connie, I saw you the other night coming out of the office, both looking like something had gone on. What about poor Nikki? She really loves you.'

Denny decided to come clean. It was the only way as Connie affected him like no other girl had. She was his future. 'I love her Sis, I have for years but I'm going to do the right thing and call it a day with Nikki. I'm meeting her tonight.'

Caroline patted his hand. 'Well let her down gently and don't go screwing over Connie, she's like a sister to me and I know what you're like with women. As soon as you've got in their knickers, you lose interest.'

Denny had the grace to hang his head. As soon as he had lost his virginity with the lovely Lesley when he was eighteen, he had literally shagged his way around the girls of North London. He wasn't proud of it and certainly wasn't a bragger but Connie was in a different league altogether. Yes she was beautiful, intelligent and confident but she was also woven into his whole being. She came from his world and more importantly she understood and accepted it. He was fast becoming one of North London's major drug barons and he needed a life partner who would be at ease with his chosen profession. He had watched Connie's mother Sonia gradually fall apart over the years because she couldn't cope with being married to a villain but he knew that his Connie (and she would be his) would take it all in her stride and be an asset to him.

'I'm going to be straight with you. I have never and I mean never been in love. Sure I've loved a girl for her tits, face, smile whatever, but I have never had that connection that makes you feel you are one half of something. I have that with Connie. I'm going to marry her Sis.'

Caroline had her doubts but at the end of the day it was their life. She had enough going on in her own life to worry about anyone else, so changing the subject she asked her brother if he fancied a Wimpy. Glad that she seemed to have accepted his words he laughed and agreed to pay for lunch feeling that today was turning out to be a good one.

As Ebony sucked on Charlie's erection he was finally feeling more appreciated. He had told her about his meeting with Alan Stewart and although she had been worried that Alan would not budge, Charlie had assured her that he had something up his sleeve that would make the man see sense. Ebony didn't really care what it was as long as she got her cut. Charlie had decided to go with his plan as Alan Stewart clearly wasn't going to part with any money voluntarily. So when Ebony had satisfied him, he jumped up, patted her on the bum and told her that he would see her tomorrow. Ebony didn't particularly want him to return any sexual favours but was still slightly miffed that he had discarded her like a used Tampax. As she heard the front door slam, she smiled to herself. Chantelle was downstairs with her neighbour Cassie so she could indulge in her favourite tv series *Dallas*. That Bobby Ewing was a bit of alright and she would rather ogle him than have Charlie slurping all over her nether regions anyway!

Denny felt a right wanker as Nikki's cute little face crumpled as he gave her the bad news.

'But why Denny, don't we have a great time together?'

'Course we do but to be honest I just don't have time for a relationship. I'm that busy and that's not fair on you, is it?'

'But I don't care, I see my mates when you're not around. I love you so much Denny. Please don't dump me.'

As Nikki sobbed, Denny couldn't help but think she was an ugly crier. Why was that he thought? As soon as a pretty girl started booing her face became a crumpled red and snotty mess. He handed her a Kleenex and patted her shoulder like he would a dog. That seemed to enrage Nikki and she roughly shoved his hand away and slapped him around his face.

'Get your hands off me Denny Draper, you're a bastard and I hate you.'

'Fair enough, I think we're done, don't you?' Denny said rubbing his face.

Nikki was sensible enough to know when she was beaten and hastily stormed out of his office at the club back to her gaggle of friends who immediately administered sympathy and told her that he was a cocky arse hole who didn't deserve her.

Denny watched from the doorway and felt a surge of relief. Closing the door behind him, he decided to go and see the one true love of his life. Like Connie he had been replaying last night's love making in his mind all day and couldn't wait to hold her and love her again.

Alan Stewart was really looking forward to tonight. It was the anniversary of Ron's death and all the old firm were coming together to toast his memory. He had taken a cab so that he could have a good drink but had sensibly decided to lay off the coke. It didn't agree with him and the mixture of the drug and alcohol gave him blackouts. He wanted to remember everything about tonight as it was a rarity that all the boys got together. As he walked into the restaurant he was immediately greeted by Ray Briggs who had been a diamond over the years, hiding stolen merchandise and crushing any evidence at his scrap yard (including bodies on occasion). Ray didn't have a record and ran a legal business so he had never come to the attention of the law. He had also been Ron's second cousin and had been fiercely loyal to the man.

'How's it going Al? I was sorry to hear about you and Sonia.'

'Oh I'm ok Mate, It's bloody great to see you!'

As they settled down for a drink, Alan looked around him and was thrilled to see so many of the old crowd. John Webb and Greg Leeson waved over at his table and he spotted Bill Smith who he used to do the door with at the club. Even Maureen Holmes, who he had worked with at the bookies, was there nursing a sherry.

As the evening wore on and everyone got more tanked up, all the old stories of Ron were told. They all laughed and cried in equal measure, remembering the man who had been such a big part of their lives.

Ron's cousin John started laughing as he told the famous stolen coat story.

'Ere did Ron ever tell any of you about the time when he stole a load of men's coats? It was one of his first jobs. He raided a warehouse in the dead of night. He'd spent weeks doing his homework and was in and out like a seasoned professional but when he checked the coats out afterwards they hadn't had the arms sewn on yet!'

Ray Briggs was howling as he spluttered, 'I had to help him chuck them in the Thames!'

As the drinks flowed soon everyone was recounting their personal stories of Ron McCardle. Alan was thoroughly enjoying himself and ran over and lifted Lily Jenson off her feet when she walked in with her son Barry. She had run the sex house for Ron and had made a damn good job of it before Ron died. Lily had loved Ron in secret for years and unbeknown to him had given birth to their child Barry after assuring him that her pregnancy had been terminated. Life had been tough for her bringing up a child with Downs Syndrome on her own but she had done a marvellous job and tonight Barry was on form making everyone laugh at his antics.

At one point he had innocently asked where Ron was which had been bitter sweet and had sobered the guests for a minute but Lily being Lily had diffused the moment swiftly. 'Bloody hell Barry, I allow you one shandy and you become all maudlin, this is a party Son.'

Secretly though she was pleased that her son still remembered the man who had fathered him and promised him another half shandy and a packet of his favourite crisps.

As the night turned into the small hours people started to call it a night and go home. Soon it was only Alan and Rob Clarke left putting the world to rights.

'How's the family Rob? You married yet?' Alan asked.

What with all that had been going on in his life he hadn't seen Rob in a while and felt guilty that he hadn't tried to find him when Rob had gone off the radar after his brother Doug had been killed by the Turks in 1978.

'Nah, marriage isn't for me but I have a nipper now. Kelly. She's the love of my life.'

Alan dutifully admired the photo of the gapped-tooth child Rob proudly presented him with and fleetingly wished that his own children were babies again. Lately he was thinking more and more of the past before life had started giving him nightmares. He often wondered that if he had his time again, would he have made the same choices but he couldn't really answer that question.

What he did know is that he still missed Sonia with a vengeance and sometimes envied her carefree life in Cornwall. These days they were friends and he looked forward to her Sunday night phone calls when they would catch up and speak about the old days before life had changed. But he also knew that living with regrets was pointless and he enjoyed the luxury that villainy had afforded him, so he would always be grateful to the man who was the focus of tonight's celebrations.

Denny and Connie had just finished making love and it had been as electric as last night. Connie had never had an orgasm like the ones Denny gave her. They seemed to go on forever and left her exhausted. There was not an inch of her body that he didn't spend time loving and she was pleased that he was such a master at knowing what a woman needed to get to that point of total fulfilment and abandon.

As the birds began to sing Denny got up from the warmth of her bed. 'I'd better make tracks, your dad will be home soon.'

Connie shook her head. 'No, I want Dad to know. I'm not hiding. Caroline seems ok now and Dad loves you, so he will be ok too.'

'Are you sure?'

As they heard the front door close Connie looked up at him and cheekily winked. 'Absolutely.'

When his daughter came into the front room with Denny who was wearing his dressing gown Alan frowned and wasn't sure what to feel.

'We've got something to tell you Dad.'

'I can see that Love.'

Denny decided to take charge of the situation and explained that he loved Connie and had for a long time. Alan could see by the glow of his daughter's face that she felt the same way.

'Well I love the both of you too, but Denny we will need a chat.'

Denny breathed a sigh of relief, he had expected no less.

When Alan lay in bed a little while later, his mind was whirring. Denny and his little girl. But he knew that she wasn't a little girl anymore. She was a woman and a beautiful one at that and he could tell that she was in love. She was also headstrong and wouldn't take any notice if he had any reservations, and he did. Denny was going up in the world, in the drugs world, and that meant risk. It also meant that he could end up with a capture. All these thoughts worried him and he knew that Sonia would go ape shit at the news. But what could they do? Their daughter had always got what she wanted in life and, by the soppy look on her face earlier, she wanted Denny Draper. Why was life always full of problems he pondered as he tried to sleep?

As he began to drift off he was oblivious to the fact that there would be another problem waiting for him on his door mat when he woke up the following morning.

Chapter 37

Alan was in a foul mood as he drove to meet Denny. When he'd read the letter that had been posted through his letterbox his heart had sunk and that evening his nightmare had returned. The nightmare where a young boy lay dead, his head blown away by the bullet fired by him. The dream was so vivid. He clearly saw the gaping hole in the boy's head and all the blood seeping out of it onto the dirty floor like a crimson river.

The letter had been a photocopy of the original, the cursive handwriting surprisingly neat and Alan had its contents engraved in his mind tormenting him.

To Uncle Charlie

I've done a stupid thing. I didn't want anyone to get hurt.

I only wanted justice for my Dad Stevie but Alan Stewart's mother-in-law died in the fire and now he will kill me for what I've done.

If I disappear then he will have succeeded.

I am not a bad person and I am so sorry.

It was signed Jason Baines and dated a week before Alan had taken a gun and murdered him. Alan had no clue how the boy's Uncle Charlie had got hold of the letter, but he had.

He tried to reason with himself that it could be a fake as it was clearly a ploy to blackmail him but, even if this was the case, Alan knew from meeting Charlie that he wasn't going to let this drop. Deep in thought, he didn't notice that he had cut up a white van until the angry looking driver began calling him a wanker as he sped past. Alan just glared at him and was gratified to see the other man look sheepish when he had realised who he was. Alan was momentarily pleased that he was still thought of as a respected face but unfortunately this did not lift his mood.

Charlie West was in a good mood as he read the morning papers. Stumbling across that letter had been pure luck which would pay dividends. He had known that his sister Doreen was back on the estate but hadn't got around to visiting. When he had decided to go and see how she and Jason were, it was too late. The old lady in the flat opposite informed him that his sister was dead and the boy had disappeared but not before giving her an envelope and instructing her to give it to his uncle should he come calling. Plan A had been to use his nephew Peter who was seeing Stewart's daughter. Charlie knew that Alan wouldn't want Connie knowing that he was a murderer so he had felt that he could blackmail him that way, however, after meeting his nephew again after so many years he found him to be a decent lad who had been through enough so Charlie lied about what he had discovered. The boy didn't need to be bogged down with the knowledge that his brother had been murdered.

Also Charlie decided that he didn't want to risk the chance of Peter taking any sort of revenge and ending up with a long prison sentence. No the letter was a better option because Alan would not want the police sniffing about even if it would be hard to prove that he was responsible for Jason's death. He felt that Alan Stewart would cough up and Charlie was determined to make some money out of his cunning plan.

Denny was feeling a little apprehensive as he waited for Alan to arrive. He was well aware that his godfather had reservations about him dating his daughter and on one level he could understand this but even so Denny felt confident that he could convince him that he and Connie were the real deal and that he would always look after her. He was disappointed when Alan walked in with a face like a slapped arse and pupils the size of saucers. He had clearly had a sniff before he had come out and Denny knew from experience that he would be a harder nut to crack because of this. So deciding against offering him a Scotch he quietly made two large mugs of coffee as Alan settled himself on the leather sofa opposite the desk in the office.

As Denny sat down opposite him, Alan gently smiled. 'Look Denny if you were a postman, worked in a bank or even a dustman, I would be over the moon for you and my girl and so would Sonia but you saw what my life did to her and my marriage…'

Denny had known what Alan was going to say and interrupted him. 'With respect Mate, Connie is way stronger than Sonia and she knows the score.'

'Maybe she does but it's just too risky this life and I don't want Connie a part of it. Look what happened in 78 with the Turks. We had casualties and innocent ones at that. What if you end up in a turf war, how are you going to protect her? What if you end up in clink or worse, dead?'

Denny sighed. 'Look Al, I am so far removed from the people on the streets that I am as safe as I can be and as for a turf war, families are usually kept out of business, you know that. You were never one hundred percent sure that the Turks had anything to do with Breda and the fire.'

Alan averted his eyes and absentmindedly looked at his shoes because now that he had received the letter he was certain that Jason Baines had acted alone on a one-man mission to avenge his father Stevie. But despite this he was still troubled about Denny's blossoming romance with Connie. 'Do you really think that my Connie will be a wife in the background who has dinner on the table for when you come home at night, because I don't? She will probably get involved knowing her.'

No Denny could not imagine the love of his life rustling up a shepherd's pie any time soon and he laughed as he imagined her in an apron slaving over the cooker. 'No of course not, but she has her hands full overseeing the rentals and helping to run the businesses when you aren't around.'

Alan had the grace to look away in shame. He had allowed his daughter to take over because after Sonia had left he had spent his days in his pyjamas nursing a hangover from the night before. Connie had proved a worthy asset but he her father had been selfish and he felt guilty. What worried him most was that although Connie looked like her mother, she was in fact a female version of him and had the same fire in her belly to earn like he had back in 1967 when he had become part of Ron McCardle's world. Connie wanted a life of luxury but how far would she go to get it he wondered? Sonia already worried about Billy who was a soldier and she would flip her lid if her only daughter took over from a life that she herself had left, a life that had driven her mad with anxiety.

Looking up, Alan studied his godson for the first time in ages. Long gone were the tight leather trousers and spiky hair of his punk rocker days. Now he wore designer three piece suits, shiny shoes of the finest leather and with his slicked back dark hair and calm confidence he looked like what he was: a successful villain.

Alan stood up to leave. 'Like I said yesterday Den, I love the both of you to bits but you have to end this before it goes too far. I can't allow Connie to be in any danger.'

Denny looked him square in the eyes and said, 'I can't do that Al, I love her too much.'

Alan held his gaze. 'Well you don't have my blessing and if anything happens to my girl, I will blame you.'

With that he downed the rest of his coffee and walked out slamming the door behind him without saying goodbye. Denny poured himself a Scotch. It saddened him that Alan felt this way but Connie had taken up residence in his heart and he could no more give her up than stop breathing.

As Alan drove away, fresh guilt and remorse weighed heavily on him. Denny's parents Geoff and Brenda would be horrified that their son was now a criminal and even worse but he had broken his promise to them and allowed it to happen with first giving him a job in Ron's club where he had absorbed every criminal activity going on around him and then investing money to help the boy become a drug baron. Putting his foot on the accelerator he felt like crying and driving into the nearest brick wall.

Charlie and Ebony were having a late lunch at her flat. Chantelle was at school and Charlie was looking forward to a quick tumble once his lunch had gone down. Ebony eyed him and her heart sunk as she knew exactly what he was planning. She couldn't even muster up the imagination to fantasise that he was Bobby Ewing when they were having sex because he was so rough. He obviously hadn't got the memo about a woman enjoying an orgasm. She would just have to try and put him off because his hairy sweaty body was beginning to make her want to vomit these days.

'That was handsome Girl,' Charlie declared patting his round tummy. 'Fancy some fun in the bedroom as the kid isn't due home for a few hours?'

As he leered at her, she said the first thing that came into her head. 'Oh I'd love to big man but it's my time of the month.'

'That's alright, you can suck me off.'

Ebony shuddered but would have to go through with it and keep him sweet because she wanted her money and Charlie had assured her that Alan would cough up any day now. Once she had her money, she had decided to get as far away from Islington and Charlie West as soon as she could.

Alan was having a drink with Rob Clarke and telling him about the letter. His friend glanced at it and laughed. 'It's got to be fake Al but how would he know all this?'

'Exactly Rob. I can't risk him taking this to the police. Even if they can't prove anything I don't need the hag. I just don't know what to do.'

Rob looked at Alan and replied, 'Well you know what Ron would have done? Dished out one of his legendary punishments. I'd say at least a number four!'

Alan laughed. Ron had administered punishments on a scale of one to five and anyone getting a five knew that they would never be going home again. 'I don't know Rob, if I give him a hiding it will only fuel the fire. I need him to disappear.'

Rob nodded and lowering his voice said, 'And I know just the fella to do it.'

'Who?'

'Me!'

Alan sipped his pint touched by the gesture. 'I can't let you do that, Mate.'

'Finish your pint and let's talk in your car, this is too public.'

Alan did as Rob had requested and listened carefully to what his friend had to say once they were out of ear shot of anyone else.

'When Doug was sliced by the Turks, it killed our mum. I watched her slowly die of a broken heart so I bided my time and eventually stabbed the son Deniz and as a stroke of luck HIS dad died a few weeks later from the shock, now that's what I call justice. Since Ron died and Irene made his businesses legal I have been working for Jerry Hart and have helped to make a few of his enemies disappear over the years. I'm good at what I do Al and I can help you for a price of course although it would be mate's rates. Did you know that my Kelly's mum is Jerry's daughter Shona?'

Alan was impressed even if a part of him was horrified that big gentle giant

Rob was now what amounted to a hitman. Jerry Hart was big time who ran the East End, and he and Ron had been friends from a distance.

'Let me have a think and get back to you Mate.'

'No worries Al but let me know soon cos me and Shona are taking Kelly to Clacton in a few weeks.'

When Alan got home Glenice was all flustered. 'Caroline has gone into labour, Connie has gone to the hospital.'

'Ah that's terrific Mum, now what's for dinner?' he joked.

Glenice smiled. Her son hadn't been right for the last day or so and she was gratified that he wanted feeding because that was always a sign that he was feeling better.

Connie and Cath were on tender hooks waiting for Wayne to come and tell them any news. Caroline had been taken to the delivery suite three hours before and just as Denny arrived carrying a giant teddy bear, Wayne emerged with a big grin on his face. 'It's a boy! Eight pounds two ounces.'

Cath immediately started crying while Wayne, Connie and Denny all hugged each other with happiness.

Inside the delivery suite, the midwife handed the baby to Caroline who had expected to feel nothing so was surprised when she looked into his little screwed up face and felt a rush of love and peace. This was HER baby. She now had someone to fill the gap that her parents had left when they had died. She had someone to love and protect. Maybe things would work out after all she thought, as she put him to the breast. 'Hello Jamie, welcome to the world sweet boy,' she whispered.

When they left the hospital, Denny told Connie about the conversation with her dad. Connie was outraged. 'He's a bloody hypocrite, he put his wife AND kids in danger when he took up with Ron.'

Denny cupped her beautiful face. 'Go easy on him Darling, he loves you and I can see his point to a degree. I've watched him over the years. He was never really cut out for the violence that this life can bring. I think that all the trouble years ago made him realise what he had given up, what he had become and I don't think he liked what he saw.'

Connie listened in silence and silently agreed, but like Denny she was adamant she would not give up on them and knew she would get around her dad, she always did.

Alan had spent all evening thinking about Rob's offer and decided that getting rid of Charlie West was the only way. It was just too risky to have him hanging around with a letter that could incriminate him. He was also worried about the connection with Connie's ex-boyfriend Peter who was the man's nephew because he knew just how the blackmail would progress if he didn't play ball. Feeling relieved that he had made a decision he went to bed and had the best night's sleep in weeks.

At breakfast the next day, Connie confronted Alan with a determined look in her eyes. 'Dad I am telling you now that I am with Denny and that's an end to it.'

'I just worry Love, I don't want you involved in anything that you can't handle. I now know that my choices destroyed your mother, I don't want that for my baby girl.'

'Dad I am not Mum and I am not your baby girl anymore.'

Alan looked at his beautiful daughter and even though she was wearing Snoopy pyjamas he could see that she was a woman who was entitled to make her own choices in life. 'Ok Love, but please promise me that you will get out if it becomes too much for you.'

'I promise Dad. I love you.'

Alan wanted to weep at history repeating itself but knew that there was nothing that he could do. 'And I love you Connie Eve, more than you will ever know.'

Connie grinned and swiping his last piece of toast from his plate rushed back upstairs. She was going to visit Caroline and the new baby Jamie at the hospital and couldn't wait!

Charlie grinned. His plan had worked! Alan Stewart had called him and asked to meet with him to discuss the letter. Alan had been polite and Charlie was sure he was soon going to be in receipt of a big pay out. Rubbing his hands together in glee he felt that today was a good day and he hadn't even had to involve Peter, which he was pleased about.

Alan waited for Charlie West to arrive like a lamb to the slaughter. As the other man screeched to a halt in his flashy BMW Alan had a feeling of unease. He had always been able to handle himself but, like Ron, had only ever used violence when it was necessary and getting rid of Charlie was a necessity. Alan couldn't risk the disappearance of Jason Baines being looked into.

Connie had recently bumped into Peter who had informed her that he was going travelling. He hadn't mentioned anything else so Alan was confident that Charlie hadn't told him about the letter.

Charlie had a big smile on his face when he got out of his car. 'Good to see you Alan, now let's get this over with and then we will never have to see each other again.'

Alan had a sudden urge to wipe the smug look off the other man's pudgy face but knew that he had to keep his cool. 'There is £50,000 in a bag in the boot but first I want the letter and a signed confession saying that you got someone else to write it.'

Charlie looked momentarily thrown but took the pen and paper that Alan handed him and began to write. He had lied to Ebony about the amount and was only going to hand her £15,000 so as he wrote down his 'confession,' he was already planning on what he would spend the rest on. As he gave the paper back Alan smirked. 'Now give me the original and you can have your money and then fuck off.'

As the business was done and Alan had what he wanted Rob silently snuck up behind Charlie. The blow to the head was swift and carried out with a precision to cause maximum damage. Charlie fell to the ground with an alarmed look on his face, twitched twice and then was still.

Rob grinned. 'Alright Al? Danny's waiting in a van, we'll sort this out for you.'

Alan shook Rob's hand and thanked him. As he got back into his car he hoped that this was the last bit of violence that he was ever going to have to be involved in.

Chapter 38

Two Years Later

As his daughter came down the stairs Alan gasped. All brides were beautiful but his Connie was breath-taking. Her dress was plain: an abundance of silk and lace which skimmed her petite frame perfectly. Tiny red roses had been woven into her dark hair which cascaded past her shoulders, matching her bouquet which she clasped in her hands. Looking at her dad's reaction she grinned. 'I take it from the shocked look on your face that you are either blown away by my dress or worried about how much this is all costing?!'

Alan laughed with her. 'Connie I am so proud of you, you look exquisite. Sod the money.'

'Well just wait until you see Mum,' his daughter said winking.

Sonia still believed that Denny managed the club. She knew nothing of his involvement in the drugs trade and Alan had told Connie that it had to stay this way to protect her. More secrets that could have tragic consequences but it was the only way and Alan would have to take that chance in order to keep both the women he loved more than life itself happy.

When Sonia appeared Alan's emotions got the better of him and he wiped a tear away from his eyes. She was a vision in pale lavender.

As she walked towards him she held out her hand and he grasped it, enjoying the feel of her. Smiling she gently brushed her lips against his. 'It's time for me to go, the cars are waiting. Billy where are you?' she called.

Billy emerged from the front room with the bridesmaids Cath, Caroline and Connie's cousin Samantha, who had all been mocking him for wearing a kilt.

'Only my son could get away with wearing a skirt to a wedding,' Alan laughed happily.

'Dad, I am a Stewart and I'm proud of my roots and my family,' Billy retorted chucking.

Alan looked around him smiling. Everyone looked amazing and laughed with him, even though he noticed that Caroline kept her eyes firmly glued to the bouquet that she was holding.

Caroline had felt tired recently. She was tired of keeping up the pretence because although she worshipped her son and although his father had been gentle and didn't seem to remember a thing about that night Caroline still felt dirty and used. Her relationship with Wayne had died. She only needed one man in her life now and that was her son. She had confusing feelings that were always rushing around her head and everyone privately agreed that she wasn't the girl she had been before the baby. As they all left the house she plastered a fake smile on to her face, determined that her brother and Connie would have the best day ever and she would keep her true feelings to herself.

The wedding service had been held at Christ Church in Crouch End followed by a reception at The Dorchester Hotel in Park Lane. No expense had been spared and Alan had paid for a fleet of cars to drive the guests to the hotel where everyone was having a day to remember. Alan had thought of everything and had two places laid for Breda and Ron and a toast had been said in their memory. All the old firm were there with their other halves and Irene McCardle had flown over from Spain with her husband Kenny Latham, who Alan liked immensely. The speeches had been heartfelt and as Denny Draper got up to tell everyone how much his wife meant to him there wasn't a dry eye in the house.

As the day moved into evening, more guests arrived and when the DJ put on Maggie May by Rod Stewart Maggie jumped up. She had been sitting with Dolly McCardle and Glenice and grinned as the song started, 'Did I ever tell you that Rod wrote this song for me?'

The other women burst out laughing. 'YES,' they shouted in unison.

'Well, come on you two, let's show these youngsters how it's done,' she urged.

Alan smiled as he watched them wheel Dolly's wheel-chair onto the dance floor and abandon themselves to the raspy tones of Rod Stewart. As he watched them he thought what great women they were. They had been through a war. Dolly and Glenice had brought up children on the bread line and all three of them had always put their families first.

In that moment Alan realised that family is what really counted in life not money, not status but the love between people who you loved and who loved you.

Later on that evening as his wife lay dozing on the sofa in their front room Alan realised how lucky he was to have her back in his life. Two years before he had been involved in another murder. He had been relieved and horrified in equal measure. As his nightmares had increased he had known there was only one person who could give him the solace that he craved and he had gone to her with promises of retirement and a quiet life. He needed to distance himself from his old life and Ebony Peters who demanded to know where Charlie was. Alan had put on a good act and said that he had paid him but he hadn't heard from him since. Ebony had been enraged but believed him, concluding he had double crossed her and had stormed off wondering what the hell she was supposed to do now?

Alan and Sonia now lived in Cornwall with Glenice and Aunty Maggie but they also had a flat in Hampstead for when they wanted to visit family in London. Although his new life suited him and he was happy, Alan asked himself if he would have changed anything because so much of his chosen life had resulted in tragic consequences. In all honesty, he didn't know because in his mind everything he had done had been for his family. He had wanted to get his family out of the daily grind of poverty. He wanted them to have a good life and he had protected them when danger came calling. He had done what was necessary and had done it for them. If he hadn't met Ron McCardle it would never have been possible and Ron had been more than an employer. He had become Alan's friend and more importantly his family. Holding up his glass of Scotch, he said a silent toast to the man who had had such a positive and negative impact on his life. The past was the past and he had everything to look forward to with his true love by his side, his Sonia.

Epilogue

1 Year Later

Caroline closed her eyes and died, surrounded by the love of her two best friends and her brother Denny as the bright day turned to dark. No one could believe the time had finally come although they knew it would descend on them like a black avenging cloud eventually. She had been diagnosed with Stage 4 myeloid leukaemia one month after the wedding. Connie, Cath and Denny had dutifully attended all of her hospital appointments until a kindly doctor had informed them that nothing could be done. They had been surprised by Caroline's acceptance of her fate. She fought the illness like a lioness with dignity until she had no fight left in her. The last few weeks had been spent around her bedside reminiscing and laughing. Everyone had tried to make her passing a joyful occasion although inside they were all screaming in pain and with the unfairness of the situation. They were determined to make her funeral a celebration of the girl they had loved.

Two weeks later Connie waved goodbye to Denny and Jamie and felt relieved that she would now have a couple of hours to herself while they went swimming. Jamie was three and lived with them full time. Caroline had ended her relationship with Wayne when he was two months old, after confessing that the baby wasn't his. She had been a decent person and hadn't wanted to lie to Wayne.

Connie settled herself on her bed and felt a mixture of excitement and guilt. Gina Davis, Cath's mum, had given each of the girls a diary for Christmas 1977. The diaries had a floral print, came with a padlock and a small key so that they could hide their childish secrets from the world. Caroline had continued to keep one for the rest of her life although the other two girls had long since stopped using theirs. Connie wasn't sure if Caroline would want her to read her personal thoughts but decided that they had been as close as sisters and had always told each other everything and she had had a desperate need today to be close to her friend so picking up the first one she began to read.

Connie laughed as she was transported back to the care free days of their childhood. It was all there: eating raspberry ripple ice cream in Brenda Draper's garden, swimming in the paddling pool, midnight feasts, first crushes on boys. Every stage of their lives had been lovingly chronicled in Caroline's large, looping handwriting.

As she eagerly read each diary Connie felt that Caroline was there with her smiling down and sharing the nostalgia. The diary of the year that Brenda and Geoff had died had been sad reading.

Caroline had poured out all her grief and pain on to the pages and also her gratitude that the Stewarts had taken her in and looked after her.

When Denny and Jamie came home the little boy was full of himself as he had jumped into the pool on his own and his Uncle Denny had bought him a Curley Wurley as a treat for being so brave. Connie looked at the child and felt a great love for him. Scooping the child into her arms Connie kissed his little button nose and told him she would watch a film with him later on. Caroline had been an exemplary mother and Connie was determined that she would bring up the boy as if he was her own. She owed it to her friend.

Later on that evening and after they had all sat down and watched *Lady and the Tramp*, Connie was once again holed up in her bedroom reading the last diary. The final entry was dated December 1986 and Connie remembered that they had gone to the pub for a Christmas drink and had danced all night long. As Connie read on the smile on her face disappeared and she began trembling. She had had no idea. She couldn't believe what she was reading but there it was:

He looked so sad so I invited him in for a coffee. I could see that he was in a world of his own, he was drunk and drugged. He didn't see ME as he started touching me. He thought I was Sonia. I tried to move but my body had seized up. Although he was raping me and that is such a violent word, he was gentle and loving.

He was making love to his wife who had broken his heart. I didn't know what to do, I was paralysed with fear so I kept quiet and focused on the photograph of Mum and Dad willing them to help me. I was still lying on the carpet staring at their photograph hours after he had gone.

Connie threw the diary across the room and ran to the bathroom where she threw up in the sink. It all made sense now: Caroline's detachment to her pregnancy, the fact that she didn't really talk to her father anymore unless she had to and more importantly the baby wasn't Wayne's. Alan had been off his head on drink and drugs in those days and had often suffered from blackouts but Connie felt disgusted by his actions even though she believed he had no recollection of the events of that night in 1986. She needed to decide what to do with this revelation.

The next day as the diary burned in their open fire, Connie felt she had done what was necessary to hide the awful truth. Denny must never find out because he would kill her father for what he had done to his sister and she couldn't put her mother through that. She would play the dutiful daughter but inside he was now dead to her. Connie would wait and one day she would seek revenge. After all she was Alan Stewart's daughter.